Letters
FROM A
PATCHWORK
QUILT

CLARE FLYNN

CRANBROOK PRESS

LETTERS FROM A PATCHWORK QUILT
Copyright ©2015 Clare Flynn

Published by Cranbrook Press 2015
London, UK

Cover design JD Smith Design.

ISBN: 978-0-9933324-1-8

In memory of Michelle Van Vlijmen 1954-2015.
A dear and true friend.

Prologue
St Louis, 2015

It was coming apart. Hand-sewn with stitches so small as to be barely visible. Meredith took it out of the battered old trunk and stretched it out on the bed, smoothing the surface with the palm of her hand. The fabric crinkled slightly, stiff under her fingers. It was a bit grubby – pretty though. The fabric shapes were in calico and cotton, in a combination of delicate shades of blues and greens. It would look perfect in the guest bedroom. Then she remembered she wasn't going to keep the house.

She picked the quilt up and took it into the study, where she rummaged about on shelves and in cupboards until she found her mother's sewing box. The quilt would have to be repaired before she could risk laundering it. She settled herself into the low armchair in front of the windows and let the autumn sunshine wash over her. Meredith couldn't remember the last time she'd sat down like this to do something for herself. To sew. To paint. To write for pleasure. The last year had been swallowed up with caring for her mother in the final phase of her illness.

Needle threaded, she calculated how to begin the repair. The quilt was a complicated design, a sampler of several different intricate patterns. She started to fold one of the

1

pieces under where it had buckled up, when she noticed the stiffness was caused by the paper pieces still present between the layers of fabric. If she was going to wash the quilt she'd have to remove them. She folded the flap of material back and gently eased out the piece of paper. It was quite thick, a lightweight card rather than paper and covered in neat, old-fashioned, cursive writing in black ink, the edges ragged where the needle had caught them as it penetrated the fabric. She set it on one side and carefully removed another piece until she had a small collection of hexagonal shapes laid out beside her on the table. Strange that the pieces had been left inside instead of being removed as the quilt was pieced together. She picked one up to read it and realised that it was part of a letter. She took the backing off the quilt and worked her way through the pieces, extracting each paper template one by one.

It took her nearly an hour to fit the pieces together, straining her eyes to read the tiny florid handwriting with its loops and curlicues. Using a magnifying glass, she worked her way slowly through the text.

1
Escape
Derby, England, 1875

Jack's eldest sister, Theresa, had burnt the porridge again. She always left it bubbling on the stove in unspoken criticism of any late risers. It was Jack's younger sister, Cecily, who'd made him late this morning. Jack had been huddled under the blanket, putting off the inevitability of rising on a morning that had frosted the window panes so heavily the bedroom was still dark. Cecily had found his precious notebook under the mattress and read bits out in a mocking tone, until he managed to wrest it from her grip. Jack wasn't ashamed of what he'd written. It was just that it sounded feeble when read out loud in a singsong tone by a younger sister, eager to gain some leverage in their sibling rivalry. He had nothing to bargain with, other than brute force – a brief Chinese burn usually kept her in her place, without causing lasting damage.

'You're late,' said their father, wiping his hand across his mouth to remove the traces of porridge from his moustache. 'What was all that thumping and banging upstairs? You been fighting again? Want me to give you both a good leathering?'

Neither Jack nor Cecily wanted to feel the force of their father's easily aroused anger and his tendency to solve all strife with a lash of his belt. Cecily slunk into her place at the table and Jack settled beside her and gave his attention to the glutinous porridge.

There was an unspoken code in that Brennan household that they didn't tittle tattle on each other, but Cecily had always struggled with it. Jack threw her a look, to warn her to say nothing.

'Our Jack wants to go for the Queen's Scholarship.' She looked at him slyly.

'Shut it,' he mumbled. Maybe that Chinese burn had been too painful – or more likely not hard enough to dissuade her from snitching on him.

'And he's been writing poems. He's got a little notebook he keeps stuffed under the mattress. Daft poems about nature and dreams.'

Jack cursed his own stupidity in thinking any place in this cramped and overcrowded house would be safe from prying eyes and twitching fingers. He should have left his precious notebook in the cupboard at school.

'Poems?' His mother, Annie, spoke, wiping her hands on her apron as she paused in washing the dishes. 'You're writing poetry, son?'

Jack forced the last mouthful of porridge down and got up from the table. 'It's for school.' If he got a move on he could be out of the house before Cecily got into her stride. He scraped back his chair.

'No it's not schoolwork.' Cecily's tone was smug. She was not prepared to give ground now that the whole family was listening to her. 'He's written a poem about how he wants to get away from here. Like this were a prison or something. He reckons he's too good for us.' She paused, looking around to be sure she had everyone's attention, then spoke in a triumphant tone. 'Says he's not going to be a priest. He's going to be a teacher.'

'Oh aye!' Their father's laugh was a deep baritone. 'A teacher! Get you, son! Well, Mother, did you ever think we'd not only have children that can read and write but we've even raised one who thinks he's good enough to teach other kids how to do it? Would you believe it?' He shook his head and wiped a tear of laughter from his eye.

Jack's mother, Annie, leaned forward and stroked his head. 'You're going to the seminary next year. The teaching you'll be doing is from the pulpit on a Sunday, lad. That's much more important.'

Jack took a deep breath. Now or never. He'd hoped to raise the subject at a time of his own choosing, but he might as well get it out of the way.

'I don't have a vocation.'

The chattering around the table stopped. His parents exchanged a look then his mother sat down beside Jack and took his hand. 'That'll come, love. If you ask for God's guidance. It will come. Say your prayers and God will help you find it.'

'I don't want to find it. I don't want to be a priest. I want to be a teacher. That's my vocation. That's what I care about.'

As soon as he spoke he wanted to suck the words back into his mouth. There was silence in the room as what he said registered. Jack gulped a deep breath and immediately felt better. He'd done it. At last. Spoken up about what he wanted. Stood up to his parents. It was out now and couldn't be taken back. He felt a surge of relief tinged with excitement.

His father got up, knocking over his chair, then banging his fist on the table so the crockery shook.

'We'll hear no more of this nonsense. You should be thankful you're not slaving away like me and Kenny, trying to squeeze out a living with the plastering. Not enough work for the two of us and there's nowt else in this town in the way of jobs.'

Jack opened his mouth to speak but his mother threw him a look.

His father carried on. 'Didn't I say being a teacher's assistant would put daft ideas in your head? – and I were right. Your mother twisted my arm, said it would help you get a fast start at the seminary. But that's it. Enough of this bloody nonsense.'

He thumped the table again.

His wife laid a calming hand on his sleeve. ' Why don't you have a word with our Dom and see if he can get the boy in right away, Bill?'

'Good idea. The brothers'll knock some sense into that thick head of his.' He turned back to Jack – 'And if you mention teaching again I'll knock your block off.'

Before Bill Brennan could leave the room he was overcome by a fit of coughing. A lifetime of plaster dust had played havoc with his breathing, and his eldest son, Kenneth was developing a cough too. Bill pulled a rag out of his trouser pocket and held it to his mouth, then tried to stuff it back quickly. Not quick enough for his wife.

'That's blood again, Bill, isn't it?'

'It's nothing.'

'You've got to see a doctor.'

'There's no money for a doctor. You know that, duck.'

'I'll talk to our Dom.'

'You'll do no such thing, woman.' The coughing fit had placated him. He leaned over and planted a kiss on the top of her head then slung his tool bag over his shoulder and went out with Kenneth behind him.

Annie Brennan grabbed Jack's arm and jerked him out of his seat.

'See what you've done now, you stupid boy. You know it makes your Da's chest worse when he gets a strop on. I'll have no more talk of scholarships in this house. I should never have let you talk me into you staying on as a monitor.

I were tempted by the two bob a week, but if you'd gone straight to the seminary you'd be a priest by now and there'd be one less mouth to feed.'

She sighed and released Jack from her grip. 'You always twist me round your little finger, our Jack, but not any more. Your Da's right. As for a Queen's scholarship, how are we expected to pay for the books? And what would you get even if you passed? Twenty pounds a year? How would that make a difference?'

Jack was about to protest but she cut him off. 'No, son. This nonsense has gone on for long enough. If you talk about it again you'll get a thick ear from me, never mind your Da.'

She turned her back on him as she scrubbed away at the porridge pan and called over her shoulder, 'Get off to school, you lot. You're going to be late.'

As soon as they were outside the house, Jack ran ahead of his sisters and brother. He didn't want to give Cecily another opportunity to taunt him, nor did he want his other siblings asking why he didn't want to be a priest. Joining his older brothers in the church was viewed as an economic necessity in the Brennans' circumstances. The family plastering business could barely sustain father and eldest son and joining the priesthood provided employment, food and lodgings, as well as building the reputation of the family within the parish.

As Jack ran through the dirty streets, he pulled his cap down to try to cover his ears and keep out the piercing cold. The piles of coal-blackened slush at the sides of the street were frozen solid. This winter was unending. Freezing fog filled his lungs and sent a sharp pain through his chest, but he kept on running. Running from the house where he felt he didn't belong. Running to the school he saw as his haven. Running so he wouldn't freeze to death. He rounded the corner of Inkerman Street and careened into the rag and bone man's cart, bruising his ankle against one of the wheels. The man yelled a curse at Jack and his tired old nag managed a half-hearted whinny. It was practically dead on its feet.

Jack ran through the school gates and past the children shivering outside the closed door; it was his job to let them in, but first he wanted to hide his notebook at the back of the cupboard where the slates and chalk were stored.

It had been four years since Jack had turned thirteen and stayed on at the school to assist the class teacher. It was hard work, but he revelled in it. Some days he had a whole class to teach and after class finished he had another three hours to be taught himself. His own tuition took place after school in the winter months and at dawn in the summer ones. The school was cold and draughty, with only a tiny coal stove in each of the two classrooms: more often than not it was unlit; coal was an expensive luxury on all but the bitterest of days.

Jack didn't care about the cold. He came alive as soon as he crossed the threshold of the school. Learning was his passion. He had an insatiable hunger for knowledge, a thirst for finding out about the rest of the world. Learning took him far away from the slums of Derby into a world where words opened doors onto magical things he would never have otherwise dreamt of. And teaching was as wonderful as learning – sharing his enthusiasm and opening the eyes of the smaller children to all the possibilities beyond this miserable industrial town. It was like a drug: seeing the small boys gathered around him, their eyes wide as he read to them from Gulliver's Travels or spun the globe and told them about faraway countries. He could never give that up to mumble Latin at a congregation most of whom were only in church out of duty, fear or habit. No, being a priest was unthinkable.

The school morning began with the only part of teaching

that Jack disliked: the catechism. The children were required to learn and recite it by rote. Jack hated the way the words turned into meaningless banalities from the mindless repetition, so that sometimes they ceased to be intelligible. Church dogma, much of which bore little or no relationship to the teachings of Christ, went straight over the heads of the children. Their little faces dropped when he tried to explain the concepts of Purgatory and Limbo. What was the point of terrifying innocent children by concepts that were beyond their experience or understanding. Secretly, Jack believed it was all a lot of nonsense – what kind of god would keep unbaptised babies out of heaven? It was hardly their fault they died before their parents managed to get them christened. He would dream of being free to teach the way he wanted to teach, inspiring the children with stories from the New Testament, instead of stuffing their heads with what he was increasingly convinced was ecclesiastical mumbo jumbo. Of course he could never breathe a word of these doubts to a living soul, or confess to this growing lack of faith in the church that was the centre point of his family and to which he was expected to devote his life.

When the children left the classroom at the end of the afternoon, in a clatter of slates which they piled up on the teacher's desk as they filed past, Jack decided to broach the topic of his scholarship with his teacher.

'Mr Quinn, you know we spoke about me going for the Queen's?'

'I think you're nearly ready, Jack. Don't you? We'll need to spend some more time on your arithmetic – that's the weak spot. But with some application and effort you'll sail through.'

Jack scuffed his shoe against the edge of his chair, noticing there was a hole in the sole. He'd need to find some cardboard to line it before his mother found out. She didn't need that to worry over on top of everything else.

'My parents say I can't sit it. They want me to go to the seminary as soon as they can get me in. They're going to talk to our Dom. They won't let me be a teacher.'

'When you've got your scholarship the school board will increase your wages. That should help. If you go to college and qualify, you could be on as much as twenty-five pounds a year.'

Jack turned away from his mentor and looked out of the window onto the small yard where a robin was pecking about in the smoke-blackened snow. 'It's not just that, sir. There's the cost of the books. And my keep in the meantime. And my Da's not in the best of health. They can't afford the doctor's bills. They need me off their hands. They'll like as not send me and our Tommy together. He's ten next month so he'll be leaving school anyway.'

'And does Tommy want to be a priest?'

'I don't think he's really ever thought there was anything else. With our Dom a priest and Bernie due to be ordained this summer, it's expected.'

Mr Quinn took a pipe out of his pocket and lit it, drawing in little sucks of air till it caught. He leaned forward, his elbows on his knees. 'And why are you so set against it, Jack? After all you'd have bed and board and plenty of free time. No wife to worry about so you can read and write your poetry to your heart's content. And if you want to teach, you could always become a Jesuit or a Christian Brother.'

Jack pulled a face. 'They want me to be a parish priest. The Jesuits are far too grand for the likes of us. And besides...' His heels scuffed at the floor again and he looked away. 'Not having a wife to worry about. That's the problem. I don't think I'm cut out to be a priest.' He could feel the blood rushing to his face and turned his eyes towards the window again.

The teacher smiled and said 'There's nothing wrong with that. Jack. You're a hot-blooded lad. I could never be celibate myself. Mrs Quinn may not be perfect but I'd not be without her, nor she me, I hope. It takes a special man to choose to devote his life to God and forgo the pleasures of married life.'

'I'm not special.'

'Maybe you are, lad, but in a different way. You're a talented pupil with a gift for words, but I reckon you're right, you're not prime priesthood material. Perhaps I should have a word with your parents. With three sons in the church, maybe they can let one of you follow a different path.'

'Would you really talk to them, sir?'

'I'll have a go, Jack. I'll give it my best.'

Jack smiled his gratitude, but while he dared to hope, his head told him it was a lost cause.

A few days later the row erupted. Bill Brennan, as was his custom on a Saturday night, had stopped for a few pints at the Catholic Men's Club with his eldest son. Bill was slightly the worse for drink when he came home, alone. The girls and their mother were sewing and Jack and Tommy were at the kitchen table, working their way through a pile of the family's shoes, trying to coax a shine out of them. There was no polish left, so they were reliant on elbow grease and spit and were making little impression.

The front door slammed and they all looked up, nervously.

Bill Brennan didn't bother with a greeting, but lurched over to the table, grabbed Jack and dragged him to his feet. Before Jack knew what was happening, his father had landed a heavy blow to his head that sent him reeling across the room. Annie Brennan jumped up and tried to remonstrate with her husband, but Bill had already lunged at Jack again, dragging him across the room by his shirt collar.

'Don't you go telling this family's business to other

people, you little snurge.' He shook his son, still holding onto his collar with his left hand and raising his right to strike again.

Annie stepped between them and pushed Jack behind her, squaring up to her husband. 'Leave the lad alone, Bill. There's no call to hit him.'

'Mind your business, woman.' He shoved his wife out of the way, sending her crashing against the wall. 'Get me the belt' he shouted at Cecily.

'What's he done?' asked Annie.

'Tittle-tattled to the teacher about not wanting to be a priest. Bringing shame on the family. He's a holy show.'

In a surge of defiance Jack blurted, 'I'll say what I like. I'm eighteen in a few weeks. I can make my own mind up. It's my life!'

'Not while you're under my roof it isn't. Not while you're eating the food your brother and I work to put on this table, you lazy little sod. I've told you already. You're going to be a priest and that's the end of it. And you can start off by examining your conscience and apologising to your mother. Then you can get yourself to confession before Mass tomorrow.'

'I'm not going to Mass.'

Bill's face distorted with rage. He grabbed the belt from Cecily's hands and turned to his other children. 'You lot get upstairs. Bed!'

Tommy looked as though he was about to protest, but Cecily pushed him ahead of her out of the room, clamping her hand over his mouth.

Annie Brennan caught hold of Cecily's arm as the children were leaving the room and hissed at her to run round to the Club and fetch Kenneth home.

Bill Brennan flexed the leather belt between his hands. 'Come here. Take your punishment like a man.' He swung the belt and brought it down hard across his son's back.

Jack cried out as the edge of the buckle hit him with force. It was like being branded with fire. Before the next blow, he tried to dodge sideways but his father caught his arm. Years of heavy work as a plasterer had given Bill Brennan a muscle mass like granite and he pinned Jack against the wall and lashed another blow down on his back. Jack bit his tongue as the pain seared through him. Don't cry out. Don't give the bastard the satisfaction. Eyes blind with tears, vision distorted. There would be more to come. Blood in the mouth tasting of metal. Sting of leather on buttocks. Buckle smashed against bone. Whole body on fire. Burning, burning, cutting. Make him stop! God, make him stop.

In a sudden rush of adrenalin, he screamed at his father. 'You're nowt but a big bully, a miserable coward and I hate you. You want my life to be as empty as yours but it's not going to be. There'd be plenty of money to pay for the books if you didn't drink it all down the Club.'

The words filled him with new found courage and he turned to parry the next blow.

His father, unused to defiance, had a face as red as a beetroot and launched himself at Jack, but a fit of coughing overwhelmed him. He sank to his knees, desperately trying to take in air but was so overcome by coughing that he turned away and was sick on the floor. Annie grabbed her son, pushing him in front of her through the doorway.

'Get over to our Maisie's. Sleep there the night. He'll have forgotten by morning.'

Jack didn't go to his aunt's house. Instead he staggered along the familiar route to the school and hammered on his teacher's door. Mrs Quinn, the teacher's plump and unsmiling wife, answered and looked at Jack with ill-concealed hostility.

'It's Saturday night. He deserves a break from school matters. You'll have to wait till Monday.'

Jack was about to answer, then, seeing the glow from the

lights inside the small house and feeling the warmth from within, he slumped to his knees and passed out in front of the astonished woman.

Richard Quinn emerged and he and his wife helped Jack to his feet and brought him inside. A cup of tea was produced, a blanket draped over his shoulders and he was led to a chair by the fire.

'What happened, Jack? You look done in.'

'My father was angry that I told you about not wanting to enter the priesthood. He beat me. Only stopped when a coughing fit came on.'

It was such a relief to be here in this quiet house, close to the warmth of the fire. Jack felt safe at last, but overwhelmed with tiredness.

'I'm sorry. I'd no idea he'd react that way. He listened when I spoke to him and I thought he was going along with your wishes. That's how it was when I left him. He was on his way to the club. Maybe he thought better of it later.'

'Maybe the drink did.'

The teacher said nothing, but exchanged a look with his wife. The woman left the room then returned with a bowl of hot water and a towel. She told Jack to take off his shirt and quietly treated Jack's bleeding back, while her husband talked to the boy.

'What are you going to do, Jack?' Mr Quinn asked.

'I'll not go back. That's it. He's gone too far this time. If the coughing hadn't started I reckon he'd have killed me. And I can't take back what I said to him either.'

'It's never too late to take back words said in haste. It's never too late to ask Our Blessed Lord for forgiveness.'

'It is if you meant every word you said and don't believe in God.'

'You're not serious about that? About not believing?'

Jack looked away, suddenly ashamed. 'No. But I'm sick of being browbeaten about the church.' He winced in pain as Mrs Quinn continued to swab his wounded back. 'I'm a Catholic but not a good enough one to want to be shut up in a presbytery with a couple of other priests and a crusty, old housekeeper, like our Dominic. Church is for Sundays and Holy Days, not for seven days a week and every day of the year for the rest of my life. Please help me, Mr Quinn. I've decided to run away.' He looked up at the teacher, unable to disguise the desperation in his voice.

The older man sighed and shook his head. 'Run away?'

'As far from here as possible.' As he said it, the idea grew more appealing.

'It's no good knowing what you're running from. You need to know what you're running to' said Mr Quinn.

'I don't know where.' Jack started to doubt himself. Where indeed would he go? He'd never set foot outside Derby before.

'I didn't say *where*. I said *what* you're running to. It's not the same thing, Jack.'

Jack looked up, his face suddenly animated and his voice excited. 'You know what I want, sir. I want to be a teacher like you. I want to keep on learning. I want more to my life than working, sleeping and going to Mass.' He hesitated then added, 'It's not only the teaching. It's writing. I want to be a poet.'

'A poet, eh? Well, Jack, you've not picked an easy road to walk. I hope you don't expect to make a living from it?'

'Not at first…' Jack looked down, embarrassed and fearful that his teacher would deride him as his family had done.

'You do have a talent, lad. I'll give you that. And it's good to have a goal in life. Something to work towards.'

Mr Quinn jumped up and moved across the room to the table and shuffled through some papers. 'As it happens, I received a letter recently from an old friend who was hoping I'd be interested in moving down south again.'

'Bart. Don't get involved.' Mrs Quinn's voice was anxious.

'I *am* involved, Viola. If I hadn't spoken to the lad's father none of this would have happened. I feel responsible.

'There's a vacant teaching post in a new school on the outskirts of Bristol. The head mistress is a nun. She's my cousin. We grew up together in Ireland. She's a good woman. They're looking for a male teacher for the boys. They'd prefer a qualified teacher, but I got the impression they're short of candidates - and they must have a Catholic, so you'll need to keep that lip buttoned and make sure you don't miss Mass.'

Jack's face broke into a grin. 'Really, Mr Quinn? You think they'd have me?'

'I don't know, Jack, but it's worth a try. I'll write you a letter of recommendation. You'll have to convince the head, Sister Callista, you're up to the job – and I can't promise it won't have already gone.'

'Thanks, sir. I'll take my chances.' Jack was overjoyed.

Quinn reached into a drawer of the sideboard and handed Jack a bag of coins. 'That should cover your train ticket and pay for some digs until you get settled.'

'Bart!' Mrs Quinn put her hand over her mouth. 'What are you doing?' She threw Jack a resentful look.

'I can't take that, sir. It wouldn't be right.'

'Consider it a little bonus for covering for me last month when I had the influenza. It's only right you should have it rather than me when you did the work.'

'Bart, that's our rainy day money. What are you think-ing of?' The woman looked close to tears and Jack felt uncomfortable.

'The lad deserves a chance, Viola. It's a rainy day for him right now.'

'I'll pay you back, sir. I promise. Every penny.'

'Aye, lad, I know you will. Only when you can afford it though. Get on your feet first. Now try and get some sleep. I'm sorry we haven't a bed to offer you but that chair's comfortable enough.'

'I don't know what to say, Mr Quinn.'

'Mind you tell your folks before you leave.'

'That's the only thing, sir. I daren't. Da will stop me. And I don't want to tell Ma as she'd get in trouble if he found out she knew and hadn't told him. Please don't say anything. Leave it between us, sir Once I'm settled I'll send news to Ma. Give it a few days then let her know I'm all right.'

Mr Quinn nodded, wished Jack goodnight and shepherded his wife from the room.

Jack sat with his feet tucked up under him in front of the fire, wrapped in a blanket, the wounds on his back forgotten. He stared into the glowing coals and felt a mixture of trepidation and excitement at what lay ahead. He was going to be a teacher. He was going to be free of the looming threat of the priesthood. In a few hours he would be far away, experiencing his first locomotive trip, his first journey outside Derby. It would be sad to leave his mother and brother and sisters, but he would not miss his father. He never wanted to see him again as long as he lived.

He felt as though he was not just beginning a new chapter in his life, but opening a whole new book.

2
Virginia Lodge

Everything happened so fast. Jack struggled to believe he wasn't dreaming. First there was the railway journey – from Derby to Birmingham and then on to Bristol. He'd never been on a locomotive before and he loved it – even the smoke and steam from the engine and the cold draughts of icy air through the windows. There was the thrill of getting on board in one place and getting off in another, of imagining the lives of the other passengers, where they were going and why, what they were escaping from, their jobs, their secrets, their hopes and dreams. He'd never left Derby before. Never been outside those crowded streets. His heart thumped with fear and excitement about what lay ahead.

Mr Quinn's letter of reference must have been glowing – or Sister Callista, the headmistress of St Patrick's must have been desperate – most likely both. The nun almost jumped for joy when Jack presented himself at the little school on the outskirts of the city. She had been teaching the older boys and girls together in one overcrowded classroom and was relieved to be able to hand the boys over to Jack. She had a broad smile and gentle eyes and Jack immediately liked her. Before taking the veil she had clearly been an attractive woman.

She arranged for him to lodge with a parishioner and his family, brushing aside his suggestion that he could stay in a working men's hostel.

'Good heavens no, Mr Brennan. We don't want you having to mix with non-Catholics. Much better that you're in a good Catholic home. I'm going to send you to Mr MacBride who is a benefactor of the school and does much for the parish. He has given board and lodging to members of the teaching staff before.'

She showed little curiosity about Jack's circumstances and why he had left the industrial Midlands to come to Bristol. He wondered if she was afraid to enquire for fear of discovering something that would prevent her employing him.

He made his way to the address she gave him, carrying the small knapsack Mr Quinn had packed with a set of clean underwear and a shirt. The house, Virginia Lodge, about a mile from the school, was set behind a high wall, and surrounded by a lawn and a dense shrubbery. Fancy. Out of his world. Jack was nervous. His skin felt clammy and he looked at his dirty, down-at-heel shoes. He'd never set foot in a place like this before. The past twenty-four hours had tipped his world on its axis. Travelling on the railway had been the most exciting thing that had ever happened to him and now here he was about to take up residence in a very grand house. He checked the piece of paper the nun had given him, in case he'd made a mistake in following her directions, then mounted the steps and rang the doorbell. He could hear it echoing through the large house and was tempted to run away.

The door opened. A young woman, dressed in black, stood on the threshold, an inquisitive look on her face.

'Mrs MacBride?' His voice sounded high and warbly to him, so he took a breath and tried to lower his register. 'Sister Callista at St Patrick's told me you might be willing to take me in as a lodger. I'm the new schoolteacher. It's all written down in here.' He thrust an envelope into the woman's hand.

'I'm the maid.' She rolled her eyes then added, 'You'd best come in and wait in the parlour. There is no Mrs Mac-Bride. I'll find out if Mr MacBride will see you.'

Blushing at his error, he followed the woman across the stone-flagged hallway and into a room so crammed with furniture that he could barely find a passageway through. The maid didn't suggest he sit, so he positioned himself in front of the ornate, marble fireplace and looked around while he waited. The fire was not lit and the room was chilly and gloomy. Heavy, green velvet curtains sucked up the pale, watery, winter light. The outside of the window was half covered with ivy. The velvet curtains were overhung by a second set of silk hangings that were draped in festoons and more elaborate than anything Jack had seen before. Exotic plants in huge pots were positioned throughout the room, some delicate and fern-like and others with droopy red flowers that hung down like icicles of blood. The furniture was over-stuffed and studded with buttons. Even the mantelpiece was decked out like the windows, covered with a patterned green velvet cloth with little silk balls dangling from a fringe all around. The dark green walls were covered in paintings and gilt framed mirrors. Jack's family didn't own a single mirror in the house back in Derby, let alone paintings. They certainly didn't have carpet or stuffed furniture or even curtains. What kind of money must it take to furnish a place like this? Jack wondered how anyone could possibly be that rich. He felt shabby, threadbare and conscious of the cardboard which was lining the inside of his shoes.

The door burst open and a portly man with enormous sideburns entered. He looked Jack up and down, then moved towards him, hands behind his back. 'You're the new teacher then?' He waved a piece of paper in the air and said, 'Sister Callista says you are highly recommended by your previous employer.'

Jack nodded, struck dumb by the man's presence.

Mr MacBride evidently didn't expect an answer, as he carried on. 'St Bridget's is a new school and there is a small but growing number of pupils. The school board and parish committee are keen that the boys have a good Catholic male teacher to counteract some of the bad influences they get at home. St Bridget's was built with my money and I'm determined I'll not see it go to waste. Understand, young man?'

Jack nodded again. As he shook MacBride's outstretched hand, he felt the sweat transfer onto his host's palm and was mortified as the man pulled a handkerchief from his pocket and wiped his hand.

'I hope I'll give satisfaction, sir,' Jack managed to stutter.

'We'll have you out as quick as you like if you don't measure up. Now you want bed and board here?' asked MacBride.

Jack was reduced to nodding again.

'Do you go to Mass every Sunday, young man? Confession?'

Again, all Jack could do was nod. Nerves had made him mute.

'We keep early hours and I expect you to do the same. No gallivanting about or keeping low company. And no overindulging in alcohol.'

'I don't drink, sir.'

'Good. Good. We live modestly. Plain simple food. There's just my daughter and me and the staff. A cook, a coachman and a housemaid. My wife passed away three years ago. Did Sister Callista explain that you will be expected to pay three shillings a week for your keep?'

'Yes sir.' His voice was barely a whisper.

'Not that I keep it. I don't need your money - it all goes back to the parish. Important that you pay your way. That's settled then. Wait here and the maid will show you to your room. We dine at six o'clock sharp. I won't tolerate lateness.'

The girl who had let him in returned and led him upstairs. After she left, he gazed around him, taking in his new home. The bedroom was as stark as the drawing room had been elaborate. There was a narrow iron bed, a small rug on the otherwise bare, wooden floor and a chest of drawers with a jug and washstand. The window was curtained in thin, black serge that may well have been leftover mourning fabric. Other than a pair of coat hooks on the back of the door and a wooden crucifix over the bed, that was it. But to Jack it was a palace. For his whole life, he'd topped and tailed on a straw mattress with his siblings: girls one end, boys the other. His parents slept in the kitchen, which was the only other room in the house. This room would be paradise: he would be left alone to think, to write, to read, to dream, with no risk of one of the little ones wetting the bed and no danger of someone's legs kicking out when they had a bad dream or because they hadn't enough space. He would enjoy this proper bed with legs, instead of the sack of dirty straw on the floor.

Jack lay on the bed trying to imagine what lay in store for him in his new life, nervous about the prospect of his first day as a proper teacher. His mind raced as he mentally planned his lessons. A gong sounded and he hurried downstairs and stood in the hall looking about him, wondering where to go. He was about to try the door next to the parlour, when he realised someone was watching him. A young woman was standing in the shadows, partly hidden by the coat stand, her voluminous skirts giving her presence away. Jack stepped forward, then hesitated. Was it polite to offer to shake a young lady's hand? Not that she was that young. At least ten years older than him, he guessed. 'You must be Miss MacBride?'

22

'You can call me Mary Ellen.'

He was surprised that she was prepared to dispense with the formalities so early in their acquaintance, but said, as was clearly expected, 'My name's Jack, Miss, Jack Brennan.'

She stepped forward into the light of the gas lamp. Her dark hair was lustrous but with a small streak of premature grey at the temples. Her features were strong and pale as if sculpted from marble. He might have thought her beautiful, but for the dullness of her eyes and the absence of expression on her face.

She put her head on one side as if weighing him up, then turned and walked away, calling over her shoulder. 'Hurry up, Jack Brennan. Papa hates lateness to table.'

He followed her along the hallway and into the dining room. Another gloomy room, although this time with a feeble fire burning in the grate. The dark green walls were hung with more paintings: mostly featuring schooners making their way through stormy seas.

Mr MacBride was sitting at the head of the table. Without looking up he said, 'Do you like paintings, Mr Brennan?'

'Yes, sir.'

'I'm something of a collector.'

'I can see that, sir.'

'Know much about art do you, lad?'

'No, sir.'

'Neither do I.' He didn't elaborate on the reason for the collection. 'Have you met my daughter, Miss Mary Ellen MacBride?'

'I've just had that pleasure, sir.'

'Pleasure? Don't be getting ideas, young man.'

Jack swallowed. 'I'm sorry, sir. I didn't mean – I was just…'

'Spit it out, man. Say what you mean. Mean what you say.'

Jack swallowed, trying to summon the confidence that he didn't feel. 'What I meant to say was it is an honour to make the acquaintance of both yourself and your daughter. I do not wish to cause offence.'

Mary Ellen, standing beside him, started to giggle.

MacBride barked at his daughter. 'Don't be tiresome, Mary Ellen. Stop that or you can go to your room.'

MacBride's tone was sharp and Jack was taken aback. The woman must be approaching thirty and yet her father spoke to her as if she were a naughty child.

She sat down, her brow furrowed by repressed anger. Mr MacBride said grace and then the supper was consumed in complete silence, punctuated only by the sound of Mac-Bride masticating his food. The meal was simple: a mutton stew with boiled potatoes and cabbage, but the portions were generous and Jack had not eaten so well in his life. He wondered whether to initiate some conversation, but decided to take his cue from his host, who ate with remark-able speed.

Jack took the opportunity to study his companions. Mr MacBride was short and stout and clearly enjoyed his food, eating with relish, while his tall, slender daughter barely touched hers, playing with it rather than eating it. There appeared to be little familial affection between them. Dinners at Virginia Lodge were unlikely to be the source of intellectual stimulation or conviviality, but, while the company may have been taciturn, Jack had no regrets about running away from home.

3

Entangled

Jack stood at the front of the schoolroom and swallowed hard. He told himself he was being foolish to feel intimidated by a couple of dozen boys under the age of eleven. Their faces were upturned towards his, with expectant expressions. He realised they were probably as nervous as he was. *The register. Start with the register.* As he called the names out, he looked up and tried to memorise the faces as each boy rose from his seat and called out, "Yes, Sir", in turn. He wondered if attendance here would be better than it had been back in Derby, where children were often absent when their families needed them to help at home or if the chance of casual work came along and presented an opportunity to add a few pennies to the family income.

The boys were ranked in rows behind their desks, the smaller ones at the front and the older boys at the back. He began the day with morning prayers, followed by recitation of the catechism, then some arithmetic drill. Maybe the pupils were on their best behaviour for the new teacher, but they were responsive and well-behaved and Jack hoped he would never have occasion to use the cane that hung on the wall at the front of the classroom.

There were two pupil monitors in the class, older boys

of around twelve or thirteen. Jack gave each of them a small group of boys to supervise as they worked at their copybooks, while he passed between them, examining each boy's work in turn. The morning passed quickly and, before he knew it, the bell was ringing to mark the two hour break for the children to go home for their dinners. Jack sat alone in the schoolroom, eating the bread and dripping, wrapped in a linen napkin, that the cook had left out for him at breakfast that morning. He swallowed it down quickly, hunger replacing the nervous energy that had fuelled him all morning. It had already been a long day, and tomorrow would be even longer, as he was expected to spend time with the monitors after class ended, teaching them the lessons they would need to pass on to the rest of the class. At least today, his first day, that would not be required.

The afternoon also went well. The children were lively but keen to learn. They recited the names of the Plantagenet kings and queens without errors and settled to draw pictures of the feeding of the five thousand with the loaves and fishes in their copy books. Jack's predecessor must have done an excellent job in discipline and teaching the basics. Before he knew it, the final bell was ringing.

Sister Callista was waiting outside the classroom door and came inside after the children had surged out. 'How did it go, Mr Brennan?'

'Well, I think, Sister.' He grinned. 'I really enjoyed it anyway.'

'That's good to hear. Children learn better if their teacher is enthusiastic. They are a bright bunch and made good progress with Miss Oxley, so I hope you will keep them on a similar track.'

'I'll do my best, Sister.'

'And so you will. You can do no more. I expect great things of you, after the confidence Mr Quinn had in you.

I would have preferred a qualified teacher, but as long as you do a good job and work hard, all will be well. I will sit in on one of your lessons, maybe in a day or so, once you've had a chance to get to know the children and get over your inevitable nerves.' She smiled and added, 'Welcome to St Bridget's. I'm delighted to have you here. Now I want you to meet the probationary teacher who is looking after the little ones.' She moved to the doorway and called out, 'Miss Hewlett, come and meet Mr Brennan, our new member of staff.'

A young woman, about his own age, entered the room. She was small, slightly built, with light brown hair and enormous brown eyes. As she stood in the doorway with the afternoon sunshine behind her, Jack was reminded of a vision of the Virgin Mary, bathed in light.

He tried to swallow and prayed his face wasn't giving away what he felt. Was that a blush suffusing her face as she looked at him? She was the loveliest creature he had ever seen. It was as though she were bathed in a radiant light. The room swirled around him, everything blurring into background. He wanted celestial trumpets to play – why didn't they? Showers of roses should be falling from the ceiling – why weren't they? Where were the choirs of jubilant angels? They were singing in his head. Jack felt an urge to rush forward and wrap the girl in his arms and crush her small body against his. Instead he coughed nervously and forced the words, 'Pleased to meet you, Miss,' out of his parched throat.

With a nod in acknowledgement of him, and a slight bob towards the headmistress, Miss Hewlett left the classroom. Jack wanted to run after her, but stood rooted to the spot, uncertain what to do or say. He'd forgotten Sister Callista was there and jumped at her voice.

'I've a school governors' meeting,' she said. 'Can't be

late for that. I'll see you tomorrow, Mr Brennan.' The nun patted his arm and left the room.

Jack gathered up his books, grabbed his cap from the hook on the back of the door and rushed outside, hoping to catch up with Miss Hewlett in the street, but there was no sign of her. To burn off his energy he ran all the way back to his lodgings, heart hammering in his chest from the exertion and his excitement. He offered up a silent prayer of thanks to his father for giving him such a good pasting and being the catalyst for the dramatic change in his fortunes. Life was good.

As he burst through the gate into the walled garden, he cannoned into Mary Ellen MacBride. She jumped aside, half stepping into a flower bed and catching her billowing skirts on a rose bush.

'I'm so sorry, Miss, I'd no idea there was anybody there.'

The woman tugged at her gown, trying in vain to disentangle herself. 'It's torn now. Completely ruined. I shall have to go and change. Will you set me free?'

Jack knelt down on the pathway at her feet. How was he to extricate her clothing from the thorns without causing her ankles to be revealed? The only way to free her was to put one hand under her skirt while the other worked the rose free from the other side, but he didn't want to do that. It would not be seemly. Swallowing nervously and looking around to make sure they were not observed, he took the fabric into his hands and shook it gently.

'That's not going to do it,' she said. 'Hurry up and get on with it. I can't stand here all day'

More conscious of the need to protect her modesty than she appeared to be, he inserted his hand between the outer layer of her gown and the multiple layers of petticoats underneath, so that there was no risk of touching her leg. It was an awkward operation and he silently cursed his fingers which had turned into a series of uncoordinated thumbs. As he struggled to disengage the fabric he was conscious of her leg pressing against his forearm. Shocked, he looked up, thinking maybe she had lost her balance. Her eyes met his but gave nothing away, yet at the same time she unmistakably increased the pressure of her leg against him.

'What's the matter?' she said. 'Stop looking at me and get on with it. I've important things to do and Papa will be going out soon. I don't want him to see me leaving. Do hurry.'

He worked the fabric free, just as the stentorian voice of Mr MacBride crashed into his ears.

'What the devil do you think you're doing, Brennan? Mary Ellen, go to your room.'

'But, Papa, I was going out for a walk.'

'You're not going anywhere. Go indoors. Look at the state of you.' A long strip of torn silk trailed from the hem of her gown.

Mr MacBride turned to Jack. 'I'll see you in my study. Before supper. At precisely twenty minutes before six o'clock.' And with that he swept past them down the pathway and out of the gate.

To Jack's horror, Mary Ellen's face was streaked with tears.

'Look what you've done, you horrible boy. He'll take all my privileges away. I'll be stuck inside this miserable house for the rest of the week and I'll go completely mad. I will. I promise you. Quite mad.' She stamped her foot on the path, sending up a small spray of gravel stones. 'It's not fair. It's all your fault.'

Her words turned into a wail as she gathered up her skirts and ran into the house. Jack remained rooted to the spot, paralysed with fear. Was his host going to tell him to leave? Would he tell Sister Callista what had happened?

Would Jack lose his job? Just as he'd landed on his feet it looked as though the ground was to be knocked away from under him. He thought of Miss Hewlett and nearly cried out with frustration. Surely he hadn't messed everything up just as he had begun to imagine the possibilities for his future?

4
Act of Contrition

Jack waited in the hallway outside his host's study. The maid, Nellie, sullen as always, had indicated the room to him. Checking the time by the long case clock in the hall, he raised his hand to knock on the door, but MacBride's baritone preempted him by booming out, 'Enter.'

The study was warm, warmer than any other room in the house, a generous fire crackling away in the grate. It was also bright, despite the wood panelled walls and the inevitable oil paintings, as the gaslights were blazing. Mac-Bride was sitting behind a large mahogany desk and there was another man sitting in the only armchair in the room. MacBride waved Jack towards a Persian rug in front of the desk, where he stood, feeling like a naughty pupil. It would not have surprised him had a dunce's cap been placed upon his head. Neither of the older men got up.

'Father O'Driscoll, this is Jack Brennan. I'd high hopes of him. He came recommended by a school in Derby, but I caught him this afternoon taking liberties with my daughter.'

The priest crossed himself and then folded his arms. He had a ruddy complexion with an even redder bulbous nose. His head was bald on top and very shiny as though he polished it every day.

'What do you have to say for yourself?' It was the priest who spoke.

'It was an accident. I meant no harm nor disrespect. I opened the gate too quickly and ran straight into Miss MacBride and caused her to catch her gown on a rosebush. I was releasing her from its clutches when Mr MacBride came upon us and I can quite understand how the situation could be misconstrued.'

'Misconstrued, eh?' the priest said. 'You are a very fortunate young man to be the beneficiary of Mr MacBride's hospitality. He has never had any trouble with previous lodgers and I trust this is not an early warning of problems with you. As the widowed father of an only daughter, Mr MacBride has placed his trust in your honour as a Catholic young man and does not want to see that trust abused…'

'No, Father.' Jack looked down, studying the intricate pattern of the Persian rug and noticing how scuffed his shoes were.

The priest went on. 'Mr MacBride has long been a pillar of the parish, but it is difficult for a man alone to be responsible for the upbringing of his daughter. Without her sainted mother – God rest her soul – to provide a guiding hand and a good example, Miss MacBride faces some difficulties and Mr MacBride and I expect you to respect her and her position. If there is ever any indication of you trying to become familiar with her, you will be asked to leave immediately and you will be dismissed from the school without references. Do you understand my meaning?'

'Yes, Father, but…'

'No buts. You are a lodger here. You are not a suitor.'

Jack thought he was going to choke. The idea of his being a potential suitor to the woman was risible.

'I expect to hear your full confession at church tomorrow after you have finished your teaching duties. In the meantime, say ten Our Fathers and ten Hail Marys and make an Act of Contrition.'

It was a moment before Jack realised the priest intended him to do it there and then. The two men were looking at him, waiting for him to start. Burning with humiliation and a sense of injustice, he dropped to his knees on the carpet in front of the desk, closed his eyes, joined his hands and began to mumble the prayers under his breath.

'Speak up, lad. God wants to hear you.'

Jack didn't see Mary Ellen again for the rest of the week. He noticed Nellie carrying a tray of food up the stairs and wondered if the young woman was to be shut away in her bedroom indefinitely, but on Sunday morning she appeared in the hall ready to accompany her father and Jack to Mass. As the three of them walked to the newly-built church next door to the school, Mr MacBride kept up a monologue detailing how he had donated substantial sums of money to fund its construction. Jack gathered that this wealth had been amassed through shipping tobacco but was wary of asking questions. As for Mary Ellen, she didn't speak to him and he didn't attempt to speak to her. Avoiding conversation seemed the wisest course if he wanted to avoid more humiliation on his knees in front of the Irish priest. Besides he had no wish to get to know her better; she seemed a troubled woman.

In the crowded church that morning there was, however, one person whom he was anxious to know better. Miss Hewlett was seated a couple of rows behind them across the aisle. Whenever the congregation rose or knelt, Jack took advantage of the mass movement to twist his head to catch a glimpse of her. She appeared oblivious to his presence. Walking back to his seat after Holy Communion, he tried to catch her eye but her head was bowed over her missal. His efforts did not go unnoticed. When Mr MacBride left the pew to pass around the collection plate, Mary Ellen leaned her head towards Jack's and whispered, 'You're sweet on that teacher, aren't you?'

He tried to pretend he hadn't heard her - but she didn't stop. 'I saw you. You can't help looking at her. Do you think she's pretty? Prettier than me?'

Jack moved away from her by shuffling sideways in the pew, desperate for her father to come back and take up his place between them. She edged towards him, closing the gap again.

'Please, Miss MacBride, your father doesn't want me talking to you.'

'How can I not talk to you when we're living in the same house?'

'We're in church. No one's meant to be talking.'

A woman in the row in front looked around pointedly, but Mary Ellen continued to whisper in Jack's ear. 'She's poor you know, that teacher. Not a penny to her name. But then you're poor too, aren't you? It must be dreadful to be poor. We're not poor. Papa is immensely rich.'

It dawned on Jack for the first time that there was something not entirely right about Mary Ellen MacBride: a slowness of wit, an absence of sensitivity. At that moment, her father returned and she bowed her head devoutly and clasped her hands in silent prayer.

When the congregation spilled outside, Jack looked around, trying to locate Miss Hewlett, but there was no sign of her. Mr MacBride was talking to the priest and summoned Jack over to join them, while Mary Ellen stood to one side, looking bored.

'I've parish business to attend to with Father O'Driscoll. Walk my daughter straight home, Mr Brennan. And mind you remember what we talked about last week. You're on your honour, lad.'

Jack was surprised and not altogether happy. He had hoped to be free to go for a walk and explore the neighbourhood and if he were being entirely honest with himself, he was hoping Miss Hewlett would be taking a walk around the parish too and he might come upon her, but he knew better than to refuse MacBride's request.

As they left the churchyard and turned the corner to walk back to Virginia Lodge, Mary Ellen said, 'Aren't you going to offer me your arm? I know you're common and poor but you should still have manners.'

'I'm sorry. I didn't mean to be rude.'

Jack held his elbow toward her and she rested her arm on his. He felt awkward and ill-matched walking beside her. She was almost the same height as him and walked with an uneven gait that caused him to keep changing pace.

'People will think we're courting,' she said.

Jack blushed to the roots. 'I don't see why.'

She stopped abruptly and pulled her arm away. Her face crumpled. He thought she was about to cry and he tried to recover the situation quickly, saying, 'I mean people might presume us to be brother and sister.'

She glared at him, looking him up and down and curling her lip at his threadbare jacket and shabby shoes. 'That's not likely.'

They walked on in silence. After a while she stopped again and said, 'Don't you like me?'

'I hardly know you, Miss, but you seem a very amiable lady,' he lied.

'But you like her better than me?'

'I don't know what you're talking about, Miss.'

'I told you to call me Mary Ellen. Well? Do you like her better? The teacher.'

'I barely know her.'

'But you were looking at her during Mass when you should have been concentrating on the blessed sacrament.'

He didn't know how to respond, so chose silence.

'Would you like to marry me?'

He laughed a nervous laugh, overcome with embarrassment, then wondered if she was trying to make a joke at his expense, but the face that looked back at him was earnest, as though she had asked a perfectly reasonable question.

'I think we'd better hurry back. Your father won't be happy if we dawdle too much.'

'Papa is an old grump. He's always finding fault with me. Ever since Mama died. It's not fair. He doesn't understand how lonely I am. I wish I was married. I want to go away and live in my own house with a husband and have lots and lots of children. But no one has asked to marry me yet. That's why I wondered if you'd like to marry me. I know you're poor but I might say yes if you ask Papa.'

He didn't know what to say. He couldn't believe what he had heard, but there was no mistake. He struggled to cover his embarrassment. Did wealthy ladies always speak their minds like this? He doubted it. There was something about Mary Ellen MacBride that he had never encountered before. Most people said what they thought people would want to hear, but she said exactly what she was thinking. And then he wondered if she was toying with him, teasing him. He looked at her face and did not believe she was dissembling. She was clearly waiting for his reply, her eyes fixed on him eagerly. If he were to treat what she had said as a joke he knew she would be offended. He swallowed, blushed and tried to look sincere and serious.

'I'm not ready to marry anybody yet' he said. 'I'm only eighteen. I've to make my way in the world first.'

'I'm twenty-nine. I'm almost an old maid and soon everyone will laugh at me. You're laughing at me now aren't you?'

'Of course I'm not, but this is not a very appropriate conversation, Miss MacBride. We've only just met. I don't think your father or Father O'Driscoll would be very happy about you discussing marriage.'

'That old devil.'

'I beg your pardon?'

'You heard me. Father O'Driscoll's an old devil. A bad man.'

'But he's the priest. He can't be a bad man.'

She snorted in derision. 'You think you're cleverer than me, Jack Brennan, but you know nothing. Nothing.'

They had reached the house and when they crossed the threshold, Mary Ellen flung her gloves onto the hall stand and ran upstairs, leaving Jack alone and puzzled in the empty hall.

5

An Object Lesson

Jack was conducting an object lesson. He held up an empty glass jar and asked the children two questions: what it was and how it was made. There were only a few raised hands for the former and a resounding silence for the latter. He chalked up an explanation of the essential ingredients and processes involved in glassmaking on the blackboard as the boys copied the notes into their exercise books. He was about to embark on a discourse on glassblowing, the various applications for glass, its impact on society and its contribution to history, when the schoolroom door opened and Sister Callista came in. She nodded to him and waved her hand to indicate that he was to continue the lesson and took a seat at the back. The pupils were unperturbed – it seemed the nun was a familiar interloper in the school-room – but Jack was overcome with nerves, stuttering and struggling to breathe, his voice rising and turning shrill like a badly played violin.

The nun smiled encouragement at him, but he was lost. The room began spinning and he could sense the children shuffling in their seats. Everything moved in slow motion. The pupils merged into a single hostile mass like a lump of cold, hard clay that was resistant to being shaped. The headmistress towered over them like the angel of death and Jack wished that the past few days had been a dream and he would wake up back in Derby on the badly-stuffed straw palliasse with his baby brother's chubby arm around his neck. Glass. Sand. Silica. Blowing. No. Not Silica. Something else. Why did it matter? What did he know anyway? He was telling them about a process he had never seen. Why hadn't he told them instead about mixing plaster? His father and Kenneth had furnished him with enough raw material to talk for twenty undiluted minutes. He coughed. He shuffled his papers. He looked up and saw Sister Callista smiling encouragement. He took a deep breath. Then another. In slowly, out slowly. And then he carried on.

This time the words flowed. He turned to the blackboard and chalked up diagrams and spelled out words and was gratified to see the boys copying them down and to hear the scratch of the younger boys' slate pencils scraping across their slate boards and the scratch of the older boys' pens as they tried to write without smudging their copy books.

At the end of the lesson the boys filed out and Sister Callista dismissed the monitors too.

'You deserve an early finish, Mr Brennan. That was a first class lesson. Well done. I'm very happy with your performance and with the conduct of the class. Mr Quinn was right to have faith in you. I will be making a very favourable report to Mr MacBride, Father O'Driscoll and the other governors.' With that, she swept out of the schoolroom and Jack's grin was as wide as the Bristol Channel.

He didn't go straight home. Instead he sat at the teacher's desk and penned a letter to his mother. He would send it care of Mr Quinn. He wanted her to know he was safe, but conscious of the need to avoid putting her at risk from one of his father's drunken outbursts, he decided to keep his location secret, merely reassuring his mother that he was safe, living in a Catholic household and pursuing a teaching career.

So absorbed was he in the writing, it was only when he was shaking the sand to blot the ink that he looked up and saw Miss Hewlett sitting at one of the desks at the back of the room. He hadn't heard her enter.

'Good afternoon, Miss Hewlett,' he stammered, then realised he sounded like the children greeting their teacher in unison. He felt the blood rush to his face and was aware that his heart was hammering against his ribcage.

She smiled at him, 'I understand you're an expert on the art of blowing glass, Mr Brennan.'

He felt a fool. She was trifling with him. But being trifled with by Miss Hewlett was a punishment he would gladly suffer.

He got up from the desk and walked towards her. 'Are you interested in glassblowing, Miss Hewlett?'

'Not at all. Are you, Mr Brennan?'

'No. Not at all.'

'So what are you interested in?'

'Poetry. I like to write poetry.'

'Love poetry?'

He felt his face grow hot. 'I haven't tried that yet. Mostly I write about nature. About life.'

'Isn't love a part of life?'

'I suppose it is. But not something I have had experience of… yet.'

'And do you suppose I have?'

Her voice was flirtatious and he wondered if the heat of his skin meant his face was red.

'I have no idea.'

'Well, I haven't. But I think I should like to.'

'I would too.'

She smiled and it lit up her whole face. 'I must be getting home. Good night, Mr Brennan.'

He moved towards her, his natural hesitancy overwhelmed by the need to be close to her and a sudden determination not to let her leave.

'May I walk you home, Miss Hewlett?'

She hesitated then said, 'I suppose I can't really stop you.'

'Do you want to stop me?' His voice was hesitant, fearing her reply. 'I don't want you to walk with me just because you think you have no choice in the matter.'

'Oh, I always have a choice, Mr Brennan. As it happens you must pass by my house on your way home to the MacBrides.'

'You know that I'm staying with the MacBrides?'

Did that mean she had taken the trouble to find out?.

She looked slightly scornful at his widened eyes. 'Everyone in this parish knows everything about everybody.' She moved towards the door, then hesitated. 'Well? Are you coming?'

Jack needed no more encouragement. He grabbed his parcel of books and followed her out of the schoolroom.

He fell into step beside her, surprised that she had a brisk walk. It occurred to him that they were taking the same route that he had walked on Sunday with Mary Ellen beside him. Remembering her comment that he had been rude in failing to offer his arm, he proffered an elbow to Miss Hewlett. Instead of resting her arm on his, she linked hers through his as though it were the most natural thing in the world.

'So, are you going to let me read them?'

'Read what?' he said, though he knew exactly what she meant.

'Your poems. I should very much like to.'

'They're not up to much. I've not shown them to anyone before. Apart from my sister, who read them without asking and told me they were stupid.'

'Stupid? How cruel!'

'She said they were too soft. She doesn't have much appreciation for nature.'

'You said they were about life too. What about life?'

'Just daft stuff. My hopes and dreams.'

'Why's that daft?'

'Well, that's what our Cecily reckoned. She's my sister. She told my parents I'd been writing about wanting to be a teacher and there was a big row.'

He paused, swallowed, then on a hunch, decided to tell her everything. 'They expected me to be a priest and I didn't want to, so I ran away. I was lucky enough to be recommended for this post.'

'A priest.' She looked amused. 'Can't see that myself. You look far too worldly for a life of prayer and devotion.'

Jack wondered if that was meant to be a compliment or an insult, but decided not to ask. 'What about you?' he asked instead.

'What about me?'

'Did you want to be a teacher? Or did you just fall into it?'

'Yes, I suppose I did rather fall into it. I certainly didn't want to be a nun, if that's what you mean.' She laughed. 'I didn't have to worry about upsetting my parents as I don't have any.'

He looked sideways at her, wondering if she was joking again.

'They're dead. My mother died giving birth to me, and my father was killed on the docks when I was thirteen.'

Jack wanted to put his arms around her and comfort her, but she didn't look as though she wanted to be comforted. She was walking along beside him, swinging her bag of books and looking as though she hadn't a care in the world. He thought about the enormity of being left alone at age thirteen. It was hard to contemplate - he had always taken for granted being a member of a large tribe.

Unable to help himself, he squeezed her arm. 'What happened to you? Who took care of you?'

'My stepmother at first. But she married again last year.

Now I have a lodging with a family in the parish. Sister Callista helped me. She persuaded Father O'Driscoll that I should be taken on as a teacher, even though I don't have the qualifications. She's a kind woman.'

'You have no other family?'

She shook her head. Then she stopped and squeezed his arm back. 'But now I have you to be my friend, Mr Brennan. At least I hope I do.'

Jack's face lit up as he grinned at her. 'You certainly do. And I think that means you must call me Jack.'

'Then you must call me Eliza.' She held her hand out towards him and he took it, feeling her small and delicate fingers through her gloves.

'Friends?'

'Friends,' she replied.

Perhaps it was because Jack had begun to feel he would not see his family again, and because Eliza had nobody herself, that the friendship between them deepened so rapidly. She waited behind after her class had gone home and appeared at the schoolroom door each evening as soon as he had completed the monitors' lessons, which kept him for two hours after he finished with the infants. Then they would talk for a while in the empty classroom before walking home together.

When the weather grew finer, during the school dinner break, they took to meeting in a nearby park, where they sat side by side under the shelter of the empty bandstand, holding hands and throwing bread crusts to the ducks.

Jack was reticent about sharing his poetry, his experiences with his sister still being raw, but one dinner hour when they were sitting together in the park, Eliza eventually prevailed upon him to let her read the poems. Jack shuffled his feet as she read, unable to control his nerves and anxious about her verdict.

'You've been on a train journey, Jack?' She looked up from her study of the pages he handed to her. 'I'd love to travel on a railway, to see the world flying by through the windows.' She read one of the poems aloud, ending with the lines:

I gazed through the carriage window's dirty glass
At the kilns and factories, fields and sheep.
I wondered what my life would bring to pass
And hoped that love, not disappointment, would I reap.

'I thought you said you didn't write about love, Jack?'

'It's not about love. It's just about the hope of it.'

'I think it's nice. I can picture you staring through the dirty window as the landscape rushes by, not knowing what the future would bring you. But why did you think it might disappoint you?'

'I don't know. Maybe because I hadn't met you yet.' He didn't look at her, but stared down at his shoes as he scuffed them against the ground.

'Are you teasing me or flirting with me?'

'What do you think?'

'I don't know, Jack Brennan. Sometimes I find you hard to read.'

'Well, I can tell you that if I'd any idea I'd be meeting someone like you when I got to Bristol I'd not have had a doubt in my head. I'd have been singing like a song thrush all the way here.'

She pushed her shoulder against his. 'You daft ha'peth.'

He grinned at her. 'I'm daft on you. That's for sure.'

'I think you should send these to a publisher or to one of the newspapers.'

'Now who's being daft?' he said.

'Why not? You have to believe in yourself, Jack. They're as good as any I've read. Why shouldn't you get them published? Wouldn't you like that?'

'I would.'

'Then send them off.'

He closed the notebook and put it in his coat pocket, saying nothing.

Eliza shook her head and he could tell she was frustrated by him. He didn't want to do as she suggested. He couldn't bear the thought of failing, of someone telling him he wasn't good enough. Better to keep the poems to himself and never risk that.

That night when he lay in his narrow bed, staring up at the ceiling, he thought of her, hoping he might carry her image with him into his dreams. She behaved as though she believed in him more than he believed in himself. He wished he had her spirit, her fearlessness, her conviction. Maybe with her he might do the things he would never have dared to do himself. Maybe he would send those poems off one day.

He knew he was in love with her, that he could love no other, that he had found his one true love.

6
Reading Lessons

One Saturday morning, after breakfast, seeing the garden bathed in summer sunshine, Jack took his notebook and went to sit on a bench under a chestnut tree. These days his poems as well as his thoughts were full of Eliza. Her image appeared as soon as he closed his eyes and every word that flowed from his pen was in some way inspired by her. It wasn't just that she was beautiful. There was something about her that made perfect sense to him. He felt he had always known her, or had felt her lack before he had known her. Their being together seemed inevitable and incontrovertible. There had never been any awkwardness between them. He supposed some might think Eliza had been forward – making it clear so early in their acquaintance that she liked him, offering her friendship without condition, suggesting they use each other's christian names. But it was so natural, so unaffected, so without guile, that to him there could be no doubt. They were meant to be together.

He sat under the tree, gazing up at the pale blue sky through the branches, which were starting to thicken out with the buds of new leaves. He whispered her name: *Eliza, Eliza.* He would marry her. Soon. Why not? She had no family to object to the match. Then he remembered he would have to wait until he had saved enough money. Once married, Eliza would have to give up her teaching post and they would both have to get by on just his salary. He had already repaid the few shillings Mr Quinn had lent him and had sent some money via him to his mother, but it had been returned with a note from his old teacher to say that Annie Brennan had refused to take his money. He'd felt sad to think of her turning the money away, too proud, too hurt, still angry that her favourite son had defied his father and walked away from the family. She would have seen it as an act of betrayal. But this sadness was tempered by a sense of relief. He could save every penny now towards the day he would ask Eliza to marry him. It would be hard. It might take years before he had enough, but once he'd set some money aside as a sign of intent, he'd feel able to ask her to commit to him.

He still hadn't kissed her. When they sat together in the park during the school dinner break, it took an enormous effort of will to keep from pulling her towards him and pressing his mouth to hers. He imagined himself drowning in the sweetness of her. But he knew that to steal a kiss was to risk her reputation and both their jobs.

He sighed a deep sigh and opened his eyes. Mary Ellen MacBride was standing in front of him, so close that her skirts were crushed against his trouser legs. Involuntarily, he leaned back.

'I need you to help me,' she said.

'Help you? How?'

'With reading. Papa says I am slow-witted and will never be any good at it, but I think you can help me get better. You're a teacher. You can show me how.'

He looked up at her, blinking into the sunlight, unsure what to say.

She moved to sit beside him on the bench. 'Move up a bit.'

He edged along to make room and she sat down,

perching at an angle on the edge of the seat so that her gown could be accommodated. She handed him a book. It was a reader, a simple alphabet reader, not unlike those Eliza used with the infants' class.

'Is this what you want to read?' he asked. 'Isn't it a bit childish?'

She looked mortified and dropped her head. 'Now you're going to make fun of me. You'll tell people I'm stupid.'

'Of course I won't, Mary Ellen. I just thought there might be something more fitting for you to read. Something more interesting.'

'I can't. It's too hard. The letters all jumble up on the page and I can't make any sense of them.'

'Didn't anyone teach you to read when you were a child?'

'Mama. A little. But she didn't really like doing it. She got cross with me. Papa says it's not important because ladies don't need to be able to read, but I feel so silly. I wish I could have gone to school and learned properly. Please will you help me?' She looked up at him, eyes welling with tears.

'Does Mr MacBride know? Did you tell him you were going to ask me to help you?'

She shook her head. Then she clasped his hands, placing hers around his. 'It's a surprise. I want to surprise him. Please, please, Jack. Help me.'

Jack knew he had no choice.

They started that morning. He quickly discovered that she had not exaggerated when she told him the letters were just jumbled shapes to her. Teaching her was going to try his patience and would eat into much of his free time. Yet he felt sorry for her. Her anguish and humiliation were real. She was ashamed and, it seemed to him, afraid. It was hard to comprehend. Reading and writing had come so easily to him. He tried to imagine what life must be like without being able to do it and was determined to help her succeed.

So it began. Every Saturday morning and for half an hour after supper each evening, except Sundays. They worked in the garden when it was fine and in the parlour when it was not. If Thomas MacBride was aware of the reading lessons, he never mentioned it. Jack did nothing to keep it secret but he did not advertise it either. Slowly, Mary Ellen improved. She would never be a fluent reader, would be unlikely to progress beyond the level of attainment of the ten-year-olds who were to graduate from his class in the summer to enter the workplace. But that in itself was a big step forward from where she started.

Despite their regular meetings he always felt awkward in her company. He was embarrassed at her slowness of wit. And he couldn't forget her strange outburst after Mass those months ago, even though she never gave any sign of repeating the sentiments.

Jack's favourite time of the week was Sunday afternoon. He and Eliza were still keeping their friendship secret so there was no walking home together after Mass. Instead they would meet up in the afternoons and take long walks together in other parts of the city where there was little risk of being spotted by anyone from the parish. Not that they were doing anything wrong or improper – but he feared that neither Mr MacBride nor the parish priest would approve of a blossoming romance between two teachers.

They were standing on the Clifton Suspension Bridge, surreptitiously holding hands, peering over the parapet to look down on the river and the gorge below. It was one of their favourite places. They liked to watch the ships passing underneath on their way to the Floating Harbour, or back out to join the Severn estuary and the open sea. The hey day of Bristol had past with the end of the slave trade, then left behind in the rapid race for growth of other more ambitious ports.

'I used to come down to the docks with my father, before he married my stepmother. He loved ships. He used to say, "Where do you think that one's going?" or, "What do think they've got on board?" and he'd make me think about how big the world out there is. Timber from Sweden. Tea from India. Tobacco and cotton from America. Silk from China. I used to wish I could sail away to places like Zanzibar and Calcutta and sail home again on a big ship weighed down with spices. Of course there was no bridge here then. We used to stand on the top of the cliffs and look down.'

'Had your father been to sea himself?'

'No. He used to say if my mother hadn't come along he'd have run away to sea, but he never got to leave Bristol.'

'I come from a family of landlubbers. You can't get much further from the sea than Derby.'

'Don't you ever wish you could sail away though, Jack? You know, just drift off into the sunset not knowing where the sea might take you?' she asked.

Jack pushed his hair out of his eyes. 'Can't say I do.'

'I'd like to,' she said. 'Not to Zanzibar or Calcutta but one day I'd like to go to America.'

'America? Why?'

'I don't rightly know. I think of it as a magical place across the ocean with great cities for me to discover. There was a man in our street left England poor as a church mouse, promising to make enough money to send for his wife and children. Two years later he was rolling in money. They went out to join him in a first class cabin.'

'How did he make his money?'

'Something to do with the Civil War. I think he was transporting goods from one side of the country to the other. Probably smuggling!' She laughed. 'Everyone in America starts out with nothing and it's up to them how well they do. I like that. The trouble with England is you have to have money and position to start with or you get nowhere.'

Jack turned sideways so he could look at her, while still leaning on the bridge. 'Does that matter to you, Eliza? Money?'

She smiled. 'Not really. I don't care at all about money itself. I just like the idea of not being held back. Of being somewhere where there's limitless opportunities. And I like the idea of new beginnings. Of having the chance to make something of oneself. Not being held back because you come from the wrong background.'

Jack turned back and looked down at the river below. 'Doesn't it scare you though? The thought of being somewhere so different? Cut off from everything you know?'

She looked surprised. 'No. I think it's exciting. Does it scare you?'

'It does a bit.'

'But you upped sticks and left Derby and came here.'

'I know. But it's one thing to get on a train and travel a few hours and quite another to sail to the other side of the world.'

'So what do you dream of, Jack, if it's not foreign lands then?'

'I like to think of making something of myself, but not in a financial sense. I'd like to do something I can feel proud of. Do a good job as a teacher. Keep writing my poems and then maybe one day find someone who likes them enough to publish them.'

'You won't get rich on poetry,' she said. 'And you can't wait for someone to come along and publish them. You have to send them off to be considered.'

'I don't care about getting rich. Just as long as I have enough to keep a wife and a family and put bread on the table.' He looked away as he spoke, knowing as he said the words that she was thinking the same thing he was. Then to break the tension that had suddenly sprung up between them he said, 'But it sounds like you want to be rich one day?'

She pushed his arm playfully. 'Now I didn't say that at all, Jack Brennan. I just want to live a happy life.'

He looked down at her face looking up at his and decided to take her in his arms and kiss her. He leaned towards her, breathing in the smell of her, her violet-scented soap, but she stepped back and, shivering, said, 'It's getting cold. We should be getting back, Jack. I'm expected back for Sunday tea at six.'

The spell was broken and he felt a moment of self-doubt. Maybe she didn't like him in that way at all? He stared down at his shoes, as usual scuffed and battered and today bearing a patina of dust from the track they had followed across Clifton Down to the bridge. He ran his hand through his hair, pushing it out of his eyes. Why would a girl like Eliza be interested in him? She was pretty enough to have her pick of the parish. He felt dispirited. Was she toying with him? Stringing him along until someone better, someone richer came along?

She slipped her hand through his arm. 'Why are you looking so glum, Jack Brennan?' She turned a smile upon him and it was as if the whole day was transformed. The sun, as though it had been waiting for the moment, broke through the cloud and lit up the sward in front of them. His spirits immediately lifted. As they walked back, Eliza pointed out the names of flowers and trees to him. He tried to remember them, thinking he might use them in a poem, a poem like all his poems now, about her.

7

Christmas in Bristol

As Christmas neared, Jack realised he was missing his family. Since he'd been in Bristol he'd tried not to think too much about them, especially since the snub he had received from his mother. His growing preoccupation with Eliza had made it easier. But Christmas had always been special. Since Dom became a priest and Bernie entered the seminary, the two oldest brothers had usually been missing for the Christmas festivities, it being one of the busiest times of the year for the priesthood. Despite their absence, it was always a convivial family time. As money was so tight Annie Brennan, determined to make the most of the festival, put aside a few pennies each week and paid them into a Christmas Club - safe from the reach of Bill on those days when he was short and pressed her for a refund of some of the housekeeping for beer money. The Christmas Club parcel usually contained enough treats to make the day memorable and special for the family.

Being allowed to stay up late for Midnight Mass was special for the younger children and Jack had loved setting out with the whole family in the dark to the church and singing carols on the way home. As he thought about past Christmases with nostalgia, Jack decided to use some of his savings to buy a greetings card to send home to them. He chose one with a small child feeding a robin in the snow. He picked it because the child reminded him of his seven year old sister, Emma. He wrote the greeting inside, carefully blotting the ink and wondering if he would be missed in Derby.

Christmas in the MacBride's household was a more solemn affair. It had been at Christmas that the late Mrs MacBride had died, the victim of a lingering illness. The only effort at seasonal cheer was a small Christmas tree in the hall, decorated by Mary Ellen.

Jack overheard Nellie grumbling to the cook about it.

'Darned nuisance that fir tree. It's me that has to clear up all the needles afterwards. They get everywhere – stick in the rugs and down between the floorboards. I were made up when he said we wouldn't be having one any more after Missus passed away and then her ladyship started her whining and caterwauling until he gave in.'

Jack was glad that Mary Ellen had made her stand. Although small and bereft of candles, the tree offered a small note of cheer, bedecked with red ribbons and hung with sweets, brightening up the normally drab hallway.

To his relief, there was no exchange of gifts between the members of the household, other than small tokens handed over with great formality by Mary Ellen to the servants, who were required to line up to receive them when the family returned from Mass.

Jack slipped away as soon as the luncheon was finished, leaving his landlord snoring in front of a fire in his study and Mary Ellen noisily practising her scales on the pianoforte. He left by the back door and made his way to the little park where he had arranged to meet Eliza. He hated the furtiveness of their meetings, the way that they had to wrap up against the cold and walk around to keep warm as there was nowhere indoors they could spend time together.

She was already waiting in the park, pacing up and down, stamping her feet beside the small duckpond, frozen over and missing its ducks. As soon as she saw him, she ran towards him, stopping just short of him, uncertain, shy, until he pulled her into his arms and hugged her. The air around them was misty from their breath.

'Let's walk,' he said. 'We'll be warmer that way.'

They linked arms and walked along.

Eliza stopped. 'I have a present for you, Jack.'

'And I for you, my dear friend.'

'You first!'

He reached into his coat pocket and pulled out a small brown paper parcel.

'Let me guess!' She was laughing as she spoke. 'A parasol? A nosegay? A puppy dog?'

'You're daft, girl. Go on. Open it.' He thrust the small parcel into her hands.

She gave him her gloves and wincing at the cold, unpicked the tight knot he had tied in the string. It was a glass inkstand.

'I've got you some blotting paper as well but I'll give you that later. I didn't want it to get crushed in my pocket.'

'Oh, Jack. That's the loveliest present. I've never had an inkwell of my own. But what shall I use it for? I'll have to start writing poetry like you.' She smiled up at him. 'No one's given me a gift since my Daddy died. Thank you, Jack. I shall treasure this as long as I live.'

'It's not much. Not as much as I'd like to give you. If I were rich I'd buy you beautiful gowns and dainty shoes and hats with feathers and a tortoiseshell hairbrush.'

'I think this is far finer than any of those things! I couldn't give a fig for a hat with a feather. You've made me so happy. Now it's my turn.'

She handed him a rectangular-shaped package. 'I saved my best ribbon to tie it.'

'Then you must have your best ribbon back. I want to see it in your hair.' He opened the parcel to reveal an inlaid wooden box. The marquetry lid showed the Clifton Suspension Bridge, straddling the Severn Gorge.

He gasped. 'That must have cost you a fortune. It's beautiful. Such fine work. Oh, Eliza, you shouldn't have spent so much on me. I don't know what to say.'

'Say nothing. And I didn't spend a farthing. My Daddy gave it to me. He carved it himself. He always wanted to be a craftsman but it never happened. He used to make little boxes in his spare time. This was his favourite. He loved the suspension bridge. I told you that, didn't I? He used to take me there. He made this the year it opened, when I was just seven. He gave it to me for my eighth birthday.'

'I can't take it, Eliza. I couldn't possibly. Is it all you have of him?'

She nodded. 'But that's why I want you to have it. To prove how much I like you, Jack. So you can think of me whenever you see it. Now open it. There's something inside.'

He opened the lid but could see nothing but an empty space.

'There's a secret compartment. In the back of the lid. Here let me show you.'

She took the box from him and slid a small panel in the lid. Inside in a tiny space, large enough only to hide a small folded letter or piece of ribbon, she had placed a lock of her hair. Jack closed the panel and looked at her. Her face was open and her eyes shone.

'I have another surprise for you, Jack. What's the time?'

'Three o'clock. You don't have to go?' There was a note of panic in his voice.

'No. We both do. We've been invited to tea. To the home of my friends, the Wenlocks. Cora was the teacher you replaced after she was married. Miss Oxley. They live with the parents of her husband Cyril in a big house up

56

in Clifton. They have just had a baby and they've asked us for tea and have promised we shall all play parlour games afterwards. And best of all, Jack, we will be nice and warm!'

The extended Wenlock family welcomed Jack and Eliza into their home as though they were part of the family. As well as Eliza's friend Cora, her husband and baby, there was a full complement of in-laws – Cyril's parents, his sister and her husband and three children, his younger unmarried brother and a older widowed sister with five children. When Jack and Eliza entered the house, it was apparent the party had already begun. There was the sound of a pianoforte coming from one room, a toy trumpet from another and one small child was spinning a top in the hallway while another ran around perched on a hobbyhorse. The hall and bannisters were garlanded with holly and ivy and mistletoe hung from a chandelier. They were ushered into a room with a blazing fire and gratefully moved closer to it.

As promised, there were assorted games after the high tea had been served and consumed, then someone suggested they do some play reading.

Ernest, the unmarried son, turned to Jack and Eliza, 'Has to be Shakespeare. Family tradition. We do it every Christmas. I vote for a tragedy.'

Cora looked up from the sleeping baby on her lap, 'But it's Christmas, Ernest! We don't want to make ourselves sad.'

'No, no, no, that's the whole point!' the young man said. 'We all make ourselves feel terribly sad then we have fun and play some more games.'

Jack looked at Eliza, doubtfully.

Ernest spoke again. 'I vote Romeo and Juliet. Act 5. Plenty of dead bodies. I'll be Romeo.'

'You're always Romeo.' His mother smiled at him indulgently. 'And not Romeo and Juliet – please, not again. Not today.'

Ernest groaned. 'I was looking forward to dying. I've been practising.'

'For goodness sake, Ernie, it's a reading, not a full performance. I won't have you throwing yourself around the floor and pretending to foam at the mouth like you did on my birthday.' She was trying to sound cross but her smile betrayed her.

Cora said, 'Let's do The Tempest. We haven't had that for a while and there's lots of parts. You can put on a deep voice, Ernie, and be Prospero.'

'Perhaps Mr Brennan would like to take the part?' her mother said.

Jack shook his head vigorously. He didn't want to be in the spotlight and was already wishing it were time to leave.

'He can be one of the courtiers.' Ernest's voice was dismissive. 'Cyril you can be Caliban. And perhaps Miss Hewlett would do us the honour of playing Miranda?'

To Jack's surprise, Eliza clapped her hands together and said, 'Can I really? How thrilling. I love play-acting.'

As Jack had expected, Ernest Wenlock read the part of Prospero with a loud, blustering declamation that betrayed his lack of understanding of the sense of the words and appreciation of the beauty of the verse. The other participants all gave a reasonable rendition of the scene, albeit punctuated by laughter. There were just two copies of the play, necessitating much elbowing, fumbling, losing of the place and missing of lines.

The hilarity ceased completely though when Miranda was speaking. Jack was astonished at the fluidity and beauty of Eliza's voice as she interpreted the part. Listening to her words, he felt transported beyond the crowded room with its blazing fire and carried away to the distant island with its airy spirits. Her voice was clear and sonorous and she spoke the role in a gentle and understated way that was in marked contrast to the braggadocio of Ernest's Prospero and the garbled, giggled speeches of the others. As he looked at her, Jack's eyes brimmed and he told himself that he had never been happier.

Sister Callista stopped Jack as he was about to enter his classroom.

'Mr Brennan, a letter has arrived for you and it carries a postmark from Derby.'

Jack had waited over six months for some acknowledgement of his Christmas greeting card so he could wait a bit longer. He'd save the letter until the dinner break.

His hope of a rapprochement with his family faded as he read. The letter was from his brother informing him of his father's death and telling him that the funeral had already taken place. Jack was stung. He had no time for his father but he was crushed that no one in the family had thought to get word to him that he was dying and invite him to pay his respects. Not even his mother. All this time and not a word from her. Over a year now. He'd spent money he could ill afford on the Christmas greeting card and had swallowed his pride in sending it. He'd even included his father in the good wishes he'd written inside. They'd not even acknowledged it. That was it then. He felt tears coming but brushed them away. Sod the lot of them.

He still had the letter in his hands when Eliza arrived in the park to meet him. He stuffed it into his pocket.

'What is it, Jack? Not bad news?' asked Eliza.

'My father's dead. Lungs pegged out. Emphysema. All those years of mixing plaster and breathing in the dust.'

'I'm so sorry, my darling.'

'He was a rotten devil.'

'Oh, Jack! Don't speak ill of the dead. He's your father. It's not right.'

'But it's true. He was a drunk and a bully and the world

will be a better place without him.'

'You'll go home for the funeral of course? Sister Callista and I can manage your class while you're gone.'

'I'm not going.'

'But, Jack, even if not for him, go for your mother. She'll be needing you. And funerals have a way of bringing families together.'

His voice was uncharacteristically curt as he said, 'Funeral's already happened so that's that.' He turned his head away from Eliza and went into the schoolroom.

8

The Parish Picnic

The annual picnic was the highlight of the Catholic diocesan year. Everyone in the surrounding parishes: parents and children, nuns, priests and teachers, old and young, rich and – more usually – poor, went on foot or took the new horse trams from the city centre, carrying baskets of food and wearing their Sunday best. Their destination was the downland above the city at Clifton.

Jack, as a member of the teaching community, was expected to assist with the supervision of the children as they participated in sprints, sack races and ran with the egg and spoon. Eliza was relegated to serving the refreshments as well as keeping an eye on the smaller children. The whole community was in high spirits and the sun had emerged from behind the clouds that had blanketed the city for days. The afternoon was becoming balmy and everyone seemed set on having a good day, enjoying a welcome respite from the drudgery of work and the deprivations of poverty.

The Down was a popular venue for the townsfolk of Bristol and the surrounding areas, commanding views across the Severn Gorge and the Clifton Suspension Bridge. The plateau was perfect for large groups and for organised games, being flat, grassy and these days grazed by no more than a handful of sheep. Once the races had been run and prizes duly dispensed, the families regrouped, seating themselves on the green sward to consume the victuals they had brought, supplemented by the additional provisions laid on by the parishes and their benefactors, including Thomas MacBride.

The occasion was intended to be a sober one, but as the afternoon wore on, Jack noticed that many of the men were swigging beer, having hidden flasks of ale about their persons. There was also an organised effort by a couple of Irishmen, who were collecting cash and orders, then deploying young lads at a penny each to run to one of the local hostelries to purchase beer. If the members of the clergy present were aware of this they chose not to acknowledge it. The combination of high spirits, freedom from work, warm sunshine and strong ale was already having an effect on many of the crowd and their behaviour was becoming more boisterous. Jack decided it was time to seek out Eliza and find out if she would be prepared to slip away from the hullabaloo for a walk to Brunel's great bridge. After several months in Bristol it had become a special place for them. Most of all he wanted to be alone with Eliza.

He wandered around the large, open upland, weaving his way between the families stretched out on the grass, some of the fathers now lying on their backs enjoying a smoke or a sleep in the sunshine, while the mothers ignored their offspring and chatted amongst themselves. There was no sign of Eliza and he began to feel anxious. Had she already left? Was she avoiding him?.

'Jack Brennan, where do you think you're going?' Mary Ellen was sitting on a wooden bench, her face slightly damp with sweat from the heat of the afternoon, despite the fact that she was holding a sunshade in one hand while frantically fanning herself with the other. 'You were about to walk right past me, you rude boy. Were you pretending not to see me?' She motioned to the seat beside her. 'Sit down,' she said imperiously.

He hesitated, looking around him, still hoping to spot Eliza and anxious that Mr MacBride should not see him with his daughter and misconstrue the circumstances. But Mary Ellen's expression made it clear she would brook no argument, so he sat down on the bench beside her.

'Are you having a pleasant afternoon, Miss MacBride?'

'I keep telling you to call me Mary Ellen,' she said, her tone testy. 'And no, I am not. It's far too hot and I don't like all these dreadful people everywhere. I feel quite unwell. I want you to take me home at once.'

He looked around again, hoping to find deliverance. 'Where's your father? Have you told him you want to go home?'

'Yes, and he said you were to take me. Didn't he tell you?'

'I can't. I have to be here for the children. We teachers are expected to be present until the end to make sure everyone gets home safely.'

'Well, it's not the end and I want to get home safely. So you can take me home now and come back again later if you must.'

'But your father?'

'He told me to use the carriage. It's waiting over there.' She batted a fly away with her fan. 'This is so tiresome. I want to go home. I don't like all these horrid people everywhere.'

Jack stood and gazed around, hoping to spot his landlord so he could seek his corroboration, but there was no sign of him. Sighing, he offered an arm to Mary Ellen and walked with her in the direction of the carriage. He climbed in after helping her inside and positioned himself opposite.

She was smiling, as though in triumph, and started to giggle. Pointing to the plush velvet seat beside her, she said in a breathless whisper, 'Don't you want to sit beside me, Jack? I might let you kiss me.'

He blushed, sat down opposite her and stared out of the window, pretending not to hear.

She banged on the carriage wall to instruct the driver and the vehicle moved off. Jack felt her foot brush against the leg of his trousers, then, when it failed to provoke a response, she slipped off her shoe and started to rub her foot up and down his shin. He twisted to one side.

She was laughing again. 'Come on, Jack. No one can see us.' She lifted the edge of her skirt and petticoats to reveal her leg as far as the knee.

'Miss MacBride. Stop that. If your father could see you…'

'I don't care. And what's wrong? It's just a bit of fun. Would you like to touch my leg? You put your hand up my skirt when you tangled me up in that rose bush. This time no one can see us so I'll let you touch my knees. Don't you want to?'

'No, I don't. Please stop. This is unseemly.'

She laughed and widened her eyes. With a jolt, Jack saw that she appeared almost maniacal.

'*Unseemly*! Listen to you! Anyone would think you knew what you were talking about. But Papa says you were born in the slums of Derby. You're just the same as all those people on the Down – just with a few more fancy words and book knowledge. I suppose you think you're better than me, because you've been helping me with my reading, but you're not. You still belong to the lower orders.'

'Please, Mary Ellen, stop this talk. It makes me uncomfortable.'

She opened her legs and placed one foot one either side of his legs and started to work her feet up and down the side of his calves, while pulling her skirts higher up above her knees.

'For heaven's sake, stop it or I'll get down from the carriage.' He reached his hand to the door handle.

'Don't be a silly boy. You'll fall out and hurt yourself.'

'Stop it then.' He looked about him in rising panic, feeling trapped inside the moving carriage. The horse was moving downhill at a pace and the carriage was lurching and he was jolted forwards almost landing in his persecutor's lap.

She held her arms out to steady him and tried to pull him into the seat beside her. Jack was suddenly angry and jerked his arms away, moving his body sideways so her feet dropped back to the floor.

She pushed her feet back into her shoes, then shuffled sideways along the seat away from him and looked out of the opposite window. The rest of the short trip was made in silence and as soon as they pulled up outside the house and he had handed her down from the carriage she ran inside.

The driver leaned down and jerked his head at Jack. 'Mr MacBride wants me to bring the carriage back to collect him but he said naught about there being a passenger.'

With a crack of his whip he pulled away. Evidently Jack's position in the household as lodger was unworthy of any deference from the coachman.

It was a full hour later by the time Jack got back up to the Down. He had to walk to the tram depot and then wait among the crowds queuing to take the trip to Clifton for a late afternoon stroll.

There was no sign of the parish picnic breaking up. People were snoozing in the sunshine, some singing, some playing ball games, others just sitting and talking. He meandered between the groups, looking for Eliza.

Eventually he spotted her, standing at the edge of the Down, near the roadway which led back to the horse tram terminus. She was surrounded by a group of about half a dozen young men.

Jack started to run towards them, his chest pounding, breathless. He couldn't bear to think of these strange men talking to her, flirting with her, charming her. Or worse, the idea of them teasing her or being abusive. He called out her name. She looked up, her face breaking into a smile that set his heart racing.

She spoke, her voice artificially loud, staged, clearly for the benefit of the men around her. 'Here he is. This is my young man. I knew he'd be here in a moment. Very nice to meet you, gentlemen, but now I'll bid you a good afternoon.' Her eyes bore into Jack's as though silently telegraphing him to keep quiet.

He looked at the men. They were youths, a few of them looked younger than he was; the others perhaps a few years older.

A tall man with a scar running across his brow, stepped forward. 'What you staring at, Paddy?'

Eliza intervened. 'Come on, Jack. We need to get back to the picnic.' She grabbed his elbow and tried to steer him away.

Jack stood his ground. 'A cat can look at a king. And this cat's not called Paddy.'

'All you lot are Paddies. Just a bunch of spud eaters and bogtrotters.'

'I was born in Derby. I've never been to Ireland in my life. And my parents were born and bred over here.' As he spoke Jack regretted his words, felt he was betraying the children he taught at school, many of whom, both here and in Derby, were from large Irish families. Indeed, his own family was originally from Ireland – even if it were a generation or more back.

Eliza tugged at his sleeve. 'Jack, please.'

The same man spoke again. 'Looks like your sweetheart's getting impatient, Jackie-boy. Better do as she says.' His face distorted with a lewd expression.

Jack was overwhelmed with anger. It was one thing to insult him but quite another to cast aspersions on Eliza's character. He wanted to smash the lascivious grin off the man's ugly face. He lunged at him, but before he could hit his target a hand gripped his shoulder, holding him back. He twisted round to see Father O'Driscoll.

'Do I know you lads? Don't think I've seen you at Mass before? Why are you lurking on the edge of things here? Come on and join in. Perhaps you'd like to help the little ones play with a football?'

A tall red-headed man spoke with a sneer. 'We're not Catholics.'

'No? Then you'd better take yourselves off and find something to do with yourselves, hadn't you, boys? Unless you'd like to become converts? I'd be happy to hear your confessions and set you up for some ecclesiastical instruction. Everyone's welcome.'

'Sod that!' said one.

'Come on, lads. Let's bugger off. I've had enough of this lot.' The speaker was the scar-faced man. He slung an arm around the shoulders of two of the others and turned them away towards the road. The other three scowled at Jack and the priest and then followed after their cronies.

Father O'Driscoll turned his attention to Jack and Eliza. 'As for you two, you should know better than to get mixed up with a bunch of heathens like that. Get back to your charges.'

He walked off, leaving them staring after him until they saw him enter a public house a couple of hundred yards down the road.

Jack reached for Eliza's hand. 'Come on. Let's go for a walk to the Suspension Bridge.'

They set off, hand in hand, skirting the large area clustered with recumbent parishioners, sleeping off the effects of the beer in the sunshine. They walked in silence until they reached the Promenade and made their way along in the shade of the avenue of beech and elm trees.

Jack was the first to speak. 'Were they bothering you, those lads? Were they frightening you?'

Eliza smiled up at him. 'Not really. They were just teasing. A bit of high spirits.'

'What did they say?' He felt his jaw tighten as he thought of the men and how they had surrounded Eliza.

'Oh, nothing much really. They were only there a minute or two before you rescued me.'

Jack snorted. 'Rescued you? I didn't even get the chance. I'd have liked to flatten that fellow. I'd have given him another scar to make his *fizzog* look a bit more symmetrical. I wish Father O'D hadn't come along.'

'Well, I'm glad he did. There were six of them and I'd like to keep you in one piece.'

'Would you?' He grinned at her. 'Wouldn't you like me if I got bashed up and looked all scarred like that fellow did?'

'I certainly wouldn't like you to get hurt and I certainly wouldn't like you to look like that fellow - not because of the scars but because if you looked like him you wouldn't look like you and I like you looking like you.'

She was blushing. Jack leaned in, about to kiss her, looking into her eyes and recognising that she wanted him to do that too, when the moment was fractured by a long, shrill, wolf whistle, followed by a slow handclap.

Jack stepped away from Eliza as though stung. The beauty of the moment was shattered. He had felt as though they were the only people in the world and now it was horribly apparent they were not. The six men were standing in a line, blocking the path.

Eliza moved back towards him, placing her body closely in front of his so he could feel the hardness of her spine against his chest as she leant back against him, making contact despite the fullness of her skirt. He reached out and put his hands on her upper arms, moved her aside and stepped in front of her.

'What do you want?' he asked the gang of men.

Eliza tugged at Jack's arms, trying to jerk him around to head in the opposite direction, back towards the open plateau and the crowds.

Seeing her intent, three of the men broke away and moved round them, spacing themselves apart to block the avenue in the other direction.

The man with the scar spoke first. 'You Catholics are at it all the time, aren't you? Like a load of bloody rabbits. Is that what you were going to do then, Jackie boy - take your Irish lassie behind a tree and give her a good banging? Aren't you scared of what that old papist will say to you in the confession box when you tell him what you've done?'

Jack could feel Eliza's small hands squeezing his arms tightly and heard her whisper. 'Don't rise to it, Jack. Just keep quiet. They'll get bored and go away.'

'I bet that's how the old priest gets off, isn't it? Whacking-off listening to all the sins you lot share with him? What a fucked-up religion.'

Jack breathed in deeply, willing himself to stay calm, trying to work out his next move. He didn't care what they said about the church, but he couldn't bear to hear them speak like this about Eliza.

The scarred ringleader spoke again. 'I've heard you Catholic girls go like a steam turbine.' He mimed the action, pumping his hips back and forth rapidly while his cohort sniggered and imitated him. 'Isn't that right, girl? He doesn't look like he'd be up to that. Just a scrap of a lad. Maybe his little balls haven't even dropped yet. I bet you'd like to do it with a real man wouldn't you, lass?'

It was too much for Jack. He jerked his arms free of Eliza and lunged at his antagonist, running at him, head down, butting into his stomach. Taking the man by surprise Jack launched him backwards so they both landed in a heap on the ground. The man tried to get up, clutching his stomach in pain and gasping for breath. Jack followed up his assault by raining punches onto his head. Thumping him. Pounding his fists into the man's skull. Pummeling him. He wanted to beat his brains out. All the repressed anger and fury at his own father came out for all the beatings he'd had. Blood on his knuckles. Sweat pouring from his face into his eyes. Blind to his own pain. Deaf to the screams of his victim.

Then he was grabbed on all sides by the other gang members, wrenched backwards and thrown onto the ground where they all set about kicking him. He was hazily aware of Eliza crying and calling his name and he curled himself into a tight foetal ball as the kicks descended on him from all directions. He tucked in his head and tried to protect his stomach and his balls but their boots pounded into him, thundering blows onto him, until it all faded into a merciful nothingness when he passed out.

He awoke to find himself lying with his head in Eliza's lap as she stroked his blood-matted hair. He was distantly aware of someone else and realised a doctor was listening to his chest with a stethoscope. He looked up into Eliza's eyes then it all faded away again.

He spent two days in bed, swathed in bandages and drifting in and out of sleep. He was nursed by a reluctant Nellie, who had a sulky expression on her face whenever she entered the room and offered him nothing in the way of conversation. Late on the second day, hearing the sound of someone knocking at the front door his heart lifted in the hope that it was Eliza come to visit him, but the footsteps on the stairs were heavy ones.

Father O'Driscoll entered the room without knocking and after looking around in vain for a chair, plonked himself down on the end of the bed. Jack moved his feet out of the way.

'How are you doing, lad? No broken bones I hear. The doctor says you're a lucky man. That was quite a kicking you took.'

Jack nodded and tried to pull himself up the bed, but gasped as a sharp pain pierced his lower back. His kidneys had taken a hammering.

The priest tutted. 'The incident has been raised with the police. Clearly a shocking example of anti-Catholic brutality. The bishop has asked me to give him a full report of what happened. If you tell me I can have a statement drawn up for you to sign.'

'I don't remember much.'

'How did they insult the church? What did they say?'

'They were trying to goad me generally. Called me a Paddy. And then they were offensive about Miss Hewlett.'

'Never mind that. She had no business walking alone with you. What did she expect? She'll get no sympathy from me. No, I want to know what they said about the church. Things have been quiet lately on that front and the bishop has been hinting about holding talks with his Protestant counterparts regarding educational issues across the city. We don't want that now, do we, Mr Brennan? We don't want interference in how we educate our children, from a bunch of Proddies. Obviously, if there is a resurgence of anti-catholic feeling, such talks will be out of the question. Do you follow what I am saying, young man? Do I make myself clear? Now, tell me what they said about the Catholic church.'

Jack hesitated. The priest was oblivious to the physical harm inflicted by the gang and hostile to Eliza. All he cared about was turning the situation to his political advantage. Jack was mindful of Father O'Driscoll's patronage and fearful of upsetting him.

Jack chose his words carefully. 'They were generally being insulting, but to be honest, Father, it was more about Miss Hewlett. They were trying to imply that as a Catholic girl she was of low morals.'

'Well, they have a point about her morality. But you say they attributed that to her Catholicism?'

Jack winced as he pulled himself further up the bed until he could lean against the headboard and look the priest in the eye. The man was nothing but a bully and one had to stand up to bullies. 'Miss Hewlett has done nothing wrong. Nothing. Do you understand me? I took on those lads because they were saying bad things about her and it strikes me, Father, you're now doing the same and I'll not have it.'

He slumped back against the pillow, adrenaline pumping through him, but a sense of satisfaction infusing his whole body.

The priest went red in the face and little globs of spit sprayed from his lips as he responded to Jack. 'Don't you dare speak to me like that. If the girl is prepared to go walking with a man, unchaperoned, she's got no one but herself to blame if she gets a reputation. She's supposed to be a teacher not a kitchen skivvy. Dr Morrison says you've had concussion so I'm giving you the benefit of the doubt and assuming that your insolence is down to its after-effects.

'I have prepared this statement for you to sign, summarising what took place on Clifton Down.' He handed a sheet of paper to Jack.

Jack read it and looked up at the priest. 'I can't sign this, Father. Not without some changes.'

'Sign it!' The priest was angry.

Jack took up his pen and struck through the offending sentences, then signed his name underneath and handed it back.

The priest scanned the paper then screwed it into a ball and tossed it across the room. 'You will regret this, Brennan.'

9
The Choir

Eliza was avoiding him. He had hardly seen her since the fight on Clifton Down. Their dinnertime trips to the park had ceased and when he went in search of her each day, she had always already left the school to eat her dinner elsewhere. In school hours they were occupied in their separate classrooms. During the quiet study periods, as his class scratched away at their slates in silence, he was reduced to moving close to the partition wall where he strained to hear the faint sound of her voice addressing the infants on the other side. When the bell rang at the end of classes she left at once, while Jack had to stay on to teach the monitors. Walking home every night he was keenly aware of her absence and tortured himself trying to think of a pretext to meet her. He walked past her lodgings, wanting to knock on her door but lacking the courage. What held him back was fear. Fear that his foolhardiness might cost her her job. Whatever Father O'Driscoll had said to her had had its effect. But underlying this was also the fear that she didn't want to see him any more: that she no longer loved him. He had been beaten by those men. He had failed to protect her and he felt weak, emasculated, ashamed and afraid that she saw him in the same way.

Even as these negative thoughts were weighing him down, the memory of her looking at him would come into his head and he was overcome with a desperate need to see her. Every time he closed his eyes he would see hers. He had to find a way to meet her outside school hours. Months of meeting only at dinnertime, on the all-too-brief walk home after school, and exchanging furtive glances across the aisle during Mass, had already pushed his self control to its limit. This current enforced separation was intolerable.

He was consumed with rage and injustice when he thought of the insults O'Driscoll had heaped on Eliza, while, on the other hand, the priest was evidently unaware of the behaviour of Mary Ellen MacBride, which merited such insults. Mary Ellen was a plaster saint, apparently regarded by the priest and her father as a virtuous woman. Jack wanted to scream and punch things when he recalled her inappropriate behaviour in the carriage. Meanwhile, he could reveal nothing of it while being forced to listen to calumnies heaped upon the head of Eliza.

When Sister Callista summoned them both to her room, a couple of weeks after the picnic, Jack was trembling with fear that further sanctions against them had been recommended by the priest. His anxiety was compounded with nervousness about being in the same room as Eliza. He was overjoyed at the prospect of being near to her at last, but terrified that she might give him the cold shoulder. When he entered the room Eliza was already there. As soon as he saw her face he knew it was all right. She still cared for him. Her eyes were smiling and she gave him a look of tenderness and concern, but said nothing, waiting for the nun to speak.

The two of them stood side by side in front of the desk, waiting while Sister Callista shuffled papers on her desk. At last she looked up.

'Do you sing?' she asked.

Jack looked at Eliza, seeking a cue from her as to how to answer.

'I can hold a tune,' the girl said.

Jack shuffled on the spot. 'We used to sing at home sometimes. Irish ballads mostly. And at High Mass – I can sing the *Tantum Ergo* well enough.'

'There's a choir starting up in the parish. We need some young voices. Every Thursday, seven o'clock until nine. You'll have to eat your suppers quickly. Rehearsals will be here in the school. We plan to be ready to perform in time for the opening of the new parish hall. Can I count on you both?'

Jack felt a surge of joy replacing his anxiety. He looked at Eliza and grinned. He wanted to hug her – and Sister Callista too. Then he remembered the priest.

'Does Father O'Driscoll know?' he asked.

'Know what?' The nun's tone was brisk.

'That we will both be in the choir?'

'Why on earth should he? I expect my teachers to set a good example to the rest of the parish and I hope that many other young parishioners will follow your example and join the choir. As no doubt does Father himself. Now, Miss Hewlett, you may go. I'd like to have a word alone with Mr Brennan.'

Jack watched as his sweetheart left the room, fighting the temptation to run after her.

'I feel it's only right to warn you that you have somehow managed to get yourself into Father O'Driscoll's bad books. Do you have any idea why?'

'I don't think he approves of me.'

'That's perfectly clear. But why?'

'He wanted me to make up things about the men who attacked me.'

She raised her eyebrows. 'Go on.'

'He wanted it to look like the reason for the attack was anti-Catholicism and wanted me to sign a statement, but what he'd written in it wasn't true so I refused. I couldn't sign up to something false. Was I wrong, Sister?'

'No. You were right not to put your name to a lie. I expect it's a case of a misunderstanding on Father's part. He seems to be unduly perturbed by the Bishop's desire to build bridges across the communities. Personally, I think what is being done by the Ragged School for the education of the poor is only to be applauded. After all, there are more children than we can handle across the few schools we have and anything that helps them to acquire some learning is to be commended, whether it be inside or outside the church.'

Jack stared at her in surprise. She was making an unveiled criticism of the priest.

She carried on. 'Last week Father O'Driscoll found out that three Catholic children, who by rights should be part of this parish, had attended the Ragged School. It was closer to their home and the children have no shoes to walk all the way here. But Father O'Driscoll gave the children a flogging and threatened to excommunicate the parents. Then as though to sugar the pill, he gave the children each a pair of shoes. You know as well as I do, Mr Brennan, the parents will as likely pawn the shoes, so what good will that do? The father in question is too ill to work and the family are destitute. Now they'll get no education at all. Sometimes I wonder...'

She turned away from him and stared out of the window as though in a dream. 'I'm sorry. I've said more than I intended but I know I can trust your discretion, Mr Brennan.'

Realising their interview had come to an end, Jack left the room.

Any hope Jack entertained of surreptitiously holding Eliza's hand in the back row of the choir was quickly disabused. The women were grouped apart from the men and all he could see of his beloved was the top of her head. But two whole hours in the same room as her filled him with joy. And he exulted in the possibility of having a legitimate reason to walk her home. As it was after dark, there was no question of her making her way home alone. At the end of the first practice he edged his way to the small group of women with whom Eliza was standing.

'Miss Hewlett? May I walk you back to your lodgings?'

She looked around her nervously, as though expecting Father O'Driscoll to materialise. 'I couldn't possibly put you to that trouble, Mr Brennan.'

'It's no trouble,' he said. 'I have to walk the same way myself.' As he spoke he noticed a couple of the younger women giggling.

The rather large matronly woman who had accompanied them on the pianoforte spoke up. 'Go on, Liza. Otherwise I'll be asking the nice young man to walk me home instead.'

Much hilarity ensued and Jack was about to retreat in embarrassment when Eliza stepped forward and nodded her agreement.

Outside, they hurried along the dark street, keeping a wide distance between them until well past the environs of the church and schoolhouse. As they reached a patch of open ground, overlooked by a terrace of rather grand houses, they stopped and looked at each other.

'Oh, Jack,' Eliza said. 'It's been awful. Not seeing you. Not being able to talk to you. I've been worried sick about you. When you missed school and were so badly hurt I didn't know what to do. I wanted to come to see you but Sister Callista told me not to. But I couldn't stand it and I went past the MacBrides and stood outside in the dark looking up at the house and wondering which room was yours and whether you might be able to see me.'

He took hold of her hands but she held them out rigidly in front of her to keep him at arm's length.

'What did he say to you? Father O'Driscoll. What did he say?'

'Not much. Just told me I was lucky to keep my employment. Told me to meditate on the Blessed Virgin and say the Five Sorrowful Mysteries of the Rosary every night.' She gave a hollow laugh. 'He accused me of being fast. Said I'd brought what happened upon you myself. You don't think I'm fast, do you, Jack?'

Jack's breath caught in his throat and he moved towards her, gathering her into his arms, but she pulled away again.

'He's not a good man, Eliza. Never mind the vestments he wears. He asked me to tell lies about what happened. Just to meet his own political ends. I wouldn't do it and I won't give you up either. What's it to him? We've done nothing wrong. Why shouldn't I be courting you?'

She looked up at him. 'You could lose your job.'

'He's bluffing. He's trying to frighten you into thinking he'll have me dismissed while saying the same thing to me about you. We've done nothing wrong. There's no law against us walking out together.'

'He said it's not appropriate conduct for two members of staff to be affectionate with each other.'

'As long as nothing happens in school. I'll act like I don't know you if that will make you happy. I'll never utter a word to you within the premises – just as long as we can see each other occasionally outside. We have little enough free time anyway. He can't object to that, can he? He won't even find out if we're careful.'

Eliza looked up at him and smiled and he reached for her hand. This time she let him take it.

They had been attending choir for about three weeks. Passing the park on their walk home one night, Jack pulled Eliza aside under cover of darkness into the recessed park gateway. He pressed her up against the stone pillar and finally kissed her. At first he thought she was angry. She looked startled and pulled away from him and his heart almost stopped beating. He'd messed it up good and proper. But she looked up at him, locked her eyes on his, then with a mumbled, 'Come here,' she fastened her lips on his again and kissed him until he thought he'd die for lack of breath and an overdose of happiness.

When the kiss was over, a wave of pure joy washed over Jack and he couldn't stop himself from jumping in the air and whooping in triumph. In a mixture of wild joy and a desire to impress Eliza, he performed a cartwheel in front of her.

'Stop that! You crazy man! Someone might see.' She was laughing. 'You'll have to marry me now, Jack Brennan. Now that you've kissed me like that. You're not going to give Father O'Driscoll another excuse to say I'm a girl of easy virtue?' She smiled and he knew she was teasing him.

'You know I'll marry you. I want nothing else. I'm that desperate to have you for mine. To be with you always. To go to sleep with you in my arms.' The darkness covered his reddening face. 'Eliza Hewlett, I love the bones of you. I sometimes think I'll go crazy if I have to live another day without you.'

She gave her little tinkling laugh, that to him always sounded as sweet as birdsong. 'I love you too. I'm so happy, Jack. I never thought I could be as happy as this.'

He flung himself onto his knees in front of her. 'Marry me. Marry me now. Let's get the banns read right away. I'll go and talk to Father O'Driscoll.'

She laid her hand on his arm and pulled him to his feet, suddenly serious. 'No, Jack. Don't be daft. We can't marry yet. You know that as well as I do. We have to save up first. We have to be patient.'

'I can't stand it, Eliza. I have no patience.'

She laughed again, then reached out and stroked his hair. 'Oh Jack, Jack, you're a good lad, but a hotheaded one. It's lucky I'm sensible enough for the two of us. We need to be patient. We have to wait. After all, our whole lives are ahead of us. You're not yet twenty and I've just turned nineteen. We've plenty of time. And the longer we wait the sweeter it will be.'

He took her hand and they walked slowly back onto the road towards her lodgings. At the door, he sighed and squeezed her hand one last time. 'I can't wait for the day when I don't have to say goodbye to you but will come home after school every night and find you waiting for me. I'll kiss you so much, girl, you won't know what's hit you. Good night, my darling one. Sweet dreams.'

'Sweet dreams to you too, my sweetheart.'

Jack set off to walk the mile or so to the MacBride house as though he were floating above the roadway. He wanted to cry out at the top of his voice, 'She loves me! She loves me! She's going to marry me.' Part of him wished he could take her back to Derby to show her off to his family. Even his father would surely have been impressed if he'd had the chance to meet her. But his father was dead and his family was also dead to him now. That made him, like her, an orphan. She was the only family to him now. He thanked God and vowed to say the rosary in gratitude to the Blessed Virgin for smiling upon him.

Jack turned the corner to take a short cut down a back alley that led to a lane just behind the MacBride house. It cut a few minutes off the journey, but there were no lamplights. There was no moon tonight either, so he trod carefully, wanting to avoid potholes in the rough unmade surface. After he'd gone a short distance he cursed his stupidity for venturing this way. Half way along the alley he paused, a stab of fear shooting through his body. There was a dark bulky shape against the wall on one side ahead of him, moving back and forth rhythmically and emitting a low grunting noise. Rooted to the spot, Jack waited, then heard another sound, this time higher, lighter, almost a cry of pain; then another long low grunt followed by female laughter. He stepped back and flattened his body against the wall as it dawned on him what was happening. He'd heard those noises before as a small boy when he'd woken with a bad dream in the night and, seeking comfort from his mother, wandered into the darkened kitchen, only to see the silhouette of his father's body moving up and down on top of her, accompanied by grunting and groaning from the pair of them. He'd crept back to bed and lain there sleepless, terrified and ashamed.

The man pulled away and said something that Jack couldn't catch. He prayed they'd leave by the other end of the alleyway so they'd not find out he'd witnessed what had happened. He felt disturbed and embarrassed, yet strangely aroused.

To his intense relief, the dark shapes moved away and were swallowed up by the night. He heard their voices fading into the distance. He waited a few minutes and once it was silent, continued on his way. At the end of the alleyway he came upon what he thought at first was a heap of rags on the corner. Moving closer, he heard whimpering and realised it was the woman. He was afraid. She must be a prostitute and he was anxious to avoid having to speak with her, yet as she appeared to be in some distress he could hardly walk by. He reached out a hand to help her to her feet.

'Get off me,' she shouted. There was something familiar about the voice.

'Are you hurt? Were you attacked?' he asked.

'Leave me alone, Jack Brennan.'

Mary Ellen MacBride.

'Mary Ellen. What are you doing out in the streets at

night? Who was that man? Let me get you home.'

He reached down to take her arm but she shoved him away.

'Leave me be. Go away.'

'No, I won't. I'm going to get you home so we can tell your father what has happened. He can summon a policeman. It's not too late to catch that man. Did he hurt you badly? Did he strike you? Did he threaten you?' He thought of the gang of men he'd met on Clifton Down.

'You stupid fool. Don't you dare tell my father. You have to help me get back into the house without him hearing me.'

Jack stood there open-mouthed, disbelieving what she was saying. 'Who was that man?'

'He's my sweetheart.' She began to wail again.

'Your sweetheart? Where on earth did you meet him?'

She didn't reply – just snivelled and sobbed.

'Does your father know you've been seeing a man?'

'Of course not. Papa doesn't let me do anything. He wants me to sit around the house all day, sewing. But I won't. How will I ever find a husband when I'm shut away all day long?'

'And tonight?'

'Papa is at a meeting in the city. I slipped out when Nellie wasn't looking. He gets her to spy on me.'

'Did you arrange to meet this man?'

'I saw him from the bedroom window. He was waiting under the streetlamp and I came out to meet him.'

Jack paused, took a deep breath then decided he must go on.

'What you were doing with him just now – you know that wasn't right? You know he was doing something an honourable gentleman would never do to a lady?'

She jerked away from him.

'Have you done that with him before?'

'Once. Why are you asking me this? It's nothing to do with you.'

'Have you arranged to meet him again?'

She began to wail, a keening noise, like an unhappy child, deprived of a favourite toy. To all intents and purposes she was a child.

'What happened, Mary Ellen? Did he hit you? Did he knock you over? Why were you lying on the ground?'

Her voice was nasal, whining. 'He said he won't meet me any more. He laughed at me and said I was stupid. Then he pushed me over and ran away.'

Jack looked around them in the gloom. There was no sign of the man. If he was running, he'd be halfway to the Bristol docks by now. Should he tell MacBride what had happened?

'We need to go home, Mary Ellen. Come on.' He took her elbow and led her out of the dark alley and onto the road that led to Virginia Lodge.

'You won't tell Papa, will you? Please, Jack. He'll lock me in my bedroom. Please don't tell.'

He wondered whether he should seek the advice of Sister Callista or ask Eliza what to do. As they walked back to the house he decided discretion was called for. Mary Ellen was vulnerable and over-trusting and he did not want to ruin her reputation.

'Will you promise me that you'll never meet anyone like that again? It's not right to do what you were doing with him. It's something you only do with your husband once you are married and then only in the privacy of your bedroom. Not up against a wall in a dark alley.'

'I like what he did to me. It felt nice inside. Like a tickle.'

'Mary Ellen! Promise me.'

'All right. I promise. If you promise you won't tell Papa what you saw.' Tears gone, her voice took on a wheedling tone. 'Wouldn't you like to do that with me some time, Jack?

You could come into my bedroom when Papa is out. Or we could ask Papa if we could get married. Then we could do it every night! Have you ever done it before, Jack? I don't think you have, have you? You'd like it. I promise you. I can show you how. Just like you helping me with my reading.'

Her eyes were staring. He felt a little afraid of her.

'What do you think?' she said. 'Or do you still like that stupid teacher more than me?'

Jack was lost for words. The woman was unbalanced. He felt incapable of comprehending her or what had happened. The happiness of the time he had just spent with Eliza was overshadowed by what he had witnessed with Mary Ellen. He was torn between wanting to protect the evidently vulnerable woman and not wanting to cause trouble for her. He knew Mr MacBride would not take kindly to the idea of his daughter having sexual relations in the street with a stranger.

He unlocked the back door and Mary Ellen followed him into the house, then darted past him and ran straight upstairs. He hung his jacket and cap on a hook in the back corridor and turned to go upstairs himself, when he saw Nellie watching him from the kitchen doorway. Before he could bid her goodnight she'd moved back into the room and shut the door.

Jack stood in the dark hall for a few moments, agonising with his conscience. Should he speak up or keep his word to Mary Ellen? He tried to imagine telling Mr MacBride about what he had witnessed and shuddered at the thought. The man would never believe him. He could scarcely believe it himself. Better to keep his counsel and hope that Mary Ellen had learnt her lesson.

10
Mary Ellen's Predicament

Jack received a summons during breakfast to go immediately to his landlord's study. He felt as though history was repeating itself when he entered the room and saw Father O'Driscoll in the armchair and Thomas MacBride behind the desk. Jack stood in front of them and waited to be reprimanded, wondering what unknown transgression he was to be carpeted for this time. It could be nothing to do with Mary Ellen. She had been avoiding him since their encounter in the alleyway several weeks ago and had abandoned their regular reading lessons.

The unknown transgression must have been serious as MacBride looked as though he was ready to disembowel him. He could hardly bring himself to speak. The words he finally spoke were shot at Jack like gunfire.

'Despicable reprobate! Loathsome creature! I opened my doors to you and welcomed you into my home. You have abused my trust, Brennan.'

Jack stood slack-jawed, not knowing how to respond.

'I trusted you. I should have realised when I caught you before, that you are a blackguard and a villain. I should have thrown you out on your skinny arse then.'

'I… I… don't under…'

'Vile wretch. Hanging is too good for you.' MacBride reached for his snuffbox, took a pinch and sneezed.

Jack was bewildered, completely at a loss as to what misdemeanour he might have committed. MacBride's rage meant it must be extremely serious. He knew he had done nothing to provoke such an outburst, but the anger of his landlord and the presence of the priest filled Jack with fear. His palms were clammy and he felt the sweat break out on his forehead.

Father O'Driscoll took over. 'You have betrayed the trust of your benefactor, your church and the whole community. You have been entrusted with the education of the boys of this parish when you are not a fit person. What do you have to say for yourself?'

'I don't know what you're talking about.' Jack wracked his brains. Perhaps he had been seen with Eliza.

'Father, I intend to marry her, but I need to save up some money first.'

'Too right you'll marry her.' MacBride spluttered. Little drops of spittle sprayed the desk and Jack's face. 'And before the month's out. She's already far gone. You've brought shame on her and this family with your immoral acts. It's a disgrace. You filthy seducer.'

Jack's blood froze. Eliza pregnant? How? Who? It wasn't possible. They had done no more than kiss. What was the priest talking about?.

The priest intervened. 'Leave this to me, Tom.' He got out of his chair and grabbed Jack by the collar. 'You're a dirty little dog. You've taken advantage of a poor afflicted woman. You should be ashamed of yourself. I'd like to beat the hide off you and kick from you here back to wherever you came from.'

Jack pulled away from his grasp and looked between one man and the other. 'I don't know what you're talking about. I've never taken advantage of Miss Hewlett. I love her and

I'd never do anything to bring shame upon her. Someone is making mischief.'

'Miss Hewlett?' MacBride's eyes were bulging and his face was the colour of claret. 'Who said anything about Miss Hewlett? Or are you telling me you've had your way with her as well?'

Jack was caught up in something he could't understand. It felt as though he and the two men were speaking in different languages. He opened his mouth but couldn't form any words. Then it dawned on him that they were talking about Mary Ellen. Before he could shape some kind of reply, the priest swung his arm out and caught him a blow across his face that sent him reeling. He stumbled back and banged into the door, catching his hipbone on the handle. O'Driscoll grabbed him and pulled him upright again, shoving him back to stand in front of the desk.

Jack tried to breathe but the room was spinning. At last he spoke, the words, slow and deliberate. 'I have never laid a finger on Miss MacBride.'

'You liar. Remember you're lying to a priest.' MacBride's voice was strident.

'I'm telling you the truth. I've never touched her. The only contact we have is when I help her with her reading.'

'You foul creature. How low have you stooped? Winning over her confidence and trust by offering to help with her reading and writing. An innocent young woman,' said the priest.

'She didn't need any help.' MacBride slammed his fist on the desk. 'What does a woman need with book learning? I only agreed to you teaching her when she begged me on her knees. And she only did that because you must have made her feel ashamed about being backward. You exploited her. You did it to gain her trust so you could shame her and bring her low with your filthy, venal ways.'

Jack was indignant. He had gone out of his way to help

Mary Ellen: he had been kind to her, devoted time to helping her, only for it to be thrown back in his face. How could they possibly think he had seduced her? 'Sir, I promise you. I swear in the name of God and my own mother, I have never laid a finger on Mary Ellen.'

The priest slapped him across the face again. 'It's Miss MacBride to you. At least until after the banns are read.'

Marriage! Were they insane? He felt the metallic taste of blood in his mouth as he bit his lip. 'I can't marry her. I can't.' Jack raised his eyes to the ceiling in supplication of heaven. 'It's all wrong. I love Miss Hewlett. I have never made any advances to Miss MacBride.'

'Oh no? Then how come she is in the family way then?'

Jack's stomach lurched and he thought he was going to be sick.

'Six months gone, according to Doctor Morrison,' said MacBride. 'She says you forced her.'

Jack's stomach lurched. 'I swear to God I never touched her.'

He felt the blow land on his head again as Father O'Driscoll swung at him. 'Don't you dare take the Lord's name in vain and blaspheme him with your filthy lies.'

The panic was overwhelming Jack. He couldn't breathe. Make it stop. Make them understand. Wrong, wrong, wrong. 'It wasn't me. Ask her. She'll tell you. I tried to help her.'

'We have asked her and she told us exactly what happened. That you promised to marry her if she let you have your way with her. You know the girl is backward. You exploited her ignorance.'

Jack couldn't believe what he was hearing. After all he had done for Mary Ellen. Why had she lied about him? 'Why would I do that?'

'Because you are filled with carnal lust. Because you are a contemptible, dirty-minded scoundrel. Because you are the lowest of the low. Shame on you.'

'It's a lie. I didn't do it.' Rising panic. Taste of bile. Sweat pouring into his eyes. Make them stop. Make them believe. Tell them about the man in the alley. No don't. They won't believe it. It will make things worse. Trapped, cornered, outmanoeuvred. No choices. No way out. Say something. 'Someone else has done this to her. I don't know why she told you it was I.'

'She told us it was you because that is the truth. She has been brought up to have no secrets in the eyes of God, to honour her parents and to always speak the truth,' said MacBride. 'I curse the day I ever opened the doors of this house to you. I let a viper into the heart of my family. I let a snake corrupt the innocence of my only child.'

The priest was pacing up and down in front of the french windows. He turned now and addressed them both. 'This blame throwing must stop now. We need to make the best of this matter. Tom, you know she'll never have another opportunity. She was destined for spinsterhood. Look on the bright side. The girl will be off your hands. If they marry as soon as possible we can get them away from here and no one will be any the wiser about the child being conceived out of wedlock.'

MacBride glared at Jack. 'I hate to think of this piece of scum getting rewarded with my daughter after what he's done.'

Jack could take no more. Enough. He had to stand up for himself. 'I won't marry your daughter, sir. Not on any account. I have told you on my honour that I have not done what you accuse me of. I plan to marry another woman and cannot go along with this. I am truly sorry about what has happened to Miss MacBride, but it has nothing to do with me.'

The priest landed another blow on his head, sending him reeling and causing him to trip over the grate. He stayed down on all fours, tucking his head between his arms as the priest began raining kicks upon him.

'That's enough.' Thomas MacBride got up from the desk. 'I don't want him going to the altar in a wheelchair. We have to make the best of the situation now.'

'You're right, Tom.' The priest fell back into his chair and ran his hands over the top of his shiny scalp. 'I have an idea,' he said. 'My cousin has a parish in the north of England in Middlesbrough. The school there is bigger than St Bridget's. I'll write and tell him to find a post for Brennan here. I'll say they've been married six months already. No one will be any the wiser. You'll have to give them some money to see them settled, but once they're gone you won't need to set eyes on the pair of them again.'

The panic was rising. Jack wanted to scream. He felt as though he was being shut up in a dark, locked room with no exit. His words rushed out in a torrent. 'You can't do that, Father. It's not right. I can't marry Miss MacBride. I have no feelings for her. I love someone else. I'm happy teaching at the school here. Sister Callista is very satisfied with my progress. I don't want to go to Middlesbrough. I want to stay here and marry Miss Hewlett.' As he said the words he knew they were the truest he had ever spoken in his life.

'Your wishes are of no interest to me. If it were up to me you'd be cast out to starve on the streets. We have only the interests of that poor, silly girl to think of. So you can shut your mouth. I will prepare a letter of resignation for you to sign and convey to Sister Callista. And I will call the banns this week.' The priest looked at Jack as though he were shit on the sole of his shoe.

MacBride spoke again. 'Once you are married you will take my daughter away and I don't want to see either of you again as long as I live. I don't want to see her child either, so don't come to me asking for money or begging forgiveness.

I'll give you thirty guineas, then you're to be gone from my life for ever.'

Then it dawned on Jack. MacBride had wanted his daughter off his hands all along. Nothing Jack could say or do would make any difference.

When at last he was released, Jack ran all the way to school. He was late. His heart was pounding and he gulped in air as though starved of oxygen. He wanted to keep on running. Running for his life. Running away from Virginia Lodge. Running towards Eliza. Oh, Eliza, my Eliza. What can I tell you? Please believe me. What shall I do? How did I let this happen? Help me, my love, help me.

The letter for Sister Callista was in his pocket. Maybe he could enlist her help? Tell her everything and perhaps prevail upon her to intercede with Mary Ellen's father and the parish priest.

His thoughts went back to Eliza. How could he expect her to believe him? Even if he were able to get out of marrying Mary Ellen, he'd never be able to convince Eliza to marry him after this. His reputation would be destroyed. Whichever way he looked at the situation it was a complete and utter mess. His life was in ruins. He looked up to the cloudy sky as he ran and called on the Blessed Virgin to help him.

Somehow Jack waited until after the morning class, impatient to find a solution to his problems but fearful of the reaction he would get from Sister Callista and from Eliza. It was hard to concentrate during the lessons as the panic was ever present. His stomach kept churning and he felt shivers running up and down his arms. Once the monitors had tidied away the slates and cleaned the blackboard, he went to see Sister Callista. She motioned to him to sit at one of the children's desks and she took up a place beside him.

'What's wrong, Mr Brennan? Nothing amiss between you and Miss Hewlett, I trust?' She smiled and her eyes were full of kindness.

Jack felt a lump in his throat. He swallowed, coughed, then fiddled with the threadbare cuffs of his shirt.

'I have a problem.'

'Well, what is it they say? A problem shared is a problem halved.' She laid her hand over his. 'What is it?'

'I'm in love with Miss Hewlett.'

'That seems to me a very nice problem to have. I think you make a delightful couple.'

'That's just it though. We can't marry.'

'If you both put aside as much of your salary as you can – and the school board has talked about increasing the stipend next year – in a few more years I'm sure you'll have enough saved to see you through. Can't you wait that long?'

'It's not the money. I can't marry Eliza – Miss Hewlett – because Father O'Driscoll and Mr MacBride say I have to marry Mary Ellen.'

The headmistress frowned. '*Have* to marry her?'

He nodded, but avoided her eyes.

'Do you mean to say she is in a certain delicate condition?'

He nodded again then quickly added, 'It's nothing to do with me, Sister. I swear I've never laid a hand on her.'

'I believe you. I know you well enough – Eliza too – to know that you two have eyes only for each other. So why do they expect you to marry her?'

He told her what had happened in MacBride's study that morning.

'I see' she said again, then cupped her chin with her two hands and stared into the middle distance. 'And do you know who is responsible for Miss MacBride's plight?'

Jack told her about the encounter in the alleyway.

'Holy Mother of God.' She crossed herself. 'And Miss Hewlett?'

'She doesn't know.'

'You love her?'

'More than life itself.'

'Yes I think you do, Mr Brennan. I think you do. And I expect she feels the same about you, doesn't she?'

He nodded, then gave a little choked cry. 'Oh, dear God, what have I done?'

'It sounds to me as though you have done nothing. Apart from perhaps being rather too discreet and respectful of poor Miss MacBride's wishes. I can see I must help you. You and Miss Hewlett must go away from here. As quickly as possible and as far as possible. Go and fetch her now. When does Mr MacBride expect you home tonight?'

'He has parish business every Tuesday. He doesn't get home until after nine o'clock.'

'Good. Now hurry, there's no time to lose.'

11
Embarkation

Eliza was still in her empty classroom, the children having departed for their dinner break. When Jack walked in she rushed over to embrace him, but he held at her arm's length.

'What's wrong, Jack?'

'You need to come with me to see Sister.'

'Jack?'

He took her by the arm and led her out of the room, ignoring her protests. He was so frightened he could barely breathe, terrified that once she knew what had happened she would want no more to do with him.

Sister Callista was waiting for them.

'We have no time to spare. I know what Thomas Mac-Bride is like when he's set his mind to something,' she said.

'What's going on? What's happened?' said Eliza.

Jack threw a plaintive look at the headmistress. He couldn't bear to break the news to Eliza. He prayed that she would realise the whole story was preposterous.

Sister Callista reached out and clasped Eliza's hands between hers. 'Miss MacBride is expecting a child. She has told her father that Mr Brennan is responsible.'

Eliza gasped and pulled her hands away. 'That's not true. I know my Jack. He wouldn't. It's impossible.'

Jack breathed again.

Sister Callista explained that Jack was expected by Mac-Bride and the priest to marry the unfortunate girl.

'No, Jack, you can't do it. You can't possibly marry her.'

'I know. I'd die first.'

'But why? Why is she blaming you? Who is the father?'

The nun took charge again. 'We don't know. Mr Brennan saw her meeting a stranger but he doesn't know who the man is. Probably a sailor. In port for just a few days then safely away on the high seas.' She turned to explain to Eliza. 'I think you are aware that Miss MacBride is a little slow-witted. The poor girl has been exploited – she has been over-trusting and naïve. It seems she's grown wild in her ways since the tragic loss of her mother.'

'But why blame Jack? Why you?'

'Because I'm there, I suppose. Under the same roof. I've been helping her improve her reading and writing and her father has made too much of that and has concluded that we've become, you know, close.'

'That's horrible.' Eliza looked at the headmistress. 'I know my Jack – he'd never take advantage of anyone. He loves me as much as I love him – and that's more than anything else in this life.' To Jack she said, 'They can't force you to marry her. I'll speak to Father O'Driscoll and tell him the truth – that we love each other and plan to marry as soon as possible.'

'No!' Sister Callista and Jack spoke in unison.

'I've told him that already,' Jack said, 'and it's served only to anger him further. They've hatched a plan for me to marry her and remove with her to another part of the country so the child can be born with no one there aware that it was conceived out of wedlock.'

'And you, Jack? What do you want?'

He looked away from her. 'You don't need to ask me that, Eliza. You know that as well as I do.'

The nun leaned forward and placed her hand on the girl's arm. 'I have told Jack I'm going help you both. Being forced into a loveless marriage is counter to the teachings of the church and not something I will sanction.'

Sister Callista hesitated for a moment, as if weighing up whether to say more, then continued. 'Years ago, when I was about your age, Eliza, I lost the man I loved. My father refused permission for me to marry and took me away from Ireland. I was an obedient daughter and had no money of my own and believed I had no choice but to comply. We swore to each other that one day we would be reunited. That is what sustained me.'

The nun patted the fabric of her habit absently, lost in her thoughts for a moment. Her face was suffused with sadness. 'When, after the death of my father, I returned to Ireland to find Angus, I discovered he had died in the famine.' She closed her eyes and crossed herself. 'That's why I never married and chose the church. My vocation, such as it is, came late and has been a consolation to me in my loss. I don't want to see the two of you torn apart as we were. I am going to assist you, so help me God.'

'But, Sister, you'll be in trouble if they find out you've helped us,' said Eliza.

'What can they do to me? I can't be hurt any more.' Her face reflected the pain she must have suffered all those years ago, but she had a look of defiance, as if she was ready for battle and relishing the prospect. 'With both of you gone they can hardly sack me without having to close the school. And what are they going to do? Throw me out of the convent? I don't think even Father O'Driscoll would go that far. I kept a small pot of money left me by my Daddy just in case things didn't work out for me in the convent – something to see me through my twilight years. I should have handed it over to the reverend mother, but somehow I never got around to it. I'm afraid you're finding out now that I'm far from being a model nun.' She gave a dry little laugh. 'But I like to think the Blessed Virgin was watching me kindly when I hid the money under the mattress. It will warm my heart to know I've helped you.'

The woman held out both hands and took each of theirs so they were joined together in a small circle. 'Now let's say a quick Hail Mary for her upstairs to look out for you, then I'll explain the plan.'

An hour later, Jack and Eliza were standing side-by-side, hand in hand, on the platform at Temple Meads railway station, waiting for the train to Liverpool where they planned to buy a passage on a steamer to America. They had no luggage – just the clothes they stood up in and the bagful of cash the headmistress had given them to pay for their onward journey.

Every few moments they turned their heads to look at each other. Jack felt an overwhelming tenderness and gratitude to Eliza, for her unshakable belief in him and her calm acceptance of their altered future. At first they had tried to refuse the nun's offer of money, but the woman was adamant. She told them that knowing she had helped them to find happiness together would bring joy to her own heart and that she wished someone had been there to make a similar offer to her all those years ago in Ireland.

The only way to leave for America directly from Bristol would have been on a small merchant ship – too risky as Mr MacBride ran his business out of the Bristol dockyards and they could have had a lengthy wait until finding a boat prepared to take them. Going from Liverpool meant being among many hundreds of others emigrating on the passenger liners. It would be easy to lose themselves in the crowd.

It was nearing nightfall when they reached Liverpool and went straight to the shipping line offices. A fellow passenger on the train between Crewe and Liverpool had warned them that they might have to wait up to ten days to secure a place onboard, but luck was with them and they procured steerage passages to New York for two days hence.

'We must be careful not to waste the money Sister gave us,' said Eliza. When Jack told her he was putting her in a boarding house, but planned to spend the night himself sleeping on a bench at the Pier Head, she protested. 'I'm going nowhere without you, Jack, not any more. Either you come with me to the lodging house or I sleep beside you on the bench.'

They settled on the lodging house, but neither got much sleep. The place was crowded, the dormitories filled with other emigrants, many of them foreigners, passing through Liverpool, most like them en route to America. It was like the Tower of Babel, with chatter in so many languages, people excited but fearful about their coming journeys.

After a sleepless night, lying fully clothed on straw mattresses on the floor of their separate dormitories, they set off next morning to provision for the voyage ahead. They bought a change of clothing, soap, dry biscuits and a pair of blankets. Afterwards, they sat with their feet dangling over the edge of the dock watching the gulls soar above them as they bit into bread and cheese. They held hands and talked, wondering what the future would bring them, curious about what lay ahead of them in America.

'I never intended it to be like this,' said Jack. 'Having to scuttle away as though we've done something wrong. I feel bad, forcing you to go on the run with me as if we were criminals.'

Eliza looked at him, her face lit up with a radiant smile. 'Don't feel bad, Jack. I'm glad, really glad, that this has happened. We might have had to wait for years before we could marry. Now we can do it as soon as we get to America. I'm excited about the future, about spending the rest of my life with you and going to America.' She squeezed his hand.

Jack bent over and planted a kiss on top of her head. She leaned into him, resting her head against his shoulder. He thrilled at the warmth of her body against his and put his arm around her, drawing her closer.

They were silent for a few minutes then she asked, 'What do you suppose America will be like?'

'Didn't you tell me it's the land of opportunity? People who never amounted to much over here go on to become rich and powerful there. Everyone's supposed to get a fair chance.'

'I'm not sure I'd like my Jack to be rich and powerful. He might not have time for his girl then. He might think he can do better for himself.'

'Never. Not in a million years. I could never do better than Eliza Hewlett and I can't wait to call you Eliza Brennan.'

They sat holding hands in the fading light until the shadows lengthened and they made their way back to their lodging house.

'This time tomorrow we'll be boarding the ship and the day after we'll be sailing away.' He took her in his arms and kissed her. He had ever been happier.

The crew were readying the ship for departure and all the passengers were on board and settling in – the well-heeled to their cabins and the less affluent, like Jack and Eliza, setting their pitches in steerage. The third class zone of the ship was stark, cramped and poorly ventilated, with bunks down each side and tables lined down the middle. They staked their claim to bunks, Jack's in the single men's section in the bows of the ship and Eliza with the women and children in the stern. Then after being dished out cups of lukewarm weak tea, they went out onto the crowded promenade deck, eager to watch Liverpool, England and all their troubles fade away into the distance as they embarked on their journey to a new life.

They leaned over the railings, watching the sailors go about their final preparations for sailing. The cargo was stowed, all passengers on board and the ship gave an initial warning blast from its foghorn. Jack was watching the crew preparing to raise the gangplank and unhitch the ropes from the huge bollards that held them in port. The engines were firing and he was filled with excitement and exhilaration. He looked at Eliza and smiled, leaning forward to drop a light kiss on her forehead. She smiled up at him, eyes shining. This was it. Soon they would be in America – free of the MacBrides and free to marry and build a future together.

Jack heard a sharp whistle, some shouting and the sound of a commotion on the dockside. The part-raised gangplank dropped back and three policemen walked up it onto the ship. At first he looked on with mild curiosity, then, just as he was about to remark to Eliza that it looked as though some poor escaping villain was about to be collared, he saw the familiar figures of Thomas MacBride and Father O'Driscoll walking behind the peelers.

Jack's heart missed a beat, then began thumping inside his chest as his throat constricted with fear. He clung to Eliza's hand, holding onto her as though if he loosened his grip she would float up from the deck beside him and drift away into the clouds. His stomach churned. He tasted bitter bile in his mouth. Dread. Fear. Panic. Eliza hadn't noticed the boarding party. She was still smiling, eyes closed, taking deep breaths of the salty air, savouring the moment. His grip on her hand tightened and she opened her eyes.

'It's too late,' he said. 'They've come for me.' His eyes filled with tears. 'I'm sorry' he said, 'I'm so sorry, my love.'

A shout went up. 'There he is.'

The policemen ran towards him. They grabbed Jack and cuffed his hands, then wrenched him around to stare into the faces of his tormentors. He wanted to be angry, but he felt defeated, beaten

'Got him!' Father O'Driscoll's voice was triumphant.

'I've done nothing.' Jack's voice was strangulated, tense, hopeless. 'You can't do this. What am I accused of?'

'Breach of promise. Theft of property.' One of the policemen spoke.

'This is wrong. Don't listen to them. I've made no promises to anyone and I've stolen nothing.' He looked about him desperately, hoping in vain that someone would intervene. A crowd of onlookers had gathered around, their faces curious, eager for this unexpected entertainment, but none of them showed any inclination for helping. 'I've done nothing,' he cried again, his voice desperate.

'In that case you've nothing to worry about, have you?' said the same man. 'You can make a statement at the police station and we'll look into it and then if you've really done nothing wrong you'll be free to go.'

'But the ship is about to sail.'

'Then it will be sailing without you.'

He felt like a man being condemned to death, just when he had believed himself to be on the brink of a new, better life. The handcuffs bit into his wrists and he bowed his head. Defeated. How had he ever dared to believe he would be free? How had he dared to think he had escaped MacBride and O'Driscoll? The ship's foghorn gave a warning blast and the policemen pushed him forward towards the gangway.

Eliza flung her arms around him and cried out, 'I'm coming with you, Jack, wherever they take you.'

One of the ship's officers approached and addressed the policemen. 'Either get off now or you're sailing with us. We're leaving right away.'

'We have a warrant for this man's arrest.' The policeman

thrust a paper under the noses of one of the ship's officers. The man gave it a cursory look then shrugged.

'Get him off my ship then. You're holding us up. We need to get underway.'

One of the policemen took hold of Eliza and pulled her away from Jack as the other two manhandled him towards the gangplank. O'Driscoll meanwhile spoke to a pair of the sailors and slipped them some coins. They grinned, pocketed the money and moved forward to take hold of the struggling Eliza, preventing her from following Jack off the ship. He turned to Eliza and shook his head. 'God bless you and have mercy on you, Miss Hewlett. I wish you a better future in America.' He winked at her and followed the others down the gangplank and off the ship.

Jack twisted his head round as he was marched off the ship. He could see Eliza pinned against the railings by the sailors the priest had tipped. He wanted to drink in the sight of her, burn her image into his brain, knowing that it could be the last time he would ever see her, but the peelers jerked him around and pushed him forward. With the sound of the booming foghorn the great ship sailed out of the dock. Jack felt lost, powerless, broken.

12
Cast Adrift

When a few yards of water separated the boat from the quayside, the sailors relaxed their hold and Eliza slumped to the deck on her knees, unable to process what had just happened. As the ship moved forward she was deaf to the screaming of gulls overhead, blind to the city behind and insensible to the sting of the wind on her face. She had never felt so alone, so lonely. Jack, Jack, where was her Jack and what were they going to do to him?

Her chest tightened as she thought about what might lie ahead. She was trapped on board a huge ship, penniless and destined for a foreign country. Until a couple of days ago she'd been a happy teacher, loving her work, loving her life in Bristol and most of all loving her Jack. The past few days had seen her world ploughed up, turned over like impacted soil after a long winter and spat out so that her future was unrecognisable and filled with fear. She knelt on the deck, clutching the railings and looking back towards the increasingly distant landmass. Jack's face swam before her eyes and she tried to focus on him. What would he want her to do? What would he do in her place? She had no answers. When she fell in love with Jack she had been prepared to do anything to be with him. She would have walked all the way to Liverpool if he'd asked her; she'd have tried to swim to America if he'd been swimming beside her. But this? All alone. Cut off from everything she'd ever known. Everything she'd ever wanted. Most of all cut off from Jack.

She cursed Mary Ellen MacBride and her father from the depths of her soul, careless of whether she was committing a sin. It wasn't right. It wasn't fair. How had God let it happen? But then God's representative on earth in the form of Father O'Driscoll had been the prime mover in the wrecking of their lives.

Eliza stayed on deck until she could no longer feel her own face, her jaw numb with cold and her cheeks streaked with salt from sea-spray and her own tears. The crowd, grown bored with the lack of spectacle, had disappeared below. She tried to force herself to think, to focus on what she was going to do next. With a dull lurch of her stomach, she remembered that Jack had the pouch with their money in. She had barely a few shillings. Not enough to pay her passage home. Not even enough to tide her over in America until she could find a job. Shivering as the bitter wind cut into her, she went below to fetch her shawl.

She couldn't remember the way back down to the steerage section. As she went down yet another companionway she was uncertain: it had not seemed so far down before. The passage was dim and it took her a few moments to adjust to the gloom after the brightness on deck. Her skirts brushed up against something and she jumped with fright as a hand took hold of her arm. She leapt away, pushing herself back against the wall.

'You know where you're going, Miss?' The voice was coarse, with a tone of mockery. 'Passengers are not allowed in the crew's quarters. We don't often see ladies this far below.' He gave a low laugh as he pronounced the word ladies with a cynical exaggeration. 'Not unless they come down here for a purpose.'

She cried out and backed away from him, banging her arm on the door to the companionway. She scrambled up the steps and emerged on another level. Breathless, she leaned back against the wall of the passage and gulped in big mouthfuls of air. Through the gloom another figure loomed in front of her and she cried out, 'Leave me alone. Get away from me.'

'Can I help you, Mademoiselle?' The accent was foreign. 'Are you unwell? What is the trouble?'

It was a bearded gentleman, with gingery blond hair streaked with silver. He looked at her with kind, sad eyes.

'I lost my way. I went to the crew's quarters by mistake…' Her voice tailed off, embarrassed, unable to find the right words about what had just taken place.

'Then allow me to prescribe a cup of strong tea. That usually does the trick when one is feeling, shall we say, *désorienté*.'

She looked at him blankly. She didn't want to talk to a stranger, even one offering her a cup of tea. She just wanted to close her eyes and, when she opened them again, find Jack beside her.

The man was looking at her quizzically. 'Mademoiselle? A tea?'

She looked at him as though he were mad.

'No. I must go.' As she spoke she felt the tears rushing into her eyes. 'Sorry. I must go.' She pushed past him and ran along the corridor her heart slamming against her ribs.

When she got to her quarters in steerage she flung herself on her bunk and buried her head in her arms and cried her eyes out. No one paid any attention. The ship was full of people with sad stories, broken dreams, shattered lives, She was no different from dozens of others.

Later on, when everyone was sleeping, she lay in the dark torturing herself, playing back in her mind what had happened on the deck earlier, over and over again, as if by doing so the outcome might be different. But it wasn't a bad dream. It had happened. Waking up didn't make any difference. Jack was gone. She was alone.

By morning she had cried out all her tears. She went through her things, searching the lining of her small travel bag, hoping in vain to find some forgotten coins. She had no jewellery. Nothing to pawn. Just the clothes she was wearing and the few provisions she and Jack had bought in Liverpool. She would either have to convince the shipping company to take her back without payment or she must find work in New York to save for the ticket home. As soon as Jack had convinced the police of his innocence he would follow her – or at least get word to her. Better to wait until she heard from him. He would come up with a plan. She must trust him, believe in him. Meanwhile she must be strong.

The following morning Eliza went out onto the deserted deck. The winds was biting and the sky grey and most of the passengers were staying below. She felt lonely, but more determined than yesterday. She kept repeating the words "Be strong. Jack will come" over and over in her head, trying to make herself believe.

Someone came and stood beside her. It was the man she had met yesterday.

'How are you today, Mademoiselle? I fear we met at what was a bad moment for you?'

'I'm sorry. You must have thought me rude.'

She forced her mouth into a smile, nodded and was about to move away, when he spoke again. 'My I then renew my offer of a cup of tea?'

She was irritated, She wanted to be alone, with her thoughts, but the idea of a hot cup of tea was appealing so she nodded.

He smiled and offered her his arm. 'Allow me' he said in a strong accent.

'You are French?' she asked, not caring what his answer might be.

'German. But I have lived for the past twelve years in Belgium.' He steered her along the passageway to the second class dining room. He settled her at a table in the empty saloon and went in search of someone to serve them. She looked around the wood-panelled room. It was very different from the cramped and overcrowded conditions in steerage. When the man returned and seated himself opposite her, she asked him, 'Where is everyone? There's no one about.'

He shrugged. 'Up on deck possibly? In the library? In their cabins?'

'You have private cabins? A library?'

He nodded. 'And a smoking room. A card room too I believe.'

'In steerage there are bunks, all together. Everyone eats and sleeps in the same place.' She didn't want to make small talk with this man but felt obliged to as he was standing her the tea. She looked around her at the empty room. 'How many people are in second class?'

He tilted his head to one side, eyes closed as he thought. 'I don't know exactly. No more than fifty or sixty.'

'There must be hundreds down in steerage. All squashed in like straw in a haystack.'

He smiled and looked as though he was about to say something.

'Did I say something wrong?' she said.

'No, no. Quite the contrary, Miss.?'

'Hewlett.'

'*Enchanté*, Miss Hewlett. Allow me to present myself – Dr Karl Feigenbaum, at your service.

The steward appeared and placed a pot of tea in front of them. The German doctor paused the conversation to serve her with a cup, raising his eyebrows when she declined the sugar and accepted the milk. 'You English are so strange with your tea-drinking. I am not so fond of it, preferring a good *café.*'

'I hope you are not drinking it on my account, sir?'

'Certainly not. You have clearly not yet had the opportunity to taste the vile concoction they serve as coffee on board.' He gave a little chuckle. 'I wouldn't be surprised to learn they use water from the bilge pumps to make it.'

She forced a smile.

'There isn't any coffee down below. Just very weak tea. From an urn. Half-cold.'

He smiled back at her and she looked down, suddenly embarrassed at being there with him.

They sat there for a while sipping their tea in awkward silence, then both started to speak at once.

'Why are you travelling to America?' he asked.

'I must go back to the steerage deck,' she said at the same time.

They both leaned back in their seats, Eliza uncertain whether to respond to his question and the doctor looking anxious that she was about to leave.

He took a deep breath then reached across the table and took her hand in his. He bent his head and grazed his lips over the back of her hand. She stiffened as she felt the tickle of his beard and moustache, and quickly pulled her hand away from his.

'I just want to say again that I am honoured to make your acquaintance, Mademoiselle Hewlett.'

She felt uncomfortable. While his continental hand-kissing was probably viewed as normal in Belgium or Germany, it didn't feel appropriate under the circumstances. They were strangers. She doubted if he would have done it were Jack present. She swallowed her annoyance and took another sip of her tea. Hot and strong, the way she liked it. Then aware again of her situation she asked herself what she was thinking of – sitting here in the second class dining room, drinking tea with a complete stranger, risking being found out and ignominiously returned to steerage? What would Jack think? What on earth was she doing, behaving as though she were at a parish social when her heart was breaking?.

'I shouldn't be here. I'm not supposed to leave steerage. I'm sorry. I must go. Thank you. Goodbye.'

Ignoring his protests, she put down her unfinished tea, scraped back her chair, gathered her skirts and ran out of the saloon, gasping with relief when she recognised the stairway back down to steerage.

Back on the small open promenade deck, she immediately regretted her premature exit. Another cup of tea would have been more than welcome and the temperature on deck was bitterly cold, despite the time of year. And the gentleman had been kind. But had she stayed, he would have expected her to answer his questions, to tell him why she was here, en route for America and all alone. Something she was not ready to share with anyone.

She didn't want to go below to the noisy crowd in the big steerage cabin, so she stayed on the deck, shivering, repeating her mantra, telling herself to be strong, to believe in Jack, struggling to suppress the little voice inside her that kept saying he wouldn't come for her. I'll be strong for you Jack. I'll be strong. Your love will make me strong.

Life on board was hard to bear. The pitch of the sea made Eliza nauseous and she passed a couple of days tossing and turning on her narrow bunk, a slop bucket close at hand for the vomiting and retching that wouldn't stop. The steerage quarters were cramped and foul-smelling, the odour of vomit pervasive, as many of the voyagers, like her, struggled to find their sea-legs. The noxious stench was mingled with the stink of unwashed bodies, cooking smells and stale breath, which combined to make the nausea harder to shake off. She lay on the narrow bunk, wishing for sleep, for oblivion – desperate for it all to be over, longing to plant her feet on dry land again. Praying that this was all a terrible dream she would awaken from and she would find herself back in Bristol sharing her bread with Jack in the park. Around her she could hear the moans of fellow sufferers, the screaming of sick babies and the raucous cries of children, frustrated at their close confinement. At night those passengers still standing tried to raise their spirits by singing, dancing, playing flutes and fiddles, banging tambourines and generally trying to turn what she saw as a voyage to hell into a cause for celebration. She put her hands over her ears and tried to shut out the noise. She replayed the events of the past week through her head. How was it possible that her life had so utterly changed in just a few days? She had gone from a happy state of loving Jack and looking forward to their future together, to being here, seasick, alone and destitute.

Three days before their arrival in New York Eliza was at last well enough to emerge from the bowels of the ship. This time she was careful to follow a couple of other women as they made their way onto the deck, avoiding any risk of straying into the crew's section.

She leaned against the railings, straining her eyes in the hope of spotting land. Not that she expected the sight of land to bring her any comfort. She would be alone and penniless in a strange city, with ten days worth of ocean separating her from Jack and everything else she was familiar with. The gunmetal grey sea stretched endlessly in front of the ship in a monotonous moving mass. She told herself that once she was on dry land she would be able to think more clearly. Perhaps she could find someone to help her. If she explained that she had been accidentally separated from her fiancé maybe someone from the shipping company could help her to get back to England. Then she thought that perhaps Jack was by now sailing on the next ship to join her. She must wait for him in New York. He would be there soon. Wouldn't he? He wouldn't let her down. He would never abandon her. But what if MacBride and O'Driscoll were holding him? She must return to help him, to prove his innocence of the charges they had laid against him. But what if they crossed each other mid-Atlantic? As she grappled with the possibilities, she felt more and more confused. It was like a horrible cosmic lottery and no matter what she chose she feared the odds were stacked against her.

'Miss Hewlett, I feared you must have fallen overboard.' It was the German doctor. 'I am happy to see that you are very much alive.'

He smiled at her with a big beaming grin, then removed his spectacles and carefully polished them with a small cloth to remove the seaspray that had clouded them. The wind blew his hair, overlong and in need of a barber's attention, up on either side of his face, giving him the aspect of Zeus or Poseidon. 'I think you will find it more sheltered on the aft deck. It's a little blowy on this side.' He nodded in the direction.

'I am not permitted to go up there.'

He extended an arm to her. 'I think you'll find you can pass quite safely with me. That is…' His face was suddenly anxious. 'That is unless you are waiting for another travelling companion?'

She shook her head, then looked about her to see if they were observed, but there was just a couple of women, preoccupied with the supervision of their children. She reluctantly rested her hand on his proffered arm and let him lead her up the stairs, hoping that the cursory wash she had improvised this morning using a flannel and half a cup of cold water would have been enough to remove the smell of several days shut up in steerage.

The second class promenade deck was much larger, despite the fact that the number of passengers were significantly fewer than in steerage.

'It's much nicer here,' she said, stating the obvious.

'I imagine the first class deck is nicer still.' He nodded upwards absently, but kept his eyes fixed upon her.

'Tell me, Miss Hewlett, you have not yet answered the question I posed the other day. Why is a young lady like you travelling alone to the United States? Are you joining your family there?'

She sighed. Better to get it over. She would likely have to tell her tale many times before she was done, so she needed to get her story clear. She knew she didn't want to reveal what had happened to Jack. She didn't want strangers knowing about his humiliation. She didn't want to talk about him at all. It was nobody else's business.

'I have no family. My parents are dead. There's no one else. I decided to start a new life in America. I read that there are many opportunities for people there who are prepared to work hard. Unfortunately my purse was stolen on the docks in Liverpool as we were boarding and I've lost all my money.'

As soon as the words were out she regretted them. He might think her a fortune hunter, or even a common beggar, preying on his goodwill. And most of all she didn't want his pity. 'I'm sorry,' she said. 'You don't want to hear about that.'

'I am very sorry, my dear. What will you do?' Still his eyes were fixed on her face and full of concern.

'I will look for employment as soon as we disembark.'

The man looked thoughtful but was silent. At last he moved his gaze from her and, leaning on the railing, stared out across the empty sea.

She looked sideways at him. He was tall and broad

and a bit stout around the middle as though he'd enjoyed rather too many potatoes or dumplings back in Belgium or Germany. His suit was crumpled and she noticed he had ink stains on his fingers. She wondered whether there was a Frau Feigenbaum and if so, where she was – perhaps lying seasick in their cabin? Clearly she didn't take too much care over her husband's appearance.

As though reading her mind, the man turned back to face her. 'I too am travelling alone.'

He was looking at her intently so she looked away.

'I am travelling to join my brother in America,' he said. 'He followed my father into the brewing trade and now lives in the city of St Louis. He works at the Drescher Brewery and suggested I come out to join him there.'

She nodded. 'You are a brewer?'

He shook his head. 'Alas no. I wish I had been. My parents wanted me to have a profession and I studied to become a doctor, like my grandfather. I often think I would have been a happier man had I become a brewer. Beer makes men happy whereas all too often a doctor has to deal with the things that make them sad.' He looked out over the sea.

'But being a doctor means you can save lives too' said Eliza. 'You can make a real difference whereas beer is just a temporary pleasure.'

He turned to her, smiling. 'You are a philosopher, Miss Hewlett. Now tell me more about yourself.' He spoke the words as if he was issuing an order.

'There's not much to tell. My mother died giving birth to me and my father died when I was twelve. I am a teacher. I was born in Bristol and have lived there all my life.'

'You are not married?' His eyes were fixed on her and she looked away, embarrassed.

'No. I am engaged to be married.'

'Why then are you travelling alone to America?'

'My fiancé will be following me soon.' She turned away from him, uncomfortable under his gaze.

'That's an unusual thing for a man to do. To send his intended alone to a strange country.'

She blushed. Why had she mentioned Jack? She hesitated then said, 'He was held up at the last minute due to a family problem and as we had already paid for the passage we decided I would go on ahead.'

'I see,' he said, but she knew he didn't believe her.

He spoke again. 'I have never married. Not from choice but from lack of opportunity. My mother, after the premature death of my father, suffered a series of apoplectic attacks and I cared for her until she passed away earlier this year. That was what took me to Belgium and kept me there for so long.'

She said nothing, hoping that he would move the conversation away from personal matters, but he persisted.

'When Mama died six months ago there was nothing to keep me in Belgium and nothing to take me back to Germany.'

He was speaking quickly, as though anxious. All the while he fixed his eyes on her face and she felt uncomfortable under the intense scrutiny

He stopped suddenly, swallowed, took a deep breath, then spoke again with the same urgent speed. 'I am what you call a confirmed bachelor. Comfortably off. I never wanted more. Or more truthfully never expected more. But…'

Eliza felt a wave of nervousness sweep over her. He was telling her too much. Where did he think this was leading? Did he think she was a woman of easy virtue? Were he to proposition her she would die of shame.

'How long until we reach New York, Doctor?' she blurted.

He paused, removed his spectacles and wiped his eyes with a handkerchief.

114

'The day after tomorrow.'

'I will be greatly relieved when we can disembark. I have found the voyage to be difficult.'

'My dear, were you affected by the seasickness? You should have sent for me.'

She turned to face him. 'You have been most kind, Dr Feigenbaum. Now I must take no more of your time.' Before he could respond she moved towards the companionway and descended to the steerage deck.

The following morning he appeared again as though from nowhere as she was standing on the deck, watching the empty sea.

'Allow me to offer you a cup of tea, Miss Hewlett. Or perhaps you'd like to try the bilge water coffee?'

The tea she had been served with her breakfast had been cold and the milk curdled. It was an offer too tempting to refuse.

They settled into seats in the second class saloon and she sipped her tea gratefully.

'Miss Hewlett, I have a question for you.'

She looked up, startled. There was something about the way he talked to her, looked at her, that she found unsettling.

'Who was the young man you were with before we left Liverpool?'

'You were watching me?' She felt sick.

'I couldn't help but see. The poor chap was removed by force from the ship. Everyone was watching.'

She gave a little choked sob.

'It was your fiancé?' He stretched out a hand and placed it on hers, but she pulled hers away.

'I don't know what he did and I won't ask you any questions if you don't want to tell me. But I can see you are in trouble and you are alone. Perhaps I can help.'

'It was all a misunderstanding. He has done nothing wrong. He will sort it out and will be on the next ship to join me.'

'I see. You sound very sure. I hope you are right.'

'What do you mean? Of course I'm right.'

'It's just that the gentlemen of the law appeared to think otherwise. I saw there was a clergyman there too.'

She put down her tea as her tears were falling into the cup. She screwed up her handkerchief and dabbed at her eyes.

'I told you. It was a mistake. Jack will have sorted it all out by now. He will have wired to New York to tell me he is coming. And if he hasn't then I will turn right round and take the next ship back.'

'I see. This Jack is a very lucky man indeed.'

'Lucky?' she cried. 'How can you say that? Lucky! He's the unluckiest man on earth for what has happened to him.'

'I'm sorry. I meant he was lucky to have your friendship and faith in him.'

She got up and gathered her skirt about her.

'You make it sound as though such faith is unmerited.'

He made the slightest movement of his head as if in acknowledgment of the truth of what she said.

'He has not only my friendship and faith. He has my undying love. Thank you for the tea, Doctor. Goodbye.'

Heedless of the stench of steerage she went back into the bowels of the ship and flung herself facedown on her bunk.

On the last evening on board, Eliza was standing on the deserted deck, watching the stars and wondering if back in England Jack was watching them too. She felt a movement beside her and turned to see the German standing beside her.

'What a beautiful evening' he said. 'I fear I upset you when we spoke last. I apologise. I did not mean to offend you, my dear.'

She gave him a brief nod then moved towards the companionway. He was such an irritating man, following her like her shadow.

He reached out and took her arm.

She spoke abruptly. 'Doctor, you have been very kind, but we arrive in New York tomorrow and I must prepare for disembarking. I wish you the best for the future. Good evening and goodbye.' And she turned on her heels and went down the stairs, leaving him alone on the otherwise deserted deck.

14
Castle Garden

Determined to avoid running into Doctor Feigenbaum again, Eliza chose to endure the conditions below decks for the remaining hours of the voyage, only emerging as the ship's foghorn gave its celebratory blast as they entered New York harbour.

She kept in the middle of the crowd from steerage, hanging back until she could see the doctor disembarking with the rest of the second class passengers. The first and second class passengers cleared the immigration process on board and were then spirited away to the mainland, while those, like Eliza in steerage, had to wait on board the ship before going through the lengthy ordeal of entry to the United States via the Castle Garden immigration centre. The vessel was quarantined in the harbour for a couple of hours – until a medical officer boarded, checked the ship's paperwork and gave the steerage passengers a cursory look-over for any obvious signs of contagious diseases. This was just in case anyone had sickened on the voyage – all the passengers had already been vetted by the shipping company's medical officer before being allowed to board in Liverpool.

When they were eventually transported by barge to

Castle Garden, Eliza joined a long queue snaking its way past the customs inspectors and another medical officer, until she entered the rotunda of Castle Garden. America was real now. She realised she had given little thought to the specifics of what it would be like. It had been just a destination, a vague concept, an uncertain future. Now, she was here she was forced at last to face up to its alienness, to grapple with the realities of entering this vast unknown continent.

The huge circular room was supported by narrow pillars, surrounding a central glass ceiling which poured light down onto the motley masses. The noise was deafening as immigration officers interviewed arriving passengers, each in their own language, creating a cacophony of sound. She looked around her: there were people here from several ships, evidently originating from different European ports. The place resembled a museum of national costume – bearded Russians in long coats and fur hats, Slavic women enveloped in embroidered shawls of every possible hue, English, Scottish or Irish men in tweedy jackets, corduroy trousers, Poles in military style jackets, Italian girls in coloured head kerchiefs and peasant skirts, Germans wearing long boots, overcoats, leather breeches, some in leiderhosen.

As she shuffled forward in the queue for English speakers, clutching the cloth carpetbag that held her few possessions, Eliza could see that completion of the immigration interview did not represent the end of the process. Some passengers were pulled aside and marked out for transportation with the sick to Ward's Island. A mother screamed and pleaded as she was separated from her husband and son and led away. But most of the assembled mass were processed and given leave to enter the United States.

After what must have been hours, Eliza reached the head of the queue and found herself in front of an immigration official.

'Can you help me,' Eliza said. 'I believe there will be a telegraph message for me from England. Where do I go to find out?'

The man looked at her without interest and spoke with a tone of voice that betokened endless repetition and boredom with his job.

'Name?'

She told him and then responded to his subsequent requests for her nationality, former place of residence, age and marital status. When she said she was travelling alone, he registered what passed for surprise on his otherwise expressionless face, by the almost imperceptible raising of one eyebrow.

'Reason for entering the United States?'

'I don't think I want to enter the United States – I was travelling with my fiancé, but he was taken from the ship when we were about to sail. I believe he will have sent a telegraph to tell me when he will join me. Please tell me where I find out? If there is no message from him then I want to go back to England to find him.'

He looked at her for a moment and she thought he was going to ask why Jack was taken. Instead he asked, 'Occupation?'

'I'm a schoolteacher.'

He wrote something on a slip of paper and handed it to her. 'Give that to the employment exchange.'

'Money?' he said, in the same monotone.

'I beg your pardon?'

'I need to see the money you're bringing in. You have to be able to support yourself.'

'I don't need to support myself. My fiancé has our money. I told you they took him off the ship in Liverpool. He will be coming to join me. I won't be staying in New York long. Just until he gets here. And if he can't get here then I will be going back to England.' She felt panic begin to grip her as she tried to explain. Her words sounded lame to herself so how must they sound to this disinterested stranger?

He looked at her impatiently so rather than argue she scrambled in her purse and produced the ten shillings and sixpence that was all she possessed in the world. He glanced at it, his face still blank.

'Not enough. That's not even three dollars. You have to be able to prove you can support yourself.'

'Anyone you know here who can lend you the money or vouch for you?'

She shook her head.

'Well, you can't come into the United States without at least five dollars. Over there.' He jerked his head towards a doorway.

'What happens now? Where do I go?'

'The holding pens till they decide if they're going to send you back where you came from. Take this.' He handed her another slip of paper. 'Move along.' Then raising his voice, 'Next!'

Eliza hesitated and stood beside the table. 'You mean they'll send me home again?' She couldn't hide the relief in her voice.

'Over there.' The man turned in his seat and gave her a shove.

She moved towards the doorway where she was met by a big burly negro with a shaved head like a convict and a nose that looked as though he'd had a head-on collision with a brick wall. He took her slip of paper and opened the iron-barred door.

'In there.'

Eliza's joy at the prospect of being repatriated was short-lived as she contemplated being shut up in a cage with this mixed rabble of people, all of whom looked as though they were beggars or thieves and none of whom were speaking English.

She remained standing, afraid to venture further inside the holding pen and unwilling to sit, like the other inmates, on the floor. The bald-headed negro guard was standing a few yards away on the other side of the barred door, so she tried to attract his attention by waving at him, to ask him how she could find out about Jack's telegraph. He ignored her for half an hour or so, then submitting to the boredom of standing sentinel when no one else had arrived requiring him to unlock the cage, he turned and looked at her at last.

'Where you from, Ma'am?'

'England. Bristol.'

'You waiting for funds to be sent?'

'No. I mean yes. I am hoping to receive a telegraphed message.'

'You all alone, Ma'am?'

She nodded.

He looked her up and down. 'You look like a nice, respectable lady. Why come to America if you don't know anyone here?'

She told him that she had been separated from her travelling companion during embarkation. 'I'm so relieved that they are going to send me back.'

'Don't be so sure of it. First they have to persuade the shipping company to take you. And if the shipping company can show that they checked you had enough money when you got on board, they'll like as not refuse.'

'What happens then?' She swallowed and looked around her at the unsalubrious crew of people in the holding pen.

'In the end they'll probably agree to send you back to where you came from, Ma'am. But it could be days. Weeks even.'

'So what will I do till then?'

'If no one claims you, you'll be sent to the penitentiary. Waiting on the British consul to visit and arrange for you to be repatriated. But you'll stay here tonight as you've missed the transit.'

'What? Here? Locked up? Where will I sleep?'

'We'll give you a blanket. Most of this lot will be out of here as soon as their money comes. Most of them had it sent from family elsewhere in the United States or have relatives who haven't turned up to meet them yet. It's often like this on a Saturday. Lots of them get drunk and forget to get out of bed to meet the ship.' He laughed and wiped his forehead with the back of his hand. 'If I were you, lady, I'd make myself a bit more comfortable and sit on the floor. It's going to be a long night.'

She was close to panic again. What was she doing here? What had she done to deserve this? She wanted to hammer her fists into the wall and scream. It was a nightmare that seemed without end. No one here cared. She was complete-lyy alone. She hated to feel self pity but she couldn't help it. It just wasn't fair. She had done nothing wrong. Why had this happened to her? When would it end? How would it end?

She looked around her, saw that the floor looked as though it was regularly swept, so took her jailor's advice and tried to doze off, leaning against the wall of the holding pen and trying to keep a distance between herself and the other inmates. Unable to sleep, her head buzzing with inchoate thoughts, her stomach churning and her skin shivering, she realised she was hungry. Not surprising as she hadn't eaten since a meagre breakfast on board. She called to the guard and asked if she could get something to eat.

'Fifty cents for a sausage in a bread roll. They'll be round in a few minutes.'

'I only have English money.'

The guard nodded towards a sign on the other side of the large rotunda. *Currency exchange*.

'I didn't get a chance to exchange my money before they put me in here. Could I go and change it now?'

'How much you got?'

She held out her few shillings.

'Tell you what, angel, you can have one on me. Welcome to New York.'

He gestured to one of the food sellers, walking around the immigration hall. She devoured the hot sausage in a bread roll as though it were her first meal in days.

'Thank you for that,' she said, wiping the warm grease from her chin with her handkerchief.

'You're all right, angel. I have a kid not much younger than you. Like to think someone would look out for her if she got into trouble.'

As time wore on, the rotunda began to empty, as each shipload of immigrants was processed and released into New York, to make their ways onward into the city and beyond into the vastness of the American continent. The sunlight through the glass roof was replaced by a gloom as the day turned to dusk.

Eliza struggled to fight down tears. How had it come to this? She wanted to curse Jack Brennan for disrupting the peaceful, happy tedium of her life in Bristol. For making her fall in love with him. For making her willing to give up everything and go with him to the other side of the ocean. For abandoning her and leaving her penniless in a strange country, surrounded by strangers. But she couldn't curse him. Not when with every fibre of her being she wanted him. Not when she knew his only crime was being too trusting and too kind. Where was he now? What was he doing? Had he been able to free himself? Might he perhaps be already steaming across the Atlantic to join her? She tried so hard to believe he was, but her heart knew that he wasn't. Something deep inside her acknowledged that she would never see him again. By now he might even be married to Mary Ellen. Would they be there when she eventually arrived back in Bristol? She didn't think she could bear the thought of seeing him with her. But the prospect of never seeing him at all was even worse.

The iron-barred door opened and her guard stood there, his wide, black face creased by a smile. 'Well, Ma'am, looks like you do have friends in America after all. You're released. Free to go.'

Eliza scrambled to her feet, pulling the shawl she had been sitting on, around her shoulders. 'What do you mean?'

'Your funds have arrived. You can collect them at the booth over there then you're free to go. It's been a pleasure to meet you, Ma'am. You're a nice lady.'

Bemused, she shook his proffered hand.

He gave her a scrap of paper. 'Here's the address of a lodging place. It's not fancy but it's clean. You won't find better for $3 a month. Tell them I sent you. It should tide you over till you find work.'

She looked up at him, smiling. 'Thank you so much. You have been so kind and I don't even know your name.'

'You're welcome, angel. And it's Clarence.'

'Eliza.'

She walked unsteadily back into the main rotunda, passing the now almost deserted booths of the railway agents, the boarding house keepers and the labour exchange. A voice called out her name from a booth at the side. The man behind it placed a piece of paper in front of her and told her to sign it, then he counted out fifty dollars and pushed them towards her.

'What's this?'

'Your funds have arrived.'

'What funds?'

'The money you've been expecting.'

'I wasn't expecting money. Who sent it?' Her heart leapt inside her ribcage as she realised Jack must have telegraphed the money to her. 'Was there a message with it?'

'Look, lady, I want to get home. That's all there is. Take your money and get out of here. Welcome to the United States.'

She put the cash inside her purse and headed uncertainly towards the exit, emerging into the open air. America.

15

Five Points

Dr Feigenbaum was leaning on his ebony walking stick and he raised his hat to her as she approached. She stopped short, too angry to speak. He smiled at her, his eyes shining behind his round-rimmed spectacles.

'What have you done?' Eliza almost spat the words at him and felt her body shaking with anger. 'They were going to send me back. Back to England.'

'I waited for you and when you didn't emerge with the rest of the passengers, I made some enquiries and they told me you had been detained and were to be deported.'

'Precisely!'

'But that would have been terrible when you have come so far.' His face was puzzled and he stroked his beard as though that would bring him some kind of revelation.

'You know that my fiancé was taken from the ship. This was my chance to get back to him. Now you've ruined everything.' She fought back the tears of anger and disappointment. Why wasn't it Jack who had sent the money and delivered her from detention? Why had he sent no word?.

'That was certainly not my intention, my dear. When I heard you had been placed in a caged cell with some very undesirable people I could not possibly stand by. They told me there was no certainty how long you would be held there and that you would likely be moved to a detention centre on an island in the Hudson River. How could I permit you to endure that, Miss Hewlett?'

Tears of frustration filled her eyes and she brushed them away with a gloved hand. 'What am I going to do now?' She looked around her. 'I have no money. I know no one.' She opened her handbag and took out the dollar bills and held them out to him.

He waved them away. 'The money is for you, Miss Hewlett. And you are not alone.'

'I can't possibly accept your money and I don't know you. I don't understand what you want with me. Take it back, please.' She thrust the dollar bills at him, but he stepped backwards and put his hands up.

'I fear I have distressed you. That is the last thing I want. Please look on this money as a small gift from a lonely old man who only wants to help you.'

'You can't go around making gifts to strange women like that.'

'But I am not, as you say, going around making gifts to strange women. You are the only woman I know here in America and I make this gift to you and you alone. It is given without conditions and I expect no repayment. But you must accept it. You won't get far with just a few dollars. You have nowhere to live and no employment. The money is just a small sum to help you get on your feet.'

Around them a crowd of people had gathered and Eliza was aware that the bundle of dollar bills in her hand was attracting attention. She felt someone take hold of her arm.

'Nice, clean lodgings, Ma'm. Only ten dollars a month. Best you'll find in town. Nice respectable place. Follow me' said a woman with a strange-sounding accent.

Eliza jerked her arm away, but a man appeared, taking hold of her other arm.

'You wanna train ticket, lady? I'll take you and your bags to the station in Jersey City. Where you wanna go? Oklahoma? New Orleans?'

Dr Feigenbaum stepped in front of them. 'On your way. The lady is going nowhere. She is with me. On your way, please.'

He took hold of her elbow. 'Let us take a carriage and get away from this area. It is filled with people out to exploit newly arrived passengers. It is safer to conduct such business inside the immigration reception, where everything is overseen by the authorities. Come on. You must be hungry.'

As he spoke, a hansom cab pulled up. Eliza hesitated, then realising that she was among the last of the arrivals and would be viewed as fair game by the circling vultures, she let him hand her up into the carriage.

The driver deposited them outside a small Hungarian restaurant and her initial resistance to accepting more charity from Dr Feigenbaum was defeated by the aroma of goulash and the sight of steaming dumplings being conveyed to the waiting tables.

They ate heartily and in silence. Eliza couldn't remember when she had tasted food so good especially compared with the watery soups and slimy stews she had been forced to eat on board ship. When the doctor finished his meal, he wiped his mouth with a napkin, but failed to remove a spot of goulash on his white goatee beard, below his bottom lip. He had also managed to stain his waistcoat.

She looked up at him and saw he was watching her intently.

He spoke at last. 'I know you may think this premature but I wish to make you an offer, Miss Hewlett. It appears we are both alone in this world and could do better were we to pool our resources.'

She looked at him in surprise, her mouth open, struggling to find the right words to shut him up and make him stop.

'Please, let me finish. I like you, Miss Hewlett. I like you very much. My days and nights since we met have been filled with thoughts of you. I have been unable to stop thinking of you, no matter how hard I have tried. I know you will think I am perhaps a little crazy. I think so myself. I have been struck by the *coup de foudre*. I never believed in such lightening bolts happening except in fairy stories but it has happened to me and I am powerless to resist.'

She tried to interrupt but he took hold of her hand, his eyes still looking into hers with an intensity that made her look away.

'I can provide for you. I ask nothing in return, other than that you give me a chance. Give me time. I am a lonely man, who had long since given up all hope of happiness and it would give me such joy to care for you. Please let me? It would be a new beginning for both of us – in the new world.'

His voice trailed away and he took off his spectacles and polished them. She realised it was the beginnings of tears that had caused them to mist over. He coughed and appeared to pull himself together. 'I have modest funds and am in retirement. I have enough to buy a small house and keep a carriage and a couple of servants.'

'Stop. Please stop.' She put up her hands, palms facing him to signal him to stop. 'I don't understand what you are proposing. I am not that kind of woman. You are mistaken.'

'No. No. Of course you are not. Far from it. You misunderstand me. I am asking you to marry me, Miss Hewlett. I want you to become my wife.'

She started to laugh. A hollow, empty laugh that bordered on hysteria.

'I can't marry you, Doctor. It's absurd. You don't know me.' She pulled her hand from his grasp. 'You have completely misconstrued my situation.'

'I know I am not a young man, Miss Hewlett, but I

can promise you I would make it my life's work to care for you and to see you want for nothing. I do understand that I am not an enticing prospect for such a beautiful young woman. I am not handsome like your fiancé. All I can offer is stability, security and my unstinting love and devotion. I would expect nothing in return but your friendship and companionship. Then maybe with time, who knows, you might come to care for me just a little.'

'Please, Doctor Feigenbaum. You don't know me at all. You can't possibly love me and I certainly don't love you. I've already told you. I can't marry you. I intend to return to England if Jack is unable to join me here. If you had not intervened I would have been able to get there a lot faster.'

He looked at her soulfully with his big sad eyes, as though weighing her words. Eventually he said, 'I never believed in love before but I have been under your spell since the moment I saw you and our further acquaintance, limited though it has been, has not altered that. And as for intervening to have you released, you have no idea what would have happened if you had stayed in that place. You could have been shut away for days, maybe even for weeks, among all kinds of dangerous and unscrupulous people. With no money. Not even enough for food. Who knows what might have befallen you? I had to step in. I could not stand by.'

She shook her head. There was no point in arguing with him. It was done now.

He looked down then raised his eyes to hers. 'If you are unable to accept my proposal I do have an alternative offer to make to you.' His voice was quiet, tentative, as though he was playing the last card in the pack. 'Would you consider accompanying me to St Louis in another capacity, as my assistant?'

She was about to speak but he placed a hand over hers. 'Please let me explain. You are a teacher, Miss Hewlett, and an educated woman. I need someone to help me with the transcription of my life's work. My hands have become stiffened with rheumatism and I find working with a pen is becoming every day more challenging.' He held up his ink stained hands to her in evidence. 'I am writing about the history of the brewing industry. Brewing has been the business of my family through three generations. I have made a long study of its origins and traditions and want to publish my findings before I die. My notes are very disordered and my eyesight is not what it once was either, so progress is slow. I think you would be the perfect person to assist me in this endeavour.

'It was foolish of me to expect that my feelings for you could be reciprocated in such a short time. I was overcome. Overcome by you, Miss Hewlett. But I still want to help you. Please let me help you? Please help me too by doing this for me.'

Eliza didn't know what to say. She picked up her linen napkin and began pleating the edge of it. She was overwhelmed with embarrassment. The last thing she expected was the attentions of an elderly suitor. She didn't even want to contemplate it. There was no room in her head for anyone other than Jack - and certainly no room in her heart. Then she began to feel angry. How dare this stranger presume to know her? How dare he think that she would even contemplate becoming his wife? How could he ask, knowing that she was distraught over the absence of Jack? But she knew the man's intentions were good. He had been kind to her. He had lent her money. He had invited her to share his meal. He was probably a very lonely man. She decided to temper her words. 'I am honoured that you have such confidence in me, Doctor Feigenbaum, although I have done nothing to merit it. I am very grateful for the kindness of your offer, but I have plans. I will stay here in New York, awaiting the arrival of my fiancé. I will find a teaching position or work as a governess and save. Should he be unable to join me here, I can return to him.'

The old man shook his head. 'If he does not come to you, my dear Miss Hewlett, there should be no question of you going to him. If a young man is not prepared to show the courage and commitment and make the necessary sacrifices to search for you, then he is not deserving of your love.'

Eliza was outraged. She wanted to thump him. 'How dare you say such a thing?'

'I say it because it is true. It is one thing to set off to a new world with your bride-to-be and quite another to embark on such a journey alone, uncertain as to whether the journey will prove fruitful. How will he find you?'

'I will write to him. I will write tomorrow and every day. And every day I will visit the port to wait for the telegraph that he will send me.'

'I see you are a very determined young lady. I just hope your young man is as resolute as you are.'

'He is. He loves me.'

'How wonderful to be so sure of another's love. I am deeply envious of that young man and I hope he deserves the trust you place in him.'

He turned away and stared out of the restaurant window into the lamp-lit street outside. 'Well then, Miss Hewlett, what is to become of you now?'

'If you are still prepared to lend some money to me I will borrow from you just sufficient to pay for my rent until I can find a teaching position. I will repay every penny, then save the money for my passage back to England.'

'I see.' He frowned.

'Now I must go and find a place to stay. I have already taken far too much of your time.'

'It is late' he said. 'I intend to stay in a boarding house tonight then take the train to St Louis tomorrow. Please allow me to accompany you there. You can take a room for tonight then seek somewhere more permanent tomorrow. Indeed I am willing to postpone my own onward journey to assist you in getting settled, my dear.'

'No.' Her voice sounded uncharacteristically harsh. 'You've done enough. I'll forward the money I owe to you in St Louis when I have it. Please give me the address.'

He tore a page out of a small notebook and wrote down the name of the brewery where his brother worked in St Louis and handed it to her.

'New York is a dangerous city and there are people everywhere who make their living by preying on new arrivals. A young woman alone is vulnerable. Please reconsider and let me help you.'

Eliza jumped up, knocking over her chair. The other occupants of the busy restaurant stopped talking and turned to look.

'I'm sorry. I must go. I have an address of a lodging house. Someone I met at Castle Garden recommended a place. Goodbye and thank you for your kindness.'

He called after her. 'God bless you, my dear. May you find what you are looking for. And remember, if you do not, my offer is open for ever.'

She ran out of the restaurant into the street. It was hot, the air clammy and debilitating, despite the fact that it was now late evening. She looked about her, not knowing which way to go, fumbling in her purse for the address Clarence had given her in Castle Garden. Kingsbridge Road. There was no one around to ask, so she set off, walking blindly, hoping that before long she would find a signpost or someone to give directions. She began to regret refusing the doctor's suggestion that she accompany him to his guest house. Conscious of the growing darkness, it was with relief that she came upon a woman, respectably dressed and with an honest countenance, holding the hand of a small child. Eliza asked if she could direct her to Kingsbridge Road.

'You're going in the wrong direction. It's miles away. What you want to go there for?'

'I was told I'd find accommodation.'

'Come with me, darling.' The woman had a soft Irish brogue. 'I'll see you right. There's rooms to be had where I'm living. I can rent you one. What's your name?'

Eliza gasped in relief and wearily followed the woman, who told her she was Mrs McCarthy, as they navigated through the grid of narrow streets and alleyways. They walked briskly, the small boy, Connor, skipping along beside them. Mrs McCarthy explained she was fetching him home after yet another episode of running away.

'The wee lad's only seven, but he has it in mind to go back to Ireland. Keeps trying to head down to the port.' She lowered her voice. 'He was a twin and his brother passed away from the fever four years ago on the voyage out. He's got it into his head that Fergus is back in Galway and keeps trying to go back there to find him. I've given up trying to get it into his thick skull that Fergus won't ever be coming back.' She stroked a hand affectionately over the tousled hair that covered the eponymous thick skull.

'Fergus was a good child most of the time. We pray for his soul every night. I keep telling this little fellow that if he keeps on running away like this he'll have a long time in Purgatory himself – or even worse end up in the other place. You a Catholic?'

Eliza nodded.

'Most are round here. Apart from the coloureds. Here we are then.' She turned into a narrow alley, signalling for Eliza to follow.

They entered a dark space, barely six feet wide between two tall buildings. Something flapped in Eliza's face and she screamed. The woman stopped and waited for her to catch up.

'Not scared of a bit of washing are you, lass? You won't

go far in Five Points without running into a washing line.' She laughed a guttural laugh and took Eliza by the arm, pushing her towards a doorway.

The light from an open window revealed that they had entered a small interior courtyard with tenement buildings surrounding it on all sides. As well as the dripping laundry, the space housed piles of wood, a pair of beaten-up old handcarts and what looked like an empty beer keg. Two mangy cats were fighting over what might have been a dead rat. There was a man leaning against the doorpost, smoking a clay pipe. He cuffed Connor over the head as the boy ran past him into the building, then looked Eliza up and down as though imagining her without her clothes on, but said nothing. Mrs McCarthy nodded at him but didn't speak, and led Eliza into the hallway of the building.

Inside it was pitch dark. Connor had disappeared into one of the rooms. There was no lighting in the hallway or on the stairs and Eliza had to fumble her way in the dark, hanging onto the bannisters and trying to keep up with Mrs McCarthy. They climbed seven flights of stairs to the top of the building and at the end of the passageway the woman unlocked a door, holding it open for a breathless Eliza to enter. Mrs McCarthy lit a candle and handed it to Eliza. The room was tiny. It couldn't have been more than eight feet long by five feet wide. The one window gave onto a narrow air-shaft that ran between the building and its neighbour. The Irish woman sat down on the only thing that passed for furniture - a wooden tea chest. Eliza held the candle aloft and looked around her. The air-shaft was only about two feet wide and when she opened the window and tried to lean out she could see nothing of the night sky above her. She had hoped for a draught of cooling air but the heat outside was even more stifling than that inside the room, and the air-shaft, far from ventilating the place, seemed to be a source of foul air in itself.

'You'll be needing bedding? I can let you have a straw mattress and a blanket for fifty cents. You may want to take it up onto the roof. The doorway's at the end of the landing. It's cooler up there. That's what most people do to get a decent night's sleep. A bit crowded on a hot night like tonight so you may have trouble bagging a space.' She laughed her throaty laugh again. 'But you'll be safe enough out there. Mostly families in this building. Decent folk all of them. Rent is four dollars and fifty cents for the month payable in advance.'

'That seems a lot for one very small room.'

The woman looked her up and down. 'Four dollars then.'

'I was told to expect to pay three dollars.'

'And there's me thinking you'd just stepped off the boat! All right. Let's say three-fifty and it's a deal. The water pump's in the yard and the privy's down there too. Best not go down there after dark on your own though.'

'Mrs McCarthy?'

'Yes?'

'Where do you live?' Eliza counted out the money and held it out to the woman who quickly checked the bills and stuffed them into a pocket of her apron.'

'Second floor. At the front. Give me a knock if you need anything. I'll send one of my lads up in a minute with the bedding.'

'Thank you.'

The woman nodded and left the room. When her footsteps on the stairs had receded Eliza slumped onto the tea chest and began to sob.

16

Attacked

Eliza awoke after a disturbed night, tossing and turning on the straw bed, bathed in sweat, with a raging thirst but too fearful to brave the dark stairwell in search of the water pump out in the yard. Her mood was no lighter, despite the arrival of daylight. There wasn't much of that anyway. Just a greyish gloom from the narrow air-shaft. She could see straight across it into a dwelling in the building opposite. A couple eating at a table in front of the window looked up and nodded to her.

There was no possibility of staying here. It was imperative that she find work and alternative accommodation, even if it reduced the amount she could put aside each week to re-pay Dr Feigenbaum and save for her passage back to England.

She made two trips up and down the seven flights of stairs, first to queue to use the privy and then, once she had borrowed a jug from Mrs McCarthy, to fetch water from the pump. Collecting the wood for the stove could wait as it was too hot to think of lighting it and she had no desire to cook anything in that place – even if she'd had the implements to do so.

Mrs McCarthy looked at her dubiously when she told

her she was a teacher, but pointed her in the direction of the nearest Catholic church and told her the name of the priest. 'If anyone can help you it's Father Connolly.'

When Eliza emerged into the courtyard it was in a frenzy of activity. Women were hanging newly-washed rags and sheets on the myriad washing lines that crisscrossed the space and rose in serried ranks, slung between the windows of the buildings at each level, like bunting on a ship. Children played, some of them holding their smaller siblings, little girls pretending to be mothers. All too soon they would be playing the part for real. Little boys played chase around the yard, knocking into each other and getting tangled in the washing, dodging the slaps that their harassed mothers dealt them when they were in range. The day was hot again, sultry, the sun covered by cloud and the atmosphere oppressive. There was a foul smell that pervaded the whole neighbourhood.

Eliza turned to one of the women and asked, 'What's the terrible smell?'

'Tanneries. They're all around here.'

'Is it always as bad as this?'

The woman shrugged. 'You get used to it.'

Eliza knew she wouldn't, couldn't. It was the stench of hell, indescribable, fetid, rancid, overpowering, nauseating. It caught at the back of her throat and made her gag. She put her handkerchief over her mouth and went out of the courtyard.

The church to which Mrs McCarthy had directed her was just a couple of blocks away, but she decided to go to the port first to find out if Jack had sent a telegraph message. There was no message. She fought back the tears. He would be in touch soon. He had to be. He wouldn't leave her here all alone like this. Would he?.

She trudged back to Five Points and walked in the direction she thought would take her to the church. The street she was walking down was quiet. She looked around nervously. Had she taken the wrong turning? It seemed different from the area around her lodgings, where people thronged the streets, going about their business. Here it was uncannily quiet. Deserted. Buildings boarded up. No one in sight. After a few hundred yards she decided to retrace her steps. Something was wrong.

She looked about her, trying to get her bearings. If only there was someone to ask. She was about to go back to the last busy road she had walked down and ask for directions, when she was grabbed from behind, a hand clamped over her mouth and another around her waist and she was dragged backwards.

Her heart wanted to catapult out of her body with fright. The sky was a narrow grey strip between tall buildings. She couldn't see her assailant but she could smell the stench of sour sweat and unwashed clothes. His hand over her mouth muffled her cries and was too tightly clamped for her teeth to gain any purchase.

He pushed her up against a wall. Her hat fell off and her face scraped against the rough bricks. He pinioned her against the wall with his chest. He was a big man. She could feel the strength and weight of his body against her. Her heart thumped in her chest and her struggle to breathe made her dizzy. Oh sweet Jesus help me! Don't let me die!.

Her head was jerked back by the hair then the hand moved away from her mouth and she sucked in great gobs of air, gasping as though she had been drowning. Her arms were twisted behind her back so she cried out in pain then he slammed her face hard against the bricks. She felt bone shatter and the taste of blood filled her mouth. She struggled again to breathe. She was going to die. Alone here in a dark New York alley. She was going to die.

The man's body continued to pinion her in place while his free hand grasped at her skirts. She tried to struggle.

To move her legs together. To squeeze them tight. Can't breathe. Can't move.

Then her racing heart and the surge of fear gave her a rush of strength she didn't know she possessed. She twisted sharply, trying to shake him off but he pressed his body hard against hers, now forcing one leg between hers. Panic gave way to anger. She'd had enough. She was damned if she'd let her life get any worse. If he was going to rape and kill her she'd die fighting. She raised her right foot up and to the side and stamped her heel down hard on his foot. He was momentarily taken off guard and as his body loosened its pressure on her, she twisted around, brought her knee up and rammed it into him between his legs as she had once seen a boy do to another in the playground with tearful consequences. Her attacker screamed in pain and bent over double. She moved to run out of the alley, but he caught her arm and pulled her back towards him, landing a punch like a hammer blow on her already broken face. Everything went black.

She awoke in an unfamiliar room. She was lying in a proper bed, under sheets and blankets. Washing hung on lines across the ceiling all around the room. She tried to pull herself up the bed, but the room began spinning and a shaft of pain burnt through her skull.

'Mam! Mam! She's woken up.' A small, half naked child with an unkempt mop of tangled curls was standing at the foot of the bed. The child crossed the room and leaned out of the open window where she yelled the same message.

Mrs McCarthy materialised at the bedside a few moments later.

'You were out cold, Eliza, love. Quite a walloping you got. Looked like you were lying there cold for some time before they found you. What happened?'

'I don't know. How did I get here? How long have I been here?' Her own voice sounded strange to her, muffled, distorted. She moved her tongue and tasted blood. She could feel a large gap in her lower jaw where several teeth should have been. As well as the sharp pain in her face, she felt a dull ache in her stomach on one side. The room started to spin and she closed her eyes. It was too difficult to contemplate what had happened and what state she was now in.

Mrs McCarthy's voice penetrated the fog. 'You were lying unconscious in an alley leading up to Mulberry Bend.'

She wanted to go back to sleep. To sleep and wake up to find this was all a bad dream. But she knew it wasn't.

'You don't want to go walking down dark alleys like that on your own, Eliza. There's men in gangs as would knife their own mothers, let alone a stranger.'

'Someone gwabbed me and dwagged me off zhe stweet down dere.' The sound of her own voice was unreal, like someone trying to speak with their mouth full.

'Whas wong with me? It hurts. My teef have gone.'

She felt the panic rising inside her as her voice distorted the words and made her sound as though she was talking with a handkerchief stuffed in her mouth. The pain in her cheek and jaw was like nothing she had ever known.

'Did you get a look at him?'

'Behind me mosh of zhe time. Happened so fass.' A sharper wave of pain sliced through her face and she cried out. 'It hurts. My face hurts.'

'Here, lassie. Laudanum. It'll dull the pain.' The woman pushed a spoon into her mouth and Eliza swallowed the medicine and felt the pain recede almost immediately to be replaced by a delicious drowsiness that numbed her whole body and filled her with a strange sense of contentment and wellbeing. She tried to smile up at Mrs McCarthy, but sleep overcame her.

When she woke again it was nightfall. Mrs McCarthy was moving back and forth slowly in a wooden rocking chair. The creaks were the only sound in the room. Eliza realised it must be the middle of the night.

The woman saw her stir and moved to the head of the bed, where she took a damp cloth and mopped Eliza's brow.

'How's the pain? Any better?'

Eliza struggled to speak. 'Do you have a looking gass? I wan see my face.'

'There's time enough for that later. You need to get your strength back first. There's a pot of chicken soup warming on the stove. You haven't eaten anything for two days.'

'Please. Bwing me a miwwa.'

The woman shrugged. 'We don't have a mirror in the house, dear.' She laughed. 'No call for it. We've more important things to spend our money on. My days of looking pretty are long gone.'

'Ank you for taking me in.' Her words were slow as she struggled to form them, conscious of the slurring and he inability to form some sounds.

'You're welcome. Gives me a bit of peace so I'm not complaining.' Again the dry sardonic laugh. 'My old man and two of my lads are sleeping upstairs in your room. It's like a holiday for me. My Paddy's a devil for the sex business, if you'll pardon my frankness. No sooner have I popped a babby out than he's shoving another one in me. That man's like a machine. Never stops. Wants to have his way all the time. I'm done in with it. Twelve kids I've carried and brought into this world and eight of them we've put in the ground. But he keeps on. No mercy. Men don't know the half of it. Don't get me wrong, Eliza, he's a hard worker. He's a longshoreman and he works his hide off to provide for the family. Barely touches the drink either. Just a few pints on a Saturday night. Sometimes I wish he was a bit fonder of the ale as he might pass out like half the street do after a good session and then I'd get at least one night's peace.' She laughed again. 'You ever been married, Eliza?'

'No. I engaged to be mawwied.'

'So where's your sweetheart?'

'England. Be here as soon ash he can. I go to zhe port. He send telgwaf.'

The woman snorted. 'I've heard that one before. Sorry to shatter your dreams, but I doubt you'll be seeing him again.'

'Why say zat?'

'Because he'd never have let you go if he meant to marry you.'

Eliza felt the tears welling up. She turned away from Mrs McCarthy. As she moved her head on the pillow, a shaft of pain sliced through her face and around her skull and she screamed in agony. The woman was there in an instant, the laudanum bottle at the ready.

'Take this and it will all be all right.'

17
Recovery

Eliza's hostess seemed in no rush to see her return to her own quarters. The pain in Eliza's face gradually subsided but she didn't know whether this was the natural healing process or the continuing effects of the laudanum. Lifting the bedcovers, she pulled up her night shift to look at the source of the pain in her belly and saw that her stomach was blackened with bruises.

As she was examining herself, Mrs McCarthy appeared. 'Yes you had a right good kicking. The doc said you must have put up a hell of a fight to get such a beating. You must have got someone pretty mad. If you ask my opinion, you'd have been better giving in and letting him have his way with you. At least it'd have been over fast enough and there'd have been no outward signs.' The woman shook her head. 'But then if you'd my luck, you'd have been knocked up in another sense!' She laughed, still shaking her head. 'Men! They have it easy.'

Eliza spent the next few days in a laudanum-induced haze until she decided that pain would be preferable to having only fleeting moments of consciousness. Pushing the proffered spoon away she said, 'I don' want any maw of that stuff. It makes me too dwowsy. I wan' be awake. I wan' get up. I must go to find news of Jack.'

'You can't just stop taking it like that. Need to do it bit by bit or you'll be as sick as a dog,' the woman warned.

Mindful of the probable cost of the medicine and fearful of its effect on her, Eliza refused to listen to the advice and that night it was as if she had entered the bowels of hell itself. The narrow cracks in the ceiling enlarged and opened up into gaping fissures. Hideous creatures crawled out and ran down the walls and over the bed. Huge rats with gigantic teeth. Cockroaches as big as cats with black eyes and red pupils. Babies with the heads of dogs. Green slime ran down the walls and a tide of filthy water swept into the room and engulfed the bed. Mrs McCarthy transformed into a cackling crone with blackened teeth and eyes that dripped blood. When Eliza looked at her it was as if she could read her thoughts – and she didn't like what they were. Her friendly Irish landlady had become a creature of terror. Then it was worse. Jack appeared, hand in hand with Mary Ellen and the pair were laughing at Eliza. She cried out to Jack but he turned away from her.

Eliza was sweating. Shaking. Skin crawling. Terrible itching. Make it stop. Go away. She screamed out for help.

'You sound like the Banshee herself. Didn't I tell you stopping the laudanum sudden, like that, was a bad thing? Here, just a wee drop to see you through till morning.' As the drops of laudanum slid down her throat Eliza slipped into a deep and undisturbed sleep.

Gradually the nightmares subsided and the doses reduced. Eliza sipped the bowls of broth her new friend brought her and even managed to swallow some bread soaked and softened in the soup. The inside of her mouth stung where her teeth had smashed into her lip and the gaps where they had been were sore and stinging and still bled.

Each morning she swung her legs out of the bed and tried to walk across the room. At first, her tentative steps took her only as far as the end of the bed before she slumped back, exhausted and dizzy. She wept with frustration.

Eventually Paddy McCarthy, whom Eliza recognised as the smoking man she had seen on her first night outside the tenement, appeared at the foot of the bed and announced that he was going to carry her up the six flights back to her room.

'And what is she supposed to do when she gets up there? How can she get herself up and down those stairs to fetch water and use the privy?' his wife said.

'She'll never be able to do it if she stops here. You and the kids can fetch and carry for her till she's well. I've had enough. I'm sleeping in my own bed tonight with my own wife. A man shouldn't have to share a bed with his sons.'

He picked Eliza up as if she were a piece of flotsam on a beach. She wanted to protest at the indignity but she knew she was too weak to walk, so she swallowed her pride and let him carry her.

She felt a mixture of relief and fear about returning to her own room. She had become dependent on Mrs McCarthy and wanted to regain her privacy and self reliance, but she was frightened. Afraid of what would become of her. Afraid of what she would see when she eventually looked in a mirror. Worried that she may never be whole again. Then there was the matter of her teeth. She would have to buy false ones. How would she pay for them? Her money had almost run out. Her attacker had stolen her purse with twenty dollars in it. What was left would be needed to pay the rent, pay Mrs McCarthy a contribution for food and board - plus the doctor's fee for the laudanum and dressing her wounds while she was unconscious.

Paddy McCarthy set her down outside her door. She thanked him and he grunted in acknowledgment and raced back down the stairs, presumably keen to ravish his wife. Once back in her miserable little room Eliza sat on the tea chest and counted the money she had left - just eleven dollars.

Now for the thing she had been dreading while she had lain in the McCarthys' bed – it was time to look in the mirror. She pulled a small bone-handled vanity glass out of her holdall and took a deep breath.

The bruising covered the whole right side of her face. It had probably already faded but she gasped in horror at the extent of it. Worse still was the swelling. The right side of her face ballooned out into a purple protuberance under a sunken eye, which itself was narrowed to little more than a slit. She touched her cheek gently with one finger and cringed with the pain. The swelling unbalanced her face making her grotesque. She tilted the mirror and turned her head – her left profile was almost normal, apart from a little bruising and a few scratches, but head-on and in right profile she was ghoulish – disfigured, damaged, distorted as though the mirror were part of a fairground attraction whose reflection transformed people into strange and fantastic sub-human beings. She flung it across the room where it hit the wall and shattered into pieces. Seven years' bad luck. She'd be lucky to get off so lightly. Her whole life was bad luck. Everything ruined. Everything lost. No future. No hope.

There was a knock on the door. Two men stood on the threshold behind Mrs McCarthy.

'You've visitors, dearie. Father Connolly and Dr Flaherty. The doc treated you when they brought you in. And Father is from Holy Innocents, where you were headed when it happened.'

'That will be all thank you, Caitlyn. I'll see you at Mass tomorrow.' The priest, a short, stocky Irishman, dismissed her friend quite rudely, Eliza thought.

The doctor put his bag on the floor and nodded at Eliza. 'You must have put up quite a fight, young lady, to come off as badly you did.' He listened to her chest with a stethoscope and took her pulse. 'Very good. You've a strong constitution. Let me take a look at that face.'

She cringed and made her hands into tight fists to stop crying out as he gently probed the surface of her damaged cheek and peered inside her mouth.

'You'll live! Get as much rest as you can. It will take some time for the bruising and swelling to go down. Are you bathing it in witch hazel?'

She nodded.

'Once the swelling's gone you'll look much better, but I'm afraid you'll never be the belle of the ball again. I don't believe in beating about the bush, Miss Hewlett. Honesty is always the best policy. Your eye socket is damaged and will likely be sunken compared with the healthy one. Same goes for the cheekbone. It's collapsed and will never be in symmetry with the other side. I'm very sorry.'

The priest spoke then. 'Never mind, my dear. What's inside is more important than outside. God sends these things to test us and we must not be found wanting. Mrs McCarthy tells me you're a teacher. She said you were on your way to ask me about finding a job when this terrible accident befell you.'

'Not an accident. Attacked by a man.'

'Yes, yes, very unfortunate. No doubt one of the Eye-ties. A good Irish lad would never do a thing like that. Those Eye-ties may be of the same true faith but they are uncontrolled hooligans. And as for the Jew boys and the coloureds? Don't get me started.'

The doctor coughed. 'You were going to talk to Miss Hewlett, Paddy, about the teaching situation. And we have to be getting a move on if we're to get the rounds done before...' He raised his hand to mime downing a pint of beer.

'Yes indeed. You're a good man, Seamus, always keeping

149

me on the path to righteousness. So let's talk about the teaching, Miss Hewlett, or Eliza isn't it?'

At last there may be something positive for her to hang onto, to work towards. The chance to start work and earn money as soon as she would be well enough.

'Much as I'd like to help you, I'm afraid I can't,' said the priest.

Eliza's heart sank.

He continued, 'We already have a full quota of teachers at Holy Innocents and the trouble is finding the pupils for them to teach. When a child can be put to work washing rags, boiling bones, or rolling cigars, there's few parents will give up the chance of a few extra dollars for the sake of an education for their kids no matter how much I tell them they should from the pulpit.'

The priest glanced at the doctor, avoiding Eliza's eyes, then shook his head. 'And to be honest, Eliza, I can't say I wouldn't do the same in their shoes. Times are hard.'

Eliza was crushed by disappointment. She didn't think she could take any more. What was there left for God to test her with? Hadn't she suffered enough?.

The priest went on. 'When you're well again, maybe you should try moving out west. People are more established there. Place more stock on education. Five Points here is full of people on the move, on the move up and on the move west. It's just a way-station. A place where folks try to set themselves up for a future out west where there's land and space and more opportunities. No time here for the niceties such as schooling. The way I see it – as long as I can get some of them along to Mass on a Sunday that's the most important thing.'

'I could shpeak to pawents. Get childwen to come to school.'

The priest looked sideways at the doctor and back to Eliza. She thought she detected a slight rolling of the eyes,

150

but in the gloom of the room she couldn't be certain.

'Well, we've plenty more sick souls to call on before we're done, haven't we, Seamus?' the priest said. He made the sign of the cross over Eliza's head. *'Et benedictio Dei omnipotentis, Patris, et Filii, et Spiritus Sancti, descendat super vos et maneat semper.'* May the blessing of Almighty God, the Father, the Son and the Holy Ghost descend upon you and be with you always. Amen.'

He reached into his pocket and pulled out a small, tin medal and placed it in her hand. 'Here you are, Eliza. It's Saint Gregory. Patron saint of teachers. Say a few prayers to him and who knows? And don't forget to say the Rosary each night before you go to bed.' He winked at her, then he and Doctor Flaherty left the room.

18
Searching for Work

In the days that followed the visit from Father Connolly and Dr Flaherty, Eliza tried to find work - but only after beginning every day with a trip to the office of the shipping line to find out whether any messages had been sent to her. The clerk there knew her by now.

'Never give up, do you, lady? Don't you think it's time to forget this fellow, whoever he is?'

She tried to hide her irritation. Every day her feet seemed to drag a bit more slowly on the pavement as she walked there, but every day as she entered his office she allowed herself to feel hope until she saw his slow shake of the head. Hope was all she had left. Hope and love and trust that one day Jack would at last get word to her.

Pain from her injuries, and her weakness after being so long confined to bed, meant she could look for a job for only an hour or two each day. She went from school to school, making enquiries but everywhere met with the same response. There was no shortage of teachers. She was also conscious of the way people drew away from her, evidently repulsed by the distorted contours of her face and the still not completely faded bruising. On top of this, she was talking with a lisp caused by her missing teeth and was as yet unable to pay for a set of dentures. While missing teeth was by no means unusual, she had always been proud of her strong, white teeth.

She was fearful of the streets of New York and recognising and understanding this, Mrs McCarthy instructed Connor to accompany her wherever she went. Eliza was unconvinced that a small boy would provide any deterrent to a determined assailant, but nonetheless took some comfort from having his small dirty hand in hers as she made her way through the unfamiliar streets of the city.

One day she asked Mrs McCarthy why she, like so many other parents, refrained from sending Connor to school.

'I'd rather he's with you. At least I know where he is then. When he does go to school he runs away. The teachers don't care. They don't even notice he's gone half the time. I'm that fed up with it.'

Eliza decided to repay Mrs McCarthy by offering to teach Connor some lessons. He was a bright lad and knew his letters and could add and subtract well enough. She asked him why he didn't like school.

'I do like it. But I want to go with Fergus. I don't want to get ahead of him. I want to wait till he can come with me. He'll be mad if I learn stuff he doesn't know.'

'You do know Fergus isn't coming back, don't you, Connor? You know he's gone to heaven?'

'No, he's not.'

'Your ma told me he took ill on the ship coming to America and he's up in heaven now. You'll be with him again one day when you go to heaven.'

'He's not in heaven.' The boy's tone was definitive. 'Father Connolly says he's in Purgatory. I want to go there and get him out.'

Eliza sighed and silently cursed the stupidity of the priest. 'A little boy such as Fergus won't have done enough to be in Purgatory for long. He'll be up in heaven now. I'm sure of it. Purgatory is mainly for grownups to atone for their sins. And once they've shown they're really sorry they get to go to heaven. Little boys, if they go there at all, will only be there for a few hours – just long enough to tell God they're sorry.'

'Father Connolly came to school and said every time we do something naughty that's another year in Purgatory. Fergus and me was always getting slapped by Da for being naughty. I worked it out and it adds up to about thirty years. And Father Connolly said Purgatory is a kind of prison. So I'm going to get Fergus out of there. I think it's in Ireland cos I know there's a big prison there. My Uncle Danny's in there. And I want to get my baby sister, Annie. She's gone to Ireland too, but she's in a different prison.'

Eliza frowned. 'What happened to Annie?'

'She died when she was just a tiny baby and hadn't had time to be baptised so she's still got Original Sin and isn't allowed into heaven. She's had to go to Limbo. Father Connolly says if you don't get baptised you can't ever go to heaven. You have to stay in Limbo. I cried when he said that and Sister Monica said it was all right cos Limbo is quite a nice place, full of little babies and they're all happy. But I don't want her to be on her own without the rest of the family. She'll be lonely. And it's not fair. She can't help it that there wasn't time to baptise her.'

'But didn't your Ma or your Da baptise her themselves when she got ill? If there isn't time for the priest to do it, anyone can do the sacrament in an emergency.'

'She died in her sleep. When we all woke up in the morning she was already cold.'

Eliza, having had no success with finding a teaching position in a school, set about looking for one as a governess. Very quickly she realised that anyone who could afford the services of a governess was not going to choose one with missing teeth and a battered face. Who could blame them? She resembled a losing, bare-knuckle fighter.

Once the swelling subsided, it revealed a flat plateau on one side of the face, a marked contrast to the high cheekbone on the other side. The bruising had gone but the right eyeball had retreated back inside the hollow of her skull, giving her a narrow-eyed shifty look. She knew that, were she to be placed in the position of those from whom she was seeking employment, she would probably be uncomfortable choosing a woman with a face so damaged. So how could she expect strangers to take a chance on her?

She went to Holy Innocents to pray. The church was silent. A cool haven away from the heat and bustle of the streets. There was a scent of incense lingering in the air, mixing with the smell of melting wax from the bank of candles. She dropped a few cents in the box and lit a candle, then knelt down in one of the pews and bent forward, her hands clasped in prayer. She asked God what she should do next. Begged him silently to give her some kind of sign, but was met with only silence. No one else was in the church. She looked around her at the fading flowers on the altar, at the heavy curtains hanging over the confessional box, at the plaster statues that stood sentry around the church and at the Stations of the Cross. She took out her rosary beads and went through all the mysteries, until her knees ached and the words of the mumbled Hail Marys ceased to have meaning. With no answer to her prayers, she left the church.

Leaving the building, her forehead damp from the holy water in the font, her foot caught a stray bottle on the pavement and it rolled into the gutter. Connor, who had been waiting for her patiently at the back of the church, bent down and picked it up.

'I'll get a cent for that,' he said.

As he was about to stuff it in his pocket, something made her ask him to let her look at it. The brown bottle was embossed on the front. Dreschner beer, from the German

Brewery of St Louis, Missouri. She swallowed, not wanting to accept what it meant, but forced to admit she had received her sign.

19
To Middlesbrough

Jack's arrest at the Liverpool docks did not lead to a lengthy detention. As soon as the ship was safely out of harbour Father O'Driscoll slipped some money to the police officers and they went away. They didn't take the handcuffs with them and Jack had to suffer the ignominy of traveling back to Bristol in MacBride's coach with the cuffs still binding him – a long and miserable journey. It was only when they were installed in Victoria Lodge that the priest removed them.

Father O'Driscoll and Tom MacBride exerted a heavy price to preserve the reputation of Mary Ellen. All the way back to Bristol they harangued him. Jack could barely make sense of what they were saying. Their words flowed over him like a river in flood, a constant barrage that formed a background to his personal grief. His brain was in turmoil. What would happen to Eliza? How could he find her again? What would she do? He was stricken with a mixture of grief and guilt. It was all his fault. She had done nothing and now she was the hapless victim of his own stupidity. He was angry with the two men sitting opposite him, but he was more angry with himself.

When Jack refused to answer their demands, the priest

set about kicking him as he sat, cuffed and helpless. Jack was obdurate in his refusal to marry the woman. MacBride threatened him with the cooked-up charge of the theft of two paintings. Jack told him he didn't care if they threw him in prison, but he would never agree to marry Mary Ellen. Then O'Driscoll played the trump card. Unless Jack agreed to marry Mary Ellen, Sister Callista would be dismissed from both her post as headmistress and cast out of the convent and the church.

That was too much. He wanted to kill the smug, red-faced bully. Bringing Sister Callista into this was despicable. He protested. 'Sister had nothing to do with this. Do what you like to me, but leave her alone. She is a good woman.'

'Stop your lies. We know she gave you money. Money she had no right to be holding. She had sworn a vow of poverty and loyalty to the church.'

They knew. Jack was desperate. 'It wasn't her fault. I made her do it.'

'Don't make things worse for yourself, Brennan. Marry the woman and Mr MacBride will forget about the paintings and Sister Callista can get on with teaching.' The priest leaned over Jack, his arms pinning Jack's shoulders back and his eyes narrowed.

'You're a smart enough lad. Wise up. Your lady friend has gone and you'll not see her again, so you'd better make the best of what's left for you. It's that or prison and with a criminal record you'll never teach again. It's time to face the consequences of your lewd actions. We're offering you a new beginning. Mr MacBride has very generously agreed to give you a decent start by paying your railway tickets, as well as giving you enough cash to tide you over for the first few months. Enough to get you started off with somewhere to live until your wages are paid. My cousin has arranged accommodation for you with a widow in the parish until you can find something more suitable for the long term.'

As he said the words "long term", Jack felt sick. It was a life sentence. He was yoked to Mary Ellen until one or other of them ended their days. Responsible for her bastard child. Forced to share his home and his life with her. He'd gladly have chosen the prison sentence – but they had made it clear it would be the ruination of the nun who had shown him nothing but kindness. He couldn't even seek Sister Callista's counsel as he was confined to the house - and as far as he knew she could also be confined to the convent. After the woman's kindness, he could not allow further sanctions against her, so three days after he was dragged from the ship, he was married to Mary Ellen.

The ceremony was rushed, with only the priest, along with MacBride and the priest's housekeeper as witnesses. There was no nuptial breakfast, no fancy carriage and plumed horses, no fine clothes or invited guests. Mary Ellen's initial joy that at last she was to be married was transformed to petulance when she found out she was to forego all the frills, fuss and finery she had dreamed of all her life.

Jack couldn't bear to speak to her. He walked into the church like a condemned man approaching the gallows. He made no eye contact with Mary Ellen or the priest. He looked around the familiar church as the sunlight streamed through the stained glass window and cast a kaleidoscope of colour over the bride's face and the floor in front of them. He struggled to pray, to find the right words of supplication, to plead to God and the saints to release him, but the words refused to form in his head. He raised his eyes to the statue of the Virgin Mary in her niche to the side of the altar, but her eyes were downcast, as though she too were ashamed at what was taking place.

The words of the marriage rite spoken by Father O'Driscoll were a mockery. Jack was consumed by anger and looked up in defiance at the priest. His look was met with a narrowing of the Irishman's eyes and Jack swallowed, remembering the fate of Sister Callista was in his hands. He spoke the required vows in a barely audible mumble and when it was over he felt his life was over too.

Over the three or four decades before Jack and Mary Ellen arrived in Middlesbrough, the town had undergone the most explosive growth of any in Britain, rising up from the empty salt marshes beside the mouth of the River Tees. The happy conjunction of deep water at the river mouth, the proximity of the coalfields and the extension of the Stockton to Darlington railway meant that what had been a tiny settlement rapidly burgeoned into a thriving port. When iron ore was discovered in the Cleveland Hills, Middlesbrough's destiny was assured, as iron foundries with their blast furnaces and rolling mills sprung up on the banks of the river. The town was now responsible for one third of the iron ore output of Britain and had become an exemplar of England's spectacular industrial progress in the nineteenth century.

The newly married couple were oblivious to this economic miracle as the train trundled towards their destination. The journey from Bristol was passed almost entirely in silence. Jack stared out of the window, unseeing, as fields and woods sped by, his enchantment during his first railway trip from Derby and the excitement and anticipation of the journey to Liverpool with Eliza, replaced by misery. Mary Ellen was confused, muddled, angry. She sulked on the other side of the compartment, sighing loudly every few minutes, presumably in the hope of eliciting a response from Jack, but he just stared out of the window and ignored her.

Jack meanwhile tortured himself over what might have happened to Eliza, constantly rewinding the events of the past days in his mind. If only they had stayed below decks, they might have escaped detection. If only they had got off the train at Crewe and stayed there for a few nights to let their trail go dead. If only he had told Mr MacBride what happened in that dark alleyway as soon as he got back to the house. If only he had not involved Eliza, but run away himself – perhaps returned to Derby until the dust had settled. But winding the clock back could not happen. Eliza was trapped on a ship, alone and without money, sailing away into a future without him. He was ashamed, wracked with guilt, filled with remorse. Powerless to do anything.

When at last the ill-matched pair exited the station at Middlesbrough, it was a sunny summer's day, yet as Jack took in the grimy, smoke-blackened streets with their crowded houses, he felt lower than he had ever been. How was it possible to be so happy one day and entering the slough of despond the next? He couldn't help his mind returning to that last night with Eliza in Liverpool, to the hopes and dreams they had shared and to their mutual excitement at an unknown future in a new world.

The lodging house that Father O'Driscoll had arranged for them, was in a tree-lined avenue with large houses, many of which appeared to be commercial lodgings. Mrs Grainger, the landlady, was a smiling, rotund lady, with dimples on either side of a generous mouth. She greeted them warmly at the door and, after raising an eyebrow when she saw Mary Ellen's condition, showed them to their room on the second floor.

Jack left Mary Ellen to unpack and followed his land-lady downstairs to a room at the back of the house, which contained nothing but a large table and chairs, where he asked her the way to the school where he was due to teach.

'It's just five minutes away, Mr Brennan. When are you due to start teaching there?'

'Tomorrow or the day after I understand. I was told to report to a Father Reilly.'

She looked at him and shook her head. 'I'm sorry to have to tell you this, with Mrs Brennan expecting a child, but the school had to close two days ago. There's been an outbreak of cholera and five children are dead already so the governors and the town council have insisted on closure.'

'When will it re-open?' Jack felt his knees giving way and he sank down onto one of the wooden chairs.

'Father Reilly will be able to tell you more than I will. If you get yourself over to the presbytery now you should catch him before he does the Novena.'

With a hollow feeling in the pit of his stomach, Jack knocked on the door of the presbytery and was ushered by the housekeeper into an anteroom, lined with wooden upright chairs around all four walls. There was a large statue of the Virgin Mary standing guard in one corner of the room, which otherwise was completely bare.

The parish priest kept him waiting for fifteen minutes, then rushed into the room, full of apologies. He led Jack into a drawing room, where he signalled him to take a seat on one of the threadbare but commodious chairs.

'Mr Brennan, it's a terrible thing that's been happening to us here. Our Lord is certainly testing our strength and our faith. Five little children have been taken back to heaven and we've lost two young women, one a new mother, and an elderly man to this awful disease. We've had no alternative but to close the school down. We have been short of funds for a long time. The bishop is trying to keep us afloat, but times are hard and there are many drains on the church's resources.'

'When will it reopen?'

'That I can't tell you. It may be some time. The town council is being as difficult as it can be and is doing little to expedite matters. Indeed I suspect they are taking advantage of this unfortunate event to put more pressure on the Catholic community, as they're mostly made up of Methodists and Quakers. While we Catholics are over-represented in the town's population, we're under-represented on the council. The post you were to fill has long been vacant and to be honest, even before the epidemic, we had come to the decision not to fill it but to consolidate the classes. I wrote to Father O'Driscoll and told him this but it seems my letter failed to reach him. I can see no possible way we can find a place for you, Mr Brennan, much as I would like to.'

Jack slumped forward, hanging his head. 'What's to become of us? My wife is to have a child soon. Are there any other schools that might be in need of a teacher? Even non-Catholic ones?'

'Do you have the qualifications?'

Jack shook his head.

'Dear, dear. This is very difficult. I am afraid the school boards here are now insisting on qualified teachers only. St Saviours was the only Catholic boys' school and it's unlikely that any of the non-Catholic schools would be prepared to take on a Catholic teacher, let alone an unqualified one.'

Jack looked up at the priest. 'What am I to do, Father?'

The priest looked embarrassed and shook his head. 'I wish I knew. I suppose you could still ask at the other schools. It's worth trying. Do you have a letter of recommendation?'

Jack cursed silently. He had not had any opportunity to ask Sister Callista to provide one or return the one written by Mr Quinn. He stood up and put his cap on, burning with humiliation and anger.

'I'll not waste any more of your time then, Father.'

That night he sat in the only chair in the bedroom, a bare wooden Windsor chair, without so much as a cushion, and watched as his new wife knelt by the bedside in prayer. She had her head lowered, resting on the coverlet and was wearing her night shift. The calico fabric was stretched tightly across her back and over her distended belly.

She paused in her mumblings and looked up at him. 'Will you not say your prayers, Jack?'

Prayers? What good had prayers done him? What kind of God was it who had torn him from Eliza and stood by as he was forced into this sham marriage at the hands of a priest? Religion had done nothing for him. He would renounce it. He would do without it. Yet there was a part of him that feared if he turned away from God he would cut off all hope for the future. Maybe this was some kind of test? Maybe if he trusted in God, then God would provide? He slipped onto his knees and took up his place on the opposite side of the bed and bowed his head. As he tried to find the words to pray he was distracted by the mumbled Hail Marys rattled off at speed from the other side of the bed. It sounded like meaningless mumbo jumbo. He wanted to pull Mary Ellen to her feet and ask her what she was saying. Ask her what she thought the words meant. Ask her how divine intercession would come from reciting the words over and over again until they became indistinguishable sounds with one word running into the next. He got up, grabbed his cap and jacket from the back of the door and went out.

He walked the streets for hours, wandering aimlessly, letting his feet take him where they willed. The town was undeniably ugly. Row upon row of slum dwellings, worse than the squalid little house he had grown up in back in Derby. Grimmer than the lodging house in Liverpool. Don't think about Liverpool. Shut it out. Close the door. She's gone. She's lost for ever. No more. He wanted to scream, bellow into the moonlit night, rage against the pointlessness of his life. Eliza. Eliza, what have I done? Where are you? What are you doing now?.

He paced the streets, wincing from the blisters caused by the new shoes MacBride had bought him to get married in and he asked himself if it was his fault. Had his defiance of his parents' wishes brought this upon him? Had he unwittingly led Mary Ellen to believe he had intentions towards her? Had he brought shame upon Eliza? He couldn't bear to think of her, his love, alone on the transatlantic steamer, then set ashore in New York. Friendless. Penniless. The money Sister Callista had given them had been in his pocket and there had been no time to hand it over to Eliza. He wanted to scream and shout at the sheer unfairness of it all and his utter powerlessness in the face of fate. He wanted to wind back time and make it all different. They had so nearly escaped. Had the police arrived just a few minutes later the ship would have departed and how different his prospects would be. It was all so random. How could God ordain this? Why did he want to punish him?

He found himself moving closer to the river, drawn towards the thrumming and banging sounds that were unending drumbeats in the otherwise silent night. Booming. Crashing. Thumping. And not just the noise. The sky in front of him was washed in the deepest purple with moving vermillion clouds of smoke overlaying it, twisting and writhing in saturnine patterns. Plumed lines of fire cut horizontally through the red clouds in bright yellows and oranges. He stopped and stared. The black bulk of buildings, chimneys and cranes were silhouetted against the multicoloured sky. It was the gateway to hell. The mouth of an angry volcano. Boom. Boom. Bang. Bang. Relentless movement of machinery. The stench of sulphur and smoke clogged in his throat. He saw it as a metaphor for the life that was ahead of him. He was a soul condemned to eternal damnation among the blast furnaces of this god-forsaken town. As he neared the waterfront to look across at the foundries, he saw white-capped waves lapping below, the rough sea indifferent to the ugly beauty of this manmade colossus of industrial might.

As the early morning light diluted the inky sky, Jack turned away from the estuary and began the long, slow walk back to the house and Mary Ellen.

Jack trudged the streets of Middlesbrough every day for three days until he had visited every school in the town. He offered to teach unpaid for a trial period until his capabilities were proven, but no one was willing to take him on. Each night, when he returned to Mrs Grainger's boarding house, he had to endure the accusatory look of Mary Ellen when he told her he had still not secured a position.

They had not consummated the marriage. At night Jack lingered in the communal dining room, pretending to read, while Mary Ellen went to bed, When at last he went up to their bedroom, he settled himself into the chair in the corner and draped his jacket over his chest.

She called out to him, her voice a whine, a desperate pleading for him to join her in the bed. He tried to shut out the sound of her and to ignore the discomfort of trying to sleep upright on a small wooden chair. The thought of lying beside her in the same bed was repugnant.

He lasted for three nights then, his body exhausted and his nerves frayed from lack of sleep and the fruitless search for employment, he slipped into the bed once she was asleep and lay close to the edge with his body turned away from her.

He awoke in the middle of the night to find her hands upon him under his nightshirt. Before he knew what was happening, she was astride him and he was inside her. He looked up at her face, her eyes closed and her features distorted with pleasure and concentration as she worked up and down on him rhythmically, her breathing jerky and ragged. Her swollen belly pressed against him, reminding him that there was a living child inside her. Another man's child. A hidden witness to what they were doing. He felt overwhelmed with shame, yet at the same time overcome by the pleasure of what she was doing to him. He thought of the time he had come upon her in the alley with that man doing this same thing. Disgust filled him, but unable to stop himself he cried out involuntarily as he ejaculated into her. She slumped forward onto his chest, then heaved her body off him and lay back, her head on the pillow beside his, and reached for his hand and placed it on her breast. He pulled away, revolted, ashamed, and confused. He was even a little frightened. Frightened of how he had felt when it was happening. Frightened of the pleasure of it. Guilty for taking gratification from this woman he could never love.

The confessional box was dim and the priest a dark shadow behind the metal grille. Jack had waited until everyone else had made their confessions. As the priest was about to emerge, Jack slipped inside the box.

'You're cutting it fine, lad. My supper will be getting cold. We'll have to add another Hail Mary for that.' The priest chuckled at his own joke.

Jack wished he hadn't come. He hoped that Father Reilly could not see him through the grille and wouldn't recognise him. He was embarrassed.

He garbled the words, rushing out the formulaic phrases. 'Bless me, Father, for I have sinned. It is three weeks since my last confession and these are my sins.' As he spoke the familiar words they sounded like a nursery rhyme and he felt foolish and childish.

'Get on with it then, lad.'

The priest's stomach rumbled loudly and Jack wanted to walk out of the confessional. He wanted to walk out of the town too, out of the marriage, out of everything that had conspired to ruin his life.

He hesitated, then taking comfort from the darkness, he plunged in and told Father Reilly that he was married to a woman he didn't love. Liberated by the anonymity of the confessional he opened up. 'I feel nothing for this woman. I despise her for trapping me into marrying her.'

'Do you have marital relations with her?'

Jack said he had done. Just once. 'And that's it, Father. I feel ashamed. I took pleasure from it. I was filled with lust.' He could feel his skin burning as he spoke, a vein on his temple pulsating, his words barely more than a whisper.

'The sacrament of Holy Matrimony is a sacred one and there is no shame in having relations with your wife. God has joined you together for the purpose of procreation and it is only natural that you should take pleasure in it.'

'But I don't love her. I can never love her.'

'Love is a gift from God. It is the greatest gift of all. Love God himself and he will help you to find love in your heart for your wife.'

'But I don't want to love her, Father. That's the point.'

'Do you lust after other women?'

'I am in love with only one woman, but she is lost to me forever.'

'And you are not tempted to go with anyone else?'

'No, Father.'

'Do you have impure thoughts about your wife?'

'No, Father. I have never thought about her that way at all – but then when she touched me last night I couldn't help but give into what she wanted me to do. And I feel ashamed about it.'

'You have no reason for shame. As long as you take pleasure only with your wife, there is nothing amiss. Your wife is there to provide you with children and keep your home and you in turn must provide for her and care for her. As long as you don't force yourself upon her?'

Jack was tempted to say that it was the other way around,

but he had already said more than he intended.

'Of course not. It's just that I feel guilty. I can't help thinking that I am using her for my own pleasure.'

The priest laughed. 'Get away with you, son! Be thankful that you've a wife who's happy to share your bed. There are many men who turn to immoral practices because their wives are unwilling. Now, as your penance say three Our Fathers and three Hail Marys and I absolve you from your sins in the name of the Father, and of the Son, and of the Holy Spirit. Amen. Now let me go and eat my supper.'

20
Employment

The money was running out. Jack was growing more desperate as every day passed and he failed to secure a position. Mary Ellen never left the lodging house, staying in their room all day, emerging only for meals in the communal dining room. Her reproachful looks were supplemented by frequent tears and angry outbursts when she blamed him for their plight and pleaded with him to take her back to Bristol.

He wrote to Tom MacBride, telling him what had happened but received a curt response requesting him not to write again, saying Jack had brought disgrace on himself and Mary Ellen and he was washing his hands of the pair of them.

He contemplated leaving her, walking out of the house and getting as far away as possible. But where could he go? Returning to Derby was out of the question - his pride would never permit it. He longed to find a way to travel to America and seek out Eliza, but he had no funds to pay the passage and were he by some miracle to get there, how would he trace her? And how could he leave Mary Ellen when she was about to give birth? He wondered whether a convent would take her in, but he couldn't just abandon her, heavy with child, on the doorstep.

Throughout it all he drowned in guilt – his conviction that he had brought all this upon himself, on Eliza and upon Mary Ellen by his failure to face up to what he had witnessed in the alley that night. Had he told her father, or sought the counsel of Sister Callista, it might have been possible to avoid the pregnancy. Then he reminded himself that it would already have been too late – she was already pregnant by the time he saw her in the alleyway.

Every night in their small room in the lodging house, he struggled with his body and his desires. He was disgusted by himself, by Mary Ellen and by what they did together. He slept in the chair for nights then, exhausted, slipped into bed beside her. The sight of her body repelled him, her hard muscular flesh, her long white legs, the growing bulge of her belly, the thick bush of hair between her legs – but in the darkness of their bed he luxuriated in her soft breasts, the warm, secret recesses of her body and was excited by the sounds she made when she reached her climax. Afterwards his own body repelled him more – his inability to control it and its blind, primitive urges that were slaked by this mindless coupling in the dark. One night, as he ejaculated, he cried out 'Forgive me' – but knew not whether he was talking to God, to Eliza or to Mary Ellen.

Several weeks after they had arrived in Middlesbrough, Mrs Grainger asked to see Jack in her private parlour. None of the paying guests were ever invited to step beyond the communal dining room. Jack was nervous about what lay ahead.

'Mr Brennan, you owe me two weeks rent. When do you expect to pay me?'

'I'm sorry. I hoped I might be able to delay it for a few days, in the expectation of obtaining employment this week.'

'And where might you be looking for work?'

He looked down, avoiding her eyes, feeling the shame burning his cheeks. 'I've been to every school in the town and many outside. I don't know what to do or where else to look.'

She shook her head slowly. 'I'm sorry for your plight. And especially with your wife being due so soon, but we can't go on like this. Even if you were able to pay the rent, I can't have a baby here. There are no families. I took you in as a favour to Father Reilly as you are a Catholic, but I understood it would only be temporary. It wouldn't be right for Mrs Brennan to have her baby delivered here. No, no, not right at all. Most of my guests are professional men, commercial travellers and the like. They wouldn't tolerate being woken by a crying baby. You do understand, don't you?'

Jack clenched his fists, feeling his fingernails cut into the flesh of his palms.

She leaned forward and tapped him on the shoulder. 'It seems to me you have to rethink your position. If you cannot be a schoolmaster then you must seek alternative employment. There's always the iron foundry. You may be lucky and get taken on there. It's worth a try.' She looked him up and down, somewhat doubtful herself. 'But you don't strike me as the sort of fellow to work in a place like that. Those fine white hands. And you don't look strong enough. Is there anything else you might do?'

Jack looked at her, his eyes brimming. 'Teaching's all I've ever done.'

She stood up. 'I've an idea. Wait here. I'll be back in ten minutes.' She left him sitting there in the stuffy parlour, which smelled of *pot pourri* and Mrs Grainger's *eau de cologne*. There was a canary in a cage. It started to sing as soon as the landlady left, as though making fun of Jack and his plight.

When she returned, she was rubbing her hands together and smiling. 'I'm so glad I thought of that. There's a public house near the iron foundries, on Colliers Street, The Tudor Crown. The publican died recently and they need to find a new tenant. The boss of the brewery, Mr Bellamy, is a parishioner at St Saviours and lives in the next street from here. His wife's a friend of mine. He's agreed to consider you as the replacement landlord. He'd lined someone up but his wife told me yesterday the fellow's let him down at the eleventh hour. The job comes with accommodation. It's above the premises but quite spacious. Jobs like that don't come along very often. He'll see you at the Crown at ten o'clock tomorrow morning. No promises, mind. If he doesn't like you he won't take you. But he's willing to give you a chance.'

Jack jumped to his feet and grasped her hands. 'Thank you, thank you, Mrs Grainger. I won't let you down. I'll do my best and I won't forget your rent.'

The Tudor Crown was a large corner pub. It was relatively recent in construction, but already had a tired look, with the windows caked in grime and the brickwork blackened with soot. The building was in a busy stretch of the road occupied by a wide variety of shops from ironmongers and boot-makers to fancy goods merchants and fishmongers. The road was intersected by a grid of residential streets, all lined by small, uniform terraced dwellings thrown up in a hurry by builders trying to keep up with demand for housing. Looking around him Jack could see no reason why he shouldn't be able to make a decent fist of running a pub here. There was certainly enough potential clientele living in these ugly, crosshatched streets.

Clutching his hat in front of him, he pushed open the heavy oak door and went into the gloomy pub, where Mr

Bellamy was waiting for him. The man had a jovial air and seemed taken with the idea of a former teacher as landlord. He pronounced that it would convey an air of respectability to the premises and he was happy to have a fellow Catholic behind the bar.

'You're very young, mind. How old are you, lad?'

Jack swallowed, crossed his fingers behind his back and decided to lie. 'Twenty-five.'

The man gave a dubious snort, then shrugged. 'And you're a bit skinny. Think you'll be strong enough to keep order if there's any trouble? I don't want the place getting a reputation for fights.'

'I can stand up for myself.'

'And there's kegs of ale to shift. That'll build your muscles.'

'I'm stronger than I look, sir.'

'Mrs Grainger tells me you're married, lad?'

'Yes, sir.'

'With a baby on the way?'

Jack nodded.

'Good. I like a family man. Last landlord had no children. Miserable bugger, with an even more miserable wife. Not conducive to drawing the drinkers in. People want a convivial atmosphere and a bit of chat. Does that sound like you?'

'Yes, sir. Being a teacher I am used to talking.'

'Aye, but don't be giving them lectures, will you? They come to the alehouse to let their hair down, have a laugh, tell a few stories and drink a few beers. Are you a drinking man, Mr Brennan?'

Jack felt the blood draining from his face. To tell the truth or to lie again? A teetotal landlord would hardly be well received, but he didn't want to give the impression he was a beer swiller when he'd never had a drop in his life.

'I like a drink when the occasion calls for it. But only

in moderation. I think that is important for a landlord – if the innkeeper is drinking as much as the customers he can't very well keep order, can he?'

'Good answer, laddie. You'll do. When can you start? Place has been shut since the other fellow died. You don't make money from a tavern with the doors locked. Wages now – four pound ten a week and if the takings improve we'll review it in a few months.'

Jack wanted to throw his hat in the air, but instead he nodded and said 'That sounds very acceptable, sir. I can start right away. I won't disappoint you.'

'Hold your horses, lad. We have to get you licensed first. There's a few formalities, but I know whose strings need pulling so we'll get you installed as quick as we can.'

Jack expected Mary Ellen to be relieved. Instead she flung herself on her back on the bed, hammering her heels and fists into the mattress.

'I won't live in a public house. I'm a lady. My Papa is rich. I won't do it. It's not fair. You're supposed to be a teacher. Why don't you teach? I won't live in a place like that. I won't.' Tears welled up in her eyes and she began to howl.

Jack sat down on the bed beside her and laid a hand on her arm. 'Calm down, Mary Ellen. There are no teaching jobs. It's either this or the iron foundries.'

With that she began to wail louder. 'I want to go home to Papa. I hate this place. I hate you. I hate everything.'

'Hush,' he said, feeling helpless and out of his depth as her body shook. She was becoming hysterical and he didn't know how to cope. 'Hush, Mary Ellen, it will be all right. We won't have to stay here in this small room and in this house with all the other people. We will have our own home with lots of rooms. You'll have your own drawing room. You won't have to come into the bar. It will be nice.'

She sat up and stopped wailing. 'Our very own house. Just for us? Just like Mama and Papa?'

'Yes. And soon you will have your baby.'

She looked away. She never referred to her pregnancy, other than to complain that she was fat. He suspected she wanted to pretend it wasn't happening – or possibly she didn't fully understand what was happening to her body.

'I want a pianoforte,' she said.

The Tudor Crown was just a few hundred yards from the iron foundries. Its proximity to the works meant there was a constant hammering and pounding from the rolling mill and a foul smell in the air. The terraced houses and the inn were all coated in a thick layer of black grime and dust.

There was one large public bar and a small snug that was rarely patronised. Mr Bellamy was there to welcome Jack, in order to hand over the keys and introduce him to the tap man and his sullen wife, who did the cleaning and cooking. He showed him the cellars, gave him the keys to the spirits cupboard and demonstrated how to change a barrel, then, with a slap on the back, a small advance on his salary to allow for the costs of the removal and a reminder that he was to give away no beer on tick, he left Jack in the hands of the tap man, a short man with a stoop and a perpetual frown, called Bob Mintoe.

The cleaner, Mrs Winnie Mintoe, a surly woman in grey, rarely spoke, except to tell people to get out of her way. She never smiled – occasionally her mouth stretched sideways into a horizontal line, which Jack at first assumed was a forced imitation of a smile, but there was no corresponding change in the expression of her eyes and he soon realised it was some kind of nervous twitch. Bob was not much more garrulous and it was clear why Bellamy had been unable to promote him into the role of landlord. But he knew the trade well enough.

Jack hired a pony and trap and went to collect Mary

Ellen and their luggage. She looked around in dismay as they left the respectable tree-lined avenues of large villas and entered the area of high density housing for foundry workers. Her expression was anxious and nervous, as though expecting armed brigands to leap upon them at every corner. Instead there were just filthy children playing in the streets and women hanging their washing out in the back entries.

'This is a slum. I won't live here.' She kicked her heels against the wooden boards of the cart and crossed her arms tightly across her chest. 'What do you take me for? I'm a lady. I can't live in a place like this.'

'We'll be living in a big house. It will be fine. Don't worry.' He gritted his teeth and tried to push away the thought that he'd like to slap her on the mouth.

As soon as they entered the pub the smell of stale beer hit him. He hadn't noticed it when Bellamy was showing him around. Maybe he only noticed it now because Mary Ellen was standing with her gloved hand clamped over her nose and her face a rictus mask of horror.

The rooms upstairs were larger than their room at Mrs Grainger's. There was a drawing room and to Mary Ellen's initial delight there was already a piano installed. She lifted the lid and thumped out an arpeggio then slammed the lid down. 'It's out of tune.'

'I'll get it fixed as soon as I get paid. Don't worry.'

Mary Ellen paced up and down, peering through the dirty windows at the street outside, running her finger along the top of the mantelpiece to reveal the dust. She scuffed her shoe at the threadbare carpet and rubbed her fingers over the grubby lace curtains, then flung herself into one of the armchairs and started to cry.

'I hate you, Jack Brennan. You should never have brought me to this horrid, horrid place. It's ugly and dirty and noisy.'

It was impossible to disagree about the dirt and

noise. With the constant hammering and banging from the foundries and the thick dust in the air, Jack couldn't remember what silence was like and what it was to breathe fresh air.

His first night behind the bar passed without mishap. He quickly learned the names and natures of the ales on tap and after a bit of practice at the pumps managed to pull a pretty decent pint. Trade was slow. Bob reminded him that the place had been closed for weeks, so it would take a few days for folk to realise it was open again. Those that did venture across the threshold seemed keen to check out the new landlord and were happy enough that Jack was prepared to pass the time of day with them. Word spread that the miserable old bugger at the Tudor Crown had been replaced with a young man who came from down south in Bristol and seemed all right. Each night the number of patrons crept up until, after a fortnight, the bar was packed out every Friday night as the iron workers raced to turn their wages into ale.

Mary Ellen never ventured into the bar during opening hours. She would come downstairs in the mornings to annoy Mrs Mintoe by walking across her newly washed floors, or putting her cup of tea down on a freshly polished tabletop. She never deigned to hold a conversation with the cleaner or her husband, who shared a small box room on the premises.

21
A Child is Born

Mary Ellen went into labour two months after they moved into the Tudor Crown. Her confinement began in the afternoon. Jack opened the tavern in the evening as usual, grateful to be occupied. He could hear the screams of his wife until the bar began to fill up. The birth was proving to be a difficult one, made worse by Mary Ellen's apparent refusal to follow any of the instructions given by the midwife.

Jack didn't want to think about what was happening upstairs. Leaning on the counter, he engaged the patrons in conversation and hoped that no one could hear Mary Ellen's yelling. It struck him as theatrical, exaggerated, unnecessary. He had twice heard his own mother giving birth: he and his brother secretly creeping up to the back door to listen after his father had banished them from the house to stay at their aunt's. His mother had cried out in pain, but it bore no comparison to the cacophony of blood curdling screams that Mary Ellen was producing. Perhaps he was being unkind and unfair to Mary Ellen. She had seemed so unaware of what her pregnancy meant and the pain must have taken her by surprise. It was also her first birth whereas his mother had already produced nine babies by the time he witnessed the birth of the two youngest.

The screams got louder and people started to notice. Jack called out to a small boy who had arrived to collect a pitcher of ale to carry home for his father, and told him he'd give him a penny if he'd run round to the house of the pub pianist. Paying for an extra shift was worth it to keep the tavern crowded and drown out Mary Ellen's screams. Music was not normally a feature of week nights and within half an hour the place was packed, as everyone gathered around the piano, joining in the singing. Jack reflected that whatever else happened, the takings would be good for a week night, even after he'd allowed a shilling for the pianist.

Since taking over the public house, Jack had started to drink the odd beer. He confined himself to just a pint a night, mindful of what he'd said to Mr Bellamy about getting the balance right between encouraging the drinking and being sober enough to restore order if necessary. At first he hadn't liked the bitter taste of the beer and made a pint last several hours, sweetening the sour taste in his mouth by sucking barley sugars. But it was not long until he grew accustomed to the flavour and began to enjoy it, relishing the way it quenched his thirst, liking the bitterness of the hops and the smell of the malt and barley as he swigged it down. He also liked the way that by the end of an evening's drinking, he stopped thinking or caring about what had happened to him. The pain of the loss of Eliza and his dreams of being a teacher was numbed a little, if not wholly forgotten.

It was approaching ten that night when the harassed midwife came downstairs and stuck her head into the bar. She signalled to him, frantically.

'It's not going well, Mr Brennan. The baby's stuck. I've tried to turn it around but I've not managed it. I need some help. You must go for the doctor. And quick. Mrs Brennan's not in a good way, poor lamb.'

Jack stared at her blankly, not fully comprehending her words.

She snatched at his arm and shook him. 'Did you hear me, Mr Brennan? You must fetch the doctor. Immediately!'

When he still didn't move, she shook her head. 'Men – you're all clueless.' Her eyes scanned the bar and she called out to one of the drinkers, 'Ollie Watson, run and tell Doctor Finch to get himself here as fast as he can manage. Tell him I need help with a delivery.'

The woman looked around the room at the crowd of men still singing their heads off around the piano, then she shook her head again and disappeared back upstairs.

A couple of men at the bar had heard the exchange.

'Your missus squeezing one out, Jack?' one of them said, nudging the other.

'First one isn't it, lad?'

Jack nodded.

'We'll need to wet the baby's head when it's here,' the first man said.

'Aye,' said his companion, 'But you look like you've seen a ghost, Jack, me lad. What you need is a nice big whisky. That'll calm your nerves quick enough. Difficult business having a bairn. I felt like I'd gone through every minute of it with the missus, with our first ween. She did that much bloody screaming. Put me off me beer it did.'

'That's right. Pour yourself a large whisky, man.'

Jack was still trying to take in the import of the midwife's words. His mind was racing. The look on the woman's face and the panic in her eyes had made him realise that Mary Ellen was in danger. He knew little enough of childbirth but enough to know it could be a dangerous business. A woman two doors down from them in Derby had died trying to be delivered of a pair of twins. They'd died with her, strangled by their umbilical cords. For a moment he contemplated the possibility. He reached behind him and found the bottle of whisky and with unsteady hand poured a large measure. He'd never touched spirits before, but he had to calm his nerves and steady his brain, which was already running away with the possibility that Mary Ellen might die and he might at last be freed from marriage and his responsibilities. Free to run away to America and try to find Eliza. For a moment he felt guilty for even thinking it, then the guilt was washed away as he drank.

The first slug of the scotch burnt his throat. He felt the hot fire searing its way down into his stomach, sending warm waves through his body. The taste was harsh, biting, alien, but the after effect was like being wrapped in a warm blanket that sent heat to every extremity and a calming balm to his fevered brain. He took another gulp, then swirled the amber liquid around the glass, holding it up so the candlelight illuminated the clear spirit: bright, pure, like topaz. He drank down the rest of the measure and reached for the bottle again.

'Steady on, Jack, lad,' said one of the drinkers.

'Leave him be. He needs a drop of the hard stuff. No easy business becoming a father for the first time.'

He'd never tasted anything like it. Cold yet hot, bitter, yet like balm. Calming. Enveloping. Wrapping him up and easing his pain. Helping him forget the woman upstairs. Helping him forget what a mess he'd made of his life so far.

It was six in the morning when Jack came to. Bob Mintoe was shaking him. His head was being smashed by a dozen hammers and his mouth felt as though a squirrel had taken up residence and died there. A shaft of sunlight came through the window and shone in his eyes. He was lying on the floor behind the bar. He struggled to remember the events of the previous night. The doctor's arrival. The continued screaming and then quiet. The eventual return of the doctor, who had laid a hand on his shoulder and told him his wife was delivered of a healthy daughter. He had a vague memory of standing drinks for the whole bar and finishing the rest of the whisky bottle himself in a fruitless quest to bring on permanent oblivion, to wipe out the life sentence that he had just received after the hope of liberation that had been dangled in front of his eyes.

As he struggled to his feet, the nausea hit him and he threw up the contents of his stomach into the bucket that Mrs Mintoe had taken out ready to fill after she had swept the floor. As the vomiting gave way to dry retching and bile, he could hear her consternation – her angry threats to leave were directed at her husband.

When he was done, he dragged his hand across the back of his mouth and went outside into the yard at the rear of the tavern, carrying the bucket. He sluiced it clean under the pump, refilled it with water, then bent over and poured the cold bucketful over his head. There was no way out now. He must go up those narrow wooden stairs to the bedroom and see Mary Ellen and the baby. The brief exhilaration he had felt that she might die was replaced by a mixture of disappointment and guilt that he had even entertained such terrible thoughts. He knew they were too terrible to share in the confessional.

It was a long, thin baby with a head that looked disproportionately large to the rest of her body. She was lying, asleep, in a wooden cradle beside the bed, where his wife was propped up against a pile of pillows, sipping a cup of tea. The midwife, who had returned to check up on mother and baby, turned to Jack. 'Can I see you outside, Mr Brennan?' Her voice was a hiss.

He nodded and stepped out of the room, feeling the floor rising up to meet him as his head continued to throb.

She followed him onto the landing. 'So you're back on your feet again? Shame on you, Mr Brennan. Passed out cold before you'd even clapped eyes on your baby and thanked your poor wife for going through torment to have her. Shame on you, indeed. You've no idea what that poor woman suffered and her having to do it with a pub full of men bellowing away like it was the greatest party on earth. She had such a hard time and so much pain. She could barely hear what the doctor and I were saying to her, poor lamb.'

Jack just wanted to see the back of the woman. All he wanted now was to lie down himself and sleep again. Sleep forever and never wake up. He said nothing but just hung his head.

'You men are all the same. A bunch of drunken wretches. That woman is worth ten of you.' She shook her head and went down the stairs and he could hear her tutting until the door slammed behind her.

He went into the bedroom and flung himself face down on the bed beside Mary Ellen.

'Aren't you going to look at the baby?'

'No. I'm going to sleep and I'd be obliged if you'd stop talking. The midwife says you need to rest anyway.'

'I'm going christen her Marian. I don't want any arguments about it. It's what my Mama was called.'

'Call her what you like. I don't care. She's not my child.'

Mary Ellen seemed not to hear him and prattled on. 'I'm glad it's a girl. We can play with dollies together when she grows a bit. It will be such fun.'

Something had died inside Jack the night before. He put his hands over his ears and fell into a deep sleep.

22
Motherhood

Since the change in the licensing laws a few years earlier, the risk to landlords of having their patrons drunk in public was heightened and should a landlord himself be found in a state of intoxication it was a certainty that he would lose his licence. The Temperance movement was gaining ground all the time in Middlesbrough and looking for any excuse to shut down a public house or strip a landlord of his licence.

After his drunken collapse during the birth of Marian, Jack stayed off the bottle. He was ashamed of what the drink had done to him. He hated the loss of control and was mortified that he had been reduced so low, bent over a bucket puking his guts up. The pounding head, nausea and exhaustion had lasted long enough to convince him that the after-effects of alcohol were not something he wanted to experience again. He shuddered at the thought of Eliza seeing him like that. Lately he had taken to using her as an extension to his conscience.

He reverted to making one tankard of beer last him all evening and when anyone offered to stand him a drink, he slipped the money in a glass behind the bar. Every night, when he cashed up, he would take the few coppers and add them to the growing stash that he kept in the little marquetry box Eliza had given him. He traced the image of the Clifton Suspension Bridge with his finger and told himself that it would mount up and one day be his means of escape from Middlesbrough to find and reclaim his love.

He thought of Eliza all the time. He had sanctified her memory, raised her onto a pedestal like the Virgin Mary in the priest's parlour. She was pure, unsullied, virginal, good – the way he liked to think he had been before Mary Ellen destroyed his soul. And yet at night his obsession for Eliza was also physical. He lay in his bed tormented with longing, imagining her body beside his, thinking thoughts about what they would do, and then feeling ashamed that he was despoiling her memory. He kept away from Mary Ellen, using the presence of Marian as an excuse to sleep in another bedroom. There he sated his hunger for sexual gratification on his own, knowing that in doing so he was committing another sin. When he was thirteen his father had sent him to talk to the priest about such matters. The kindly old fellow had winked at him and said, 'If you should wake up with an erection, Jackie lad, just say one Our Father and three Hail Marys and it will go away.' Jack had found that advice to be erroneous.

He turned to poetry again. He had not had the stomach to write anything after he had been separated from Eliza but now he devoted himself to pouring out his feelings for her in verse. He remembered every tryst they had enjoyed and captured each one in a poem. The critic in him knew they were overly sentimental, but turning those feelings into words on paper gave him comfort. He would sit at a table in the corner of the bar when the pub was closed, scribbling away undisturbed – Mary Ellen avoided the public rooms, complaining of the stink of stale beer. When the weather was fine he would sometimes walk, leaving the town and heading for the hills, strolling through Albert Park or wandering along the shore away from the grinding and smoke of the iron works. He would find a sheltered grassy spot and sit, smoking and filling notebooks with his poetry, scratching out lines and rewriting in a constant pursuit of perfection, trying to pin the memories of Eliza onto the page.

Sometimes I fear, how slender is the thread
That holds me anchored here upon the ground
And now my love that you will ne'er be found
I long to cut it and the marriage bed.

I feel you near, that with outstretched hand
I might reach out to catch you ere you fall,
Press you to me, needing no words at all
Then have you join me in this empty land.

Mary Ellen did not take well to motherhood. Her hopes that the baby would be a living doll for her to play with evaporated as soon as she realised she was expected to feed, wash, change and comfort the child. Marian cried incessantly and suffered from colic but was resilient and robust and thrived despite her mother's neglect. The parish was supportive and there were always other mothers and parish do-gooders on hand to help Mary Ellen, stepping in and taking over when she forgot something or couldn't be bothered.

Mrs Mintoe threatened to withdraw her services as a cleaner when she realised Mary Ellen expected her to empty the bucket full of soaking nappies that she kept in the corner of the bedroom.

The cleaner confronted Jack in the public bar, before opening time. 'I'm not cleaning up after a baby. I'm employed to keep the tavern clean and do some light cleaning upstairs. I didn't mind helping out while missus was still abed but I'm a cleaner, not a skivvie or a nursemaid.

I don't do washing and I'll not empty that stinking bucket of baby rags in the bedroom. You can tell her upstairs that from me. She left the lid off the pail again yesterday and the pong carried all the way down here. Not right, it isn't. And in this hot weather. Not healthy. It'll bring a miasma. My Bob and I have to live here too and I don't want to catch some horrible disease from breathing in bad air from a baby's business.'

Jack was annoyed and impatient, but couldn't risk losing the services of the cleaner, especially as it would mean the departure of the tapman too. He tried to be conciliatory. 'Mrs Brennan is taking a while to adjust to having a child. I'm sure –'

The woman interrupted him before he could finish. 'Taking time to adjust? I'll be kicking up the daisies before she adjusts. You need to hire some help. A nursemaid. Someone to care for the baby because she certainly isn't going to.'

'I'll think about it, Mrs Mintoe.'

'You'll do more than think. Otherwise my Bob and I will be seeking alternative employment. Then see how you'll get on!'

Jack bowed to the pressure and hired Sally, a cheerful sixteen-year-old, who seemed delighted to take on the care of one small baby instead of her eight siblings in exchange for two shillings a week.

The entry of Sally into the household eased things. As soon as she arrived and was confronted with the urine-drenched sheets in Marian's cot and the overflowing bucket of unwashed nappies, she assumed control.

'Let's get this cot stripped and the sheets washed. Me Mam lays our babbies on straw. Much easier. We can just throw the mucky straw out and no washing.'

The girl was even sanguine about the red-raw nappy rash that covered the baby's nether regions. 'A nice dollop of lard'll sort that out in no time, Mrs Brennan.'

Sally took over the care of the baby completely. Mary Ellen would ask for the child to be brought to her in the early evening and dandled her on her lap for a few minutes before bedtime, but otherwise delegated all aspects of her care to the girl. She took little interest in anything other than playing the pianoforte, which she did without any flair, going to Mass, which she did most days of the week, and reading penny dreadfuls, which she devoured, even though they often gave her nightmares.

One night, when the child was about six months old, Jack lay in bed worrying. It had been quiet lately and the pub's takings were low. The Temperance people had been out campaigning. Several days had passed since he'd had any money to add to the marquetry box. He needed to do something to drum up custom.

The door creaked open, then closed again quickly and he made out his wife's shape in the darkness of the room.

'Go back to bed, Mary Ellen, the baby might wake up. She'll be needing you.'

'She won't wake. I put a few drops of Mrs Winslow's Syrup on her tongue. She'll sleep through till morning.'

Jack drew himself up the bed and clutched at the covers, drawing them around him protectively. Mary Ellen had not been near him since the child was born.

She reached down and jerked the bedding back. Before he could react, she cupped a hand around his balls. 'Move over. Make room.' She began stroking him.

'Stop that will you?' His voice was faint, half choked, his mind trying to exercise control over his body. 'Go back to bed, woman.'

'I want to sleep with you. You're my husband. It's your duty. You're supposed to sleep with me. And anyway, you know you want to, Jack.'

He was hard now. He groaned then let his body take over, moving on top of her, thrusting into her, pumping into her, full of anger. Her face under his was distorted and her breath came out in little gasps that turned into grunts. He thrust harder, trying to hurt her, inflict pain on her for wanting him, for making him want to do this, but instead she became more excited. She tangled her hands in his hair, pulling his head down, pressing her mouth onto his, but he moved his head to one side. Not that. Never that. He pushed his face into the pillow beside her as his hips continued to jerk up and down on her, trying to punish her, damage her, wanting to kill her.

When he was spent she started to laugh. 'We needed that, didn't we? It's been a long time, Jack. I'll move your things back into the other bedroom in the morning.'

'No.' His voice was laced with panic. 'Not with the baby. Best leave things be.'

'I've asked Sally to move in. She and the baby can sleep in here. Marian's sleeping better now I'm dosing her. She'll do fine.'

'No. It's not right to keep pouring medicine down her. A little thing like that. She's too small to be dosed up every night. It's wrong.'

She gave him a puzzled look. 'What are you talking about?'

'I mean Marian needs you. Just like you needed your mother. She wants you. You're the most important thing in her world. Every baby needs its mother.' He saw the doubt in her eyes so he added, 'You mustn't keep pushing her away. She loves you already. Anyone can see that. She wants to be with you.'

Mary Ellen frowned then smiled. 'Maybe you're right. When Mrs Avery next door was holding her this morning she cried for ages and only stopped when I took her.'

'See what I mean. You're the only person that matters

in her world. She loves you and she needs you. You're her mother.'

'She needs you too. You're her father.'

He turned away from her. 'I'm not her father. You know that. Her father was a stranger who had you up against a wall.' The words were out before he could contain them.

She started to sob. 'You're her father. You're her father, Jack. You have to be. You're married to me so that makes you her father. I don't know what you mean by talking about a stranger. There was never a stranger. You're a mean nasty man, Jack.' Her sobs turned into whining. 'It's not fair. Why are you always so horrid to me? I try to be a good wife but you just ignore me. Is it because I'm not clever enough? Is it because you still think about that teacher? It's all your fault. I didn't want to come to this horrible smoky town with all these dirty, common people. I never asked to live in a public house. I'm a lady and it's not fair that you don't treat me like one.'

She lay back on the pillow beside him and stared up at the ceiling. 'You're just the same as Father O'Driscoll aren't you? You think I'm a slut.'

Jack sat up. 'He called you a slut?'

She started to cry again and he reached to where his trousers hung over a chair and fished a handkerchief out of the pocket and handed it to her.

Sniffing loudly she went on. 'Yes, he did, but it's not true. You know it's not true. When he said it first I didn't know what it meant, so I asked Nellie and she told me a slut is a bad woman who gives her body away to anyone. But I didn't, Jack. I didn't give my body to anyone. Only to Father O'Driscoll. And since we got married, to you.'

She told him everything. How the priest had first touched her a few years earlier when her mother was dying. He would visit the house during the day when her father was at work, to administer the sacrament to her mother. Afterwards he would come to Mary Ellen's bedroom where he would fondle her. In all her twenty-five years no young men had ever come courting and she had been flattered and pleased that this important man was spending time with her. She had been shocked by his reaction to what he did to her – the way his breathing quickened, the way he pushed her away after he had touched her as though she were on fire and muttered prayers under his breath. It had made her feel oddly powerful to be able to bring about such a change in this aloof man, who usually barely deigned to speak to her and acted as though she were invisible.

Jack, knowing the extent of his wife's sexual needs, was not surprised that her finding an outlet for them might have seemed like a release, a kind of freedom. What surprised and shocked him to the core was that it was the Irish priest who had been the man who had brought about this sexual awakening.

Bile rose in his throat and his stomach roiled. He staggered over to the chest of drawers and threw up in the china washing basin, over his shaving brush and flannel wash cloth.

Mary Ellen sat up in the bed and stared at him, uncomprehending. 'Are you ill, Jack? Did you eat something bad. What's wrong?'

The room was spinning. Indeed it felt that the earth was spinning out of control. He clutched his stomach and slumped into a chair. 'So he was the man in the alleyway with you that night. The man who was ramming you up against the wall like a prostitute?'

She nodded.

He wanted to be sick again but his stomach was empty and nothing came out. 'How long had it been going on? How often did you meet him in that alley?'

She looked affronted. 'Only that one time. He used to fiddle with me when Mama was sleeping, but he never put his thing inside me. He stopped coming to the house when she died except to see Papa and he ignored me. It made me sad.'

'So why were you in the alley with him that night?'

'One day Papa was out and Father O'Driscoll called at the house and asked me to go with him to the presbytery to collect some papers for Papa. While I was there he put his hand up there again. You know. Touched me. It always made me laugh when he did that because it tickled. I told him it was nice and asked why he didn't come to the house and do it to me any more. He said I was bad and would go to hell for being a slut. He told me leading a priest into temptation was a mortal sin, like Eve with the serpent. Making a priest commit a sin was worse than doing your own sins or getting an ordinary person to commit a sin. I started crying because I don't want to go to hell and he got angry and hit me round the head. I fell over and he got down on the floor on top of me and pushed his thing inside me. It hurt at first. Just to begin with. I cried but he put his hand over my mouth and told me to shut up so his housekeeper wouldn't hear.' She pushed her lips out into a pout.

'Go on. What happened next?'

'Nothing that day. He just told me to go home. He ignored me for weeks, but then later, the night you found me, I looked out of the bedroom window and saw him standing outside our house under the lamp post and I went down to meet him. We went to the church and prayed together. He told me I had to pray that God wouldn't send me to hell for being a slut. I was scared. It was dark so he said he'd walk me home. I asked him if I would really go to hell and he said if I said a full novena of the rosary every night and said nothing to anyone then God might forgive me. He told me as I'd led a priest into temptation it was up to me to give him relief – I'd put the lust in him and had to help him get rid of it. So he did it to me again leaning against the wall. Put his thing inside me. He told me I had made him sin and so I had to atone for *his* sins as well as my own. What we'd done was a secret and if I ever told anyone I would burn in hell.' She started to cry. 'I won't burn in hell for telling you, will I, Jack? You're my husband – I'm supposed to tell you everything.'

Jack held his head in his hands, scarcely able to comprehend what she was telling him.

After a while he looked up. 'Do you know how babies are made, Mary Ellen?'

'They grow inside you when you get married.'

'What we just did tonight and what you did with that priest, that's what makes babies. That night in the alleyway you and Father O'Driscoll made a baby. That's how Marian was conceived.'

'Conceived?' Her face was uncomprehending.

A wave of pity for her washed over him and he patiently explained to her the basic facts of procreation.

'So Marian isn't your baby at all? Not even a little bit?'

'Not even a little bit.'

'But Father O'Driscoll isn't my husband.' Her face was creased by a frown and her eyes filled with tears.

He reached over and took her hand. 'Priests can't get married. You know that, Mary Ellen. They are not supposed to do what he did to you. He is the one who is the sinner. Not you.'

'But he's a priest. Priests don't commit sins.'

'It seems they do. Well, that one did anyway. He is a disgrace to the priesthood and deserves to be punished.'

'Are you going to tell Papa?'

Jack looked up at her, at her startled eyes and bewildered face. There was no point. Thomas MacBride would never believe him. The two men were thick as thieves. O'Driscoll was protected by the dog collar around his neck, his ceremonial vestments and the whole weight of the church, which would never accept that a man of God was capable of performing such acts.

He wanted to kill O'Driscoll. To tear him limb from limb. To pound that smug face into a pulp. To shame him in front of his whole parish. The man who was the father of his wife's child. The man who had destroyed his life and condemned Eliza to a life in exile.

Jack swore he would never enter a church again.

23
Journey to St Louis

Eliza didn't write to say she was coming. She wanted to keep the possibility of changing her mind until the last possible minute.

She visited the shipping office one last time and left the address of Dr Feigenbaum's brother with the clerk, who shook his head but nonetheless pinned it to the noticeboard behind his desk. She said her farewells to Mrs McCarthy and, with a tug of sadness, to Connor. The little boy ran after her when she left the tenement and pressed a handful of wilting, wild flowers into her hand. 'I wish you weren't going away, Miss.'

'So do I, Connor.'

'Why do you have to go then?'

'I need to find a job.'

'You're not going to purgut'ry then?'

She smiled and ran her hand over his tousled head. 'No, Connor. I'm not going to purgatory. I'm going to a place called St Louis.'

'What's it like there?' he asked.

'I suppose it's like New York. Full of people.'

'If it's like New York why don't you just stay here?'

She struggled to answer that, then said, with a forced

but false optimism, 'There'll be a job for me there. I haven't been able to find one here.'

She waved him goodbye and took the ferry across the Hudson River to Jersey City to buy a one-way ticket to St Louis.

Jersey City was awash with hundreds of newly-arrived immigrants, who had come straight off the ships from Europe, negotiated the trials of Castle Garden and were now heading for the railroad station. Eliza looked around with a half-formed hope that she might see Jack among the hordes. Three months had elapsed since she'd arrived in New York and every day that passed made seeing him again less likely. She knew he was married to Mary Ellen and settled in Middlesbrough. She had written to her friends, the Wenlocks, and they had broken the news to her. Even though it was written down in black and white, she didn't want to believe it and she couldn't help praying every night for a miracle, for it all to prove a horrible mistake and for Jack to turn up one day to tell her they could at last be married.

People pushed and shoved each other, as though this might be the last train ever to leave the city. Eliza was swept along in the crowd, tired before the journey had even begun. Children were crying and people shouting and more than once she cried out in pain as someone crashed into her shins with a piece of luggage.

As she settled herself into the cramped and spartan railway car for the journey to Philadelphia, where she was to change trains, she wondered if she were making a terrible mistake. Dr Feigenbaum was a stranger. She was already beholden to him for the money he had lent her. St Louis was hundreds of miles away, taking her deep into the heart of the United States, away from the ocean and her route back to England and Jack. But what choice did she have? She could get no work as a teacher. Her missing teeth and malformed words ruled that out, not to mention the damage to her face that would likely be deemed to frighten the children. The only alternative had been to become a seamstress – ruled out when on her day's trial she proved to be too slow and ham-fisted. Otherwise the options were unthinkable – scavenging the streets with the rag and bone collectors or turning to prostitution.

The journey was almost as bad as the Atlantic crossing, redeemed only by the absence of the tossing ocean and its consequent impact on the stomachs of passengers. Instead of hammocks or straw mattresses, passengers were expected to provide their own bedding and washing kit and the only place to sleep was upright on the hard wooden benches. When the occupants of the car thinned out Eliza managed to push two benches together to form a makeshift bed. But sleeping on the hard wood planks, with the train rattling and jerking along, was impossible. The temperature was cold, as autumn was giving way to the beginnings of winter. The cold should have been lessened by the presence of a small stove in the centre of the railcar, essential for the brewing of tea and coffee by passengers but, while rendering the accommodation stuffy and smelling of smoke, it had little impact in heating the space.

Eliza was in a car reserved for women and children. A harassed Irish mother, with five children all under the age of eight, offered to let her share their washing bowl, soap and towel, in gratitude for assisting with the unruly children. Washing her face and hands was no easy task with a towel already damp from the children and while trying to keep her balance on the outside platform of the rail car. Apart from the few words she exchanged with the Irish woman, she spent most of the journey in grateful silence, looking out of the window as they sped along. The journey was complicated by the need to de-train whenever they reached a state border, where they were expected to drag their suitcases across the state line in order to embark on another train.

When she eventually arrived in St Louis, exhausted after three days and nights travelling, she ignored the street cars and hansoms outside the railway depot and asked for directions to the Dreschner German Brewery, making her way there on foot, stopping every now and then to change the hand carrying her carpet bag. It was about two miles from the station. She trudged along past newly built houses and churches, stopping to buy an apple when she passed a large, bustling market. She looked longingly at the baked patisserie, bread, and sweetmeats and drank in the aroma of melted sugar and the tang of cheeses, but she had only two dollars left and didn't want to contemplate what would happen if she failed to find Dr Feigenbaum. To her consternation, the area to which she had been directed was home to a large number of breweries and it took her some time before she came upon the right one – like all the others, a big redbrick building. She walked to the front entrance and asked for Mr Feigenbaum.

'He's busy,' was the curt response from the porter. 'You got an appointment?'

'No. I'm sorry. I've just got here on the train from New York.' She tried to speak as distinctly as possible, conscious as always of the lisping caused by her missing teeth and grateful that the veil Mrs McCarthy had attached to her hat was covering the scars and distorted contours of her face.

The man looked at her with curiosity. 'Mr Feigenbaum will be finished in an hour. Wait there.' He indicated a wooden bench, then added, more kindly, 'He's testing the day's batch. Be done by five. You a relative?'

She hesitated then decided to tell the truth. 'To be honest, I don't really know Mr Feigenbaum himself. I just want to ask him for the address of his brother, Dr Karl

Feigenbaum, who is an acquaintance of mine. We crossed from Liverpool on the same ship.'

'Why didn't you say that right away? Dr Karl lives opposite the German church. Back the way you've come – about half a mile. Here you are, Miss.' He scribbled the address and some rough directions on a scrap of paper and handed it to her, looking her up and down with interest.

Eliza took the paper, relieved that the doctor was at least here in St Louis.

'You Dr Feigenbaum's intended then?' the man asked, unable to restrain his curiosity.

'Certainly not,' she answered.

'No offence, ma'am. I can tell you're much younger than the doc, but you never know these days. My uncle married a girl fresh out of school. Can't have been more than sixteen and him pushing sixty. Mind you it probably helped that he had a thousand acres of fine cotton-growing land. He's dead now. She sold up and scooted off to Boston and we never heard from her again.'

Eliza stared at him, open-mouthed, in horror.

'Sorry, ma'am. I wasn't saying you're a fortune hunter. Me and my big mouth.'

'Good afternoon,' she said, frostily, 'And thank you for the address.'

It was an unprepossessing, square-shaped house, attached to its neighbour and with an arched, recessed porch. It was built with the red bricks that characterised most of the construction in the city. There was a small patch of overgrown grass and a large tree that must have made the rooms in the front very dark. Opposite was a church with a sign outside in German.

Eliza took a deep breath, then walked up the short flight of steps to the door and rang the bell. A small, plump woman answered. She had very red cheeks and grey hair, in braids wound around her head. The woman said nothing, but just looked at Eliza, her head tilted to one side.

'Good afternoon. I am looking for Doctor Karl Feigenbaum. My name is Eliza Hewlett.'

Before the woman could reply, the door swung wide open and there was the doctor. Almost elbowing his housekeeper out of the way, he took the bag from Eliza's hands and placed it behind him in the hall, leaving him free to grasp her hands in his.

'Come in, come in, Miss Hewlett. I am so happy to see you. Why didn't you telegraph to tell me you were coming? I would have come in the carriage to the station to meet you. Marta, bring tea. Miss Hewlett takes hers with milk in it. And bring some of those little *kuchen* you baked yesterday. Miss Hewlett, this is my housekeeper, Marta Bauer. Marta, I had the privilege of making Miss Hewlett's acquaintance on the voyage.'

He took Eliza by the arm and led her into the drawing room, directing her to one of the chairs in front of the fireplace. 'Please take off your coat and hat, my dear. Come in and get warm. It has suddenly turned cold today.'

She slipped the coat off her shoulders and let him take it, standing beside her with it draped over his arms as he waited for the housekeeper to return. Eliza hesitated a moment, then deciding she must get it over with, she sat down, lifted her veil and eased the hat off her head.

He flung her coat aside onto a chair and moved across to kneel beside her. She looked at him and saw his eyes were misted.

'My dearest lady, what has happened? Did you have an accident?' He took her hands in his, but she pulled them away and shrank herself deeper into the armchair.

'I was set upon by a stranger who stole my purse. There are parts of New York that are very dangerous and it happened soon after I arrived and before I understood which streets were safe and which not. I know you warned me so you have every right to say *I told you so.*'

'Your teeth? Your poor face? Are you in pain? My dear, this is a terrible thing to have befallen you.'

'The pain is gone now. I came here, doctor, to find out if you're still prepared to offer me employment as your secretary. I've tried to find a teaching position in New York but no one wants to employ a woman whose face is likely to frighten the children. I used the last of your money to pay for the train ticket, so I will work without remuneration except food and board, until I have repaid you every last cent.'

He waved his hands in dismissal. 'Never mind about that. We must get you to a dentist. We will purchase a new set of teeth for you. As beautiful as your own were.'

'No,' she said, 'I cannot accept more from you. When I've repaid you I will save up to buy some teeth and until then I will manage well enough without.'

He shook his head. 'We will talk of it later, but I warn you, I am going to insist. Apart from anything else it will help my poor old German ears to hear you better. If you are to work for me it is essential that we can understand each other perfectly. Is that not right, Marta?'

The housekeeper was standing beside the table, laying out cups and saucers. She nodded and carried on with her task.

Dr Feigenbaum proved to be a man who, once his mind was made up, would brook no argument. The next morning he took Eliza in his carriage across town to the premises of a dental surgeon, Edward Larkman, who, after taking wax impressions of her remaining teeth, promised to fashion her a dental bridge before the end of the week. He told her that he used only real teeth, and those of the finest quality. The walls of his surgery were hung with certificates demonstrating that he had qualified as a dental doctor at the Baltimore College of Dentistry and that he had served as a dental officer in the Confederate army during the civil war.

'I acquired an excellent collection of teeth from healthy but unfortunate young men who lost their lives in the war,' he told Eliza in his slow southern drawl.

She didn't want to know, but was powerless to stop him as he reminisced about his wartime experiences and the haul of teeth he had amassed at Harper's Ferry.

'No use to them when they're dead. Y'all a lucky lady, Miss Hewlett. Just two missing and both from the bottom incisors. No one will be able to tell the new teeth apart from your own. Y'all soon get used to wearing them. Made a set for my wife last year and she says she don't even notice she's wearing them. I can see you brush your teeth regularly. Be surprised how few people do. The Union army didn't even issue toothbrushes to their men. I may have fought on the losing side as an American citizen but I was on the winning side as a dentist.'

Eliza was relieved when she was able to leave, but uncomfortable about the prospect of having a dead man's teeth in her mouth and horrified at the cost of the treatment.

When they were outside and in the carriage, she began to cry.

'What is the trouble, my dear?'

'I don't know how long it will take me to repay you, Doctor. I am never going to be out of your debt.'

'I have told you, I do not expect any repayment. It is my pleasure.'

'No' she said. 'I can't accept that. I intend to repay it all.'

The dental bridge, when it was fitted a few days later, was comfortable enough and she overcame her scruples about having a dead boy's teeth in her mouth and began to appreciate the restoration of normal speech.

The dentist called her back as she was leaving the surgery.

'If you ever want to get that face looked at, Ma'am,

they're doing fine things at the hospital here in St Louis. The surgeons here had plenty to practice on with fellows back from the war. I reckon one of those doctors might be able to make some improvements to the appearance of your face, with surgery. Seems a shame for such a fine-looking woman as you.'

Eliza shuddered at the thought of anyone operating on her face. She'd rather look the way she did. Why would she care anyway? Not now Jack wasn't around to see her.

'Or you might want to see Mr Pozzoni. He's a hair-dresser over on 6th Street, at the new Lindell Hotel. He has a bit of a sideline in face powders. Reckon he might be able to rustle one up for you that would help disguise that scar. And just to show what high quality products he makes I'm going to present you now with a free sample of his vegetable tooth powder, to keep those new teeth looking beautiful.'

Once Eliza got to grips with the hieroglyphics and frequent inkblots that characterised Dr Feigenbaum's handwriting, she found that working for him was not arduous. In the mornings, while her employer took his daily constitutional in the nearby Lafayette Park, she ploughed her way through the backlog of his notes, transcribing them. They were in a mixture of German, French and English and consisted of a mixture of lengthy essays and short scribbled scraps. The pages were out of sequence – Dr Feigenbaum had been in the habit of sweeping them off his desk onto the floor in fits of impatience when he was trying to find a particular reference. He seemed oblivious to the fact that this was creating the very problem he was trying to solve. Eliza had no knowledge of either French or German, so she transcribed as best she could, with the help of the dictionaries in his study. The doctor's intent was for the work itself to be written in English. In the afternoons, while he turned her transcribed notes into prose and chapters, she set up a system using index cards to keep track of topics, sources and themes for the eventual compilation of the book's index and bibliography. She found she enjoyed the work and began to recognise frequently recurring words in French and German, writing a list of them each day which she memorised before going to sleep at night, after saying her prayers.

The content of Dr Feigenbaum's book was a mixture of dull and arcane chemistry and only slightly less dreary explanations of brewing processes, mixed in with history and geography lessons on the development and spread of the brewing industry across Europe. Eliza found it strange that a medical doctor should make this his life's work, and wondered why he hadn't followed his father and brother into the brewing business. One day she plucked up the courage to ask him.

He looked up from his newspaper and smiled, evidently pleased that she had asked him a question of a personal nature.

'My maternal grandfather was a medical practitioner and it was Mama's wish that one of her sons pursue that profession. Papa was insistent that one of us join the family business and I was, I admit, a better student than Alphonsus, so it was decided that I would train to be a doctor and he a brewer. Growing up with the scent of fermenting hops in the air, it was hard to resist the desire to go into brewing myself but I was always the dutiful son.'

He gave a wry smile, as though ashamed of his own compliance to filial duty. 'As a child I haunted the brewery, trailing after Papa as he tested the batches, riding out on the drays when the deliveries were made. I confess I have never felt the same excitement for general medical practice.'

Eliza smiled to herself. It was hard to imagine Dr Feigenbaum getting excited about anything. Almost as hard as it was to imagine him a small boy.

The doctor worked on in silence and Eliza began to relax more in his company, both of them quietly getting on with their work, accompanied only by the ticking of the clock, the scratch of their pens and the crackling of the fire in the grate.

They fell into a steady routine. Every Wednesday afternoon and at weekends, Eliza was free to do as she wished. The doctor insisted that she took the time off and she was grateful to escape from the house and his presence. Mealtimes were awkward, with long silences. Eliza was unwilling to attempt to fill them herself so they sat at opposite ends of the table, staring down at their plates, as though the food that Frau Bauer served was a source of endless fascination.

The evenings were a trial, as her host expected her to join him in the parlour after supper. She would have preferred to spend the time with Marta Bauer in the kitchen, but the housekeeper, while courteous enough to Eliza, made it clear that she did not want to develop a friendship. This felt peculiar to Eliza as her own background was closer to the housekeeper's than to the doctor's. They were both employees and she was embarrassed that the doctor treated her in a different way from the older woman.

Every evening Dr Feigenbaum would read the St Louis newspaper and a local weekly magazine for the dominant German population of the city; Eliza sat by the fireside, occasionally sewing, regardless of her inadequacy at the task, determined to appear occupied; sometimes she would read – the only available reading matter being slim volumes of translated German poetry, a copy of Darwin's *On The Origin of The Species* and a number of dictionaries. There was not even a bible in the house. In a city with a population heavily biased to German Catholics, Dr Feigenbaum informed her that he was an atheist, despite being born and raised as a Roman Catholic. Eliza was shocked but slightly thrilled by the idea and by the frank and unashamed way he told her.

One evening Dr Feigenbaum laid aside his newspaper and asked Eliza to read aloud to him. He handed her the poems of Josepf Von Eichendorff, translated into English.

She looked up in surprise. 'This is an English translation.'

'I know and love the poems well and would like you to experience them too. It would give me great pleasure to hear you read.' He leaned forward, smiling encouragement.

She started to read, hesitantly at first, then moved by the lyricism of the poems, the gentleness, the quiet of them. They made her think of England, with their references to nature, to birds, to falling leaves, to the calm and quiet of evening. Feigenbaum listened, eyes closed, an expression of enchantment on his face.

She was reading a sad poem about autumn, enunciating the words carefully, trying to do justice to them, conscious that they probably fell short of the German original for him. Then her voice broke as she said the words *"whoever loves me is far away"*. She closed the book.

'I'm sorry. My voice is tired. I think I will retire now, Doctor. Good night.'

He half rose from his chair, his face etched with sadness. She could feel his eyes following her as she left the room. She cursed her own stupidity.

On Sunday mornings she crossed the street with Frau Bauer to attend Mass at the German church. The language made little difference during the Mass itself as it was in Latin, but it meant that the sermon went entirely over her head. Once a fortnight she walked a couple of miles to the Irish church to make her confession to a priest who could understand her, but otherwise she enjoyed the anonymity of attending a church where everyone else spoke another language. England and Jack felt very far away.

One morning as she was leaving after the service, a

young woman tapped her on the arm.

'You're staying with Dr Feigenbaum, aren't you?' The woman was about the same age as Eliza, smartly dressed and wearing a fashionable hat. She smiled and stretched out a hand. 'I'm Helga Strauss.'

'Pleased to meet you.' Eliza hoped that her new dentures were not as obvious to the woman as they were to herself. Sometimes she felt as though if she spoke too quickly they might fall out. She was still wearing a veil to cover her face.

'You're English?'

'Yes, from Bristol. I arrived in America about five months ago.'

'What brought you here to St Louis? Did you already know Dr Feigenbaum? Is he your guardian? Only most people who come to St Louis are German, although there's quite a lot of Irish people too. And Poles, now I think about it. Oh no. There I go again. Asking too many questions and giving you no time to answer them. You must think me very rude.'

'Not at all. And no, I did not know the doctor. We made our acquaintance on the voyage out.'

There was an immediate raising of the eyebrows and a little giggle from the woman. Eliza regretted her own lack of equivocation. She cursed herself for not going along with the guardianship story. Now half of the parish would be making assumptions about the propriety or lack of it in her relationship with the doctor.

Helga Strauss didn't dwell on it, but breezed on. 'You must be very brave. Coming here on your own. I was born in St Louis, but my folks still speak German at home. They told me how absolutely terrifying it was deciding to emigrate here - and they had each other. How on earth did you cope all alone? My folks are terribly old fashioned. They're over there.' She pointed at a crowd of people standing chatting. 'Papa works in the Lemp brewery. He's an accountant.

I'm a teacher in the elementary school on Western Street.'

'I used to be a teacher too.' As Eliza said the words she regretted them. Better to let the past lie. Stop resurrecting things that can never be the same again. She wanted to kick herself. Helga would want to know why she'd stopped teaching and she didn't want to tell her about the attack. 'Now I am employed by the doctor as his secretary. He is compiling a book on the history of the brewing industry.'

'I suppose Dr Feigenbaum pays you lots more money than you could earn as a teacher. I'd love to have a higher paid job. But then I will be stopping teaching soon.' She slipped off a glove and held out her hand for Eliza to inspect her engagement ring. 'I will be married in the spring. That's him over there.' She nudged Eliza and nodded her head in the direction of a bespectacled young man with pock-marked skin and a tangle of dark hair. He must have been a good three inches shorter than his intended bride.

'Not much to look at, I know. But Peter's a good man and he's recently been made a senior salesman for the Anheuser-Busch brewery. After we're married we may have to move to another city if he gets promoted again. It seems like all of America is crazy for lager beer from St Louis.'

Frau Bauer appeared at Eliza's side and gave her a silent signal that she was heading home.

Eliza seized the opportunity for escape. 'It was nice to meet you, Miss Strauss. Good morning.'

The woman clutched at her arm. 'Do call me Helga. You must come for tea. Next week. Sunday afternoon. About four. Mama always bakes on a Saturday. She makes a delicious *sachertorte*!' She slipped a visiting card into Eliza's hand. 'See you next Sunday, Eliza.' Then she was gone.

Frau Bauer gave an almost imperceptible roll of her eyes and the two of them crossed the road back to the house.

24
Letter from America

November 1878
St Louis, Missouri

My darlingest boy, my love, my Jack,
I ask myself why I am writing this when I will never send
it and you will never read it. I wrote many times before – care
of the school and the MacBrides, but when you did not reply I
wrote to the Wenlocks and they told me you had married Miss
MacBride. Oh my darling, how did they make you do that?
Why did you not run away and come to find me? I'm sorry that
is not a fair question. I know you would never have agreed to
the marriage if you had been left with any choice.

As I write this I have decided to imagine that somehow you
will know what I have written. That you can read my mind.
That my words will reach you. I know it is foolish, but I cannot
help myself. If I do not try to talk to you I shall go mad.

So much time has now passed since that terrible day when
you were dragged from my arms and taken away to your fate.?
I had prayed that you would have convinced Mr MacBride and
Father O'Driscoll that Mary Ellen has been telling lies and that
one day you would join me here. Now I know you are in in the

north of England and I will never see you again. I do not think I am strong enough to bear that.

I am living in a place called St Louis. It is on the banks of the Mississippi River. The city is a fine one and growing rapidly. There is a big iron bridge here that crosses the Mississippi and opened just two years ago. It makes me think of Mr Brunel's iron bridge in Bristol and of course that means thinking of you (but, dearest Jack, I think of you all the time anyway – I do not need a bridge to remind me).

My employment here is as the assistant to a German doctor. I transcribe his notes on the history and development of the brewing industry – it is his life's work and you can imagine it is very dull indeed. Doctor Feigenbaum (who is German but speaks excellent English) has been very kind.

My love, there is something else that I must tell you. I am no longer the girl you knew in Bristol. Something happened to me before I left New York – indeed it was the reason I left New York as it prevented me from getting employment as a teacher. My face was disfigured in an accident and I am afraid that were you to look upon me now you would not love me any more. But then I tell myself that no matter what happened to you I would still love you just the same and so perhaps, my love, you would be able to look beyond my face to the person inside, the girl who still loves you with all her heart and soul.

I can only say these things knowing you will never read them.

I wrote twice to Sister Callista. She was always a good and kind woman and I prayed that she might be able to send some news of you but there was no reply from her either. I hope and pray she has not been punished for trying to help us.

My beloved, you are always in my thoughts, from the moment I waken until I close my eyes at night. And of course you are always in my prayers. Will we ever be together again? I pray every day that you will find a way to get in touch with me - that God or the Blessed Virgin Mary will send me a sign so I will know you still care for me and think of me.

Now that I have written this and cannot send it to you I have decided to sew it inside a quilt I am making. I have always disliked sewing but concealing my letters to you will make me look more kindly upon it as a pastime and when I sleep beneath it I will feel closer to you, my beloved.

With fondest love,
Your own darling girl,
Eliza Hewlett

25
Tea with Helga Strauss

Helga was clumsy. She managed to pour almost as much tea into the saucers as the cups. She wasn't at all apologetic and kept up a constant flow of chatter. Eliza was the only guest, but the other members of the Strauss family had gathered in the hallway to greet her when she arrived and look her over with ill-concealed curiosity.

Eliza had felt obliged to accept Helga's invitation, but had approached the house with a sinking heart: she was conscious of her face and dreading being asked to remove her veil and having to explain her injuries.

Once they were alone in the drawing room, Helga's monologue ranged from listing the names, ages and occupations of each member of her family to her favourite books and songs and descriptions of every concert she had attended in the past year. In between these autobiographical exposés, she subjected Eliza to a barrage of questions about her own tastes, but barely listened to her responses.

'Do you like music, Miss Hewlett?'

'I do, but I have had little education in it.'

'I play the pianoforte and the violin. And I do love to sing. Do you sing?' Then without waiting on Eliza's reply, 'My favourite song is *Take me Mother in thy Lap*' She jumped up. 'Shall we sing it now? I'll play and you can turn the pages.'

Eliza said, 'I don't read music and I don't know the song.'

Helga looked askance. 'How frightful for you, Miss Hewlett, but never mind – I'll tell you when to turn the page.'

She settled herself on the piano stool and began to sing and play. Eliza looked at the clock on the mantel and wondered when she would be able to leave without appearing rude.

After about half an hour, Helga closed the lid of the pianoforte and in a conspiratorial whisper said, 'Is there something the matter with your face? You always wear a veil and Mamma said that Frau Bauer told her you had been disfigured in a terrible accident in New York City. Will you show me? I promise I have a very strong constitution. I won't faint with shock, no matter how hideous you look.'

Eliza stiffened. Helga's choice of words offered no comfort. Letting her see her face felt like an invasion of privacy. Eliza didn't want this woman treating her like a curiosity, a member of a freak show. She didn't want to be seen as ugly. She didn't want be taken back to that day in New York. Was it vain to have such scruples? And she couldn't spend the rest of her life hiding behind a veil.

'Please.' Helga laid a hand on Eliza's arm.

Eliza lifted the veil over her face on to the top of her hat. 'There you are. Take a look.'

Helga's hands covered her mouth, her eyebrows shot up and her chin jutted forward. 'Oh goodness gracious. That's a mighty fine battering you've had, Miss Hewlett. No wonder you wear a veil. It must be very hard as I imagine you must once have been quite pretty. How horrible to be blighted by such an affliction. Did it happen in some kind of accident? I suppose now you will never be able to marry. Maybe some kind-hearted man will be willing. Looks are not everything. I should know, shouldn't I, as my Peter is not handsome, but he does make up for it in other ways. Especially in his prospects. Prospects are so important, aren't they, Miss Hewlett? A prosperous man is a handsome man, as my grandmama used to say. But it's not the same for a woman, is it? Our future prosperity is in our faces. Oh dear. You poor, poor thing. How ever do you bear it?'

Eliza tried to choke down her anger. Being the object of this woman's pity was too much. 'I bear it well enough as I don't think about it at all, unless or until someone draws attention to it, which I am happy to say, until this afternoon, nobody has.' She rose from the chair. 'Thank you for the tea, Miss Strauss. I wish you good day.'

She left the room as the voice of her hostess followed her. 'Well, really! There's no need to be so abrupt. I was, after all, being kind.'

Eliza went back to the doctor's house, still seething with anger, but glad she would need no excuses for avoiding Helga Strauss's company in future. Going straight to her room, she sat down in front of her dressing table and studied her face in the mirror. Maybe she'd got used to it, but it didn't seem so bad to her. She traced the scar with a finger and turned her head sideways, peering at her reflection. Yes, one eye was recessed more deeply than the other and her left cheek lacked the definition around the cheekbone which the right one showed, but each side looked normal enough in profile and it was only head-on that the imbalance was evident. The main problem was the scar. The skin was still raised and livid and ran from her eye down to the side of her mouth, making her look as though she had just emerged from a cat fight.

On her afternoon off that week, Eliza made her way on foot to Mr Joseph Pozzoni's hairdressing emporium next to the Lindell Hotel. Having explained her predicament to Mr Pozzoni, she was shown into a room at the rear of the salon.

'I am so glad you have come to me, Miss Hewlett. Many women are over cautious about the use of cosmetic powders and creams. There is a feeling that perhaps it's not appropriate for a woman of good background, but I can assure you all that is changing and I predict there will come a day when all respectable women will happily apply potions and creams to their faces and possibly even colour to their lips and cheeks. Now, let me look at you.'

He showed her to a chair and Eliza lifted her veil.

'Yes, yes. My product can work wonders for you. I have only recently gone into production with my medicated complexion powder, but already it is outselling my wigs and perfumery products. All the druggists in the city are selling JAP powder and I'm expanding distribution to other cities later this year. Now, I am going to apply it for you and show what a difference it will make to your lovely face.'

Eliza sat back as he applied vanishing cream into her skin and then, using a powder puff and a small sable brush, worked the powder onto her face to conceal the raised red scar. When he was done he stepped back and appraised his work and, with a sigh of satisfaction, spun her chair around to face the mirror.

'There, Miss Hewlett. What do you think? Quite a difference, eh?'

She gazed at her reflection and had to admit that he had worked wonders. As well as covering up the scar he'd used a tiny amount of coloured powder to create an impression of the lost contours of her cheekbones.

'I can't claim I work miracles, but I think it's as near to one as you'll ever get without surgery – and I wouldn't be recommending that for a beautiful young woman such as yourself. Far too dangerous and painful.'

Eliza leaned closer to the mirror, searching in vain for the red and white line that had so badly disfigured her face.

'Thank you, Mr Pozzoni. Thank you so very much.'

When she joined Doctor Feigenbaum at the table that evening he looked over his newspaper and remarked, 'My dear you look particularly lovely this evening.'

As she took her new protective mask off with cold cream that night she marvelled at how a little cream and powder could make such a difference, not only in her appearance but also in her spirits.

26
Christmas In St Louis

Dr Feigenbaum left the house early, unconcerned by the heavy snow that had begun to fall during the night – indeed it seemed his sortie was inspired by it. Over breakfast Eliza had tried to dissuade him from venturing outside, but he paid no attention.

'Just a light flurry, my dear. Nothing like the amount we used to get in Bavaria. I do love the snow. I am delighted that our first Christmas in St Louis will be a white one.' He rubbed his hands together and smiled at her, his eyes lit up like an excited child's. She tried not to think about his use of the words *our* and *first*.

Two hours later he returned, riding on a brewery dray cart pulled by a pair of Clydesdale horses. Eliza looked out of the window as they approached and saw him sitting beside the driver, his scarf blowing behind him like a Medieval pennant, the bottoms of his trouser legs sodden and his nose as red as a cherry. His beard was flecked with snow, giving him the appearance of Santa Claus. On the flatbed of the cart behind them was the most enormous fir tree Eliza had ever seen. The doctor and the drayman grappled it off the cart with some difficulty and dragged it into the parlour, leaving a trail of broken branches and pine needles in their wake.

Frau Bauer had evidently been forewarned, as she appeared from the kitchen bearing trays of gingerbread men and brightly painted salt dough stars, each one with silk thread inserted, ready to hang on the tree.

'Ah! You have baked the *lebkuchen*, Marta,' said the doctor.

'There's *stollen* too and the *glühwein* you asked for. Everything's ready,' the housekeeper replied.

'We shall have a proper German Christmas,' he said, 'especially for Eliza.'

The drayman left, rewarded with several pieces of *stollen*. As the three of them set about dressing the tree, Eliza thought about Jack. That Christmas they had spent together seemed a lifetime away. How happy she had been then, sharing gifts with Jack, walking together in the freezing cold then joining in the festivities at the Wenlocks. She remembered the look on his face when she was reading the part of Miranda – the tears that had brimmed in his eyes. What would he be doing now? Did he and Mary Ellen have a Christmas tree? Would they be standing in their own parlour, tying ribbons on it and lighting candles? Then it dawned on her that Mary Ellen must have had her baby by now. She paused, a stick of candy cane in her hand and gazed out of the window watching the snow falling, her eyes glazed with tears. She didn't want to think about Jack holding that baby in his arms, cradling it, looking into its eyes, maybe even loving it. Who could fail to love an innocent baby? Even one conceived with a stranger in an alleyway and borne by Mary Ellen.

'Are you all right, my dear?' said Dr Feigenbaum. 'You're looking pale. Why don't you sit down and rest for a few minutes? I've been working you too hard. You must be tired. Marta and I can finish this.'

She shook her head. 'I'm quite well, Doctor, thank you.'

She didn't want to sit down. She didn't want time to

think. Grabbing some candy canes from a box on the table, she set about hanging them on the tree, making herself work out the optimal spacing between each, varying the colours of the striped paper wrapping – anything to stop herself thinking about Jack and his new family back in England. And anything to stop herself thinking about the baby she longed to have herself one day and probably now never would. Her hand moved over the sunken contours of her face – no one would want her now. No one except the doctor and she could never contemplate marrying him.

When they were done, Dr Feigenbaum crossed to the sideboard and poured three glasses of the warm *glühwein*. The housekeeper looked shocked when he handed her a glass.

'I couldn't possibly, Herr Doctor. It wouldn't be right.'

'It's Christmas, Marta. I think we can make an exception.'

He smiled at Eliza and raised his glass and she realised that he had only included Marta to legitimise the situation and prevent any awkwardness between them.

'To Christmas!' he said, adding, 'And to friendship.' He moved around the tree closer to Eliza. 'And to the future, here in America. In Saint Louis.'

She looked at him in alarm. She didn't want to drink a toast to remaining here. She wanted to sail back across the Atlantic. Back to Jack. Back to the life they were supposed to have together. Her eyes welled up, her throat closed and she struggled to swallow.

'Drink!' he said, fixing his eyes upon her, his tone pleading. 'Drink and be happy!'

On Christmas Eve Alphonsus Feigenbaum, the doctor's older brother, with his wife and two sulky children, descended on the house for the festive meal.

It was Eliza's first meeting with Alphonsus. The

thin-faced and frowning man was quite unlike his avuncular brother. There appeared to be little love lost between him and his wife and children. Frau Feigenbaum spoke no English and barely spoke at all, other than snapping occasional irritated instructions to her children in German. The children, a boy and a girl, adolescents of indeterminate ages, sat in bored silence as though the evening was a trial to be endured.

After dinner, the party retired to the parlour. Herr Feigenbaum took Eliza aside.

'My brother is impressed with the work you have done on his book, Miss Hewlett. I understand you are even teaching yourself German?' Before she could reply he continued. 'How did you meet? My brother has always been vague about the circumstances which led him to offer you employment.'

'We met on the voyage from Europe.'

He pursed his lips and leaned his head to one side as though doubting her. 'On the voyage? I see. And who were you travelling with?'

'I was alone, sir.'

He shook his head and frowned. 'Alone? My brother is a very trusting man. He has led a quiet life and is not – how shall I say? – well-versed in the ways of the world. I fear his kind nature has made him vulnerable to those who might seek to profit from his generosity.'

Eliza gasped.

'I think you understand what I am saying, Miss Hewlett? I just want you to know that I am firmly in – what is the expression? – my brother's corner. I will be watching out for his interests. Do I make myself clear?'

'I understand you perfectly, Herr Feigenbaum, and resent the implication. I am very mindful of Dr Feigenbaum's kindness and would never take advantage of it. I am indebted to him but you can rest assured that as soon as I have discharged that debt I will be returning to England.'

He nodded. 'Good. I hope I have not offended you. I believe it is always the best policy to spell these things out. I would not like you to be under the illusion that your employment here might lead to something else, something more permanent.'

Eliza's face burned. She struggled to find the right words, feeling powerless, unable to retaliate. Did everyone see her that way? Did Marta Bauer? Helga Strauss? Was the whole town talking about the disfigured Englishwoman setting her cap at the German doctor?.

The following morning when Eliza came down to breakfast she found a small tissue-wrapped box waiting for her. The doctor was already seated and rose to greet her.

'What's this?' she asked, embarrassed and thinking of Alphonsus Feigenbaum's words the previous night.

'Merry Christmas. Open it, my dear.'

'There was no need for you to give me a gift and I'm afraid I have nothing for you, Doctor.'

'Please.' He smiled and shook his head. 'Your presence here is all I want.'

She hesitated for a moment, then unwrapped the parcel and opened the box to find a small brooch inside a velvet pouch. Two interwoven strands, one of diamonds and the other of emeralds, set into a gold clasp. She put it back into the pouch and held it out to him.

'I can't accept this.'

'I want you to have it, my dear.'

'No. It's not right. It's too much. I can't.'

He moved around the table towards her. 'It cost me nothing, Eliza. It belonged to my mother.'

She shrank from him, horrified. 'I can't possibly accept your mother's jewellery. It wouldn't be right.'

'Here. Let me pin it on for you.' He took the brooch.

'No!' Her voice was sharp, panicked. 'I'm sorry, Doctor.

I'm grateful for your kindness and deeply honoured that you should think to give me something that belonged to your late mother, but it's not appropriate. It would be wrong for me to wear it.'

His eyes reflected his hurt and he put the brooch down on the table in front of her and went back to his seat.

They sat in silence for a few minutes. Eventually Eliza spoke.

'It is the most beautiful brooch I have ever seen. I am honoured that you should think me worthy of it but you must understand that by accepting it, it would imply that our relationship was more than that of employer and employee and I have always made it clear that as soon as I am in a position to repay you what I owe, I intend to return to England.'

He continued to eat his breakfast without responding.

'Please, Doctor. I would hate for there to be difficulty between us. Surely you can understand that were I to wear this it would be seen by others as – '

'Alphonsus has said something? I knew it. What did he say to you? I saw you talking. That's what this is about.'

'He only said what others may be thinking. That he believes I am a fortune hunter, out to lure you into marrying me. You must see that accepting such a gift would convince him that is the case. Can't you see that?'

'I can see only that my brother is misguided. He treats me as though I am still a boy, not a man nearing sixty. As I am sure you observed last night, he has not been fortunate in his choice of wife. Liesel is a difficult woman. She has turned him against marriage. I suppose he wishes to prevent me making his mistake. When he knows you better, Eliza, he will see how wrong he has been.'

'Please, Dr Feigenbaum, do not speak again of marriage. I have told you I will *never* marry you.'

She moved towards the door, but the doctor stepped in front, blocking her path.

'Let me speak. Please?' He gestured towards the table and, reluctantly, she sat down again.

'I will say this now and then never speak of it again. I love you, Eliza, and I want to marry you. I realise I can never presume to replace your fiancé in your affections but I want to care for you. I expect nothing from you in return except your companionship. I don't give a damn for what people think, including my brother. I have never been happier in all my life than these past months since you have been living under my roof. If you do decide to return to England I will be a broken man, but I will never stand in your way. What you want matters more to me than anything in this world. I gave you that brooch but I give it without condition. I live in hope that one day you might feel more kindly towards me and want to wear it, but whether you do or not, I would like you to have it. I can see that what I am saying is distressing for you so I promise you this. I will not repeat my request for you to become my wife, but if some day you think you might be willing to do me that honour I want you to know that my offer will stand. I love you, Eliza, and will always love you, whether you marry me or not.'

27
The Confessional

The Irish church was gloomy and draughty. Eliza waited in the pew, shivering, running the rosary beads through her fingers. She was kneeling away from the rest of the attendees. She wanted to be the last into the confessional box so that she would not be overheard and would feel less hurried by a queue of penitents waiting to unburden their sins.

The priest had a heavy Irish brogue that for a moment made her breath catch as it so resembled the voice of Father O'Driscoll. Eliza rattled off her sins: the usual catalogue – vanity and regret for her lost looks, impatience with her employer, lack of gratitude, covetousness of a gown she had seen a woman wearing in the street, lack of concentration during holy Mass. Then she gritted her teeth, squeezed her fingernails into her palms and decided to speak the words she was afraid to say.

'Father, I have loved a man for a long time. We were engaged to be married. He was falsely accused of fathering another woman's child and compelled to marry her against his will. As he did not enter into the marriage freely, does that mean it is valid?'

'Ah, now, there's a tricky one. And not really one for the confessional. Let me see if there's anyone else waiting.' The priest stuck his head out of the curtain, then turned back to her. 'You're the last, so why don't I give you absolution and penance and then we'll pop next door to the presbytery for a nice cup of tea and I'll try to answer your question.'

Ten minutes later they were seated either side of a fireplace in the drawing room of the priest's house, with the housekeeper dispensing cups of tea.

'So this fella didn't want to go ahead with a marriage to this other woman, but she was already expecting a child?'

'Yes.'

'And he said it wasn't his child?'

'Yes.'

'Now, Miss. It is Miss isn't it?'

'Yes. Miss Hewlett.'

'Are you so sure he wasn't the daddy?'

'Yes.'

'Forgive me asking this, but do you know how babies are made?'

Eliza flushed and twitched at her skirt in annoyance. 'Of course I do.'

'And you're absolutely sure he couldn't have … you know?'

'I am sure.'

'What were the circumstances of his acquaintance with the woman he married?'

'He lodged in her father's house.'

'She was under the same roof?'

'Yes.'

The priest shook his head and rubbed his chin with his hands. 'Put it this way, Miss Hewlett. If he wasn't the father of the child and was compelled to marry under duress, the marriage would be invalid *ab initio* – from the start – and there would be definite grounds for annulment as the marriage would be deemed not to have taken place. Consent is a key requirement of the sacrament of marriage.'

She squeezed her hands together and leaned forward. 'So he would be free to marry again?'

'He would be free to marry as the first marriage would not have been a marriage at all. But may I ask another question, Miss Hewlett? How long ago did this forced marriage take place?'

'About two years ago.'

'And the fella had already promised himself to you?'

'Yes.'

'Then I have to wonder why he hasn't done exactly what you've just done – as any priest would have told him the same thing.'

'Perhaps he has.' Eliza felt a little surge of hope and excitement inside her.

'Then why has he not sought you out?'

She looked down.

'I presume he has the means to do so?' he asked.

'He's in England. We were parted as our ship was about to sail. He doesn't know where in America I am.'

'I see.'

There was a moment's silence while they sipped their tea.

'Does this fella know anyone else who's in contact with you? Has he any way of tracking you down?'

Eliza put down the teacup and looked away from him, thinking of the Wenlocks. Jack could have found her if he'd tried. 'Yes, I suppose he has.'

'Then I'm sorry to say it looks like he was perhaps not the innocent man you have presumed. Maybe he was prepared to face up to the consequences of his sins and stand by the woman he had illicit relations with.'

Eliza stood, gathering her skirts around her. 'I know he's innocent. He did not have relations with the woman. I know him. He wouldn't.'

The priest sighed and shook his head. 'How many times

have I heard that? Perhaps you're right, Miss Hewlett. I wish I had your faith in human nature. In that case, the only conclusion I can draw is that he decided to stand by the woman anyway in her hour of need. He made an honourable sacrifice and that implies he went willingly into the contract of marriage. Either way, after two years, it looks unlikely that he has invoked nullity proceedings. I'm very sorry. Look on the bright side, Miss Hewlett. Plenty more fish in the sea. And if not, the church is always looking for young women with a vocation. Have you ever given thought to becoming a nun?'

Eliza left the presbytery and walked the streets of St Louis for hours, churning the possibilities through her mind. She wandered down to the banks of the Mississippi and looked up at the Eads Bridge, thinking of the times she had stood on the Clifton Bridge with Jack.

Her Jack would never have seduced Mary Ellen. She was sure of that. But what had the priest said? He'd heard it all before. Maybe Jack's intentions had been noble but Mary Ellen had visited him in the night. No. Hadn't he told her about coming upon Mary Ellen with a man in a dark alley, having intercourse against a wall? Jack had been as shocked as she was. He had told her he was a virgin. She believed him. Mary Ellen's child was not Jack's. She would stake her life on it.

Why then had he not sought an annulment? The priest had been clear that there were grounds. According to the Wenlocks he'd gone with Mary Ellen to the north of England – far from the threats and influence of Father O'Driscoll and Mr MacBride. Yet he hadn't done anything about it. The Wenlocks had received no enquiries from him and heard no news. It was as though he had drawn a line through their courtship, wiped it out and removed all traces, like cleaning chalk off a blackboard.

As she walked along beside the Mississippi, Eliza examined everything she knew of Jack, challenging all her assumptions about him. She realised she knew little of him, of his background, his family, his life before Bristol. She remembered how he had received the news of his father's death. His family had buried his father without him. He hadn't returned to visit his mother. She had been shocked at the time but had brushed away the thought, assuming he wanted to think only of the future. His father had been violent and prone to drunken rages – understandable then that Jack would want no more to do with him. The hurt must have run deep. Yet why punish his mother? Surely he should have gone to pay his respects and support his mother, to be reunited briefly with his siblings? There was something cold and selfish in this decision and how he had refused to talk about it with her. She who had no family at all found it hard to understand how he could shrug off his like a snake sloughing off its skin. Then she reminded herself they had held the funeral without him. He must have felt excluded, hurt, shut out. Oh Jack, my poor, poor Jack.

She thought back to the day on Clifton Down when he had stood up to those ruffians and defended her. Wasn't that proof of his inherent goodness, of his strength of character? He had taken blow after blow to protect her, heedless of the way he was outnumbered.

Yet the priest had planted a doubt and it was burrowing through her brain like the invisible worm inside William Blake's rose. Poetry. She didn't want to think about poetry. Jack's poetry. How so much of it had been about her. She had been overwhelmed with love for him, bowled over by his outpourings of devotion on the page. But now as she thought about it perhaps there was something unhealthy, almost obsessive about his words. From the time they had met he had written about nothing but her. It was all very well being on top of a pedestal – until the man who had placed you there went away and left you up there unable to get down.

Eliza sat on a bench beside the Mississippi, close to the great iron bridge. Here the river was wide and grey and flowed like a sluggish giant through the low, flat land. So different that other iron bridge, spanning the Severn between high wooded cliffs. A wave of homesickness washed over her. She felt abandoned. Displaced. Alone. Abandoned by Jack. Abandoned by God.

She knew she would love Jack Brennan until the day she died, but she could not escape the fact that he had made no attempt to contact her. Whatever his reasons, he had turned his back on her. He was never going to come for her. They would never be together. She could only conclude that he hadn't loved her enough.

28

The Decision

Dr Feigenbaum glanced up at the clock on the wall behind Eliza. 'Won't you be late for church, my dear?' he asked.

'I'm not going' she said.

'Are you unwell?'

'No.'

'Has something happened?'

'I won't be going any more. Ever,' she said.

'Might I ask why?'

'God has let me down.'

The doctor shuffled the pages of his newspaper, but said nothing.

She spoke again, her voice expressionless. 'I want to have a child.'

He put down his newspaper.

'I will marry you,' she said. 'If you still want me.'

'And your fiancé?' he asked.

'He has let me down too,' she said.

They were married two weeks later. The witnesses were Alphonsus Feigenbaum and Marta. When the doctor told Eliza his brother had agreed to be his groomsman her heart sank.

'Don't worry, Eliza. I told you he would eventually understand why I want to marry you.'

'You're sure he's not going to make a scene?'

'Of course he is not. He knows how much I love you.'

She looked away. She hated him persisting in his attestations of love. As far as she was concerned the marriage was a contractual arrangement. Her only hope of motherhood. She was worried about Alphonsus being there. She had always ensured she was out of the house or stayed in her room when he visited.

Her dread was unjustified. When they arrived at the city hall Alphonsus was waiting for them. He bowed his head low over Eliza's hand, then clasped it between his. 'I owe you an apology, Miss Hewlett. May I be permitted to address you now as Eliza?'

She nodded, still nervous.

'I have had time to realise how happy you make my dear brother. He speaks of nothing but you when we meet. He has also explained how hard he worked to persuade you to marry him. I regret what I said when we first met, but trust you will understand that I had only his interests at heart.'

'Thank you, Herr Feigenbaum.'

'And you will forgive me for saying that I trust you will not disappoint him?'

Eliza bit her lip. He had such a strange way of phrasing things. So blunt.

Dr Feigenbaum, who had been speaking to the clerk, returned and clapped his arm around his brother's shoulders.

'I hope you are not telling her about all my faults, Alphonsus? I do not want Eliza to change her mind!'

The clerk ushered them into the office and in two or three minutes the whole thing was over. So quick. So easy. Eliza swallowed and forced a smile onto her face but felt as though she had just signed her life away.

Afterwards they gathered in the drawing room to drink

a glass of champagne, then Alphonsus left the two of them to eat supper together as usual.

Dr Feigenbaum chewed in silence and Eliza played with the food on her plate, trying to disguise her nervousness. When Marta had cleared the table and they retired to the drawing room, she was conscious of his eyes watching her as she sewed the patchwork quilt she was making. Uncomfortable, she looked up and met his eyes and he looked away, picking up a volume from the table beside him and pretending to read.

'You would do better if you had your reading spectacles on, Doctor,' Eliza said, knowing that without them he was almost completely word blind.

He didn't comment that she had referred to him by his professional title rather than using his name as he had asked her to do after the ceremony.

He coughed, got out of the chair and went back into the dining room to find the glasses he had left on top of his folded newspaper. He came back, sat down and picked up his book, but after a few seconds put it down again, rose and stood in front of the grate where, unnecessarily, he began to stab at the healthily burning fire with a poker, sending sparks flying into the hearth. He replaced the poker and paced slowly up and down in front of the fireplace, pausing to adjust the framed photographs of his dead German relatives, moving each one pointlessly a fraction to the left, then edging it back again into its original position.

Eliza bent her head over her sewing. His nervousness intensified her own. She stabbed her finger with the needle and watched as the tiny drop of blood appeared on the surface of her skin. She sucked her finger, knowing she should put aside her quilting and stem the bleeding properly, but she was afraid to move, to get up, in case it prompted him to speak to her.

After a few minutes, seeing that she had managed to

make a blood stain on the cotton fabric, she muttered under her breath in annoyance and put her work into the sewing basket. 'I think I'll go to bed,' she said.

The doctor jumped as though stung, then coughed and took off his spectacles and began to polish them with the handkerchief he kept in his pocket for the purpose. 'I will follow shortly,' he answered. 'Just as soon as I've wound the clocks and checked my appointments for tomorrow.'

Eliza knew he was dissembling. He had no appointments. He rarely left the house apart from his morning constitutional through Lafayette Park. But she was grateful. She would have been mortified at going up to bed together. She could not imagine how it would feel to get undressed in the same room as him, to sit at the dressing table and brush her hair out while he watched her. This way she could prepare for bed in private and await him there, though that would mean she would have to watch him undress instead.

Entering his bedroom for the first time, she saw with relief that there were a pair of damask-covered screens at each corner of the room opposite the bed. Frau Bauer had placed a large bowl of lilacs on the dressing table and Eliza's hairbrush and hand mirror were waiting for her beside it. She undressed quickly, washed, took off the mask of Pozzoni's make-up, slipped on her nightgown, applied her night cream, brushed her hair, and climbed up into the enormous bed, pulling the covers around her. The candlelight cast shadows across the ceiling and she wondered whether she should put the candle out. But Dr Feigenbaum might think she was asleep, or even that she had returned to her small single bedroom. She lay there agonising over the embarrassment of it all and wishing he were a more forceful and confident man, or that they were closer in age and might be able to laugh about their mutual shyness. Wishing was a dangerous path to follow – that could lead her to imagine she were lying here waiting for

Jack Brennan and she didn't want to think about that. No, just focus on getting through tonight. On doing what must be done. On what it would lead to – the baby she was now desperate to conceive.

Eliza lay motionless for what seemed like an age, watching the shadow-play from her candle on the ceiling, mentally tracing imaginary lines between the plaster ceiling rose and the corners of the room, dissecting the space into geometrical shapes. Dr Feigenbaum's uneven step sounded on the stairs and after a discreet warning cough, the bedroom door creaked open and she snuffed out her candle. He padded across the room and went behind one of the screens. She listened as he fumbled his way out of his clothing and into his nightgown, his body casting a new shadow across the ceiling. Eventually he moved back across the room, placed his candle on the night stand and climbed into the bed. She saw him hesitate for a moment, then he extinguished the candle and the room was bathed in a comforting darkness.

They lay there in silence for a few moments, both of them on their backs, side by side with a gap between them, each unconsciously modulating their breathing to the other's. Eliza wanted to giggle – she felt like an entombed mummy or one of those marbled husband and wife pairings from an old English church.

At last Dr Feigenbaum spoke, his voice disembodied in the darkness. 'May I hold you?'

'Yes,' she said, glad that she was unable to see his face.

He edged closer and she did the same until she felt his hip against hers. He moved onto his side and reached across her, laying one arm over her stomach. They lay there, unmoving, for what seemed like an eternity, but couldn't have been more than a minute or two, then she spoke, conscious of the loudness of her voice in the empty room.

'Have you done this before?'

'Once,' he said, 'Do you mind?'

'No.'

His arm tightened slightly around her waist and she felt the warmth of his breath on her neck.

'I was a young man. To mark my graduation from the university my brother arranged for me to have an experience with a woman.'

'I see.' She was glad the darkness hid her blushes. Relief that he was not as completely inexperienced as she was, mingled with a feeling of disgust that he was telling her this. She didn't want to know the details.

'Alphonsus paid her. My two best friends came with me. She dealt with us all, one after the other. I was the last.'

There was silence again, then he said, 'She was a lot older than me and at first I was repelled by her and didn't want to go ahead. So I understand how you must be feeling now.'

Eliza mumbled a negative, but knew it didn't sound convincing.

'She must have been used to dealing with young graduates as she was kind but very matter of fact. She was wrapped in a sheet which she dropped and showed me her body. I told myself that I was now a doctor and that made me feel better. It became more like a scientific experiment and I could be detached and stopped feeling ashamed. She gave me a glass of *schnapps* and that helped even more and before long she got me to laugh and then the whole thing was over before I'd even realised it was getting started. A bit of a disappointment. Before that day I had presumed I would only do something so intimate with someone I loved and ever since I swore I would not do it again, unless and until it were with someone I cared for.'

His head was resting against the top of her arm and she felt the scratch of his beard through the linen of her nightgown. She reminded herself that she had to view this as practically as Dr Feigenbaum had all those years ago. It was a necessity. Something to be got out of the way. An essential pre-requisite to becoming a mother. She eased up her nightgown, moved her legs apart, took his hand and placed it between them. He gave a small choked cry, then moved his other hand and laid it against her damaged cheek, stroking her face tenderly.

'I'll try not to hurt you, Eliza, my love. You have given my life back to me, my darling girl. You have made me so happy. I love you with all my heart.'

She squeezed her eyes shut and tried to reimagine the patterns that she had seen on the ceiling, to shut out the temptation to pretend that it was Jack Brennan who was lying on top of her. Her body was rigid, her eyes closed and her arms by her sides, like a corpse. As he pushed himself into her she almost cried out with the pain, but bit her lip instead. It hurt like hell. The sharpness of the pain seared through her, but then gave way to an uncomfortable ache as he worked in and out on top of her. She began to count the thrusts in her head, hoping that it would distract her from what was happening, that it would help her get through this. She reminded herself that she was doing this to have a baby. But it felt demeaning, degrading. Like animals. So embarrassing. It didn't seem right. Not when Dr Feigenbaum was such a dignified person, so quiet, so private, so closed. But here he was now, grunting like an animal on top of her.

He lifted his head and looked at her in the dark, then bent down and kissed her forehead. Drops of sweat fell from his face onto her own. 'Breathe,' he said. 'Breathe deeply. Slowly.'

She did as he asked and as she exhaled, she felt the tension leaving her limbs. She kept her eyes shut and carried on with slow deep breaths as the pain faded. Just as she was starting to become accustomed to the rhythm of his movement inside her, beginning to feel a small answering sensation each time he moved in and out, he gave a terrible cry, like a stuck pig, then fell away from her, leaving her suddenly empty, a sticky mess seeping between her legs.

He rolled over and reached for her hand. 'I didn't hurt you too much, *liebchen?*'

She mumbled a response of sorts, shy, awkward, hoping he would go to sleep. What they had just done seemed beyond belief. It was too intimate. How could she ever look him in the face again?

When she was sure he was asleep, she slipped out of bed, put on her dressing gown and crept downstairs to the parlour, where she sat on the floor in front of the hearth watching the dying embers of the fire. She wondered whether what Dr Feigenbaum had done had already made a baby inside her. She hugged her knees, conscious of the stickiness that he had deposited on the top of her thighs. It was disgusting. And yet? She slipped her fingers under her nightgown and touched herself down there, provoking her hips into a sudden and unexpected jerk. When her stepmother had walked into the bedroom and caught her touching herself there when she was about fourteen, she'd told her it was a mortal sin and if she did it again she would end up in hell. How was that possible when, according to the church, what Dr Feigenbaum had just done to her was seen as part of the sacrament of marriage? It didn't make any sense. Her hand wandered back and she stroked herself again, this time letting her fingers go inside, touching herself where he had been.

The following evening Eliza waited for her husband again in the darkened bedroom. This time however, he dropped a light kiss on her forehead and wished her goodnight, going quickly to sleep. She lay in the dark beside him, feeling a mixture of relief and disappointment. Had she done something wrong? Who could she ask? Was once enough to bring about a pregnancy? Could she ask him? He was after all a doctor and presumably would be accustomed to such questions. Perhaps after all he found her unattractive. But then he had only made love once before in his entire life so maybe he would not expect or want to do it again so soon. How often were they supposed to do it? She mulled these and more questions over in her head, lying on her back staring at the moonlight leaking into the room above the curtains. Eventually she drifted into sleep.

The following morning she awoke to him stroking her breasts. Shocked, she started to sit up but he pushed her back down gently.

'Let's stay here a while.'

He moved one of his hands down and laid the flat of his palm on her, then his fingers moved between her legs, probing and stroking. She turned her head away, embarrassed by what he was doing, her breathing fast and uneven. Then she relaxed and let herself give in to the sensations. It felt strange that those long, ink-stained, spatulate fingers that she was used to seeing gripping a leaking fountain pen, were now touching her down there, causing her to make little cries. It was better than what she had done to herself in front of the fire. Her face was burning and she kept her head turned away from him, overcome by the intense sensations.

He leaned over her and asked her if she was all right, or if she wanted him to stop.

'Don't stop!' she said. 'Please don't stop.' Then suddenly. 'Yes stop. Inside me. I want you inside me!'

She didn't know where the words had come from. What was happening to her? What had he done to her? When he positioned himself on top of her, she grasped him with both her arms, pulling him into her, bringing her knees up and her legs wrapping around his back. She groaned as he entered her, moving her arms to hold him tighter as they started to move together. He looked down at her, his face frowning in concentration, his eyes out of focus, unrecognisable as though he were in a mystical state of trance.

When it was over, she turned on her side away from him, her body wet with sweat, her breathing rough and uncontrolled. She was drowsy, sated. She had never imagined it would be pleasurable.

Then Feigenbaum started coughing: uncontrollable coughs that made him struggle for breath. Alarmed, she piled the pillows behind him to prop him upright. Eventually he settled and they sat there, side by side in the bed and Eliza suddenly felt ridiculous. It was absurd, undignified what they had just done together. Embarrassing. She had lost control. She hated that. He was practically an old man and judging by the coughing fit, possibly not long for this world, particularly if he exerted himself the way he had done just now. So undignified.

He reached for her hand. 'I love you, Eliza,' he said.

She squeezed her eyes tight shut. She didn't want to look at him with his white hair, his white, loose skin, his small paunch. And she certainly didn't want to look at those ink stained fingers now stroking her hand.

They sat in silence for a few minutes and Eliza wondered when it would be appropriate for her to reclaim her hand and get out of bed, But she knew he would look at her. Watch her as she went across the room. Take in her body with his eyes just as he had taken her body with his own.

'What are you thinking about?' he asked.

'Nothing really,' she said.

'Tell me.'

She took her hand back from under his and pretended to adjust her hair. 'When we were in that restaurant in New York why did you ask me to marry you? You barely knew me.'

'I knew you.'

'That's not possible.'

'It was recognition. I saw in you something. A strong feeling. A connection. Recognition is the best word.'

'I saw nothing,' she said.

He flinched.

'You were just a stranger. Kind-hearted, yes, but a stranger.'

'And now?'

'You are a kind man.'

'But no longer a stranger?'

She could sense the hesitance and hope in his voice.

'I know more of you, but…'

'Yes?'

'I think I will always feel apart from you, distant.' As she spoke she knew her words were knife wounds but she felt compelled to twist the knife further, to regain some separation, some distance after the strange, primeval intimacy of their love-making. 'I don't know you at all.'

'You haven't tried to know me.' His voice was sad rather than accusatory.

'Perhaps I don't want to.' She knew she was being cruel, but couldn't help herself.

'I wish it were otherwise.'

'Do you still believe you love me?'

'I do love you.'

'How is that possible? Love must travel two ways.'

Without waiting for his answer, she swung her legs over the side of the bed, reached for her dressing gown and went to the bathroom, leaving him propped up against the pillows, his eyes rheumy and sad.

29
Birth of an Empire

Dr Feigenbaum's book was almost complete. Eliza was typing up the final chapter. She had the glossary and index to prepare and then it would be ready for publication.

She had become increasingly absorbed by the task. The doctor's style was ponderous and florid and she had taken it upon herself to recast some of the writing to make it flow more smoothly.

He was alarmed when she told him. 'You've changed the text? How? Why?'

'Not all of it. Just the opening chapter. For you to consider. If you like it, well and good and I can work on the rest; if you don't, then I still have your original draft here.' She brandished a handful of papers.

'Read it aloud.'

She began to read and he listened, his expression inscrutable. When she finished the chapter, he nodded and smiled. 'You have worked wonders with my clumsy syntax. Thank you, Eliza. Please continue with the rest of the manuscript. It will be a better book for what you are doing.'

The next evening he went out to his weekly chess club. Eliza looked forward to those evenings when she had the house to herself. She still found his presence awkward and struggled to reconcile the man who puffed at his pipe and read his German newspaper with the man who did embarrassing things to her body in bed and could make her cry out with pleasure. In the darkness of the bedroom she was able to relax, but she could not imagine a time coming when she would feel comfortable in conversation with him.

When he arrived home that night, he came into the parlour without taking off his coat, so eager was he to speak.

'Something amusing happened this evening, my dearest. I was extolling your virtues as an editor when Edward Larkman – you remember him? – the dental surgeon – he is working on a volume outlining the techniques and methods of modern dentistry – he asked whether you would be willing to transcribe and edit his book and prepare the index, footnotes and glossary. Of course, I told him it was out of the question for you to take on work now that we are married. But I thought you would be amused, my dear.' He took his coat off and flung it absently on the chair, eager to continue. 'Then, Felix Montague, I don't think you've met him – he is a breeder of racehorses – he said he'd a mind to write his memoirs – a record of his past triumphs and his training methods. Once the two of them had started, several of the others announced that they had writing plans and were in need of the services of an editor. By the end of the evening there were tomes in the making on matters as diverse as palaeontology and numismatics. Oh – and a history of the Cahokian tribal lands!' He reached for his pipe where it lay on the mantelpiece. 'Eliza, Eliza! You have inspired a flowering of technical writing in St Louis as has never been witnessed before!' He chuckled as he stuffed the bowl of his pipe.

'Why should it be out of the question because I'm married?'

He raised his eyebrows. 'A married woman does not work, Eliza. Not if her husband is able to support her. You know that. Before long we both hope you will have children to occupy your time.'

'Why can't I do both?'

He looked puzzled.

'I enjoy the work I've been doing for you. I think I am good at it, so why would I want to stop?'

'You are certainly good at it. But no woman chooses to work if she doesn't need to.'

'This woman does. I think I should be bored if I were expected to deal with nothing but household matters. Anyway, Marta has all of those under control. I think I should be perfectly capable of bringing up children while continuing editing. In fact I would be positively overjoyed. I have been dreading finishing your book.'

A tone of defiance had crept into her voice and he looked at her, smiling.

'I see. Then far be it from me to stand in your way. I will share the good news with my fellow authors. But don't say I didn't warn you! At the rate they are clamouring for your services I think you could be overwhelmed.'

She thought for a moment. 'How are they intending to publish their books?'

'I suppose the same as I am. Our friend Gunter Hoffman has a printing press.'

'That's all very well but what about distributing them?'

'Ah! You are ahead of me, my dearest, I had not thought of that challenge.'

'It occurs to me that if so many of your friends and acquaintances are planning to write books of this kind – text books, works of a scientific or specialist nature – there may be advantages in grouping together to print and distribute them. Perhaps a partnership?'

'Indeed! We could form a publishing company. Here in St Louis.'

Eliza clapped her hands together and smiled at him. 'Now wouldn't that be something!'

'But how would this be achieved? Neither of us knows anything of such matters.'

'You are a clever man, Karl. And you have connections throughout the city. The breweries would all be interested in your book and I imagine the same will be true of dentists and horse breeders and such. And there are the universities. Not just in St Louis but in the state. Why even the whole darned country! We just need a plan to reach these people, to make them aware of the books we offer. But first of all we must speak with your Herr Hoffman and find out if he wants to join the enterprise.'

She carried on, buoyed up by an enthusiasm she hadn't experienced since she had been in America. Feigenbaum played devil's advocate but the longer they talked the more his excitement mirrored hers.

'We have proved to be good partners in working on your book, so why not in a larger enterprise? I think we complement each other well,' she said.

'In so many ways.' Overcome, he flung his arms around her and hugged her tightly. 'I think a toast is called for.'

Thus was born Feigenbaum & Hoffman, printers and publishers of text books and academic works. That night, Christabel Feigenbaum, the first of their two daughters, was also conceived.

Eliza's feelings for Karl Feigenbaum changed the moment she watched him holding their first born in his arms. The expression on his face, the pure undiluted love, moved her. She shivered.

He looked up at her and smiled. 'You have made me so happy. You have given me the greatest gift. When I boarded that ship in Liverpool I had no idea that everything would change so much. I was an empty old man, a weary, wizened creature who thought life had passed him by in his Belgian backwater. I never dreamed I would one day be a husband and a father. My dear, dear girl, Eliza.' He brushed the tears from his eyes as his voice broke with emotion. 'I love you so much.'

She leaned forward and squeezed his arm, then let her hand stroke first the head of the baby girl and then rest against his cheek.

'Thank you, Karl. Thank you. You too have made me happy.' She paused, took a deep breath then said the words. 'I love you too, Karl.'

He gasped and still cradling his daughter, reached for Eliza's hand and squeezed it. 'I thought I would never hear those words from you. I told myself to be content with your kindness, with your presence, your companionship. I never dared to hope that one day you might come to love me.'

Now she had spoken, she could not take the words back. Had she been overwhelmed by the moment, the hormonal rush of giving birth, the joy of holding her own child? How could she possibly love this strange German man, with his Franco-German accent and Santa Claus beard? The sunlight shone through the bedroom window and lit up his face as he gazed upon his child. It was a kind face, now a familiar face and one she had come to like looking back at her across the table at mealtimes.

She watched him as he stroked his daughter's head, humming a German lullaby, his eyes still damp with unshed tears.

He was the person who cared for her more than anyone. He had rescued her from detention, lent her money, given her refuge and work. He had paid for her teeth to be fixed. He had told her she was beautiful every day since they married, even though she knew she wasn't anymore. He had built with her the publishing company that already was in profit in less than a year. Her respect for him had grown and she had found an unexpected pleasure in working so closely with him. While there was no doubt that Eliza was the creative force behind the business, she struggled to imagine how she would have got it off the ground without him and how she would have made such progress without his wise counsel, encouragement and boundless enthusiasm. He had given purpose to her life. What was love anyway? She had always thought of it as a grand passion, an agonising rush of desire. Now she was not so sure. Perhaps love was the accumulation of small things, little acts of consideration, the persistence of a man in loving even when he receives nothing in return. Day after day, loving her by doing, being, caring, giving. What resistance did she have in the face of that? It was inevitable that in the end she would start to love him back. She tried to imagine life without him. It was not an appealing prospect.

He was looking at her, still holding their child, his eyes fixed on Eliza, waiting. She wondered if he could see the hesitation in her eyes, and she knew he expected her to tell him again, to remove all possible doubt.

'I married you believing I could never love you, never care for you.' She could see the hurt in his eyes, the slight twitch of his mouth as he prepared himself for her to retract her declaration. 'I was wrong. I do care for you. Very much. And now with Christabel I am a part of a family. We are a family. Thank you for that, Karl.'

He was about to speak but she silenced him with a finger on his lips.

'For the first time in a very long time I have hope for the future, a sense of purpose, a sense of belonging. You have given that to me, Karl. I know at times I was unfair to you, cold, distant, ungrateful. I am sorry for that. I was angry. I took my anger out on you, when all you ever did was show me kindness. I was superficial, valuing things that I now know don't matter, and overlooking those that do. It took me a long time to see you for who you really are, but now that I see that person, I know I love him.'

Speaking the words made her surer, as though giving voice to the feelings anchored them, tethered them to her, made them real and irrefutable. She smiled and the baby made a gurgling noise as if in approval.

30
Gertrude Logan

Over the years, Jack's family grew. Mary Ellen's confession about Marian's parentage softened his feelings towards his wife, just as it hardened his hatred of the Irish priest. He felt pity for his Mary Ellen, but it was mixed with guilt that, like the priest before him, he was using her as a vessel for his lust. Their marriage lacked companionship, friendship or any meeting of minds. The lives they lived were mostly separate, there being no common ground between them, apart from in the marital bed.

The year after Marian's birth, Jack's first child, a daughter, was stillborn. Mary Ellen couldn't understand how or why the baby she had carried inside her for so many months and laboured to bring into the world was dead. She swaddled a waxen faced doll in the layette intended for the baby and carried it around between cradle and chair, pretending to nurse it. This tragic charade was broken by the arrival of the next baby, a son, Anthony. Over the following five years Francis, Jane, then another still-born daughter and Ursula followed in rapid succession.

Mary Ellen saw her children as confirmation of her place in the world. A validation of her. She was a mother. She had produced lives. But her love for them was abstract and collective – she seemed incapable of appreciating them as individuals. She was happy to delegate their physical well-being to Sally, while their personal and emotional needs increasingly fell to Marian. Perhaps to make up for the lack of love or affection she received from either parent, from a very tender age Marian took on the role of little mother to her siblings, overseeing their washing and dressing, ensuring their attendance at school later and enforcing what little discipline existed in the household.

Jack's feelings for his children were ambivalent. Every so often he would be jolted by a shock of recognition at a facial expression, a tone of voice or a sudden movement that recalled one of his own siblings or resembled what he saw in the mirror. On the other hand, he recognised that his growing family was tethering him forever to his life with Mary Ellen and to this ugly northern town.

Having grown up in a large family, he was comfortable having a lot of children around. He was absentmindedly indulgent towards the girls, Marian excepted, but a strict disciplinarian with the two boys. He looked for evidence that his own shortcomings had been inherited by the boys, whereas he never felt that way about the girls, whom he saw as light, delicate, sparkling creatures, flitting about him. Jack treated them as distant acquaintances, pleased enough to see them if he happened upon them, but never going out of his way to seek their company and uncertain how to handle them. The boys were different. Every time they made a noise he barked at them. Every time they laughed he sent them away to read their books, fearful that they would inherit the slow wits of their mother.

Soon after Ursula was born, the two boys died within days of each other from whooping cough. It happened quickly. Jane too was infected but her little body offered more resistance and she made it through the crisis. Mary Ellen, pregnant with Alice, took their deaths badly, taking to her bed, howling and weeping for days and inconsolable at the graveside. Jack refused to let himself grieve. He saw his wife's outpouring of grief as insincere and undignified and he refused to let his own mind dwell on his dead sons. He was sorry that they had been snatched away so young, but in some ways he saw their deaths as a blessing, an escape from a world that he increasingly believed held no joy, meaning or purpose.

As for Marian, he barely looked at her and completely ignored her. When he did let his eyes rest on her in an unguarded moment, he saw in her long oval face, heavy chin and over-large nose the irrefutable signs of her parentage. For her part, Marian worked hard to gain affection and attention from the man she believed to be her father. She would try to show him her drawings, offer to bring him tea, ask him to look at her letters, holding her slate up to him eagerly, but to no effect. By the time Clementina was born in 1892, when Marian was sixteen years old, she had stopped trying and had retreated, hurt and cold.

Childbirth and the years had impacted Mary Ellen's looks. The tall slender woman had become stooped and had thickened heavily around the middle. Her once shining hair had greyed and roughened in texture. She looked older than her years. When he looked at her, Jack felt repelled by her and what she had become. But in the darkness of their bedroom he sank into her amplitude, losing himself in the abundance of her soft flesh.

Jack met Gertrude Logan soon after Clementina was born. He was accustomed to walking out of the overcrowded town with its hundreds of narrow streets, teeming with people. He often headed to the coast at the mouth of the Tees and was walking there in the sand dunes when he came upon her. He almost fell over her as she was half sitting, half lying amidst the marram grass.

'I'm sorry, Miss. I'd no idea there was anybody there.'

He raised his hat to her and was about to carry on walking past her onto the beach, when she spoke.

'You're Mr Brennan from the Tudor Crown in Colliers Street aren't you?'

He nodded.

'I thought I recognised you. I've been in a few times to collect a jug of beer for my husband when he wasn't up to getting there himself. I'm Gertrude Logan. My husband's Bill Logan. He's a foreman in the foundry.'

Jack nodded. 'I know Bill.'

He looked at the woman, her skirt tucked under her and the wind blowing her dark hair out of the loose bun she'd tied on top of her head. There was something about her that reminded him a little of Eliza and he felt that familiar stab of pain at her memory. It wasn't that she looked like her – this woman was not pretty like Eliza and was as dark as Eliza was fair, but there was something in her manner, the way she spoke or held her head – he couldn't quite put his finger on it. Rather than walk on, he hesitated a moment, trying to place what it was exactly that stirred the memory.

'Where are you heading?' she asked.

'Just out for a walk.'

'Same here. I stopped to look at the sky for a while. I love to watch the clouds. Sometimes in town you can't even see the sky for the smoke.'

Jack looked up. The sky was azure blue fading to paler blue near the horizon and faint wisps of lacy cloud were scudding across it at speed. He could hear gulls screaming and smelt the salty tang of the sea.

'It changes all the time,' she said. The colour of the sky and the shape of the clouds. They're always moving, forming new shapes. Sometimes the whole sky looks dark and grey because of heavy clouds and then suddenly a gap opens and the rays of light shine through. It's as if you're catching a glimpse into heaven. That's why I love it. Like looking into a kaleidoscope. I had one when was I was small. My father won it for me at the fair, but … it got broken.'

Jack saw a sadness in her eyes, but then it was gone and she was laughing. 'Listen to me! Chattering away. You must think me strange, when we don't even know each other.'

'Not at all.' He knew he should say goodbye and continue on along the sand dunes away from her, but he was rooted to the spot. 'I like to watch the sea, myself,' he said. 'Same reason as you and your clouds. It's always changing. I was born in Derby which is slap in the middle of the country so I didn't see the sea until I was eighteen and moved to Bristol. And even then it was the Avon Gorge rather than the sea itself. But here it's like your clouds. One day waves crashing on the shore and the next calm as a millpond. And the smell of the salt. You don't get that from looking at picture books.'

She studied his face for a moment, then said, 'You don't talk like a publican.'

'And how's that?'

'I didn't think men who ran public houses would like walking at the seashore and watching the waves.'

'I was a teacher,' he said. 'I've always loved being close to nature.' He smiled. 'Probably comes from growing up in an industrial town. You don't get a lot of chance. I used to write poetry.'

'Used to? Why did you stop?'

He shrugged and turned away to look out at the sea again. 'When the waves wash up on the shore it makes me think that maybe that particular bit of water has travelled right across the world. All that water moving around. I've often thought of putting a message in a bottle and throwing it out there to see where it might end up.'

'I heard about one being found that came all the way from France,' she said. 'The boy who picked it up couldn't understand what the message said. It was in the newspaper last year. It was near Hartlepool he found it. You should do it. Write a message and see where it ends up. Or a poem! Why not?'

He shrugged. 'No point.'

'Why's there no point? It's worth a try, surely.'

'The only reason to send a message is if you want someone specific to read it. And throwing it into the ocean isn't the best way to do that.'

'Ah. You've no romance! You have to believe. You have to trust.'

'I stopped doing that a long time ago' he said.

'How sad.' She looked up at him, a frown creasing her face.

There was silence between them for a moment, then Jack said, 'I'd better be going. Good to meet you, Mrs Logan.' He moved off down the dune, the sand sliding under his feet so he was almost running by the time he reached the bottom.

She called down to him. 'Mr Brennan, if you see my husband, please don't mention you met me here. He doesn't like me being out here on my own.'

He raised a hand in acknowledgement and walked away down the beach. For a moment he wondered whether her remark about her husband was a hint that for him to offer to walk her back to town, but then reasoned that if Logan didn't like her to be here alone he'd probably like even less for her to be out walking with a man.

As he paced along the open sands, he was overcome by loneliness. The brief conversation with Gertrude Logan had highlighted the emptiness of his life. Just a bit of pointless banter, but every word somehow seemed precious. It was not so much what was said but the way it was said: her words offered up with a sense of trust. A spontaneous sharing of what was on her mind at that moment. It was banal, yet curiously intimate and it made his heart ache for everything he missed with Eliza. In the years he'd spent with Mary Ellen they had never had a conversation like that. They had barely had a conversation at all.

Jack avoided the sand dunes for a while after that. He didn't acknowledge to himself that he was avoiding meeting Gertrude Logan again, but he was. There was something about her that disturbed him, unsettled him. The emptiness of his marriage to Mary Ellen, his failure to fulfil the dreams he'd cherished since boyhood and the vast hole Eliza had left in his life preyed on his mind since the encounter with the woman on the shore. And his poetry? What had once been his passion seemed foolish and impractical since he stopped teaching and started pulling pints. The notebook in which he wrote his poems was tucked away on the bookshelf, beside the volumes of poetry and the novels which he no longer read. He remembered that morning all those years ago when Cecily had found his poems and made fun of him. That had been the trigger for his running away. What high hopes he had then, arriving in Bristol and landing on his feet. It had all proved a sham. But there was something about his brief conversation with Mrs Logan that made him want to fight back. Losing Eliza forever did not have to mean losing the rest of his dreams. Why shouldn't a publican be a poet?.

Next time he went to the coast, he took a pencil and his notebook with him in his pocket. Watching the waves crash onto the shore he remembered what he had said to the woman about the sea travelling across the world, and he thought of Eliza standing on the coast of America, staring out over the ocean and thinking of him.

He pulled up his coat collar and settled down in the sand with the notebook propped on his knees and began to write.

The sea that touches here the land
Has travelled far, who knows from where?
Watching waves break upon the strand.
I wonder is she watching there?

Her lonely figure on the shore
Of a distant unfamiliar place
Looks out to watch the seagulls soar
Sadness covering her face.

He began to write a third verse but crossed out the lines almost as soon as he wrote them. He chewed on his pencil. What was the point? Ever since he'd met Eliza his poetry had been for her and now she would never read it. The words mocked him. They were inadequate, commonplace. His feelings of loss and loneliness were too great to be captured in a few lines of doggerel. The fault lay in him, in the feebleness of his imagination, in the banality of his words, in his failure to bring the image of her alive. He broke the pencil in half and threw away the pieces.

One day, on a whim Jack took the ferry across to Port Clarence on the north side of the Tees and walked past the foundries alongside the salt marshes towards the sea. He was leaning on a wall looking out to the sea when he realised someone was standing beside him.

'You were in a trance there, Mr Brennan. Been seeing a hypnotist?'

He turned to face her. Her expression was of amusement and he realised that the features he'd remembered as plain, were much improved when she smiled.

'Mrs Logan, I'm sorry, I didn't notice you were there.'

She laughed. 'That's me. The Invisible Woman - no one noticed she was there until she was gone! That could make a good story for the penny dreadfuls, don't you think?'

'I wouldn't know,' he said. 'My wife loves them but I've never read one.' He wanted to eat his words, realising how pompous he sounded, but she appeared unconcerned.

'My husband reads them. Can't say they're my taste - but I've been known to scan over the pages before I light the fire with them.' She raised her eyebrows at him and gave a little shake to her head.

Jack laughed. 'What brings you over here? It's a pretty desolate spot,' he said.

'I saw you on the ferryboat. My husband left his dinner box behind so I had to come over to Port Clarence to bring it him. I thought I'd come and look for you and see if you wanted to walk back with me.'

Jack was surprised and felt slightly uncomfortable. It seemed odd that a woman, another man's wife, should seek out his company for a stroll over the salt marshes. He looked at her, wondering if she was testing him in some way – or teasing him. Her face betrayed nothing. Just that same open gaze he had noted when they met before, and an air of calm that surrounded her like an aura. She looked a bit older than he was, but then most of the women here looked older than their years, worn down by poverty, poor health and unhealthy living conditions in the crowded terraces.

'Come on,' she said. 'Looks like it might rain later. We need to make the most of it.' She set off walking briskly in front of him, then looked back over her shoulder. 'You coming then?'

He had little choice but to follow, half running to catch up. She hitched her skirts to clear the wet grass and he caught a glimpse of her ankles over the top of her boots and felt an unexpected lurch in his stomach. What was wrong with him? She wasn't beautiful at all. Plain if anything. Couldn't hold a candle to Eliza. Yet he felt a sudden desire for her, a longing to reach out and grab her, lean her over the stone wall and take her right there. Then she smiled at him, oblivious to what was going through his head and he felt ashamed.

'When my mother was a little girl there was nothing here,' she said. 'Just empty marshes as far as the sea. Collecting salt was the only industry. Nothing between here and the hills. Just a few houses. It's hard to imagine that now, isn't it? All those ugly blast furnaces and smoke stacks. Ships everywhere. In her day there were just a few fishermen lived on the coast. She was a shepherd's daughter. Not many sheep round here now.'

'She grew up in Middlesbrough?'

'Born here. Before the railway came.'

'Your father too?'

She looked away, staring across the river. 'No. He came over from Ireland. For the work. He was an iron man too. Like my husband and most of the men in this town.' Her voice had an edge to it but before he could ask her anything else she turned her gaze back to him. 'What about you, Mr Brennan - you said you came from Derby?'

'Born and bred there.'

'And Mrs Brennan?'

'Bristol.'

'Is that where you met?'

Now it was his turn to look away. As though she sensed his reluctance to talk about Mary Ellen, she said, 'I'm sorry. It's none of my business. It's just I have so little chance to talk.' She laughed, a brittle, ironic laugh. 'My husband's not much for conversation.'

Before he could stop himself, he blurted, 'Nor is my wife.'

They were silent for a pregnant moment, then she spoke again. 'I had a feeling we were kindred spirits, Mr Brennan. I think we will be friends.'

'Friends?'

Friendship between a man and a woman, each married to other people was unthinkable - and yet he knew he wanted nothing more.

'Why not?' she said.

He looked down at his feet. He was wearing his good shoes – the leather was stained with mud. He mentally cursed his stupidity for wearing them today.

'It's just that…you know… people would talk.'

'Let them. We've nothing to hide, have we?'

'Of course not. It's just… the other time when I saw you…you asked me not to tell your husband.' He felt his face reddening.

'It's just that he doesn't like me walking out alone. The beach is a lonely place in winter. He worries I might fall and hurt myself and no one would know. He's a powerful imagination has Bill. Must be all those penny dreadfuls.'

'So you'll tell him you met me?'

'Of course I won't. I told you. He's got a powerful imagination. No point in encouraging him to use it. You've spoilt those nice shoes, Mr Brennan.'

31
Friendship

They began meeting two or three times a week. They would walk on the beach, along the banks of the Tees or cross over the river on the steam ferry to walk on the sands or beside the salt marshes. On these walks they saw no one, except for the odd fisherman, all the men of the town being occupied inside the foundries or shipyards and the women working in their homes.

When the weather was fine they would sit side by side on a sand dune or a stone wall to watch the oystercatchers wading in the shallows and dipping their long orange bills to pick up cockles. Sometimes they would sit quietly as the grey seals basked on the sandbanks, soaking in the sunshine at low tide. Gertrude encouraged Jack to listen to the bird-song and taught him to distinguish between the different species. It reminded him of the afternoons spent with Eliza when she had painstakingly pointed out the names of wild flowers.

'When I was a little girl it was so different here. Every year it seems there's more furnaces and smokestacks, more noise, more stink, fewer birds, fewer seals. Soon there'll be nothing here but machinery and ugly buildings to house it.'

'It's progress, I suppose. Means jobs. Means money. You

can't stand in the way of progress, can you?' he replied.

'You sound like my Bill. He's blind to anything that's not to do with iron and steel. He doesn't look. Doesn't see. Doesn't care.'

'I care,' he said.

She didn't answer and they walked on in silence. Jack liked the way it didn't matter whether they spoke or not. There was no awkwardness between them.

'They're reclaiming most of the river. They've run out of land to put their ugly buildings on. All that over there,' she pointed across the river, 'that was once water. They dumped tons of slag from the blast furnaces to fill it in. Gets rid of the waste and creates new land to build on. Kills two birds with one stone, they reckon.'

'They'll have killed more than two birds before they're done. Some days I wonder how the birds can fly through the smoke and fumes – you can't even see the other side of the river,' he said.

'I long to be free of this place. Of this whole life,' she said. 'It's why I like coming out here by the sea where I can still breathe. In the town and at home there's no escaping it. The dust gets everywhere. On every surface. Inside your clothes. Up your nose. Ingrained in your skin. In your eyes and your food. Inside you. The machinery throbbing away till you think your brain is going to burst with the sound of it, the clanging of the trucks shifting the pig iron, the stink of the sulphur and the smoke from the coke ovens. Smoke and dust burning your throat.'

She stared back at the town which was under a pall of smoke. 'It's like living inside hell. The furnaces never go out. Just keep on burning, day after day, night after night, week after week. For ever. Burning away. Melting iron ore into money. Money that stays in the pockets of the rich men in their big fancy houses while the rest go hungry, get sick, work till they're so tired they drop. Then all that's left is to die.' She sighed. 'You think I'm wrong to complain, I expect.'

'Of course I don't. I find it hard living here too. And I have it easier than most with living above the pub. We have space. I don't have to work in the foundries. I can't imagine how hard that must be.'

'You never get used to it. I've lived here all my life but it's got worse in that time. Much worse.'

She stopped and looked at him, studying his face intently. 'Why did you come here, Mr Brennan?'

'What?' His voice was full of surprise. 'Why do you ask that?'

'You look sad. Sometimes it feels like you're not really here. Like you don't want to be. Like you're far away in another place.'

He shook his head, uncomfortable that she had switched her attention to him.

'Is it very beautiful in Derby? Or in Bristol? Do you miss those places? Is that why you're sad? Being stuck up here in the middle of these filthy steel mills and furnaces?'

'I don't like to dwell on what's past.' He spoke with a hard edge to his voice, wanting to stop her line of questioning.

'You are sad then? You don't have happy memories?'

'I told you. I don't like to think about the past. Good or bad. The past is dead. Gone. Buried.'

'You're not the only one to want to forget, Mr Brennan. The past can be painful for a lot of us. I married Bill Logan for one reason only. I'd no idea it would be out of the frying pan and into the fire as my mother used to say.'

'What do you mean?'

'My father was a violent man. He'd come in late on the night he was paid. Blind drunk and he'd have spent most of his wages in the ale house. He thought my mother and I were blaming him, criticising him for leaving us short. We never said a word of complaint, but we didn't need to.

It was his own guilt I suppose. My mother had to take in washing and I had to help her when I wasn't at school. The pair of us lugging buckets of water in and out of the house, the kitchen full of steam so you couldn't see in front of you. Washing hanging everywhere. Hurrying to get one load out of the way so we could start on the next. It never ended. Back-breaking work. No wonder she went to an early grave. When my father was sober he'd feel bad about striking her but it didn't stop him getting drunk and doing it again the next time. When she died and he switched to hitting me I'd go to bed early on pay day and pretend to be asleep in the hope he'd go straight to bed when he got in. Sometimes it worked but other times he'd come home full of beer and bad temper and drag me out of bed just to give me a thrashing.'

'Oh God, Gertrude, that's terrible.'

Neither of them noticed he had used her given name for the first time.

'You get used to it. Doesn't stop it hurting though. Hurting in your body, and hurting even more in your head – that your own father hates you so much he wants to beat you night after night. Although the truth is I think he hit my mother and me because he hated himself even more. Hated his miserable life and the way he'd never amounted to anything. He missed Ireland too. Came from a small village and when he was sober he'd talk about how beautiful it was, how green and with the coast all wild and rocky.'

'How long did the beatings go on?'

'Until I left home to marry Bill Logan. And then after a while it all started up again.'

'Your husband let your father beat you?'

'No. It was Bill. He started hitting me after we were married a couple of years and I'd given him no children. Not that he'd have wanted the extra mouths to feed - it would have meant less money for him to spend in your tavern. No, it's his pride. He doesn't like that people might gossip about us having no children. He thinks people would say he wasn't man enough, so he takes it out on me. Calls me a shrivelled old fruit.'

Jack said, 'I'm sorry I never thought to ask. I suppose I presumed you had children.'

'Don't feel sorry. I never wanted children. Not with him anyway.'

'Does he still hit you?'

'Sometimes. Not so much these days. On pay nights I mostly leave a jug of beer and some food on the table and a fire lit so if he comes in hungry he'll stop to eat and if I'm lucky he falls asleep in the kitchen in front of the fire without waking me. It works most of the time. Not always though.'

'I'd like to clobber him.' Jack squeezed his hands into tight fists, his knuckles white. 'Hitting a woman. Hitting his own wife. It's a dreadful thing to do. He'll not be welcome at the Crown any more.'

'No!' She raised her voice and grabbed at his sleeve. 'You mustn't ban him. You mustn't let him know that you know. It'd make it worse for me.'

'But I can't let him beat you. I can't just stand by and let it happen.'

'You're not standing by. You're not supposed to know. No one knows. Well, I suppose the folk next door know - but there's many the night I can hear them screaming through the walls when their husbands have had a few too many and come home spoiling for a fight – or when cross words are exchanged when the rent money's due. It's a way of life in Middlesbrough. Probably half your customers go home and knock the stuffing out of their wives.'

She reached her hands up to her neck and opened the top buttons of her blouse, to reveal an ugly bruise across her collar bone. Jack stepped backwards, his hand clamped to his mouth. Then he moved towards her, his fingers reaching out to trace the bruising on her skin but, anticipating him, she buttoned herself up

She laughed a dry laugh. 'Bruises fade. And so far he's not broken any bones. I've got quite canny about it now. When I think there's a likelihood of him wanting to thrash out I make sure the lodger's around. He doesn't like to hit me in front of him. I try to stay one step ahead of him and most of the time it works. But then something triggers him and he goes off like a roman candle.'

'How long have you been married?'

'Thirteen years. I was sixteen when I married him and he was forty-nine. He was a widower. Married to his first wife more than twenty years. He was my father's friend. I should have known that they'd be as bad as each other, but I were that glad to get away from my father I didn't think straight. I didn't know then what marriage involved. You know. What women have to let men do to them. In bed. My mother never warned me. If I'd known I'd never have married him. Better to be beaten up by my father than have to put up with all that business as well as the beatings. On the wedding night I cried myself to sleep. I did a lot of crying at first. Then I realised there was no point.'

Jack looked down, avoiding her eyes. Her frankness embarrassed him but at the same time moved him. He wanted to take her in his arms and hold her, feel her head against his chest while he smoothed her hair and comforted her. Instead he kicked at a clump of marram grass and looked at his watch. 'Best be getting back. I have to open up in an hour.'

That night in the bar he looked over at the corner table where Bill Logan was sitting with a group of foundry men. Jack's fists clenched involuntarily. He wanted to stride across the sawdust strewn floor, pick up the tankard in front of Gertrude's husband and throw the contents in his face before beating seven bells out of him. Logan was short and stocky, with a beergut straining his work clothes at the seams. His face was pinched – narrow eyes and a sullen slit for a mouth. Why would any man pick a fight with a woman? Jack clenched his teeth and swallowed. He hated the thought of that brute climbing on top of Gertrude in the darkness and forcing himself on her. It was strange. When he looked at the woman he didn't find her attractive at all, but their afternoons together were the high points of his life. There was a vulnerability about her that made him want to protect her, to be with her. He told himself it wasn't love. That would be impossible. He could only love one woman. As his thoughts switched to Eliza he felt a stab of pain and guilt.

'What's up with you, Jackie lad? Look as though you've the cares of the world on your shoulders.' The speaker was a regular, Paddy Flanagan, a voluble Irishman, who propped up the bar of the Tudor Crown, night after night.

'Oh, nothing. Just wondering if I need to get another barrel up.' Jack nodded over towards Logan. 'You know that fellow, Paddy? Bill Logan - what's he like?'

'Old Bill? Nasty piece of work if you get on the wrong side of him but a fair man if you work hard and look out for the rest of the crew. Saved the life of a young lad who slipped and almost fell into the furnace a few years back when they were doing maintenance on one of the bells. If Bill hadn't been so quick off the mark the lad would have been roasted alive. Risked his own life to grab him. Another fellow wasn't so lucky and slid right in. Hotter than the fires of hell itself inside a blast furnace.' Paddy crossed himself. 'They fished his remains out but there wasn't much left of him to put in the coffin. Pretty hard on the wife and children. He'd ten little 'uns. We had a whip round but she went and spent all the money on the wake. Ended up on the game, poor lass. Children in the workhouse.'

The man swigged back his pint and handed the mug to

Jack for a refill. 'Have to feel a bit sorry for old Bill though. Married to his first wife for nigh on twenty years and no children. Everyone reckoned Gwen Logan were barren, including Bill himself. Used to slap her around all the time. Then when she kicked the bucket he married a young lass and either he's the unluckiest man in the world to wed two barren women or else he hasn't got what it takes. I know what I think.' He chuckled and leaned forward speaking *sotto voce*. 'My missus has given me seven children and she reckons Bill's wife is no more barren than she is. No, you can't blame his women. There's no lead in his pencil.'

The next time Jack met Gertrude she was quieter than usual. He asked her what was the matter.

'I spoke out of turn, Mr Brennan. It was disloyal of me to speak of my family like that.'

'You can trust me, Gertrude. I'll never tell a soul what you told me, but I'd like to help you.'

She gave him a forced smile. The wind caught her hair, blowing strands out of the loose bun she had pinned up on top of her head. She reached up and tucked it behind her ears.

'You can't help me. And I don't need your help anyway. I told you. I'm no different from half the women in this town. Getting a bit of a slapping every now and then is no more than to be expected. I'll survive. I've managed to put up with the beatings for the past fifteen years, ever since my mother died.'

'Who does your father hit now you've gone?'

She shrugged. 'I wouldn't know. Whoever he has his way with at the back of the Three Dogs on a Saturday night.'

They didn't speak for a while. They were walking along the breakwater at South Gare and the wind off the North Sea made talking almost impossible. When they reached the end of the sea wall they sat down side by side in the shelter of the lighthouse.

Jack reached for her hand but she snatched it away.

'Don't.'

'I'm sorry. I was just…'

'Please. Don't touch me. I don't want to be touched. I don't want us to be like that. I want you to be my friend for talking, for walking, for just being together. Don't spoil it, Mr Brennan.'

'I see.'

'I don't know what I'd do without our meetings. If my husband found out he'd stop me and I couldn't stand that. I count the hours until the next time I see you. Do you understand?'

He looked at her, puzzled, confused. 'I suppose so, but I thought…'

'You are my dearest friend. My only friend. You are the only person I feel I can be myself with. The only person who has ever treated me as a friend, who cares for me. You do care, don't you?'

'I do care for you. Oh I do, Gertrude.'

'The only other person I was close to was my mother. I feel peaceful with you. Do you understand?'

He looked into her eyes, still confused. 'Then why won't you let me hold your hand? That's not much to ask.'

'Mr Brennan, Jack. How can I make you understand? I hate all that. It's what *he* does to me. Touching me. Pawing me. Using my body. It's horrible. I hate it. I don't want it. I love being with you because we can just be. Just be! We don't even need to talk. We're just together. Besides, you're married, and that should make it easier for us to have a friendship that is of the soul, not the body. You're the brother I never had. Please say you understand.'

He picked up a stone and threw it into the roiling sea. 'I understand,' he said. But he didn't.

32

Temperance

Mary Ellen and her eldest daughter, Marian became closer and, by the time Marian was eighteen, they had forged a strong alliance. Their solidarity stemmed from a shared purpose. In defiance of Jack's occupation as a licensed victualler, mother and daughter embraced the growing Temperance movement with zeal. Where once Mary Ellen had stayed upstairs in the family drawing room, banging on the floorboards if the noise from the bar grew too loud, now she and Marian went out every evening to Temperance meetings. They became active members of the League of the Cross, urging total abstinence on everyone they met.

Mary Ellen had been the tallyman's best customer, frittering away money from their limited household budget on knick-knacks that were neither useful nor decorative. She had appeared to equate the accumulation of possessions with her position in society, raging against her humiliating descent down the social ladder. The upstairs parlour had become crammed with items that she had no practical use for – a large empty birdcage: the pair of canaries that had resided therein having perished when she forgot to feed them; three separate sets of china dogs; a Singer sewing machine that she never bothered to find out how to use; a series of empty gilded picture frames – she had never got around to arranging for the family photographic portraits she had intended would fill them. Just as Jack had come to the conclusion that he would be repaying the tallyman for his wife's inessential indulgences for the rest of his life, she stopped spending. She barred the tallyman from the door and neglected the shops that she had once haunted.

Meanwhile, Jack continued to eschew the temptations of alcohol. Standing behind the bar night after night seeing a procession of men drinking away money that by rights should have been taken home and handed over to their wives for feeding and clothing their families, hardened him against alcohol. He felt guilty that the bright lights and roaring fire in the bar acted as a siren's call to men trudging home tired from their labours at the docks, steel mills and iron foundries. As well as the lure of beer and spirits, there was the attraction of the billiards table, where each man had to pay a penny a game, with the loser funding the winner's charge. It was easy enough to notch up serious losses before Jack called time at the end of the evening. He was careful to keep trouble out of the premises, now that the law determined the publican would be liable himself for any public drunkenness. Middlesbrough had a public house on every street so the competition should have been fierce, yet the demand meant that all of them thrived. Whether customers consumed their beer on the premises or carried it home, there was no sign of trade falling away as the town continued to expand.

Mary Ellen and her daughter's growing conviction that the closure of all public houses was an essential element of their campaign against the demon drink, caused inevitable friction. The resentment Jack had felt for his wife causing the ruination of his life, returned with a vengeance. The fact that she was united with the priest's bastard daughter in railing against him deepened his anger.

In response to the constant complaints of the two women, Jack's own drinking began to creep up. The one sociable pint of bitter that he once managed to stretch out through the whole evening was soon supplemented by two or three others, but he was careful to steer clear of the spirits. Every time he put his empty glass under the beer pump and primed it again, the image of his late father would cloud his brain and remind him that drink led to violence. Many mornings he woke feeling thick-headed, tongue furred and stomach churning, and each time he vowed he would lay off the beer that evening. When evening came, these resolutions fled and he grew adept at convincing the little voice of conscience in his head that a drink was deserved – a reward for his hard work.

Drinking was also the means of forgetting. The alcohol flushed away thoughts of the life he might have been having if he had escaped with Eliza, granting him a temporary acceptance of his lot. But his increasing retreat into alcohol was more than matched by Mary Ellen's opposition to it.

One evening as he was getting ready to open up the pub, she and Marian entered the bar, carrying the silk Temperance banners they had been occupied in embroidering for the past six months. Mother and daughter were cloaked and bonneted and ready to set out on their nightly mission to protest outside the taverns of the town.

'Get that stuff out of my bar,' Jack snapped. 'You can take your protests elsewhere.'

'We are committed to visiting every public house in Middlesbrough. Why should this one be an exception?' said Marian

He was polishing glasses behind the bar and slammed one down so hard that it smashed into pieces. He cursed and sucked at the blood that had started to pool on one of his fingers.

'It's drink that puts the food on your table. It's drink that pays for the clothes on your backs.'

'I married you when you were a teacher,' Mary Ellen said. 'I didn't marry a publican. You can always be a teacher again. I'm ashamed every time I see the priest or carry this banner. My own husband is shaming the family and the church by encouraging people to drink.'

'I don't encourage anyone to drink. It's still a free country as far as I know. If people choose to forget about their miserable lives by paying for a bit of comfort then who am I to stand in their way?'

'If this place were closed they couldn't drink here,' she said.

'If this place were closed they'd cross the street and drink in the White Horse.'

'Look, Father, we have to make a stand.'

It was rare that Marian addressed him directly and he hated it when it she referred to him as Father. He could hardly tell the girl to desist; nor could he reveal the truth of her parentage, but as always when he looked at her he felt the familiar anger bubbling inside him. Years of Mary Ellen's sermonising and the constant undermining of his role as breadwinner by his wife and daughter had worn him down. He looked at them and felt a burst of defiance.

'Make a stand? I'll make a stand.' He reached behind him and grabbed a glass and poured a large measure of whisky into it, downing it one. It felt good and he filled the glass again.

'Are you happy now, the pair of you? There's at least one man in this town you've driven to drink. You're like a pair of cockerels that won't stop crowing. Well, you can go and do your crowing elsewhere. This is a public house and my customers will be arriving any minute and they don't want to look at those banners and your sour, sanctimonious faces.'

Mary Ellen opened her mouth to respond, but Marian took her mother by the sleeve and led her towards the door.

That was all it took. One whisky led to another and Jack

soon became accustomed to drinking steadily throughout the evening.

Jack wasn't expecting Mary Ellen to lose her previously voracious appetite for sex, so it came as a surprise when it happened. It was one thing to accept the offer of his wife's body the way that he had done throughout the years of their marriage, and quite another for Jack to seek her out and demand his conjugal rights. His pride was too great for that, so he lay alone in bed, conjuring images of Eliza as he tried to satisfy himself, remembering how, when he was a small boy, his mother had warned him against fiddling with himself for fear of madness or blindness. He wondered whether he should seek the services of a prostitute – a simple financial transaction for services rendered. There were enough women who would be only too ready to oblige, not only the professionals, but housewives and widows who were struggling to put bread on the table – why not return some of the money their menfolk spent in his bar? While he no longer went to Mass, a lifetime of being indoctrinated by the church was enough for him to fear that this would be a sin too far.

He went to the doctor, embarrassed as he tried to explain his predicament. 'My wife,' he said, 'no longer wants to have children and has closed the bedroom door.'

The doctor nodded. 'How old are you, Mr Brennan?'

'Thirty-nine.'

'Still a young man then. It's unlikely the urges will pass for some time yet, even if they have in your wife. She's younger I presume? How many children?'

'My wife is fifty. We have six living children. Two died as infants and two were still born.'

'I can perhaps see why Mrs Brennan is reluctant to continue with her matrimonial duties. A woman does get tired, I suppose. Nonetheless, Mr Brennan, you are completely within your rights to demand that she permits you to fulfil your duty as a husband or, if she refuses, to take her by force. But I presume since you are sitting here you have already ruled that out of the question?'

Jack nodded.

'Yes, some men do have qualms about such matters. Can't say I understand myself. A wife has little enough to do that she should wish to withhold from her husband what's rightfully his. It's a well known fact that most women are untroubled by sexual desire of any kind and so gentlemen often have no alternative but to force the issue. Times are changing and not for the better in my view. So, Mr Brennan, if you are not prepared to persuade your wife, it appears to me that you have little choice in this matter. There are but two options. Abstinence or seeking satisfaction outside the matrimonial home. Self-pleasuring must be avoided at all costs. It is now an undisputed fact that masturbation leads to insanity, physical weakness and flabbiness of the body and frequently brings on consumption.'

'There's no medicine you can give me for my wife? To make her willing to do it again?'

'Alas, no. I would be a very wealthy man if I could lay my hands on a potion such as that. My advice to you, sir, is to try to curb your urges by taking regular exercise. When the need to relieve your desires becomes overwhelming, discreetly seek out a woman who can provide you with what you need. Make sure you choose a clean woman, free of disease. The old adage *"You get what you pay for"* is as relevant in financial transactions such as this as in buying a horse.

Jack tried it just once. She was a woman who had come into the Tudor Crown a few times in the past to try to encourage her husband to return home at the end of a long drinking bout. The husband in question was now off sick from the ironworks, suffering from blood poisoning. The lack of wages coming into the already straitened home caused the woman to seek alternative means of feeding the family during his illness.

She approached Jack in the street when he was returning to the Tudor Crown before opening time.

'Mr Brennan?'

He turned to look at her, surprised.

'My husband's one of your regulars but he's been off sick for three weeks already and no sign of him going back. Money's tight. I thought he were paying his dibs into the sick club every week but turns out he wasn't. I'm desperate, Mr Brennan. I'll take on any work. Do you have any cleaning jobs going? I'm a hard worker.'

'I'm sorry. We already employ a cleaner.'

'Look. I'm also willing to do a bit of *the other*, you know? You get my meaning? I don't want to stop people on the street. But if you hear any gentlemen in your pub saying they want some *you know what*, maybe you could send them round to our house? It's 21 Nelson Street. Needs to be late – after the pubs close. Don't want the neighbours knowing. I'd be ever so grateful. I'm a good wife. I hate to be doing this. But things are really bad. I have to feed my kids.'

Her despair was palpable and Jack felt sorry for her. She had a pretty face but it was pale and lined and she was painfully thin. He asked her if he might call on her himself that night after he'd shut the tavern and she looked so grateful he felt even more guilty about what he was about to do.

He knocked on the door to her small two-up-two-down terraced house and she showed him into a tiny, cold room. He could smell the damp in the air and the grate was empty.

Jack looked around him at the bare room. Barely a stick of furniture. It was clear she had started to pawn their possessions. 'Where?' was all he could say.

'Here,' she said. 'There's nowhere else. The children are

upstairs.' She nodded towards a door at the rear. 'My husband's sleeping in there. But it's all right. He knows what I'm doing. He knows we've no option.'

She lay down on the floor and lifted her skirts up and spread her legs wide. 'Hurry up. I hope you're not one of the noisy ones. I don't want Fred to wake or the kids to come down.'

He hesitated, shame at what he was doing welling up inside him. How had it come to this? He looked down at her. Her fair hair was matted and dirty and her eyes were sad. For a moment he thought of leaving the money on the table and walking out of the house, but he knelt down between her open legs and lowered himself onto her body and took her there quickly on the dirty kitchen floor. When it was over and he was hurrying away, head bowed, down the street, he realised he hadn't even asked her what her name was.

33
The Seduction

Jack vowed he would never again seek sex from a prostitute or a despairing mother. Uncertain what to do, he considered seeking the counsel of Father Reilly. He brushed aside the fact that the man was O'Driscoll's cousin, instead remembering that, when he had talked to him in the confessional box, he had been down to earth and practical.

Since he had stopped going to church, Jack's only contact with Father Reilly was when the priest called in at the Tudor Crown. Mary Ellen had insisted he come to bless the house and during Lent invited him to their home to say the mysteries of the rosary with the family. These visits were outside licensed hours but Jack always excused himself, although always showing courtesy to the Irishman. He felt embarrassed, being in the company of the priest and Mary Ellen, remembering what he had told the man about their marital relations, in the confessional box.

Occasionally the priest dropped into the public bar for a pint of ale.

'I don't hold with all that temperance nonsense, Jack. A little bevvie in moderation never did anyone any harm. I don't approve of men getting blind drunk but we shouldn't be trying to shut down the public houses. That's punishing the many for the sins of the few. All due respects to Mrs Brennan and your daughter, Jack, but you'll not be seeing me carrying a banner through Market Square any day soon.'

Every time he saw Jack, the priest would say the same thing. 'And will I be seeing you at Mass on Sunday, Jack?'

And every time Jack would offer the same reply. 'Not this Sunday, Father.'

Jack knew he couldn't bear to have sex the way he had done on that kitchen floor again. It had felt like exploitation. He knew the woman was grateful for his money but it had been sordid and humiliating for both of them. Perhaps with a proper prostitute it might be easier. The *toffers,* as the better class of prostitutes were known, used private rooms to conduct their business with their more affluent clients. He could never take a woman in a dark alley, behind the pub, or at the back of the railway station as he knew so many men in the town did – he would never do what O'Driscoll had done with Mary Ellen, a quick and furtive "*thrupenny upright*" against a brick wall.

He got as far as the church door and stood on the threshold looking at the rows of kneeling women and the few men, waiting their turn in the confessional. These people were about to share their innermost secrets with Father Reilly. Telling this unmarried Irishman about their money troubles, their petty jealousies, their lust, their anger. Seeking his counsel on all these matters. Begging him to intercede on their behalf with God. As Jack watched them going in and out of the curtained box, his jaw began to ache. No wonder people were in thrall to the Catholic church when it allowed them to go out and sin all week, only to be fully absolved in the confessional box in exchange for a few Hail Marys. *Go in peace your sins are forgiven. Ego te absolvo a peccatis tuis in nomine Patris, et Filii, et Spiritus Sancti.* Men like Bill Logan who beat up their wives then asked for absolution only to go out and do it again.

He breathed in the lingering smell of incense from last night's Benediction. What was he thinking? It was a folly. He must be deluded. Asking the advice of a celibate man about sex? Jack walked away from the church, hands thrust in his pockets.

There was only one solution. He realised he'd known it all along. He must take a mistress.

There was only one candidate. Now he needed to work out how he was going to convince Gertrude. He walked alone along the sand dunes, mulling the idea over. He didn't love her, nor did he suppose she loved him. That meant he wouldn't be hurting her. They would each embark upon the affair with their eyes open. She owed no fidelity to that brute of a husband. Hadn't she told him many times how much she hated him?.

But there was the matter of her refusal to let Jack touch her. It was not going to be possible to touch her or kiss her and let one thing lead to another. He wondered if her sensibilities on this count reflected a coldness in her, a lack of feeling. She'd already told him she didn't want him to touch her at all. She hated the idea of sex. But surely making love with him would be a very different proposition to having to endure it with her fat old husband? Yes, he reasoned. He'd be doing her a favour – showing her that she could after all have pleasure with a man. She would be grateful to him. They would find comfort in each other.

Eventually he decided there was only one way to set about it. He would have to be honest with Gertrude – appeal to her reason. He would tell her what he proposed and then set about convincing her to agree to his plan. It would not be straightforward. It would require patience. It might take some time.

It was a Thursday afternoon. The first dry day after weeks of rain. After not seeing Gertrude for so long he had missed her. He missed her smile, her open countenance – her expression that reflected her trust in him. The way she said exactly what she felt without dressing it up.

As he walked along the pathway towards Coatham Sands, he felt his heart racing and his walking pace speeding up at the thought of seeing Gertrude again, of beginning his seduction of her. Why did he feel this way when he didn't love her? Didn't even really desire her? Not the way he'd desired Eliza. He certainly wouldn't have picked her out in a crowd. And yet, she had a way with her. A wild spirit that drew him to her. Her love for the sea, for the sky, for the birds. Her visceral hatred of the town and what it represented.

He was nervous at the prospect of making love to Gertrude. Perhaps a bit guilty? He wouldn't be planning to seduce her if there was any alternative. And he'd be doing her a favour, wouldn't he? Showing her that sex was not always unpleasant and to be endured.

As he walked on, the image of Eliza appeared before him. He was about to betray her. Having sex with Mary Ellen hadn't counted. He'd had no choice about that. The quick fuck on the floor with the stevedore's wife didn't count either. He'd felt nothing. It was just a transaction. Expediency. But making love to Gertrude would be different. He may not love her but he did care for her. She was his friend. His confidante. Eliza wouldn't like that. That would be a kind of betrayal. But then hadn't he already betrayed Eliza by allowing this secret friendship with Gertrude to flourish?

He reached the beach but there was no sign of her. He looked back towards the town and saw her coming towards him, her figure silhouetted against the skyline as she walked along the Gare. The smoke stacks rose behind her, the plumes of smoke from the foundry chimneys blowing sideways in the wind like ostrich feathers in a fancy hat.

She is a good woman, he thought. Don't hurt her.

They walked for half an hour, then sat down side by side in the lee of a wall.

'I brought you some bread and jam,' she said. 'The jam's homemade. Remember I picked some blackberries, last time we met?'

He opened the waxed paper-wrapped parcel and bit into the bread and jam with a hunger he hadn't realised he was feeling.

'Good,' he said. 'Sweet but with a bit of a tang.' He looked at her and added, 'Like you.'

She frowned. 'Don't talk like that, Jack. I don't like it. We never talk that way. We don't need that.'

'Need what? I don't understand.'

'That flirting stuff. It doesn't sound sincere and I don't like it. It's shallow and meaningless.'

'I was just trying to be nice.'

'Nice!' Her tone was scornful. 'I don't want nice. Talk to me properly or don't talk at all.'

He sat in silence for a few moments. A large flock of dunlins flew past and landed in the field behind them, digging for insects in the sandy soil. He listened to their cries: a series of light, high-pitched squeaks, insistent, then a softer more plaintive note. Their sound was sad and intensified the loneliness of the place. Jack looked around them and could see no one. Just the two of them, the diminishing sands of the beach, the gunmetal grey sea, flecked with white as the tide rose towards them, and the dozens of hungry birds.

He took a deep breath then said, 'I need you to help me, Gertrude.'

'Help you? How can I help you?'

'I've ruined my life, Gertrude.'

'Don't be silly. You've plenty to be thankful for.'

'I've nothing. It's all wrong. I never wanted to be in this town. I'm stuck in a job I don't want to do. I'm married to a woman I never wanted to marry. I have an empty meaningless life.'

'What do you want then?' she asked.

'I want you to help me.'

'I can't help you, Jack, you have to help yourself. You have to believe in yourself. I believe in you, but I don't think *you* believe in you. If things aren't working out the way you wanted them then you have to change them. Either that or make the best of what you've got. Look around this town and you see people facing far worse every day than you'll ever face. Maybe you should count your blessings.'

This wasn't working out the way he hoped. He decided to try a different tack.

'Have you ever loved anyone, Gertrude? I know you don't love your husband. You told me that. But has there ever been anyone else?'

'Why do you ask?' Her voice sounded brittle, nervy.

'Because it's important we're honest with each other.'

'If you want me to be honest you must be honest too. You go first,' she said.

'Very well. Yes, I have been in love.'

She said nothing for a moment, gathering the fabric of her skirt in her hand and crushing the cloth under her fingers. Then she turned to look at him. 'And are you in love now?'

'I am,' he said.

'But not with your wife?' Gertrude looked down, her hands nervously pulling the fabric of her dress down over the top of her boots, a smile playing about her lips. 'Oh, Jack, I don't know what to say.'

Her voice was tremulous, but Jack didn't seem to notice. He went on. 'Her name is Eliza and I will always love her. I may never see her again but I will love her until I die.'

Gertrude gave a little choked cry. 'Why are you telling me this?' Her voice was strange, strained.

'Because I want you to know all about me. Because you are my friend. My true friend. My only friend.'

'And this Eliza? Is she not your friend?'

'Of course. More than friend to me. But she is far away from here. Gone forever. In America.'

'And you still love her?'

'Of course. I love her with all my heart and soul. I promised myself to her. We were separated from each other against our wills and I was pushed into marriage with my wife. Not a single day goes by when I don't think of Eliza. I know I may never see her again but I can't stop loving her. She's everything to me.'

'Everything?'

He nodded, oblivious to her distress. 'It's the tragedy of my life. Being torn from her. Being separated for ever. I know she feels the same.'

'You write to her then?' Gertrude's voice was barely a whisper.

'No. I don't know where she is. I've written poems about her. To her. Dozens of them. One day I pray she will read them and know how I feel. But I know they're not good enough. They don't do her justice. No matter how hard I tried. So I've stopped writing them now.'

She swallowed and brushed tears from her eyes. 'The wind is strong today,' she said.

Jack was blind to her wretchedness. 'Now it's your turn. Have you ever been in love?'

She was silent. Jack pushed her shoulder gently with his own. 'Come on. Tell me, Gertrude.'

She sighed. Pulled her knees up and hunched her shoulders down, resting her chin on her knees as she stared out to sea. 'I thought I was in love once, but not any more.'

'Did he love you?'

'He did not.'

'Foolish man.'

'Perhaps. I know now that he was a vain man. A clever man. But I can see now he lacked imagination. He was incapable of entering into another person's feelings and understanding them.'

'Then he didn't deserve you.'

She shivered. 'It's getting cold. I should be getting back.' As she stood up the flock of dunlins rose as one and flew off. Jack reached for her hand and pulled her back down beside him.

'Since we are both disappointed in love, why don't we find some consolation in each other?' He pulled her into his arms and kissed her before she could stop him.

Gertrude pulled away from him and pushed him back against the wall. 'What are you doing? What are you thinking of?'

He reached for her again. 'Please, Gertrude. Neither of us has any happiness in our marriages so it's only natural that we should look for comfort with each other. There's no one to get hurt. My wife no longer shares a bed with me and you've told me your husband's embraces are not welcomed by you. What harm is there? And I want you, Gertrude. I really want you. You can make me so happy.'

'You don't love me.'

'Don't you see? That's why it's perfect. That's why we should do this. We like and respect each other and we will make no demands on each other.'

'You're making demands now.'

'Not demands! We mean so much to each other. We share so much. Why not this too? Please, Gertrude, if you care for me at all, please let me have you. Please let me touch you. This is how you can help me. Let me hold you in my arms and make love to you. I promise I won't hurt you. I'm not like your husband. It will be different. I swear to you. Please, if you care for me at all, do this for me?'

'You want to use me?'

'No, I want us to use each other. I want it for you too. I want to give you pleasure.'

'Pleasure?' Her voice was a sneer. 'And what about this woman you love, this Eliza? What would she think of what you are proposing?'

He turned his face away from her. 'She wouldn't like it. But she would understand. She wouldn't want me to suffer like this. She wouldn't want me to be in pain. She would forgive me. I have tried and tried to be faithful to her memory, but I am a man and I have needs. It's different for women. I believe she would understand.'

'And me? Why should I do this?'

'Because you too understand me, Gertrude. Because you are a woman of great understanding. Because we like each other. Because you can help me. Help make my life a little better. Help to take away some of the misery. Don't you want to make me happy? I want to make you happy.'

He leaned into her and cupped one of her breasts in his hands and squeezed it gently. 'Like this.' He placed his other hand on her leg, under her skirts, and began stroking her thigh, moving his hand higher. 'And this'

She didn't resist, but made a choked sound that he took to be desire. He pushed her back onto the sand beneath the wall. 'Thank you, my dear Gertrude, thank you.'

She let him do what he wanted with her, lying under him, unmoving. After it was over he took a small tin from his pocket and rolled himself a cigarette, watching her as she pulled her clothing together.

He stood up and held his arms open. 'Come here. Let me hold you a moment,' he said.

She moved towards him.

'You have saved my life,' he said. 'I needed that so much. Meeting you is the best thing to happen to me since I came to Middlesbrough years ago. I knew you would help me, dear friend.'

285

Gertrude stood unmoving while he held her. He stroked her hair and tucked the stray strands behind her ears and kissed the top of her head. 'You're a good woman, Gertrude.'

When he released her from his hold she stepped away from him, gathering her shawl about her. 'You've spoiled it all. You've wrecked everything. But you're too selfish to understand why.'

Jack screwed up his eyes in puzzlement. 'What do you mean? You wanted it too.'

'I never wanted it. Not like that. And I never want it again. Before now, I had dreams. You have stolen my dreams.'

She swung her arm around, pointing down the beach. 'All this too. You've spoiled all this for me. Being here was all I had. Being here! This place was my refuge. I shared it with you and now you've ruined it. I can't come back again. I've nowhere now. I hope you're happy.'

'Gertrude! What are you talking about?'

'I loved you. Really loved you. You were too stupid to even notice. Too wrapped up in yourself. I'm ashamed that I let myself be hoodwinked by you and your charm. Then when you trampled over my feelings, flaunting your love for another woman, I saw you as if for the first time. I was no longer blind. You're a selfish man, Jack Brennan.'

Jack was stunned. He swept his hair back from his brow and stared at her, shaking his head. 'But why? Why did you let me?'

'Surely you don't think I wanted it? I let you do it to punish myself. To hurt myself so that I'd never ever forget how stupid I've been. I wanted to know if you were so unseeing and uncaring that you'd still have your way with me, even though I didn't want it. And you were. You looked very satisfied with yourself afterwards. I don't suppose you even care how it was for me. Well, I'll tell you anyway. It was horrible. Worse than with my husband. He puts the food on the table and the clothes on my back so it's only fair he expects to get something in return. But having you use my body for your own pleasure with no regard to my feelings was the worst thing. After telling me about your love for another woman. A woman you know you'll never see again. If you cared so deeply for her why didn't you go after her? Tell me that, Jack? Why? You're a weak man. Passive. You allow the world to shape you. You do nothing to shape it yourself. But you've succeeded in doing one thing. You have broken my heart. Goodbye, Jack. Don't come near me again.'

Half running, she stumbled along the beach. Jack stood rooted to the spot, watching her until she disappeared, swallowed up by the soot-stained bricks of the town.

34
Repercussions

All the way back into town Jack puzzled over Gertrude's reaction. She had let him have his way with her – how was he to know that she didn't want to make love? He thought they were both seeking comfort in each other. A convenient arrangement. And he'd had no clue that she was in love with him. She had given no hint. She had been a friend to him, never coquettish. How was he expected to read her mind?.

He walked on, quickening his pace, feeling more aggrieved with every step. Gertrude's behaviour was unreasonable. She was an intelligent woman so should understand that he could never offer her love when that was reserved for Eliza alone – but why not share some pleasure, intimacy, closeness? He was, after all, fond of her. He liked her. Very much. Why was that not enough for her?

He would give her a few days to calm down, then call on her to make peace. Perhaps he'd rushed her. If they returned to their platonic friendship he could smooth things over and maybe after a while she'd come round. He just needed to be patient.

When he got home that evening, Mary Ellen, unusually, was standing in the bar waiting for him.

'There's a gentleman coming to see you this evening and I want you to be polite to him.'

'I'm a publican, Mary Ellen, we're polite to everyone. Unless they're mafficking or causing bother.'

'Mr Vickers won't be doing any of that. He's in the League of the Cross. And he doesn't want to enter a public house so he'll knock at the back door at about seven and you're to bring him upstairs to the parlour.'

'And why should I be doing that? I've no truck with your Temperance friends trying to put me out of business. If you weren't so daft you'd have worked that one out.'

She ignored the barbed comment. 'He's coming to ask for consent to marry Marian.'

'He doesn't need to ask me. He's welcome to her. If he wants permission he'd better bugger off to Bristol and ask that old priest.'

'Don't be uncouth, Jack Brennan. You're a disgrace. Mr Vickers is a good Catholic and he's doing what you were supposed to be doing. He's a schoolmaster.'

'Bully for him.'

'Jack!' She narrowed her eyes. 'Don't you dare bring up those lies about not being Marian's father.'

There was no point in arguing with her. Long ago he had accepted that Mary Ellen had re-cast her own story.

He sighed. 'Very well. I'll see the lad.'

When Jack opened the door to Malcolm Vickers he realised it was no lad who was asking for the girl's hand. The man looked a few years older than Jack. He was tall with a slight stoop, clean shaven and wearing a pair of round, horn-rimmed spectacles.

They sat down in the empty parlour. Jack was about to offer him a drink, but remembered there was no point. The man was a teetotaller and Jack wasn't going to offer a peppermint cordial to someone who was set upon undermining his livelihood.

'You know why I'm here, Mr Brennan?'

Jack shook his head, determined not to make things easy.

The man coughed, and Jack thought he looked annoyed. Good.

'I'd like to marry your daughter.'

'Which one? I have several. Although I think Clementina may be a little young for you. Come to think of it, they all may be a little young for you.'

Vickers gave another nervous cough. 'I'm forty-six. I've never been married. I spent ten years in a seminary in Ireland but before I was ordained I realised that God had not blessed me with a vocation so I became a teacher. I am employed at the Reformatory of Saint Dominic near Northallerton. The boys there are all sinners but we pray that by the good example of the Brothers they will salvage some small good in their misbegotten lives. I have put by some money and feel that the time has come when my work there would benefit from having a wife, a helpmate, someone who can share in my life's mission. I believe that Miss Brennan will be most suitable.'

'And what does Miss Brennan think?'

'I thought it best to seek your consent as her father before asking her.'

'How do you think Marian will feel about living in a home for criminal boys?'

'I believe she will view it as I do. As a means of bringing sinners closer to God. Miss Brennan has all the qualities to make a good Catholic wife. She is devout, sincere and tireless in her work for the League of the Cross.'

'Take her then. If she'll have you. I'll not stand in your way.'

The man looked astonished at his abruptness.

'I'm needed downstairs soon. I've a pub to run. It may have escaped your notice, Mr Vickers, but this family is supported by the proceeds of liquor sales. I'll get her in here and you can ask her.'

He called out and Marian entered the room with Mary Ellen in tow.

Jack spoke first. 'You know why Mr Vickers is here?'

The girl shook her head. Jack turned to Vickers who was standing in the middle of the room, frozen like a startled deer. Jack sighed. The poor fellow would have done well to have a large whisky first to whet his courage.

'He wants to marry you. Will you have him?'

She looked up and nodded, dropping her head again quickly, but Jack thought he detected a smirk on her face.

Jack sat on the steps of the parish hall and ran his hand round his collar. It was too tight and the day was unusually hot. He reached in his pocket, pulled out a hip flask and took a long slug of scotch.

Mary Ellen had made it clear that this was to be a completely dry wedding, serving only tea and cordials. That morning when she saw him filling the flask she had tried to wrestle it from his hands.

'One day. Just one day. Can't you do without the drink for one single day? For your daughter's wedding. For our eldest.'

'My eldest child is Jane, now the boys are gone.'

'Stop that!' She looked around, terrified that someone might overhear, but the bar was empty.

Now here he was, forced to lurk outside to imbibe a tot. He hadn't wanted to be there at all, but Mary Ellen threw one of her tantrums, screaming at him, insisting that he give Marian away. The ceremony brought back the nightmare of his own marriage, twenty years earlier and it was as much as he could do not to take a drink in the church itself.

Now sitting here, he let himself wallow in self pity. If God existed he was a cruel and merciless deity. What had he done to deserve the life he had been given? Losing the only woman he could ever love, losing the only profession he wanted to follow, living in this godforsaken town, forced to play the role of father to the bastard daughter of a priest – the very man who had ruined him.

He took another swig, and brushed the hair out of his eyes, blinking in the sun, then closed his eyes and leaned back against the stone steps.

He opened his eyes to see Clementina, his youngest, sitting beside him. She said nothing. Just slipped her tiny hand into his and leaned her head against him.

'Why are you all on your own, Dadda?'

'I just needed a bit of air, Clemmie, love.'

'Will you tell me a story, Dadda? The one about the naughty boy who ran away from home.'

'Come here, lass.' He lifted her onto his lap and stroked her hair.

Clementina. The only one of his children who had managed to get under his skin. The only one he'd lay down his life for. The only one who understood him without question, deaf to her mother's often-voiced criticisms of him. Clementina, who had inspired a fierce love in him, without even trying.

He had tried to see Gertrude: night after night for several weeks after their last meeting he'd slipped out of the Tudor Crown and gone round to her home in Lawson Street, stepping into the narrow alleyway behind the houses and knocking on her back-door. He knew she was inside but she didn't answer and he was afraid of causing a scene and alerting the neighbours. After a few weeks he gave up.

There was a limit to how much pride a man could swallow.

One evening, a few weeks after Marian's wedding and six months after his argument in the sand dunes with Gertrude, Jack had just unlocked the doors to the pub and was polishing glasses behind the bar, when his first customer of the night, Paddy Flanagan, appeared.

'Give me a pint, landlord, and one for yourself,' said the Irishman. 'It's a bad business that's gone off, isn't it?'

'Lost on the horses again, have you, Paddy?'

'No. Haven't you heard?' He nodded towards the empty corner table, where Bill Logan usually sat. 'What's happened with old Bill.'

'What about him?'

'Arrested. They took him away this morning. He's to stand trial at the assizes in Newcastle for murdering his wife.'

Jack continued to pump the beer, oblivious to the fact that it was spilling over onto the floor.

'Yes. Shocking. You could have knocked me down with a feather too, Jack. Hey – I think that pint's poured, mate!' Paddy reached for the brimming tankard. 'I know Bill had a temper and word was he used to knock his woman around, but I'd never have thought he'd go so far as to do her in.'

'He's killed her?' Jack leaned against the counter for support.

'Beat the living daylights out of her. Poor soul. The neighbours are feeling bad, I can tell you. They heard her screaming but did nothing. Reckoned it happened quite a lot. It was only this morning when she didn't open the door to clean the step that they went round to check. Looked through the window and saw her. Lying in the hearth, covered in blood. He'd kicked her in the belly and hit her over the head with a poker. Knocked the bells of Shannon out of her. Her skull was all stoved in. Hey, you all right, landlord?'

Jack turned away from the bar and was sick in the sink.

'Good lord, Jackie boy, you've a weak constitution. Did you know the lady?'

Jack wiped his mouth on his sleeve. He shook his head. He couldn't frame a response. He wanted to push Paddy Flanagan out of the bar and slam the bolts of the door shut, but he knew he couldn't. Dead. How could she be dead? Not possible. A mistake. Wrong, wrong, wrong.

Two men entered the pub and greeted Paddy.

'I was just telling Jack here about what happened over in Lawson Street.'

'Terrible. My missus said it was because she'd been doing the deed with another man.'

'Usual story.'

'Can't blame old Bill then. He'd not stand for another fellow tupping his wife. Who can blame him?'

'How did he find out? Did he catch the blackguard?'

'Seems she were up the duff. And we all know that can't have been on account of old Bill. Married to two women for more than thirty years and never managed to put a bun in either oven. Bridget Bailey who lives next door to them says Gertrude were trying to hide it but at six months the penny finally dropped with Bill that she wasn't just eating too many pies!'

The men all laughed. Jack could feel the sweat on his face.

'Can't say as I'm surprised she had a fancy man,' said Paddy. 'Bill was more than thirty years older than her. A young healthy woman like that. Stands to reason she'd be getting it elsewhere if he couldn't hoist the mainsail!'

They all laughed again.

'Not that she was much to look at.'

'No oil painting for sure.'

'Still, she had a nice pair of diddeys.'

'And you don't look at the mantelpiece when you're poking the fire.'

Jack flung the cloth down and rushed out of the bar.

'What's up with the landlord then, Bob?' someone asked the tapman.

The coroner examined the body and confirmed that the victim was carrying a child. Logan was charged not only with the murder of his wife but also of his unborn baby. When he read this in the newspaper, Jack felt sick with the knowledge that it was his child. One quick fuck in the sand for him to make her conceive a child, after more than ten years of Logan trying. One quick fuck in the sand was also the cost of Gertrude's life and probably Logan's too by the time the courts finished with him. Jack didn't want to think about it, didn't want to accept that it was true. He kept hoping that it was all a terrible nightmare and he would wake from it.

Gertrude's funeral was paid for by the parish. Jack didn't go to the service, which by all accounts was packed. Nothing like a good murder to pull in the crowds. While the rumours continued to circulate about Gertrude's infidelity and the paternity of her unborn child, they didn't appear to have reached the presbytery and the general consensus was that Mrs Logan was the hapless victim of a belligerent and drunken husband. This view was widely propagated by the League of the Cross and the Temperance League who held a joint rally to draw out the lessons on the evil consequences of drink.

Jack didn't go to Logan's trial either. He knew he wouldn't be able to bear hearing the gory details of Gertrude's death and he didn't want to see the man in the dock. There had been a half-hearted attempt to reduce the charge to involuntary manslaughter while of unsound mind but, as the cause of his loss of reason was assumed to be alcohol, this went nowhere.

The day Logan was hanged, Jack drank as though the temperance campaigners had won the battle and alcohol would no longer be available. He got through a whole bottle of whisky. He drank to forget, trying to sluice away the knowledge that he had been the cause of Gertrude's death. Bill Logan may have been the one who wielded the poker that cracked open her skull, and whose hobnailed boots had kicked to death the baby in her swollen belly, but Jack knew that Gertrude would still be alive if he had not seduced her on the beach that wintry afternoon.

He kept trying to make sense of what had occurred. She had lain down, opened her legs and let him take her. What could he have assumed other than that she wanted it as much as he did? Why hadn't she told him she was expecting his child? Now she was dead he wished he had persisted in his efforts to see her again. He had given up too easily.

If only she'd told him she was expecting his child, he could have run away with her. Couldn't he? Wouldn't he?.

But he knew he wouldn't. She would have known that too.

He was haunted by the picture of her trying to keep the pregnancy a secret from her husband. Perhaps she had attempted to abort it? Jack clenched his teeth. He didn't want to think about it. He wanted to close his eyes and forget he had ever met Gertrude Logan. The only way to forget was to drink. The amnesia didn't last long but it helped for a while.

The nightmares were the worst part. Rather than Gertrude, he would be lying in the sand dunes with Eliza, making love, her body yielding, soft, tender, excited, moving under him – then as they climaxed together her body changed. Hard, cold, heavy-limbed, broken, bloodied. Dead eyes open in a smashed and battered face – Gertrude's eyes, sad, accusatory, disappointed. He would wake, tangled in sweat-soaked sheets in the small hours, unable to fall asleep again, night after night – until he discovered that if he was heavily drunk he fell into a sleep more akin to a coma.

Late one night when he locked the pub and stumbled up the stairs, Mary Ellen was standing on the landing, waiting for him. He slumped against the wall, pushing his hair out of his eyes and struggling to focus.

'You're drunk.'

He said nothing, just leaned against the wall as the floor rose up to meet him.

'You should be ashamed, Jack Brennan. You're a holy show. Don't you care that you're setting a terrible example to your daughters? Don't you care that you're shaming us all? You're blind drunk. How do you think it feels that everyone in the League knows my own husband is a drunk?'

'How do you think I feel that my wife is trying to get us thrown out of our home and me out of a job?' His words were slurred.

She curled her lip in disgust. 'Then you'd have to get a proper job. Become respectable, not a common landlord who serves liquor to men while their families go hungry. Your daughters and I could go into church without bowing our heads in shame.'

He laughed an ugly, hollow laugh. 'You're as likely to hang your head in shame as the Pope is to come to Middlesbrough and run naked round Albert Park. Shame's never been high on your list, has it? You've never felt it and you've never shown it. Not even when you let that old devil of a priest shove you up against the wall and grind away. Not even when you let your father force me to marry you when I was committed to someone else. Or when you hitched your nightgown up and forced yourself on me.' He jerked his head and the sudden movement caught him off balance and he slumped back against the landing wall.

Mary Ellen's face was rigid with pent up rage. 'You're my

husband. It was your duty to give me children.' She hissed the words through clenched teeth as she choked back the tears. 'Be quiet or the girls will hear.'

'So you do have some shame? You don't want them to know that their mother is a hussy who lifted her petticoats for the parish priest. Have you told that to Father Reilly in the confessional yet? What would your sainted son-in-law think if he knew Marian was a priest's bastard?'

She lunged at him, but in his drunkenness, he slithered down the wall to the floor. Her momentum carried her forward. She tripped on his legs, which were stretched out in front of him, and hurtled over him down the stairs.

She screamed as she was falling, then crashed to the bottom of the stairs, landing in a crumpled heap at the bottom. The noise brought Ursula and Alice onto the landing.

'What's happened, Papa? What was that noise?'

He looked up at his daughters standing side by side in their nightdresses, then looked down the stairs to where their mother lay limp, splayed out on the floor like a discarded rag doll. Ursula stepped over him and pattered barefoot down the stairs.

'Oh dear Lord, I think she's broken her neck. She's dead. Oh, Mama.' Her words turned to a cry of fear.

Jack remembered little of the rest of that night. There was a flow of people in and out of the pub - neighbours, the Mintoes, the doctor, a pair of policemen and Father Reilly. Someone sent word to the Reformatory to break the news to Marian. Through it all, Jack nursed his aching head and tried to piece together what had happened. He told the police he and Mary Ellen were going up to bed and she had slipped at the top of the stairs and fallen. Alice and Ursula, if they had heard the arguing, said nothing, but he felt the pressure of their silent judgment.

When Marian arrived in the early hours of the morning

with her husband, she saw at once that Jack was drunk. After looking at the body of her mother, now laid out on tables in the saloon bar, she turned on him.

'If you hadn't been drunk you could have saved her. You could have caught her before she fell.'

'Now, now, Marian,' said the parish priest, 'You can't say that. You weren't even here. Those are steep stairs and the wood is very worn and slippery. Accidents happen.'

'He forced her to live in this filthy den of iniquity. My poor mother hated it. She couldn't bear living above a public house, breathing in the stink of beer every day. It's all his fault.'

Malcolm Vickers took his wife by the arm and led her away, nodding to Jack as they left.

He lost his licence. The police and the town council acknowledged that there was no evidence of foul play, but Jack's evident inebriation was enough for them to determine he was not to be entrusted with a liquor licence. He heard the news the day before Mary Ellen's funeral.

It was a bitter blow. He'd come to enjoy life as a landlord. As well as the ready access to alcohol he'd liked the banter with the men who gathered at the bar each night. It had been a welcome escape from Mary Ellen as she had rarely ventured into the public rooms. The temptation was to walk away, to leave Middlesbrough at last. To set off for America. He might never find Eliza but he might find a new life, a new sense of purpose.

Tempting as the idea of flight was, Jack knew he had to face his responsibilities. He had three daughters at home, depending on him. He couldn't just leave them.

He stood at the open graveside as Mary Ellen's coffin was lowered. The woman whom he blamed for the complete ruination of his life was gone forever. It had happened so quickly. He'd not intended for her to fall, but now that it had happened he silently cursed that he had not thought of this as a way to dispose of her years ago. As the sods of earth tumbled onto the lid of the coffin he imagined how different his life would have been if he had pushed her down the stairs soon after they'd arrived at the Tudor Crown. He fought the urge to spit on the coffin.

Malcolm Vickers approached him as they walked away from the graveside. 'Mr Brennan, I understand you're leaving the Tudor Crown?'

Jack looked at his son-in-law, suspecting that the man was crowing over his ignominious dismissal. 'They're looking for another landlord, but we can stay on until they find one.'

'What will you do?'

'Do my best to keep the family out of the workhouse.' Jack spoke with bitterness, but was filled with shame and humiliation. Just a few months earlier this man had stood before him asking to marry Marian. Jack had had the upper hand. Now, Jack suspected Vickers wanted to crow at the expense of his father-in-law.

Vickers persisted. 'Marian tells me you used to be a teacher.'

Jack nodded.

'I was wondering if you might consider taking up a teaching post at The Reformatory. At present I am the only lay teacher, but Father Ignatius, who is the principal, has expressed his agreement to my proposal we take on another.'

Jack looked at Vickers in astonishment, unable to speak.

'I am willing to put your name forward,' said Vickers. 'As long as you sign the pledge and turn your back on alcohol, I will keep the matter of you losing your job between us. God rejoices in the salvation of every soul from the evil of drinking.'

Jack was open-mouthed.

'The school inspectors have complained that there is insufficient emphasis on the traditional elements of the school curriculum. The brothers are exemplary in their moral and spiritual guidance for the wretched sinners who are under their care, but one man alone can't cope with teaching two hundred boys, try as hard as I might. There would of course be some conditions before I could put you forward for the post. As well as remaining teetotal you will be expected to attend Mass with the rest of the school and to do all you can to reinforce the Catholic values we hold dear. Marian has told me that you are rather lax in your churchgoing?'

Jack swallowed. 'It's been difficult. Running a public house… Sundays are our busiest days.' Why was he trying to justify himself?.

The thought of being under the thumb of the church once more was anathema. He didn't want to be obliged to Vickers, or to Marian. And giving up drink? He hated the thought of those smug Temperance people. Hated the thought of Mary Ellen exacting a victory over him even in death. He ran his hands through his hair and closed his eyes. What should he do? His career as a landlord was over and this was a chance to do again what he most loved to do. He had his daughters to think of. Clementina was only four.

Do you think I've a chance then?'

'The decision is Father Ignatius's but I do have his ear. The fact that you are Marian's father will certainly help. He has been very impressed with her and so I'm sure he will be willing to consider taking on her father.'

Jack swallowed again, then took a deep breath. He nodded at Vickers's. 'Thank you, Malcolm. I appreciate it. I won't let you down.'

'Understand me, Mr Brennan, I do this for Marian and her sisters, not for you. I trust you will not let them down.'

35
The Cricket Match

Clementina had spent the last eight years living in a boy's reform school. Even though she didn't like being surrounded by so many boys, with no girls to play with, St Dominic's wasn't so bad. Most of the time she was free to do what she pleased. She'd mostly forgotten her mother, who'd died when Clem was five. Her other sisters had gone to heaven too. Her big sister, Marian, tried to act as though she was her mother, but Clem wasn't very happy about that. At least she still had her father.

Clem was sitting on the stone steps at the front of the reformatory, trying to play cat's cradle. Every time she got past four or five of the stages she went wrong. She kept trying, getting increasingly frustrated with her own ineptitude. Whenever she thought at last she'd got it, as soon as she pulled her hands apart, the string fell loose and she was back to the beginning. It was no good. She would have to ask Tommy Kelly to show her again. She'd have to find a time when Marian wouldn't see her talking to him. Marian always got angry if Clementina went anywhere near the boys, reminding her of their badness, that they were destined to go to hell; how they were common and badly brought up. Clem just felt sorry for them, with their big, sad eyes, threadbare uniforms and scabbed knees. She was particularly sorry for Tommy, but she knew he'd be angry if she ever showed the slightest hint of pity for him. He was proud, defiant and frequently on the punishment roster for his acts of insubordination.

The first time she'd spoken to him, she'd been walking along the boundary that separated the school grounds from the surrounding farmland, dragging a long stick aimlessly through the hedgerow. She heard an angry shout and a word that she knew to be bad even though she didn't know what it meant. She stopped and walked back a couple of steps, poking her stick into the depths of the hedge.

'Leave off will you? That were nearly me eye you just poked out.'

She looked into the thicket and saw two big blue eyes staring back at her.

'Why are you sitting in the middle of a hedge?'

'None of your damn business.'

'Shouldn't say that word. You'll have to tell it in confession now.'

'What's it to you?'

'I want to save you all those extra Hail Marys. I think a word as bad as that must be worth at least fifty.'

'Don't care. Now buzz off.'

'What are you hiding for?'

'I'm waiting till dark then I'm going to run away.'

'That's daft. No one ever escapes. They'll catch you and lock you up.'

'That's why I'm runnin' away. Just done two days in't dark cell and I'm never going back there again.'

'Why did they put you in the dark cell?'

'I talked back to Brother Bellamy, when he were giving me the stick for pulling another lad's hair.'

Clementina considered his words for a moment, then sat down on the grass in front of the hedge, crossing her legs neatly and pulling her gown down over her shoes to make sure he couldn't get a glimpse of her bloomers.

She folded her arms. 'You need a plan. Otherwise they'll catch you and put you straight back in the dark cell and that doesn't sound very nice at all.'

'It's not. I'm not going back. Never. I'll kill meself first.'

'You can't do that because it's a mortal sin and you'll definitely go to hell and burn for ever and that will be much worse than the dark cell, won't it?'

'S'pose so,' he conceded.

'How old are you?' she asked.

'Twelve.'

'I'm older than you. I'm thirteen,' she said. 'So you should listen to my advice and experience.'

'You're Mr Brennan's lass, aren't you?'

'Yes. I'm Clementina Brennan. And who are you?'

'Tommy Kelly.'

'What did you do to get sent here, Tommy?'

'Stole a handkerchief. One month in prison and four years here. I've done two of them.'

'Didn't you know it's a sin to steal?'

'Course I did.'

'So why did you do it then?' She tilted her head on one side and tried to see his face through the dense foliage of the hedge, but all she could make out was the brightness of his eyes in the darkness.

'The little 'uns was hungry and there was nowt to eat in the 'ouse.'

'Didn't your father provide for you?'

'Dead.' His voice betrayed no sentiment. Just a bald statement of the fact.

'I've got lots of dead people in my family too,' she said. 'My two brothers died before I was born, then my mama fell down the stairs and broke her neck. And then my sisters died. Not my biggest sister. She's Mr Vickers's wife. But all the others died not long after we moved here.'

'How did they die?' he asked.

'They got sick. Ursula and Jane died of consumption and then Alice got pneumonia. I hope I don't die next. Marian, that's Mrs Vickers to you, says I have to keep away from the infirmary and I'm not supposed to talk to any of the boys. So we have to make sure no one sees us.'

'Do you miss them?'

'Yes. It's lonely. Now I've no one to play with. Is your mother dead too?'

'In the nick. She were caught stealing herself. Week before me.'

Clementina absorbed the weight of what the boy said, nonplussed for a moment. 'You should have gone to the church. I'm sure a priest would have helped you out.'

The boy snorted. 'Yeah. And put us all in the workhouse.'

'Who's looking after the children now?'

'Dunno. In the workhouse after all I 'spect.'

'Mmm. Which rather proves my point. Crime doesn't pay. You'd have been better off trusting in God and the church to take care of you. Look at you now. All on your own locked up here. Do you think your mother knows where you are?'

'Dunno. Look, Miss, I wish you'd stop talking and get on yer way. You're going to give me away, sitting there like that talking to a hedge.'

'I'm not going anywhere. Not until you come out and go back inside. It's almost time for Benediction and then supper. They'll notice if you're not there. Anyway you'd be better off having supper before you go or you'll be hungry.'

'I won't. I stole some stale bread from the kitchen.'

'Oh no. Silly boy. You'll be for it now.' She thought for a moment. 'Look. I have a plan. Give me the bread and I'll take it back to the kitchen when cook's not looking. If anyone sees me I'll just say I was going to feed the birds.

You can run round now and wash your face and be in chapel in time for Benediction and no one will be any the wiser. You can have my apple.'

She fumbled in the pocket of her apron and pulled out an apple, polishing it on her skirt before holding it out towards the hedge. There was silence. She reached into the pocket again and pulled out a toffee.

'Tell you what, Tommy, as I quite like you, I'm going to give you this toffee too. I'd been saving it to eat on Sunday, but I'll let you have it instead.'

The offer was too tempting to ignore. The boy burst through the hedge, knocking Clementina backwards onto the grass as he grabbed the fruit and the sweet. Before she could scramble to her feet he was running off in the direction of the wash house.

After that first encounter, Clementina spent time with Tommy whenever she thought there was no risk of being observed. He appeared to shun the company of the other boys and avoided them during the two brief periods of recreation they enjoyed each day. The pair would meet under a large elm tree at the side of the school buildings, away from the main lawned area where the other boys usually kicked around a battered old football or played tag. With endless patience he demonstrated how to perform the cat's cradle, but all his efforts were in vain as, unless he stood over her barking instructions, she was unable to replicate the process alone. With more success, he showed her how to whittle a stick. He worked every day trimming pieces of wood for the production of matches – one of the industries the boys were being trained in. While match-making, carpentry and farming were the principal trades of the reformatory, the work undertaken was more akin to exploitation than an apprenticeship, to prepare the boys for rehabilitation into the world after their sentences. As far as Tommy was concerned, cutting match wood was better than working on the farm as it kept him dry, if not warm, and meant he had access to tools and the opportunity to indulge his passion for carving small wooden animals. Clementina became equally adept under his tutelage, her small fingers flying as she chipped the wood away to reveal the strange and beautiful creatures that lay sleeping within. Her works were always fantastical – mythical creatures with plumes, scales, horns and tails – while Tommy's were accurate and perfectly executed common animals and birds.

Clem knew Marian would be horrified if she were to find out that her sister was consorting with one of the inmates. She doubted her father would care. He treated the boys kindly, if absently, avoiding the judgemental approach of his son-in-law and most of the brothers.

The growing bond between Clementina and Tommy was forged in mutual loneliness, curiosity about the natural world and a shared sense of somehow being out of place, here in this ugly collection of buildings in the midst of nowhere.

It was Easter Monday, two years after Clementina befriended Tommy. In recognition of the Easter festival, the boys were permitted extra recreation and the headmaster decided a cricket match would be a good way to mark the day. The work in the fields and workshops was scheduled to end an hour early and the boys assembled on the lawn behind the main building.

It was a hot day and the air was heavy. Clem had slipped away and found a shady spot under a large elm tree safe from the eyes of her sister. She lay on her stomach in the grass and settled down to watch the game.

It was to be a match between the boys and the lay staff – not a fair contest, as the latter were better fed and enjoyed more comforts than the inmates. The boys were plagued with chest infections and coughs, all were undernourished and often sleep-deprived. The work they had to do, labouring on the farm or working in the match factory, book bindery and tailor shop, was arduous and frequently rewarded with beatings when their output was judged below par.

Clem knew Tommy was excited. He loved any form of physical sport and was fast on his feet. On top of this he had only another few days to go before his sentence would be over. She didn't know what she'd do when he was gone. While she'd graduated from cat's cradle long ago, the pair continued to seek each other out and would sit on the grass behind the elm tree, talking about what the future held for each of them.

As she watched the game she grew drowsy. Easter was late this year and the afternoon was warm and the atmosphere soporific. She sat up, leaning her back against the trunk of the tree as Tommy took up position at the crease. He smashed the ball with such impact that it went straight over the improvised boundary. Fifteen minutes later he'd scored almost forty runs. After a conversation between the staff, her father stepped up to bowl. Clem had never seen him play cricket before. She was afraid he was going to be an embarrassment. He paused, polishing the ball, narrowing his eyes as he scoped out his target, then began his run up to the wicket. He moved with a grace she hadn't expected, hair flopping into his eyes, his movement to the crease fast and powerful. Tommy struck out at the first ball but it was too fast for him. He hit it but it bounced off the bat and rolled straight towards one of the fielders. No runs. Jack readied himself for the next ball. This time he served it with his arm parallel to the ground. It flew through the air like a shot from a cannon.

Clem thought at first it was too high and readied herself to witness her father's humiliation. But the ball didn't pass over Tommy's shoulder as she'd expected. There was a loud thwack. Tommy was on the ground. Flat on his back. For a moment there was silence. The world was frozen. Then people were running towards the boy, bending over him, trying to raise him up.

Clem got up. She ran across the lawn, holding her skirts above her ankles so she wouldn't trip, uncaring of who might see. She pushed her way through the crowd of boys and masters standing mute around her friend. He was lying on his back, the impact captured in a glassy-eyed look of shock, a bloody gash above one of the surprised eyes.

'Tommy, Tommy! Can you hear me, Tommy? Speak to me. It's Clem.'

She dropped on her knees beside him. She felt someone's hands on her shoulders trying to pull her back, but she shrugged them off. Still the same glassy, vacant look of surprise in her friend's eyes. She remembered that look. She'd seen it when she witnessed her mother's body lying at the bottom of the staircase. The realisation hit her like a hammer blow, just as the cricket ball had struck him. Tommy was gone. Clem gave a cry of pain that was so loud, so shrill, that everyone stepped back. Then she flung herself across the boy's inert body, convulsed by sobbing.

'Tommy, Tommy. Don't die.' She began to shake him. 'Please wake up, Tommy. Please…you can't be dead. Not now. You're going home next week. You're getting out of this place. Please, please, Tommy! Speak to me!' She clung to him, her head buried in his chest, where her tears and snot dampened his dirty threadbare shirt.

'What do you think you're doing, Clementina? Get up at once. Get off that filthy boy. You should be ashamed.' Marian's voice was cold. She grabbed at her sister's collar and dragged her off the dead boy's body, giving her a shake as she did so.

Clementina jerked away from Marian's hold and ran across the lawn towards the gate that led to the open fields behind the reformatory.

'Come back at once, Clementina. Do you hear me? Come back at once.'

Jack Brennan laid a hand on his elder daughter's arm. 'Leave her be.'

'But she's making a holy show of herself. What will people think?'

'That she's unhappy I suppose? That she's shocked.'

Marian looked at him with contempt. 'Unhappy about a boy? An inmate? A horrible little criminal? Did you know they were friends?'

Jack shook his head.

'Of course you didn't. You don't know anything, do you? You're that wrapped up in yourself. You've let that child run wild. If it weren't for Malcolm and me, she'd never get any moral guidance, let alone go to Mass. I don't understand you, Father. What kind of man are you?'

Jack closed his eyes, then bent down and lifted the body of Tommy Kelly into his arms and carried him towards the school buildings, past the shocked and silent boys and his stunned colleagues.

They brought Clem home that night. They'd found her lying shivering in a dry ditch. Her eyes were red raw and she refused to speak. No one could penetrate her silence. When Jack opened the door, she walked past him without even looking at him.

He leaned forward to touch her arm. 'I'm sorry, Clemmie. I'm so sorry.'

She pulled away from him and walked into her bedroom, closing the door behind her.

It didn't make sense. She couldn't understand how God had let it happen. Just when Tommy was at last to be free of this horrible place. Just when he was about to start a new life, find his brothers and sisters and maybe his mother.

Her own father had killed him. She blamed him. She hated him.

Clem stopped eating. Jack, normally oblivious to domestic matters, was keenly aware that she was refusing to eat. He was desperate for her to wake up one morning and be once again the sunny-natured little girl he loved so much. After a week, Marian intervened. Her threats to force-feed her sister were conveyed so categorically that Clem decided it was easier to comply than to engage in protracted warfare. She ate as little as possible, but enough to avoid giving Marian cause to speak to her. Instead she began a process of silent compliance – doing the bare minimum to avoid having to account for her actions or lack of them.

36
The Dormitory

Tommy Kelly's death was entered in the principal's log book as an accident. The death certificate from the local doctor said the same. Just another boy to add to the reformatory's roll call of deaths. What did it matter if it were death by poorly aimed cricket ball, or by cholera or tuberculosis? It was the twelfth mortality already that year.

The day after Tommy died, when work was supposed to resume after the short Easter break, his fellow inmates were angry. While not popular – he was too much of a loner for that – Tommy had been respected by his peers, not least for his stoical attitude to the frequent punishments meted out to him, especially by Brother Charles. Rumours began to circulate that Mr Brennan had deliberately struck him down to eliminate the boys' strongest player from the game. Their anger took the form of a refusal to return to work.

Jack was on duty in the dining room when they staged their revolt. The bell rang to summon them to the work-place and instead the boys stayed in their places and began to thump the top of the tables in unison. Jack looked about him, not knowing what to do. He tried to reason with them but his voice could not be heard above the clamour.

One of the boys called out, 'Killer Jack!' The rest of them

took up the cry, repeating the epithet in a rhythmic chant.

Jack couldn't disagree with what they were saying. He *was* a killer. He didn't know how it happened. How he had managed to wield the ball with such force? How had he aimed it so badly. He wanted to wind the clock back and bowl the ball again. He'd do it underarm this time instead of trying to be clever. Better still he'd refuse to bowl at all. Now he had two accidental deaths on his conscience – this young boy's as well as Mary Ellen's. Why was God testing him in this way? Hadn't he suffered enough all these years? Just as he'd found some kind of peace here at the reformatory his life was shattered again.

Sensing weakness and smelling victory, the clamour of the boys grew louder. Jack stood transfixed, unable to move, unable to respond, as the shouting drowned out his thoughts. He put his hands over his ears to shut out the noise.

'What's going on here? Silence! Immediately!' The voice of Malcolm Vickers cut through the din and the boys shut up at once. He was accompanied by Brother Charles and both of them turned their eyes to Jack, who was standing with his hands clamped over his ears.

'Get to work at once or you'll all go without food tonight.' Vickers' voice was strident and the boys began to move towards the door to do his bidding.

One of the older ones, incensed at the sudden capitulation, ran at Vickers and head-butted him in the stomach, knocking him to the floor. Before the boy could seize the advantage, Brother Charles grabbed him by the scruff of the neck and dragged him off to the dark cell. When a winded Vickers got to his feet he threw a look of absolute contempt at Jack, then left the hall without another word to his father-in-law.

When work details and lessons were completed that day, Father Ignatius summoned Jack to his office and told him that he needed to exercise greater discipline over the boys or risk the termination of his contract.

'You are too soft, Mr Brennan, too lax. It is important that the boys make progress on the path to virtue and the only way to do that is by exercising strong discipline and close attention. You treat the older boys as though they were your friends. That's a poor state of affairs. These are common criminals and need to be shown the way towards the goodness of Our Blessed Lord. You seem to take little interest – it appears you even allowed your own daughter to consort with the dead boy. It won't do, Mr Brennan. It won't do. Mr Vickers told me it was pandemonium in the hall this morning. Complete insubordination. You were on duty and were responsible. He told me you did nothing to restore order. I would commend you to follow the example set by your own son-in-law and by Brother Charles. Both of them stress the importance of Catholic virtues and both of them are unstinting when it comes to rooting out bad behaviour. The only way these reprobates will learn is through strict discipline. This is a final warning. Do you understand me?'

Jack was listless. He barely took in the words being said to him. The tone of voice was enough to tell him he was being reprimanded. He didn't know what to say. He didn't know what to do any more. He was consumed with guilt about what happened on the cricket pitch. This morning he had faced the silent condemnation of his own daughter. It was more than he could bear.

'Mr Brennan?'

'Yes, Father.'

'Do I make myself clear?'

'Yes, Father.'

Tommy Kelly's was the only inmate's grave in the small burial ground that showed evidence of being tended.

Clementina was as assiduous in visiting and placing small tokens on his grave as she was in tending to those of her sisters. She placed wild flowers on it, little piles of acorns, a toffee she'd been saving in her pocket for him. Sometimes she would sit down in the grass beside his earthen mound and wooden cross and read aloud. He'd always loved her stories. She liked to imagine him up in heaven listening to her, maybe smiling, laughing even. Of course Marian had told her he'd probably be burning in hell now because of all his bad deeds – at the very best he would be confined to purgatory for at least a hundred years. Clem refused to believe her. Tommy was a good person. He had shown her more kindness than anyone else in this world. His only crimes had been in trying to do the right thing for his family and then attempting to run away so he could go and find them again. God wouldn't let him suffer any more. Surely. He must let him into heaven to sit with the Blessed Virgin and the saints. She pictured him, wearing clean white robes with washed hair and a clean face, the callouses on his hands healed and his missing teeth replaced with straight and shiny ones. Then she remembered that God had let him die. Right before he was due to be released. She wanted to hate God, but was afraid to. Instead she decided to hate her father.

Jack had been trying hard to avoid trouble. Keeping this job was essential. He had to provide a home for Clemmie. He had to be responsible. He was trying to cut back on the drinking too, but so far without success.

The first year of being at the reformatory, haunted by the death of Mary Ellen so soon after Gertrude's and knowing of his own part in that, Jack had managed to eschew the alcohol. Being away from the pub helped. While he paid only lip service to his Catholicism, the confined nature of the isolated reformatory removed easy access to temptation.

The tragic deaths of Ursula, Alice and Jane, not long after the family had relocated to Saint Dominic's, pushed Jack to the edge and after burying Alice he had walked away from the graveside and taken the short road down to the public house in the village. At first he went only occasionally, but the death of Tommy and his part in it and his beloved Clementina's continued rejection of him, sent him in the direction of the Raven every night.

He'd sit tight through supper in the communal dining room then, unless he was on dormitory duty, once he knew Clementina was in bed, he would slip out of their quarters and walk the half mile in the pitch dark to the Raven for a drink. He sought oblivion, to wipe out all the things that made his life unbearable, that made him long for it to be over. The only good thing that had happened to him since he was dragged off the boat in Liverpool was Clementina. And now she too had turned against him.

He sat at the bar, chasing each pint of ale with a shot of whisky. Fred Butler, the landlord, eyed him, keeping watch to make sure he didn't fall off his stool, but otherwise showing the tolerance and kindred spirit that exists between those who have stood for years behind the bar.

Jack stared into his pint as if he expected to see some kind of revelation in the depths of the dark liquid. But sacred revelations only happened to pious, peasant girls on hillsides or in caves, not to washed-out drunks in public houses. He wasn't a bad person. Not fundamentally. Just unlucky. Why did life keep throwing misfortune at him? Why was he being punished? He thought about Gertrude. She'd been a good woman. A true friend. If it hadn't been that he'd already given his heart to Eliza he might even have grown to love her. He tossed the rest of the pint back and signalled to Fred to fill it up again.

The walk back to the reformatory was more of a stagger,

but the sharp wind coming off the moors helped to sober him up. As he walked along in the darkness he swore it would be the last time. He'd give up the drinking. Turn over a new leaf. Start writing poetry again. Save up the money he was frittering away on booze so that one day, when Clemmie was married and off his hands, he could sail to America and search for Eliza. Even if it took him forever, he'd damn well do it. And if she were married? And why wouldn't she be? – a girl as beautiful as she would have been snapped up in no time. How could she have been expected to wait for him for ever? Yes, even though she'd be married he'd hunt her down if it took him the rest of his life. Just to say sorry. Just to explain. To let her know he'd had no choice. But deep inside a little voice told him he'd always had a choice.

He crossed the lawn towards the side door leading to the staff quarters and noticed the light from a flickering candle in one of the dormitories. The rules were clear – the dormitories were to be in complete darkness after lights out.

Conscious of the headmaster's warning, he decided this was his opportunity to redeem himself, to show some backbone, to exercise some discipline, to identify the guilty party and make sure they were appropriately punished. He'd never wielded the stick before, not even on his own children, but if he were to make a new start it might as well be now.

The doors to the dormitories were always kept open. He stood on the threshold. The light was no longer evident. One of the beds was empty. He walked slowly towards it, anxious not to waken the other boys. As he neared the empty bed he heard muffled sobbing from the bed next to it. When he moved towards it the boy inside curled himself into a tight ball, pulling the covers up around him.

'No. Please no. Not again. Don't hurt me.'

He leaned down and pulled back the thin blanket. A lad of about fifteen with a shock of red hair stared at him in terror.

'What's the matter, Billy? Why are you crying? And where's the boy from the next bed?'

The only answer was more muffled sobbing.

'Who is it and where has he gone?'

The boy's eyes were bloodshot and when he turned away, Jack noticed there was a large, fresh weal across his skinny back. He touched the spot gingerly and the boy jack-knifed away. His whole back was crisscrossed with welts.

'Who did this?'

'No, sir. Please, sir. I can't say. Just leave me alone. Don't tell. Please don't tell.'

'Where's the boy from the next bed?'

This time the child's eyes moved reflexively towards a door at the far end of the room where a faint glow showed under the doorframe. It was a store cupboard where bedding and chamber pots were kept. With a sudden sense that something was very amiss, Jack crept across the room and wrenched the door open.

37
The Condemned Man

The boy was kneeling on the stone floor. He was wearing only his drawers and his small body was shivering. Brother Charles had his back to the door and must have assumed the interruption was from one of the boys as he continued to hold the boy's head to his crotch as he spoke, his fingers tangled in the boy's matted, unwashed hair.

'Get back to bed before I leather you,' he said, without turning round, his words breathy and punctuated by grunts.

Jack couldn't believe what he was witnessing. 'Brother Charles, what in God's name are you doing? Let that boy go. Stop! Now!'

The monk took his hands away from the boy's head and the lad grabbed the opportunity to scramble to his feet and run out past Jack.

Brother Charles tucked his penis back inside his robes. 'Go to bed, Brennan' he said. 'This is no concern of yours.' He pushed Jack aside and walked out of the dormitory.

Jack went after him. Outside in the corridor he gripped the sleeve of the monk's cassock and jerked him to a stop.

'What the hell were you thinking of, Brother Charles? You're supposed to be a man of God. And that other lad, the red-headed one? Did you do that to him too or did he refuse to cooperate, so you beat the living daylights out of him instead? I saw his back. It's red-raw and bleeding.'

The Brother narrowed his eyes and sneered at him. 'These boys are filth. They're all sinners. They get what they deserve.'

'And what do you call what you were doing to that boy? Is that not sin? And sin of the worst kind? It's a perversion. It's scandalous. Shame on you.'

The brother spun round and grabbed Jack by his lapels. 'You're drunk again, Brennan.' Then he pushed him away, knocking Jack off balance. 'You can't even stand up straight.'

Overcome with tiredness, Jack went to his quarters. He must tell Father Ignatius. But it could wait until morning.

He overslept and woke with a throbbing head. There was no sign of Clementina – she must have already left for school. Jack groaned and swung his legs over the side of the bed. He would definitely be giving up the drink. This time for sure. This time would be different. He staggered across the room and pissed in the pot. It seemed to go on forever. His head was pounding and a wave of nausea flowed over him. He wanted to crawl back into bed. What time was it? He cursed, realising he was already late for class. His coat was hanging on the back of the door and he remembered he'd got Fred in the Raven to fill his hip flask for the walk home. There might still be some left. What harm could it do? One small swig. Enough to get the day started. Enough to make the throbbing in his head stop and loosen the tightening metal vice that was compressing his skull. He unscrewed the top and slugged the whisky back, feeling the tension soaking away as it burned a path down his throat. He'd need a bit of dutch courage to tell Father Ignatius what had happened last night.

He dressed hurriedly and left the room, bumping into his son-in-law in the corridor. 'Malcolm. I need to tell you some-thing. Something terrible has happened. I need your advice.'

'Where've you been, Jack? You were due in class ten minutes ago. I've come to find you. The boys are making merry hell in there. You don't need to give Father Ignatius any more cause for complaint.'

Jack grabbed at his sleeve. 'Wait, listen. I saw Brother Charles last night. He'd been beating the living soul out of a boy and then I caught him with another one, doing… doing… an immoral act.'

'What?' Vickers' expression was full of disgust, as though somehow in the telling Jack was as culpable as the perpetrator. 'How can you say such a shameful thing?'

'I'm only telling you what I saw. What should I do?'

'Do? Do nothing. You can't go around making allegations like that.'

'It's not an allegation. I saw it. I found him in the laundry closet. He had the boy in front of him on his knees and was making him–'

'Stop! I don't want to hear such filth.'

'Nor did I want to see it. I have to tell Father Ignatius.'

Vickers looked at him for a moment as though weighing up the veracity of his words. 'Don't do anything yet. Let me think. We'll speak again after lessons.'

He placed a hand on Jack's shoulder, then pulled back from him as though stung. 'Good lord, Jack. You've been drinking. It's not yet eight-thirty. Have you no shame, man?'

The bell rang to mark the end of classes. The three hours of lessons had seemed interminable. At one point Jack had excused himself and run along the corridor to the latrines where he threw up. When the boys filed out of the classroom to wash before the midday meal, he reached into his jacket pocket and found the flask. He tilted his head back to drink but there was only a dreg left. How was he going to get through until this evening when he could slip away to The Raven?.

'Mr Brennan?' The unmistakeable voice of Father Ignatius. 'My office. Immediately.'

Jack followed the principal along the draughty corridor, past the heavy wooden crucifix and the statue of Saint Vincent de Paul. As he walked he rehearsed what he was going to say, wishing he'd had a chance to confer properly with Malcolm beforehand.

When they entered the headmaster's study Jack pulled up short, surprised to see both Vickers and Brother Charles already waiting there. He looked from one to the other and then to the headmaster.

'I am not going to dismiss you, Mr Brennan,' the head said. 'That would involve a lot of paperwork and a discussion with the bishop. Instead I would like to receive your immediate resignation.'

Jack's throat dried up and another wave of nausea hit him. 'I don't understand.' He turned to his son-in-law as he tried to fight the rising panic. 'Malcolm?' But Vickers lowered his eyes and avoided his gaze.

The head spoke again. 'Brother Charles has told me how he came upon you last night in a state of drunkenness, in which you were performing a loathsome and unnatural act upon one of the boys. Further it appears you beat another boy most cruelly with a walking cane, presumably because he had refused to comply with your wicked purpose.'

Jack tried to swallow, but his throat was parched. He needed a drink desperately. What was happening? The room was spinning and a pain shot through his ears like a bolt of lightening. He slumped into a chair. *Oh God help me. Please sweet Jesus. Let me wake up from this nightmare.*

'That's not true,' he said, his voice barely a whisper. 'It wasn't like that at all. It was *him!*' He pointed at the brother, who responded with a shake of the head and a look of disgust.

'I told you, didn't I?' said the monk to the headmaster.

'So drunk he was practically insensible.'

'I wasn't drunk. I wasn't.' But as he said the words they sounded hollow.

There was a collective intake of breath, then Father Ignatius spoke again. 'Mr Brennan, I can smell the drink on you now.'

'I have a mouth ulcer. I gargled with some surgical spirit this morning to numb the pain.'

'Don't make it any worse. Sign this letter of resignation and that will be the end of it. You're a fortunate man. I could have taken this up with the Home Office inspectors and the bishop and destroyed your reputation. Instead I am giving you the opportunity to walk out of here with a little dignity – which is more than you deserve under the circumstances.'

'Malcolm? Tell him! Tell him what I told you this morning. You know he's lying.'

'Mr Vickers cannot help you. We are all too aware that you made this disgraceful allegation about Brother Charles this morning. You are disgusting. Not only evil enough to perpetrate such acts but trying to transfer the blame to a man of God. Shame on you, Brennan. While you sloped off drunk to your bed last night, Brother Charles came straight to see me and told me what he had witnessed. He did not name you but instead asked to pray with me this morning in the chapel to seek divine guidance. Only then did he tell me the terrible truth. Since then Mr Vickers has checked with the landlord of the local public house who confirms you were there all of last evening until he showed you the door after last orders. He said you were the worse for drink. Now my patience is running out. Sign the letter, man, and let's be done with it. I want you out of this place.'

'You can't do this! It's all wrong. It's all lies.' He tasted bile in his mouth. 'If I'm out of a job how will I get another? What's to become of Clementina?'

'It is only because of Clementina and Mr Vickers' intercession on your behalf that I agreed not to dismiss you. He urged me to do everything to avoid her name being tarnished by yours. He has kindly offered to take responsibility for the child and care for her himself with Mrs Vickers, where she will be safeguarded from your depravity. You should be grateful to your son-in-law. It's more than you deserve and I hope will not be too late to prevent that young lady from being corrupted by your lack of a moral and spiritual compass.'

'She's my daughter. She's all I've got left. You can't take her away from me. She'll never agree.'

'She already has. Mrs Vickers spoke to her this morning, explained you would be leaving the reformatory and asked her if she wished to stay or to go with you. She has elected to stay with her sister and Mr Vickers.'

'I don't believe you.'

The headmaster nodded his head at Vickers who left the room. While he was gone the headmaster took a piece of paper and thrust it across the desk to Jack. 'Sign it.'

'I won't. It's a lie. I'm innocent and this man knows it.' Jack pointed at Brother Charles who exchanged a 'told you so' look with the principal.

The door opened and Vickers re-entered the room, this time accompanied by Marian and Clementina. The girl avoided looking at her father, fixing her eyes instead on Father Ignatius.

'Clementina, your sister has explained to you that your father will be leaving the reformatory today?'

The girl nodded, still avoiding looking at Jack.

'And you understand that you may stay on here living with Mr and Mrs Vickers and their children?'

'Yes.'

Jack jumped up from his chair. 'Clem! I don't want to leave you here. And I'm not going anywhere. It's all a mistake. I'm going to sort it out.'

Marian took her father by the arm and shoved him back into his seat. 'That's enough, Father. Don't make this hard on Clemmie. Don't embarrass us all further. You've done enough.'

Jack slumped in the chair, his eyes welling up.

Clementina stepped forward and looked at him for the first time. 'I don't want to see you any more.' Then with a little strangled sobbing noise, she ran from the room.

It was over. He could fight no more.

38
Ticket to America

Jack sat on his bed, in a state of shock and still suffering the ill effects of the alcohol. Malcolm Vickers was folding his few items of clothing into a battered suitcase.

'Why?' asked Jack. 'You know it was Brother Charles. We're supposed to be family. I thought you were my friend.'

'You're a drunk, Jack. It's time you faced up to it. Otherwise it's going to destroy you.'

'Sod the drink. I'm telling the truth and you know it as well as I do.'

'You're losing touch with reality. I think you actually believe Brother Charles did it. You're a sick man. You need treatment. I know it's been a while since Mrs Brennan died, but, Jack, for heaven's sake, you have no business taking out your frustrations on boys. It's vile. Rotten. And to malign the name of a man of God – it's unthinkable.'

Jack wanted to roll over on the bed and sleep until his head stopped hurting and his stomach stopped heaving; until he woke up and found this was all just a drink-induced nightmare. But it wasn't. It was happening and he couldn't stop it.

'I want to say goodbye to Clemmie.' He pulled himself upright and started to move towards the door.

Vickers reached out and took his arm and eased him back down onto the bed. 'She doesn't want to see you any more, Jack.'

'Clem doesn't know? Please tell me she doesn't know. About…'

'Of course she doesn't. Neither of them know what you did in that linen cupboard. They've both been told it was for the beating you gave Hudson.'

'I didn't beat the lad.' His voice was faint, the fight gone. Then he jumped up. 'Why don't you ask him? The boy. Ask both boys. They'll tell you the truth.'

'Everyone knows Brother Charles is a strict disciplinarian while you are easily manipulated by the boys. It's obvious they'll lay the blame at his door, which is why we won't be asking them. It would imply there was a doubt in the matter. Neither Father Ignatius nor I want any shadow to be cast over the good name of one of the brothers.'

'And what about my good name?'

Vickers snapped the suitcase closed and turned to face Jack, shaking his head, his face taking on a look of disappointment, almost sadness.

'What good name? You lost that long ago, Jack.'

They paid Jack his wages and sent him on his way. It was just starting to get dusk when he walked out of the reformatory grounds for the last time. He went along the path past the chapel and looked over at the little graveyard. He made the sign of the cross and trudged down the driveway to the road, forcing himself to turn right rather than taking the left turn which led past The Raven.

He promised himself he would never drink again. Maybe he'd been using the drink as a consolation for the way his life had turned out, but he knew it had now become the catalyst for his own self destruction. He walked on, gulping in the cool evening air, hoping it would ease the after effects of the alcohol. Maybe Malcolm was right and he did need help.

He kicked a clump of grass growing out of the edge of the road, then bent down and picked up a large pebble and hurled it over the wall into the adjacent field, letting out a cry. 'Why?'

His life was ruined. He'd tried to trust in God. He'd been a good Catholic since he'd been at the Reformatory. He'd done his best. He'd tried to atone for his sins. Hadn't he? He hadn't let Father O'Driscoll colour his view of the whole church. But he'd been betrayed by another bad egg in the ecclesiastical basket.

If he'd been able to stay with Eliza might he have been a better man? It felt as though he only had the capacity for goodness when he had someone to love.

He would trust in God now. Maybe this was all part of God's plan for him. All this suffering would at last lead to its reward. He had atoned for his sins and now it was time for something good to happen. He was going to find her. His Eliza. There had never been a right time to do that before. He'd had to be there for the girls. As their father it had been his duty to give them a home.

He was stung with pain at Clemmie's rejection, but he was going to look on it as a disguised blessing. It freed him at last to find Eliza. It might take him years but he would manage it somehow. Once he'd tracked her down he would then effect a reconciliation with his daughter. Plenty of time for that.

As night fell he found a farm outbuilding, far enough away from the farmyard as to be out of sight of the farmhouse and out of earshot of any dogs. He sat on the bare ground, draped his coat over him, then ate the bread and dripping Malcolm had brought him from the kitchen.

Warmed by the food, he drifted off into a deep sleep.

When he awoke the next morning his hands were shaking. He was desperate for a drink. He dusted the straw off his trousers and set off walking again, his legs unsteady. There were few people about on the country roads and those he did encounter just gave him a curt Yorkshire nod and went on their way without words. He was grateful.

He needed a plan. He'd just ten pounds to his name. He began talking to himself out loud as though he were a separate person, trying to knock some sense into his head. If he were to call into a public house the money would be gone in no time. He had to make it last. He had to hold on to enough for the passage to America. Rather than use any form of public transportation he decided to keep walking.

Eventually the rhythm of the road helped to clear his head, helped him think with more clarity than he'd done since he'd married Mary Ellen. As he walked, lines of poetry began to form. That hadn't happened in years. Not since Gertrude and Mary Ellen died. He felt a sudden surge of joy. He was reclaiming his life. Yes, he'd lost all those years, but it didn't matter any more. What was important was to build a new life. A new beginning. Let all the filth and poison of the past go. Let it drift away like the clouds that raced across the top of the moors, gathering together and then dispersing. It didn't matter. All that mattered was finding Eliza. Telling her he had always loved her and always would. Expecting nothing in return. Atoning. Being cleansed. The words of the *Confiteor* came into his head and he began to say them out loud, instinctively striking his breast as he reached the climax: *mea culpa, mea culpa, mea maxima culpa* before he begged for the intercession of the blessed Virgin Mary, Michael the archangel, John the Baptist, the apostles Peter and Paul, and all the saints on his behalf. He stopped and looked up at the sky, expecting to see a sign, an acknowledgement of his contrition, but there were just the same old clouds scudding through the pale blue sky, casting shadows over the distant hills.

When Jack reached the Liverpool docks he had eight pounds nineteen and sixpence in his pocket. The steerage fare to New York was three pounds ten. He paid the money, his heart thumping as the ticket was handed to him. It was happening. He was going. Into the unknown. To Eliza. At last.

A sudden chill of fear gripped him, making his stomach lurch. What would he do when he got there? How we would he find work? How would he find Eliza? It was an impossible task. Like searching for a lost farthing on the seashore. America was vast. Where would he go? How would he support himself? He knew nobody there. Then he reminded himself that Eliza had faced all that completely alone twenty odd years ago – a young woman who'd never set foot outside Bristol before – and she'd had to do it without any money.

A ship was scheduled to depart in two days time. He wanted to conserve his remaining funds so he elected to sleep on a bench. He found one near the spot where he and his beloved had sat hand in hand on the quayside, so full of hope, so full of love, so young. He lay prone, his coat laid over him and his shirt folded over the suitcase which he used as an improvised pillow.

'Budge up, mate.' Someone was shaking his leg. 'There's room for one more on there.'

Jack resisted the urge to lash out at the man, a dirty-faced fellow with a clay pipe dangling from his mouth.

'Off to America?' The man grabbed Jack's legs and swung them off the bench and deposited his skinny frame beside him. There was a familiar smell that it took Jack a moment or two to recognise as alcohol.

Jack pushed his hair out of his eyes and faced the stranger. 'Look here. That was my spot. I'd just managed to nod off.'

'Where's the sign saying it's your personal, private property then? I must have missed that.'

'Haven't you heard that possession is nine tenths of the law?'

The stranger laughed. 'I hadn't as it happens, but it looks like I'm in possession of this half of the bench now so it's all right, isn't it?'

The man laughed, revealing a mouth with several missing teeth and the rest badly discoloured and chipped. He was unshaven, the collar of his shirt was filthy and the rest of his clothes were torn. 'Where are you heading?' he asked.

'New York.' Jack looked about him to see if he could spot another empty bench, then decided to pick up his bags and walk away from the Pier Head to find somewhere else in the town where he might sleep undisturbed.

The man grabbed his arm and pulled him back down on to the seat. 'What's the hurry, man? Your ship's not sailing yet. Why not share a wee dram with an old sailor. I can give you some advice about New York.'

'You've been there?'

'Aye. You need to ken where to go and what to do or they'll eat ye for breakfast. Place is full of villains. Eyeties and Paddies that'd sooner slit your throat as say good morning. Lots of them nigro fellows too. Not to be trusted.' The man reached into his pocket and pulled out a bottle of whisky. He took a slug then passed the bottle to Jack.

'I don't drink.'

'Get away with you! Everyone drinks.'

'Not me. Not any more.'

The man looked at him intently. 'A wee drop won't do you any harm. We should drink to your future. To America.

To good fortune. And I'll give you some tips to see you right when you get there.'

Jack looked at the bottle doubtfully. 'One little drop maybe, just to take the chill off the night.'

When he woke up someone was driving rivets through his skull. He tried to sit upright but the bench felt as though it was tipping away. A lone seagull was watching him, standing on the ground in front of him as though challenging him to get out of her space. He moved his legs out and off the bench, and as he tried to place them on the ground his foot caught something – an empty bottle which rolled away towards the seagull. The bird looked at it with disdain before flying off to perch on a nearby lamppost. Jack bent down and put his head between his knees to try to stop the dizziness. From that vantage point he saw that there was another empty bottle lying under the wooden seat. He groaned. How had he let that happen? The events of the previous evening were a blur.

Then it hit him. A sharp pulse of fear through his stomach, like a knife. The bench beside him was empty. His suitcase gone. Everything he owned had been in that.

The ticket. Where was the ticket? He felt inside his coat pocket. There was nothing there.

39
The End of the Road

Nothing in Jack's life had prepared him for being destitute. Yes, he'd been born into poverty, he'd struggled to find work and he'd never had the luxury of spare cash at the end of the week, but there had always been food on the table, no matter how frugal. Now he was stuck in Liverpool without a penny to his name, his only assets being the clothes he stood up in.

The labour exchange had no work to offer him as either a teacher or a publican. He lowered his sights and tried for a job as a clerk in a grocery store, but the post went to a younger man. Sleeping rough and forced to try to keep clean using the public toilets near the Pier Head, his appearance grew more dishevelled every day, further limiting the work opportunities open to him.

Having nothing to eat was bad at the first. Jack's stomach screamed for food. Walking past a restaurant, the smell of cooked meat was so hypnotic that he stood outside for half an hour breathing the aromas in and trying to imagine eating a plateful of stew, piled up with potatoes. Thinking about it just made the hunger worse and after a while he felt sick and ran into an alleyway where he tried to throw up, but there was nothing to vomit.

Eventually his stomach shrank and the hunger wasn't so terrible any more. He found that if he drank water from a drinking fountain the pain and the hollow feeling diminished. It was as if his stomach was full. Jack saw his reflection in a mirror in the public lavatory. He looked like a stranger, gaunt, hollow-cheeked, hair unkempt and face shadowed with stubble.

Weak, but desperate to find work, Jack went along at dawn to try his luck at the docks, where gangs of men were hired every day to load and unload cargo. The demand for work greatly outweighed the supply, and the crowds seemed to grow bigger every morning. Even those chosen for work had little cause to be grateful, as it was just for one shift and they needed to return to try their luck again each day. Without being known to the foreman, the chances of getting picked were minimal. The odds were well nigh impossible in his case now that his appearance was so scruffy and his body so emaciated. He knew that even if by some miracle he was selected, he wouldn't have the strength to lift the sacks of grain.

To keep warm and pass the time after his fruitless daily trip to the labour exchange, Jack went into the library to read. The librarians watched him with distaste and suspicion, worried that he planned to pocket books. He tried not to mind. The place was a sanctuary and for the few hours he spent there each day, his head buried in a book or perusing the newspapers, he felt as though he was leading a normal life again. He lost himself in poetry, alternating between reading verses to uplift his spirits and those that made his own plight seem universal.

After ten days of sleeping rough, starving and failing in the quest for work, Jack admitted defeat. He begged for help at the labour exchange and was told to go to the workhouse. At least he would have shelter and some form of nourishment, no matter how basic. When he got to the poorhouse at Brownlow Hill he was told it was full.

It was the last straw. He'd had enough. His reserves were spent. His strength sapped. No more. He wanted to die. I've had it with you, God. Stop toying with me. You've punished me enough. Take me now. Get it over. Let it be done.

He staggered down the steps of the building, blind to his surroundings, then sat slumped at the bottom of the stairs, his head resting on his folded arms.

Someone tapped him on the shoulder and said, 'There's another place over in Walton, mate. They may have space there if you're lucky.' He gave Jack directions.

It was a long walk from the centre of the city. Jack's shoes had virtually no soles left. He did what he had done as a child and found some cardboard in a dustbin at the back of a shop and lined the shoes with it, then trudged off to Walton. As he trailed along, he had to stop every fifty yards or so to rest, leaning against a wall to get his breath back. His chest felt tight and he kept coughing.

The Walton Hill workhouse was a redbrick building, and like most of the buildings in the city, blackened with smoke. It had a central clock-tower with wings on each side, one for women and the other for men. The children were quartered separately. Jack walked up the pathway, feeling defeated, broken, but he told himself to rise above it. All he needed was a few days to get back on his feet, get some food inside him, have a good sleep, regain a bit of strength and he would be ready to resume the hunt for employment. He pushed the fact that he'd been coughing blood to the back of his mind.

Jack was in luck. There were one or two places left and they agreed to take him in. All inmates were expected to work inside the institution in exchange for their bed and board. The Master, on admitting Jack, assigned him to work in the carpentry shop. As Jack was leaving the room, the Master called him back.

'I am curious, Mr Brennan – you have an educated manner and your clothes, although they've seen a lot of wear, are made of good cloth. What brought you to this state? What was your occupation?'

'I was a schoolmaster, sir,' said Jack. 'In a reformatory in Yorkshire.'

'How did you come to be here? Why did you leave?'

Jack hesitated.

'Spit it out, man. Why did you leave?'

'They accused me of being drunk.'

'Accused you, eh? Are you saying you weren't?'

'I had the odd drink now and then, but I wasn't drunk in class.' Jack swallowed, feeling the humiliation of his dismissal all over again. 'My face didn't fit.'

'And do you still like a drink?'

'I haven't touched one in weeks. Not since the night I arrived in Liverpool. I swore then never to drink again. It's brought me nothing but ill. I've learnt my lesson.'

The man nodded. He was portly, with a red nose that Jack suspected indicated he might not be averse to a tipple himself. 'Do you have references?'

Jack shook his head.

'Did you like teaching?'

'More than anything, sir. It's all I ever wanted to do since I was a lad.'

'Were you any good at it?'

'I think so, sir. The school inspectors gave me good reports.'

'Did they now.' The Master shook his head and picked up a sheet of paper from the desk.

Jack assumed he was dismissed and was about to leave the room when the man spoke again, 'I believe everyone deserves a second chance, Mr Brennan. As it happens, we're in need of a second schoolmaster here and have struggled to fill the position. Until we can find a suitable candidate

I am prepared for you to assist in teaching the children instead of working in the workshops. Only until we fill the position, mind.'

Jack squeezed his hands together and his face broke into a grin. It was the first time he had smiled since the death of Tommy Kelly and the discovery of Brother Charles in the linen cupboard. He felt tears of joy and gratitude rising.

'Thank you, thank you, sir. You won't regret this. I'll do a good job. I promise you.'

The Master waved him away and Jack left the room, his step light and his heart rejoicing.

The brown paper parcel bore a Liverpool postmark. Clementina didn't know anyone in Liverpool. She didn't know anyone outside the walls of the Reformatory, apart from her father, but the handwriting was not his and she had heard nothing of him since he had left the reformatory almost three years earlier. Inside the package were a threadbare pair of trousers and a grubby jacket with a torn collar. On top of the clothing was a letter.

Walton Hill Workhouse,.
Rice Lane.
Liverpool.
December 15th 1909

Dear Miss Brennan,

It is with regret that I have the sad duty of writing to inform you of the death of Mr John Brennan. He was admitted to the workhouse in June 1907, penniless and in a poor state of health, suffering from consumption.

Mr Brennan was invited to provide temporary assistance to the schoolmaster and acquitted himself well. Last year he was awarded a full-time position here as a teacher, but regrettably was forced to retire after only a month due to his worsening health.

Although it is not normal practice to forward possessions post mortem, the Guardians and I took the decision to send his few possessions to you in the light of Mr Brennan's contributions to the wellbeing and education of the unfortunate children we have in our care here. He gave your name and address as his next of kin on admission.

Mr Brennan was buried in the Parochial Cemetery in Walton, Liverpool at public expense.

With condolences,
Michael Prendergast, Master.

Clem sat on the bed with the parcel of old clothes beside her. She had tried not to think about her father since he'd left, but as the time passed, her anger over Tommy's death had faded and she had begun to feel remorse about her failure to say goodbye, and her too-ready acceptance of what Marian and Malcolm had told her about her father hitting the boys. Her Papa may have had a lot of faults but beating children was not one of them. Now she would never have a chance to tell him she believed him. Never see his face again. She tried to remember it, to force a picture of him into her memory, but it was already fading. Not so much as a single photograph to remind her. He'd had a wide smile though, one that lit up his whole face. Whenever he smiled she'd always felt the world was a bit brighter. Now she would never see that smile again.

Her eyes filled with tears. She would never have the chance to tell him how much she loved him. To say sorry for not believing him and standing by him.

She touched the threadbare fabric of the jacket. Fit only for the bin. Not even worth giving to the poor. Then she reflected that he was the poor. Her own father dead in a distant workhouse, buried in a pauper's grave. How had she let that happen? Why had she never tried to track him down? Why had he never written to her?.

But she knew why. He had left here in disgrace. She had spurned him, refused to say goodbye to him. Refused to stand up for him. And he wouldn't have wanted to ask for help. He had always been a proud man. An unhappy man, but always too proud to ask anyone for help. He would have hated his daughter to know that he had ended up in a workhouse.

She picked up the jacket and held it to her face, trying to evoke some memory of him, but it smelt stale and unpleasant. She began to cry, wiping her eyes with the back of her hand. Through the mist of tears she noticed there was something else in the parcel. Nestled beneath the jacket and the trousers was a little wooden box with an inlaid picture of a bridge, an envelope and small pile of loose papers. The pages were stained and grubby, but covered with his familiar spidery handwriting. She picked up the envelope. It was addressed to her.

My dearest Clementina,

I write this to you, knowing that if you are reading it I will be gone. I have nothing to bequeath you, other than my words, my verses, but it is through these that I have tried to live a better life. My best legacy on this earth though is you. You are my only source of pride, the one perfect thing I leave behind.

I know I have been a weak man, a neglectful father, all too easily swayed by the pursuit of impossible dreams, but believe this, Clemmie, I have always loved you. My life did not take the path I had hoped to follow. Instead of making the best of what life offered, I let myself wallow in self pity and sought consolation in alcohol. These last few years though I have tried to redeem myself by seizing the chance that was offered to me to teach again. I have loved every minute of teaching and can die in peace, save for the fact that I die without your blessing.

Many years ago, I lost someone I loved and this shaped the rest of my life and blinded me to the needs of others, not least you. When I was betrayed (as indeed I was) by my son-in-law and the brothers at St Dominic's I lost the only two things in life that I still valued – my daughter and my good name. I have lost them in my life. You have the power to restore them to me in death. Please forgive me.

Your loving father
Jack Brennan.

Clem let the letter fall into her lap and pulled the pile of papers towards her and read the poems through her tears. She knew what she must do.

Epilogue
St Louis, 2015

Meredith moved the paper pieces from the old quilt around on the table, fitting them together as best she could, using a process of elimination, careful not to tear the thin paper. Slow work. Eventually she had the text of a letter in front of her. Someone had scrawled in a different hand across the top "Return to the sender"

St Louis, 1915

Dear Jack,

I am overcome with joy today. Amelia, my daughter, brought me some poetry books as she knows how much comfort I have drawn from poems since I lost my husband. As well as works of Mr Longfellow and Mr Wendell Holmes, imagine how I felt to pick up the third volume and find it was a collection of works by a contemporary English poet and that it was you! Oh Jack, I cannot tell you how it felt to know that you never gave up, that you carried on writing, that you have at last found the success you always deserved. I have thought of you so many times over the years, imagining you hunched over a notebook, writing lines, crossing them out and writing again, always searching for the right word, the right metaphor, the right rhythm and cadence.

I was so overcome when I saw your name upon the printed page that I wept. I told Amelia that reading the poems had brought back memories of my girlhood in England – my daughters know nothing of our friendship. I am writing this letter to you care of your publisher and I hope he will forward it. It is the first I have ever posted – but far from the first I have written. I do not want to hurt Amelia and Louisa, who honoured and respected their late father, so I have kept the unsent letters safe where they will not find them. Now I pray that, at last, one will be held in your hands and may be the means of me hearing from you.

Now you are a celebrated poet, a man of respect in England, I have no wish to disrupt your life. I am sure you too have children and grandchildren and will not welcome anything that might upset the equilibrium and peace that I hope you have found.

I can say this now as so many years have passed and the anger and disappointment I felt towards you for not coming to find me, for not even attempting to know what happened to me, has long passed. I have had a happy life and a happy marriage (as I hope was true for you too) and now, looking back would not wish my life any other way.

But grant me this at least. Please write me a few lines. Just to let me know that you are happy, well and at peace. I hope and pray the war raging over there is not impacting you or any of your children and that it will end soon.

My fondest wishes to you,.
Eliza Feigenbaum (née Hewlett)

Meredith knew of no Eliza, nor of Jack, Amelia and Louisa. The letter was a hundred years old. How little she knew of her family's history. The trunk and its contents had been handed down to her mother, who had evidently never explored them. Meredith turned back to the pile of paper and began to sort the sheets into some kind of order, hoping to piece together Eliza's story. As she picked up one of the paper cut-outs she noticed it was a different, thinner, paper stock. Like the others it was covered with Eliza's spidery copperplate, but this one carried indentations. She flipped it over. The other side was typewritten, the edges folded in to make the shape of the template, rather than cut to size. She turned back the corners, touching the paper gingerly and read the short missive.

Russell Square,
London, 1915

Dear Mrs Feigenbaum,
I regret to inform you that I am unable to forward your letter addressed to Mr J Brennan and I return it herewith. Mr Brennan died prior to the publication of "Thoughts from the Fireside" and Bromley and Bradgate had communications only with his daughter, Miss Clementina Brennan. It would be inappropriate for Bromley and Bradgate to forward your letter to any other recipient than that to whom it was addressed. If you wish to write specifically to Miss Brennan we will be happy to pass such correspondence on.
Yours faithfully,
Wm Bradgate Esq.

Meredith turned the paper over.

Oh Jack,

My heart is breaking. I thought I would know if something happened to you – that the world would feel emptier – or stop turning altogether. How could I not have known you were gone? And yet you have always been gone. Ever since you were dragged from the deck of the ship.

Why did you never come to find me? I was waiting. I longed for a message from you. Why did you not send me so much as a line to let me know how you were and to explain why you could not come after me?

Oh my darling, I feel ashamed writing to castigate you when you are no longer here to read my words. I have no right to accuse you when you are not here to defend yourself. The Jack I knew , the Jack I loved, the Jack I will always love would have done what he believed was the right and honourable thing, even if it broke his heart.

I am writing this now to get my feelings for you off my chest and to clear my conscience about always loving you while being married to another. I am going to hide this letter away with the other letters I have written to you by sewing it into a patchwork quilt where my daughters cannot find it. I want to leave something in the world, something solid but secret to testify to how much you meant to me.

I have had a happy life, despite losing you, Jack – I would be wrong to try to deny that. I married a good and kind man whom I loved. It was not the same as the love I had for you, but he made me happy, cared for me, gave me two beautiful daughters. At first I didn't care for him and only agreed to marry him because I was desperate to have a child and knew I had no hope of seeing you again. Yet over the years I became fonder of him and grew to love him. He died thirteen years ago and I miss him every day.

So what of my life without you, Jack? I think you would be surprised to know that your Eliza became a successful business-woman. Yes, Jack, your former sweetheart is head of a company that publishes books across the whole of the United States. Imagine! I have become a wealthy woman. I have loved this part of my life and to my astonishment have proved quite good at it. My husband supported me in the business while he was alive, but it was mostly my enterprise. Now I hope that my daughters and their husbands will continue to make the business prosper.

The books we deal in are academic tomes – sadly not poetry – but imagine my joy when I discovered that your poems were at last published. The publisher told me that your daughter

344

submitted the work after your death. She must be as proud of you as I am. I am so sad that you did not get to hold the book in your hands, to see your words printed on the page. I have been reading the poems every night before I sleep and I draw so much comfort from them – even though I blush at how many are addressed to me. Reading those words fills me with joy to know that you went on loving me. But, dearest Jack there are also poems that have brought me to tears. I do not know what caused such pain but you write of being wrongly accused and of battles with alcohol. I wept when I read those. What brought you to that? Who could have been so cruel to you?.

I wrote to your daughter, Clementina, and told her that we had been teaching colleagues many years ago. I did not mention our attachment. She said you died in Liverpool under straitened circumstances. Oh, Jack, if only I had known, I could have sent you money, helped you to get back on your feet. It is a cruel world. Sometimes I think God tests us too much.

I do not think it will be long until I join you, as my sickness is advanced. I have been ill for some time and am rarely able to venture outside the house these days. I have not been the best Catholic, but I pray that God will have mercy on us both and that we will finally be together in heaven.

Your loving friend,
Eliza.

Meredith leaned back in the chair and sighed. This little glimpse into these long-dead lives was so sad. She wanted to know more about Eliza and Jack and their tragic love affair. She rummaged through the trunk. It was mostly old bills and papers relating to the sale of Feigenbaum and Hoffman. There was an old photograph album but this appeared to be from the 1930s and must have belonged to one of Eliza's daughters. At the every bottom of the trunk she found a faded copy of the St Louis Post Dispatch from 1925. She unfolded it and there it was, the obituary of Eliza Feigenbaum. There was a grainy photograph of Eliza that

345

appeared to have been taken some time during the first decade of the last century. She looked about fifty. Unusually for a photographic portrait, her face was in profile. She had been a fine-looking woman. As Meredith read the eulogy, she was impressed by her ancestor, who not only founded a publishing empire but had also been a leading campaigner for women rights in St Louis.

It was after midnight when she closed the lid of her laptop and went to bed. Her online research had thrown up few facts about her great-great-grandmother and her lost love, but enough to whet her appetite for more information.

She discovered that Eliza's two daughters had sold the publishing company in the late 1930s after the depression had destroyed much of the value in the enterprise. It was evident that the two sisters and their husbands had lacked Eliza's business savvy. One of the daughters, Amelia, had died childless, and Christabel was Meredith's great grand-mother, her mother's grandmother. There were no other surviving relatives.

She sipped a whisky as she sat in bed thumbing through the slim leather-bound volume of poetry that she had found under the quilt in the trunk. One of the poems caught her eye. It must have been the one Eliza had referred to, detailing Jack's struggles with alcohol. It was titled, For My Daughter.

'My end draws near and much fills me with shame
My children whom I long neglected.
Others sought to lay at my own door the blame
A love for drinking, ne'er corrected.
And so I have lost it all, e'en my good name.

But dearest daughter, try not to think too ill of me.
A sinner yes, but not of sins so base as those
Of which I was accused. To thou my plea –
Forgive me for the paths I chose
So that in eternal life I will be free.

Meredith wondered what were the sins of which poor old Jack had been wrongly accused. Whatever they were, she hoped his daughter had forgiven him. The fact that she had submitted the poems for publication indicated she had. They were over-sentimental for Meredith's twenty-first century sensibilities, but presumably they had fitted their times. And the outpouring of love for Eliza left no doubt that Jack had loved her as much as she him.

The Bellefontaine cemetery was to the north of the city. Meredith had never visited it before and was surprised at the extent of the place and the splendour of the mausoleums. Some of the tombs must have cost a fortune to build. It was an architectural mashup – classical, Gothic, Egyptian, Roman, obelisks, domes, arches, lions, eagles. She walked past the last resting places of politicians, beer barons, civil war generals, magnates and pioneers, all laid out in extensive parkland. She felt bad that she had never visited before, nor shown any curiosity about her forebears.

At last she found Eliza's grave. It was much simpler than many in this necropolis: a simple marble plinth with a book carved on the top on which were inscribed the names, Karl Feigenbaum 1828 – 1902 and Eliza Feigenbaum 1858 – 1925. Eliza's belief that she was near to death in 1912 had proved wrong.

Meredith laid a bunch of calla lilies on top of the grave. 'From Jack,' she said, 'And me.'

It took Meredith longer to locate the last resting place of Jack Brennan. After weeks of often frustrating research she flew to England and took a train up to Liverpool and then a taxi to Walton. Jack had been interred in a pauper's grave in a disused cemetery close to where the poorhouse had been in Liverpool. She felt terribly sad to discover that the poet was buried in an unmarked, communal grave with other destitute people. When he had been shovelled in there, the poor chap would have had no idea that he was on the brink of becoming published. He would have never known that the woman he loved would read his poems on the other side of the ocean.

The old parochial cemetery was now the home to a city farm. Here, in the middle of the urban sprawl of Liverpool, it was a green oasis, with goats, sheep and pigs – a popular place for families to visit. Meredith liked the idea of Jack being in this woodland setting, surrounded by playing children and grazing animals. It was better than the usual serried ranks of ugly gravestones in most modern cemeteries.

There was nothing to indicate the spot where Jack's body lay. The former graveyard housed ancient tombstones from the 1700s and some graves of servicemen killed in the first world war. Most of the old cemetery was overgrown and wild – open stretches of grass under which were many unmarked communal graves. Meredith looked around and chose a quiet spot under the shelter of a tree. She opened her bag and took out a trowel and dug a hole in the ground; into it she placed a wooden box containing Eliza's letters and the newspaper photograph of Eliza Feigenbaum.

Meredith sat on the grass and read a few lines from one of Jack's poems from *Poems from the Fireside*.

Those joyful days are now long gone
When you and I, not two, but one,
Danced in the dying August sun.

She laid the poetry book on top of the box of letters and covered them with the turf. 'Rest in peace, Jack Brennan,' she said.

THE END

ACKNOWLEDGEMENTS

To Jo Ryan, Anne Caborn, Clare O'Brien, Susanna Sewell and Anne-Marie Flynn, my band of brilliant beta readers. Your advice and input was truly helpful. Thank you.

To my wonderful editor, Debi Alper, who, quite simply, rocks.

Thanks to David Chidgey, Martin Levy and their Facebook friends for cricketing advice. I hope I did justice to the roundarm technique you described, Martin.

To all my Facebook friends for your advice on covers – and to Jane Dixon-Smith for designing it.

To all my readers. Thank you.

ABOUT THE AUTHOR

Clare Flynn is the author of **A Greater World**, set in Australia in 1920 and **Kurinji Flowers**, set in India in the 1930s and 40s. She is a graduate of Manchester University where she read English Language and Literature.

After a career in international marketing, working on brands from nappies to tinned tuna and living in Paris, Milan, Brussels and Sydney, she ran her own consulting business for 15 years and now lives in West London.

When not writing and reading, Clare loves to splash about with watercolours and grabs any available opportunity to travel - sometimes under the flimsy excuse that it's research.

Get in touch with Clare

Website http://www.clareflynn.co.uk

Twitter - https://twitter.com/clarefly

Facebook - https://www.facebook.com/authorclareflynn

Amazon Author Page http://www.amazon.com/Clare-Flynn/e/B008O4T2LC/

Goodreads https://www.goodreads.com/author/show/6486156.Clare_Flynn

Pinterest - https://www.pinterest.com/clarefly/my-new-work-in-progress/

If you enjoyed reading Letters From a Patchwork Quilt please consider leaving a review on Amazon. Reviews are really vital to authors and help more people discover the books. Thank you!

Get a FREE short story

Get an exclusive short story from Clare Flynn, set in Victorian London during the Great Exhibition of 1851.

Not available elsewhere.

To get your FREE short story go to Clare's website, www.clareflynn.co.uk or use the QR code below. You will be the first to know about new book releases, special offers and freebies.

ALSO BY CLARE FLYNN

A Greater World

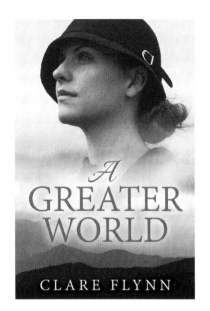

When Elizabeth Morton's father asks her to travel across the world to marry a stranger, she thinks he's crazy. This is 1920 and a woman has rights - she's not going to be subject to an arranged marriage. But she's reckoned without her brother-in-law, who brutally shatters her comfortable world, leaving her no choice but to sail to Australia

When Michael Winterbourne, a lead miner, wakes up with a hangover after his engagement celebrations, he has no idea he is about to cause a terrible tragedy that will change his life and destroy his family

When Michael and Elizabeth meet on the SS Historic, bound for Sydney, they are reluctant emigrants from England. They hope their troubles are over, but they're only just beginning

A Greater World is set in the early 1920s, and moves from the dales of Cumberland and the docks of Liverpool to Sydney and the beautiful Blue Mountains.

A Greater World is a B.R.A.G Medallion Honoree and is Ascribe Approved.

ALSO BY CLARE FLYNN

Kurinji Flowers

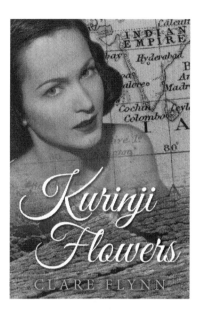

It is 1936. Ginny Dunbar, an 18-year-old debutante, has been exploited for years by a charismatic, older man and is under the thumb of a well-meaning but bossy mother. When she is caught up in a scandal, her marriage prospects are ruined - until a new start in India offers another chance to find love and happiness.

But Ginny's own inner demons, her new husband's expectations, the shallow, lifestyle of the expatriate British community and her mother in law's bullying conspire to turn her dreams of happiness sour.

When Ginny meets Jagadish Mistry, she's forced to question her own prejudices about India and its people. But then the outbreak of war changes everything.

Set in the beautiful tea growing uplands of South India during World War II and during the struggle for independence, Kurinji Flowers traces a young woman's journey through loss, loneliness, hope, and betrayal to unexpected love and self-discovery.

Kurinji Flowers is a B.R.A.G Medallion Honoree.

PRAISE FOR
KURINJI FLOWERS

"A sweeping, lush story – the depiction of India in all its colours, smells and vibrancy is pitch-perfect in its depiction. You will be grabbed from the first chapter" *The Historical Novel Society*

"You would enjoy Kurinji Flowers if you are drawn – as I am – to stories of individual human relationships." *The Review Group*

"A beautiful story of betrayal, love, sacrifice and redemption all framed by the gorgeous countryside of India. " *Amazon reviewer*

"Kurinji Flowers is a lovely, joyful, heartbreaking novel. Oh, how I wished this story could go on and on!" *Amazon reviewer*

"This is a brilliant book, Clare Flynn has recreated the atmosphere of pre-, and post-, war London and India really well - it is as if you are actually remembering it, instead of reading about it." *Amazon reviewer*